MONUMENT ROAD

Michael Wiley

This first world edition published 2017
in Great Britain and the USA by
SEVERN HOUSE PUBLISHERS LTD of
Eardley House, 4 Uxbridge Street, London W8 7SY.
Trade paperback edition first published
in Great Britain and the USA 2018 by
SEVERN HOUSE PUBLISHERS LTD.

British Library Cataloguing in Publication Data
A CIP catalogue record for this title is available from the British Library.

ISBN-13: 978-0-7278-8743-6 (cased)
ISBN-13: 978-1-84751-857-6 (trade paper)
ISBN-13: 978-1-78010-917-6 (e-book)

Typeset by Palimpsest Book Production Ltd.,
Falkirk, Stirlingshire, Scotland.

For George and Sally Wiley, who taught me the shadings between.

ONE

On the night that the Bronson boys died, I went fishing. At midnight, before the clouds moved in, a sliver moon hung over the Fulton Landing Boat Ramp like a hook that would snag the whole world and reel it in. I stood in the ocean at the bottom of the ramp, and I cast a finger mullet on to a sandbar in the deeper water. The bait settled until it touched sand – I felt it touch as if fingers neared my skin and the air between us had heat and friction.

A fish hit the bait. I whooped at the moon, snapped the rod up, and reeled in. I whooped again because the world was so full of such wealth that an eighteen-year-old boy could stand waist deep in the warmth and everything he needed would come to him. I could close my eyes, and still it would come.

And two hours earlier, as we partied on our driveway, Trina smiled at me, and that pleasant confusion, which felt like a change of tide, flooded my head.

I could have.

I knew in my head and my bones that I could.

Could have. But *didn't.*

Then the Coronas ran out, and my brother Jared took Trina's hand and led her inside to his bedroom, though she looked over her shoulder as if it was me she desired.

The world was full of such things.

Not that I was afraid of Trina.

Or Jared.

Now, at one a.m., with the hook-moon buried behind a black cloud and a warm mist falling, I reeled in a second fish, a flounder. Thirteen inches long, if one. The Florida minimum limit – twelve inches.

I pulled out the hook, the barb ripping the rough skin around its mouth, and brought the fish so close to my face I could kiss it. I stared at its wandering eye. Then I lowered it to the ocean surface

and released it. Because I was basically a good kid. Because, as
Dad once said, I had a wild spirit but a soft heart. Because I was
a boy becoming a man. Because the world was full of wealth and
keeping a fish just an inch bigger than the minimum seemed greedy.
Because Trina smiled.

Really, I didn't know why.

And one uncertainty bred another.

I put a new finger mullet on the hook and, with the next cast,
reeled in an eighteen-incher.

Sometimes the world worked that way.

At two a.m. on the night that the Bronson boys died, the rain came
hard and harder as the ebb tide went slack and the flood started
to rise. In three days, I was due to start a job at the Rayonier
cellulose plant. I would inventory boxes that came off a machine
that made absorbent pulp out of pine fiber. Another company
would turn the stuff into diapers. From my trustworthy hands to
a baby's butt.

But on a night like this, the sweat of adult life seemed far
away. The ocean water swelled around my belly and the rain
poured down, stinging my eyes against the dark, and there was
no better sting than that. I hooked another finger mullet and tossed
it into the dark. With the battering and noise of the rain, I never
felt the bait touch bottom, but I reeled in and cast again – and
again – until a fish struck and my rod bent and tensed as if it
was made of muscle.

That night, I had faith. I could have taken off my clothes
and stood barefoot on the jagged oyster shells, bare-skinned in
the world. I *knew* I would live and be strong. The world was
my world.

At a quarter to three, I put the fish in the trunk of my dad's
car next to his .22 rifle. I carried the bait bucket down the boat
ramp and waded into the ocean. I poured the fingerlings and the
slop into the sea. I rinsed the bucket in the saltwater and, after
standing for a minute longer in the rain, trudged up the ramp and
got into the car. I didn't pray then or ever, but I closed my eyes
and was grateful. Then I turned the key and punched the accelerator
to the floor.

TWO

Eight years later, homicide detective Bill Higby came after me like a wolf, though Judge Peterson had said, *Get out of jail free*, and the newspapers and magazines had said, *Oh, the injustice – three years on death row and five more in Supermax for a crime he didn't commit –* and Jane Foley and Hank Cury at the Justice Now Initiative talked about a hundred thousand per incarcerated year plus damages, and even the governor said, *Something should be done to make him whole.* So I rented a room at the Cardinal Motel on Philips Highway. Weekly specials. Hourly rates available. Jimmy marks on the doorjamb.

'Why the hell there?' Jared asked. 'Hookers and pimps for neighbors.'

'Who else will rent to me?' I said.

Bill Hopper, the motel owner, was a foul-mouthed, born-again ex-con, famous for taking in men like me. *60 Minutes* did a segment on him. He asked the reporter, 'You think if Mary and Joseph had felony records, the stable wouldn't have kicked them out on their asses?'

'The judge let you go,' Jared said.

'I could stay with you,' I said.

He laughed.

'I wasn't joking,' I said.

'I don't think that would work so well, Franky.'

'I didn't think you'd like it.'

'In fairness, you did this to yourself.'

'Maybe we shouldn't talk to each other anymore,' I said.

'We would probably kill each other,' he said.

A man who'd gone through what I'd gone through didn't joke about these things.

'You'll always be my brother,' he said. 'That doesn't change.'

As if he'd given me the gift of shared blood.

So I was at the Cardinal Motel when Detective Higby came knocking. With a fist like a club of wood.

I opened. What did I have to be afraid of? I was free.

But freedom meant little when a man like Higby blocked the only exit from a room. 'What?' I said.

'Just checking on you,' he said. He was a big man. His thinning hair – black when he sent me to jail – was mostly gray now. His back – broad and straight when he lifted me by the collar and held me against a wall – seemed narrower. The last eight years had been hard on him too. 'Just letting you know I know where you are.' He peered into the room, dark except for the flickering TV. 'You aren't going to invite me in?'

'The judge said I didn't do it.'

'No, the judge said we didn't *prove* you did it, Franky. Big difference. Lack of proof means still to be proved. It doesn't mean innocent. Your blood was on the boys. That doesn't go away.' With the glisten of sweat on his forehead and the weight he carried around his middle, he looked like he should smell.

'You've got no right to harass me,' I said.

'I'm halfway there,' he said. 'More than halfway. This time you won't get out.'

'The State Attorney says she won't try me again.'

'I don't know where you get your information,' he said. 'She'll do whatever the evidence tells her to do. When I'm done, the evidence will tell her to retry you. Count on it.'

I tried to close the door, but he held it with a fist.

'The damage you did to those boys,' he said, 'it haunts me.'

'I didn't do it,' I said.

'You *told* me you did.'

'You made me say it. If I could go back, I would let you kill me before saying I did something I never did. I was a dumb kid.'

He shook his head. 'There's a difference between dumb and having no soul.'

THREE

'Y ou're the smartest client we've ever had,' Jane Foley told me six years ago when the Justice Now Initiative first took on my case.

'Thank you,' I said.

'That doesn't make you especially smart,' she said. 'Just the smartest we've had. Even that might be too much. Smart men manipulate people. They game the system, or try to.'

'You would rather I was stupid?'

'In many respects, yes,' she said. 'IQ below seventy, and you would be easy.'

'Sorry,' I said.

'Don't worry about it,' she said.

I did half the research that got me off death row and three-quarters of the research that freed me to the outside five years later. As Jane Foley said, smart prisoners gamed the system. We gave the guards something they wanted, if we had anything to give. I gave the one thing I could give, the thing they got too little of in a place where the funniest joke was splashing a cup of month-old piss on a passing uniform. They wanted respect. Which was different from fear – there was plenty of that. If I treated a guard right, he might allow me an extra fifteen minutes in the library or even forget I was there for a whole afternoon. Or, if he'd come to work after fighting with his wife and kids, he might brutalize me for the hell of it.

On the days that I went to the library, I looked up the names of wrongly convicted men who, after ten or fifteen or thirty years, got their freedom. Like me, most of them were on death row for rape and murder. I read their stories over and over until I could recite them, and I studied the mistakes they made as they tried to get someone to listen. I wrote down the names of the people who finally paid attention. Then I wrote letters to those people, telling my own story. I read the news articles on my case, and they made me look so bad that, by the time I finished, I worried I might be guilty after all. So I stopped reading the old news and put in a request for my court records. They came eighteen months after I asked for them. I also requested the police records. They never came. From the court records, I learned one thing my trial lawyer should have grabbed on to and wrestled to the ground but didn't, as if he feared getting gored. Aside from pointing out my blood on the older boy's shirt, which I explained a hundred times, the prosecution never took the next step. They did a DNA profile on the blood from the car battery and the blood on the shirt, but if they ever did a rape kit, no one mentioned it.

In my letters to the prisoner rights people and to the journalism professors who used people like me to give their students real-world, high-stakes investigative experience, I dropped phrases like *missing serological report* and *post-conviction relief*, and that got some attention, though it also made Jane Foley say I might be too smart for my own good.

'If I'd been smart when they arrested me, I wouldn't be where I am,' I said, 'and we wouldn't be having this conversation.'

'Smart answer,' she said.

The doubt she sowed when she told the court that the public defender failed to ask about a rape kit – ineffective counsel, if ever – got me off death row. After that, she and Hank Cury filed six requests for the investigation records before another court ordered the Sheriff's Office to turn over a box of them. The records showed that a rape kit *had* been collected but never tested. Then the Sheriff's Office said they lost the kit but, eleven months later, said they found it again. So Hank Cury asked for money to test the kit, but the State Attorney said there was no need – they already had their man – and two courts agreed until one didn't, and when the test came back, it said the man who raped the boy was ninety-nine-point-nine-to-the-fifth-decimal percent *not me*.

Judge Barbara Peterson ordered the state to let me go and praised the Justice Now Initiative for its work. Then Jane Foley offered me a job at the JNI. On occasion, they would ask me to speak about death row prisoner rights, she said, but mostly they would pay me to investigate other convicts' claims that police and prosecutors coerced confessions or railroaded them. A dollar above minimum wage, she said, but with insurance benefits that would include sessions with a reintegration counselor. When the settlement came through, I could decide whether to continue as an investigator.

The stink of prison hung in my nose. I wanted nothing to remind me of the life I had lived for the past eight years. But I needed money for food and my rent at the Cardinal Motel.

'You get shared use of a computer,' Jane Foley said. 'We're low-budget. Lower than low. We survive on grants and contributions. That means some weeks Hank and I don't get paid. But we pay the receptionist, and we'll pay you.'

'I'll think about it,' I said.

'You barge through closed doors. You don't let anyone turn you away. That will make you good at this.'

'I said I'll—'

'You need this,' she said. 'You'll fall apart without it. It's well documented.'

You have no idea what I need, I thought.

Then Detective Higby came knocking and pointed his fat finger at me and said, *Your blood your blood your blood.*

And I said, 'Only the worst kind of man can't admit he's wrong. That man thinks he's God. He thinks whatever he says is true must be true – even if it means putting an innocent kid like me to death.'

'You're no kid,' he said. 'Even when you were eighteen, you were as old as evil.'

So I went to the JNI office. They worked in donated space above an empty storefront near the old courthouse. They had two metal desks, one for Jane Foley and one for Hank Cury, and a wooden desk for the receptionist, whose name was Thelma Friedman. Bulletin boards, covered with thumbtacked letters and court orders, and white boards, scrawled over with names and dates, hung on the walls. When I arrived, a clock by one of the white boards said 8:28 AM, but already Jane was yelling into one phone, and Hank was yelling into another. Thelma Friedman was speed-freaking on a computer keyboard.

I stood and listened as Jane and Hank swore about exhausted appeals and death warrants – words that burrowed like acid in my ears – and Thelma Friedman leaned toward the computer screen as if it would suck her in. The clock ticked to 8:31 and then 8:38 and then 8:47. I could have disappeared in sparks and smoke, and no one would have noticed. But at 8:48 Hank slammed down his phone, and a minute later Jane hung up and wiped her eyes. Thelma stopped typing. They looked up at me as if I was a confusing problem.

Then Jane asked, 'Do you know a man named Samuel Thomas?'

'Sure,' I said. 'He was already on the row when I arrived. We called him Sam Nines. *Nines* as in nine-millimeter pistol. He's the only man I've ever met who told the truth a hundred percent of the time. I liked him.'

'The governor just signed his warrant. He dies tonight.'

I felt bile rise in my throat. I stared at her and Hank and Thelma, and they stared back. 'I can't do this,' I said, and I turned to go.

Thelma said, 'You also know Jamar Manheim?'

When I first went to prison, Jamar lived in the cell next to mine, except when the guards put him in solitary for threatening them or fighting in the yard. Like me, he was thin, and he taught me how to survive – mostly through examples of what *not* to do. 'Yeah, I know Jamar,' I said.

'He's the daddy of my little girl,' she said.

I went back to her desk. She was a thin-faced woman, her hair done up in cornrows with yellow beads. 'No offense,' I said, 'but he never mentioned you.'

She had hard, dark eyes. 'I couldn't let my little girl grow up with that in her life. I cut him off when he went in.'

'But you're still working here?'

'I've got to do something, right?'

I knew Jamar's story. He'd shot an old man and his wife while robbing their convenience store. He seemed to have no regrets. 'You think he's innocent?'

She gave me a sad smile. 'No,' she said. 'That man was born guilty.'

So Hank pulled a second chair alongside her desk, and for the rest of the morning I used her computer to try to track down four witnesses who'd testified against another death row inmate – Thomas LaFlora – who'd been convicted on charges of killing a couple of crackheads twenty-five years ago. LaFlora had a date with the needle in seven weeks, but Hank thought the police coerced the testimony against him. After the witnesses testified, the prosecutor – Eric Skooner, who'd since risen to become chief appellate judge – dropped drug charges against them, and one of them went on to testify in two more capital murder cases. As I made my searches, I found that three of the four were now dead, including the repeat witness. But if I was right, the last one, the only woman among them, lived with a husband in Callahan, northwest of the city.

'You'll go with us to talk to her later this week?' Hank asked.

Sweat bristled on my back. 'I don't know about that.'

'A man like you, with your background, you could persuade her. One look from you and she'll come clean.'

I tasted bile again. 'Right.'

After lunch, Jane and Hank closed the office so they could drive to the state prison in Raiford and stand with other protesters who would hold a vigil for Sam Nines until the execution team hooked him up to the pentobarbital.

The afternoon was hot and getting hotter, and as I rode a bus back to the Cardinal Motel, my skin felt like it belonged to another man. My sweat stung. I could hardly rip off my clothes on the bus or tear at myself with my fingernails, so I pulled my knees to my chest and rocked back and forth until the other passengers stared at me and one went forward to talk to the driver. I got off a mile from the motel and walked up the highway shoulder, clawing at my arms, telling myself that I was not Sam Nines and I was not Thomas LaFlora – I was Franky Dast and I was free. I looked at the sun in the hot July sky. The glare bounced from the metal of passing cars. Heat rose from the pavement. I dug my fingernails into my arms. As I walked past a bus stop, an old black hooker standing in the shade gazed at me and said, 'Hey?' but she didn't mean it.

'Free,' I told her, and she shrank deeper into the shade.

By the time I reached the yellow sign with the big red cardinal at the motel, I'd sweated through my new pants and shirt. I planned to go inside and stand in a cold shower, though if I could have slipped from inside my skin and crawled out bloody and new, I would have done it.

But in the parking space by my door, Detective Higby waited for me again. He sat in a blue Pontiac, the windows closed, the engine humming. As I approached, he got out, squared his feet, and crossed his big arms over his chest. He stared at me from my feet to my face and grinned. 'What's wrong, Franky?' he asked. He moved so he blocked the line to my door. 'You having a hard time adjusting? I hear it can be tough. Even if you've got no conscience, your body knows where it belongs.'

'Get out of my way,' I said, and the words tasted sour in my mouth.

'You know what's worse than prison bars?' He tapped his forehead. 'The bars in here. Those ones'll drive you crazy.'

'I'm free,' I said.

He looked disgusted. 'You'll *never* be free.'

I tried to step around him, but he moved toward me – then stopped. 'Jesus Christ, you smell,' he said. He wiped his hands on his pants as if he'd touched me.

So I slunk into my room and locked the door.

I turned on the TV full volume and went into the bathroom. My face in the mirror was pale – prison pale, the pale of sickness and death. My hair was slicked down with sweat. I had prisoner's eyes. The eyes of a camp survivor. A dying man. I stripped off my clothes and looked in the mirror again. I'd done pushups in my cell, hundreds a day, and I'd lifted weights in the yard. I'd done squats, and I'd run in place for hours at a time. I'd done sit-ups on my skinny bunk. My body was strong, muscled. My skin – which had felt loose and foreign on the bus – looked taut. I still wanted to rip it away and tear off the muscles until all that remained of me was bone. But I turned on the shower, cold, and stepped under the stream. *Free*, I thought – *free* – though I worried that Bill Higby might be right that I'd lost that possibility of freedom on the day he accused me of killing the Bronson boys, or maybe even before that – maybe on the night when I pulled over to check on the boys and their broken-down car. I blamed Bill Higby for my loss. If I could go to death row for a rape and murder I didn't commit, why shouldn't Higby suffer for taking away my freedom?

That thought comforted me. It gave me enough strength to step out of the shower, dry myself, and get dressed.

What should a free man like me do? I stared at the TV. A talk show panel was discussing bisexual bombshells.

I watched for a half hour, and then my skin started to creep again, so I turned the TV off, checked through the window, and went out to the bus stop. I caught the number seven back toward downtown. When it reached Atlantic Boulevard, I got off and transferred to a bus heading to the beach. The reintegration counselor Jane and Hank set me up with – a man named Dr Patel – said I should return to the activities that gave me pleasure before I went to prison. 'Spend time with your family,' he said.

'My mom died when I was a baby,' I told him. 'My dad died when I was locked up. And pleasure's not the word I think of when I think of Jared.'

Dr Patel nodded thoughtfully and said, 'Sex is also good.'

That ache, raging at first, had deadened over the years. 'Maybe,' I told him.

'For some men, the desire never comes back,' he said. 'For others, when it comes back, it slams into them like a truck. You're still young. Be ready for it.'

More than anything, when I was in prison, I missed the woods and the water. When I was a kid, I would run on the paths that snaked from my backyard into a slash pine forest and, deeper, past loblolly bays and live oaks. I would skip over the tangles of roots, my shoes denting the sandy soil, sinking in where a path dipped low toward the swamps – unless I sped up and skimmed over the wet ground as if I was floating or flying. Or sometimes Dad would put Jared and me and a bunch of cast rods into his car and take us to the beach, and we would surf-fish in the salt and bright spray.

Pleasure, Dr Patel said.

I would find it at the beach. Or if I didn't find it, I could strip off my clothes, peel off my skin, and drown myself. *No*, the doctor said, 'Beware of dark thoughts. In a month or two – or a year – you'll see the difference. Your life will look like a kaleidoscope, spinning from dark to light. Resist the dark. Refuse it when it comes, because it *will* come. Look forward.'

Into the salt and bright spray.

Wishful thinking. Halfway to the beach, in a gray stretch of boarded-up car dealerships and fast-food restaurants, I got out of my seat and walked to the front of the bus. The beach seemed too much – too much water, too much sound, too much air. A crushing weight. When the bus stopped at the Regency Mall, I got off.

When I was a kid, the mall drew shoppers from around the city and south from the Georgia border. In the days before Christmas, traffic would back up for miles. On summer nights, you couldn't get a ticket for a new release at the AMC Cineplex unless you came three hours early.

But now the Regency was dying, the parking lots almost empty. I kicked gravel as I crossed the hot pavement toward JCPenney. This time of year usually brought afternoon thunderstorms with lightning that jagged the sky and made ceilings shake even in a bolted-down prison. Rain would come hard and pound the buildings, and you just knew that it cleaned and renewed someone somewhere. But this afternoon the sun hung in a cloudless sky, and renewal seemed like an impossibility. I went around the side of the store, kicked more gravel, passed a truck loading zone and a Belk department store.

At the other side of the lot, the Cineplex looked just as it did before my troubles started – a block of pale yellow concrete with inset brick-red pillars, like a too-sweet cake.

A poster in the ticket window advertised an Afternoon Kids Classics Series with *Home Alone*, *Mrs Doubtfire*, *Toy Story*, and *Karate Kid*. Today the Cineplex was screening *Honey, I Shrunk the Kids*.

'One,' I said to the man in the booth.

The theater smelled of sugar. I felt my way to a seat, sank low on the cushion, breathed deep – and closed my eyes. The smell, the dark, and the air-conditioned cool could have been anywhere and anytime. I could have sat in a theater in a different city, a different state, a different country – far from this place that had tried to kill me. Or I could have sat in *this* city but long before I went to prison, when, hanging out with kids from the neighborhood, I cracked jokes in the dark as a movie started, booting the seats in front of mine to tease my friends, laughing and laughing – until Jared lit a cigarette, cuffing it in his palm, and then a man with an AMC logo on his shirt came and kicked us out.

When the screen lit up, I opened my eyes.

Only two others sat in the theater – a woman with a young boy.

The movie started and Rick Moranis shrank his kids with a ray gun shrinker. Within five minutes, I felt happier than I'd felt since before Bill Higby arrested me. When Rick Moranis threw the shrunken kids into the backyard like trash, I laughed and yelled at the screen, 'That's right. Goddamn it, that's right!' The woman with the little boy hushed me, and I tried to stay quiet, but something was happening inside me – something that felt good. When Rick Moranis's son got picked up by a bumblebee, I laughed so hard I couldn't breathe. I got up from my seat and fled to the corridor.

A teenage usher stared at me as if no one would grin so wide outside a theater unless he was on drugs or insane or both. I caught my breath and said, 'Sorry.'

The kid said nothing.

'You see, I just got out of prison,' I said.

I was making matters worse, so I wandered to the concession stand.

The girl who got my popcorn had straight blond hair that hung to her shoulders, and brown eyes. I guessed she was eighteen or nineteen. She wore a metal stud on one side of her nose and three rings in her left eyebrow. A tag on her shirt said her name was Cynthia.

When she gave me my change, she said, 'You look like you're having a good time.'

I stared at her eyes and wondered if I would feel a truckload of desire if I looked at them longer. 'I'm having a blast.'

I returned to the movie, and Rick Moranis's son rode back into the house on a dog and fell into his dad's bowl of Cheerios. When Moranis lifted his son to his mouth in a spoonful of cereal and milk and almost ate him, I felt an excitement I couldn't account for.

As I left the Cineplex after the movie, I looked back at the concession stand. The girl who'd sold me popcorn was watching me. When she waved with the tips of her fingers, I rushed out into the afternoon heat.

I rode the bus back toward the Cardinal Motel but got off halfway down Philips Highway, went into the Sahara Sandwiches Shop, and ordered a gyros from a bald man with a moustache. I ate outside at a picnic table as the sun dipped behind the building. Fumes from trucks on the highway blackened the evening, but I felt as contented as I figured I ever would again.

I walked to the motel then, and the hooker I saw earlier had left the bus shelter, though a wooden walking stick leaned against the wall where she'd stood, as if holding her place. At the Cardinal, the parking space outside my room was empty, and that made me happy too. I let myself in, stripped off my clothes, and did seventy-five pushups on the carpet. Then I turned on the TV and did a hundred fifty sit-ups. When I finished, I did two hundred squats, then another hundred sit-ups, and then more squats. An hour and a half later, when the ten o'clock news came on, I was still exercising, my body slick with sweat.

I ran in place as a thick-shouldered anchorman said the twenty-six-year-old son of the chief appellate judge in Florida's Fourth Judicial Circuit died earlier in the evening in a police-involved shooting. I'd seen the judge's name that afternoon. Eric Skooner. Twenty-five years ago, as a young prosecutor, he sent Thomas LaFlora to death row for killing two crack addicts. Now, after giving a few details about the shooting death, the anchor noted that Judge Skooner had once been named Jurist of the Year by the American Board of Trial Advocates, but also that he'd once been arrested, though never prosecuted, for striking his now-deceased wife. The judge's dead son, Joshua Skooner, had an arrest record – including two convictions – reaching back to when he was twenty, all for drug- and alcohol-related crimes.

The police weren't identifying the officer who'd shot him, but news cameras showed an evening scene with police tape cordoning off a patch of a tree-lined street where a body, draped under a white sheet, lay on the pavement near two cars that had hit hard enough to mash their hoods. One of the cars was a yellow Mustang with a black door stripe. I figured that must be Joshua Skooner's. The other was a blue Pontiac. A big man in a golf shirt stood next to it talking with three uniformed cops. He seemed to be bleeding from a cut on his chin, and he looked dazed. When I realized he must have been driving the Pontiac – and most likely had shot and killed Joshua Skooner – I felt the breath punch from my lungs. I moved close to the TV screen. The dazed and bleeding man was Bill Higby.

I laughed. And I said, 'That's right. Goddamn it, that's right!'

FOUR

Eight years earlier, on a rainy July night, the White Stripes played 'Fell in Love with a Girl' on my car radio – tore the song apart, Jack White ripping his fingers bloody on his guitar, Meg White punching holes in the drums. I turned the volume up, up, up until the speakers distorted. I crammed the accelerator to the floor. My car skidded around a bend on Monument Road, the rain coming hard and harder, the headlights glinting off the black asphalt, and I didn't care. Pine and oak forest slashed past. The roadside would reach out and pull the car in if I didn't take my foot off the gas, and I didn't care. I remembered then – like a punch in the gut – once, when I was six years old, after a hit-and-run driver came through, the body of a hitchhiker rotted for three days in the palmetto undergrowth and no one was the wiser until another hitchhiker happened by and *oh, the smell.*

Why, on a night like this – the rain falling hard and harder, Jack White ripping and Meg White pounding, my fishing rod, Dad's .22, and three flounder in the trunk – *why* did that dead hitchhiker come to haunt me again? I was eighteen years old, I had a Buick Skylark that Dad let me drive when Jared didn't need it for school, and I had a load of fish that I would fry on the stove so that when Dad woke in the morning he would smell breakfast and maybe, just maybe, come into the kitchen laughing.

Twelve years of daytime sun and night-time rain had burned and washed the smell of that dead hitchhiker into the sandy soil, and he had no business coming to wreck my mood now. I eased my foot off the gas, though the music kept playing and a jet of rain smashed against the windshield. I eased the gas, that's all – I didn't touch the brakes and I didn't second-guess the joy I felt as I blasted into the blind dark – but that's when my life went to hell.

If I'd kept my foot on the gas, I might've flown past the Bronson brothers and their broken-down Chevy Cavalier. Another car – all tail lights and brake lights to me – slowed for them and then sped away as I came up behind it. I might've done the same. I might've looked in my rearview and waved *Bye bye bye*. Or my tires might've slid on the pavement, and the boys and I would have risen through the rain on a cloud of gasoline flames.

If a hit-and-run driver knocked the ribs of a hitchhiker into his lungs and kept going, why didn't I go, go, go?

The truth is, I stopped to help.

'You're always answering the door when you should stay in the kitchen,' Dad said more than once. 'Always picking up the phone when you don't know who's calling.'

Only a guilty man or a coward worries about who's at the door, I thought. *What worm is going to crawl through the phone into my ear?*

But honestly, I could have kept driving. Should have.

I stopped, turned off the music, asked from my window, 'Problem?'

Two boys stood in the rain. Kids. Too young to drive. Too young to be out alone on the side of Monument Road at three a.m. The hood of the Cavalier was up, the engine steaming. Black rain fell against the black night.

'Um,' said one of the boys, the smaller of the two, blond hair slicked down by the rain.

'Yeah,' said the other. Thick face, black hair.

'You steal this car?' I asked.

'Nah,' the big one said.

'Right. How old are you?'

'Seventeen.'

'Right.' I got out and looked under the hood. Blood on my hands from the fish. The wet gravel silent under my shoes. The rain slapping my face. In the dark – no flashlight – as if I knew what I was doing. As if I could help. Joyous in the late night. Free the way I felt at that hour. 'The battery?' I asked.

'Don't know,' said the big one.

The little one asked, 'Can you fix it?'

Engine steam might mean the radiator – even I knew that much. I touched the cap. Hot. 'You have a cloth?'

The big one stripped off his T-shirt.

I wrapped it over the cap and tried it. Pressure held it tight. I tried again. Tight. I leaned into it and wrenched it with my weight. My hand slipped, and my knuckles raked across a metal bracket.

I swore. Shook my hand, the rain stinging the cut skin. Sucked the bloodiest knuckle. Wiped my hand on the T-shirt and threw the shirt on the ground.

The little one said, 'Can you—'

I said, 'It's a mile and a half to the closest gas station. I'll give you a ride.'

The little one wanted the ride. The big one wanted to stay with the car.

The rain came hard. The palmetto fronds on the roadside looked like slick black leather. 'Decide,' I said, 'because I'm leaving.'

The little one looked at the other one and said, 'Please.'

The big one balled his fists as if he might hit him, but he picked up his T-shirt and put it on, then walked to my car and got into the front passenger seat.

The little one said, 'Thanks,' and ran to the back seat.

I knew of a Shell station that I thought stayed open twenty-four hours. As we drove, the big kid hunched into himself. I guessed *he'd* had the idea to steal the Cavalier and he knew the blame would come down on him. When I glanced at the rearview mirror, the little one stared back with wide, nervous eyes. He was skinny, almost pretty, almost a girl.

'You're brothers, aren't you?' I said.

'We don't look it,' the little one said.

'Yeah,' I said, 'but I can tell.'

The tires hissed on the wet asphalt. The wipers snaked across the windshield. Our bodies steamed inside the car. The big one smelled of sweat and rain and cigarette smoke. You would have thought anything could happen.

The Shell station had closed for the night. But the neon yellow glowed like a bar of gold. Icy light shined from inside the empty minimart.

I drove under the pump canopy, and the rain silenced. Sheets of water poured from the canopy and the roof of the minimart. 'Tough luck,' I said.

The little one leaned over the seat. 'Duane?' he said to the big one.

'Shut up,' the big one said.

'Don't you have a phone?' I asked.

Neither answered.

'You can use mine if you want,' I said.

Again, no answer. I figured the big one was deciding how to get out of the mess. I figured the little one was waiting for the big one to decide.

'If you want to hang out here, the station will open in a couple of hours,' I said.

'Can you give us a ride?' the big one asked.

'Where to?'

'We live by the airport,' the little one said.

Twenty miles at least. 'What were you doing over here?'

'Driving,' the big one said. 'Some nights we do.'

'Our dad used to live over here,' the little one said, 'before he moved to Miami.'

'Shut up,' the big one said.

I said, 'I can't take you all the way to the airport.'

They sat, silent in my car, the big one smelling of sweat and cigarette smoke, the little one looking like fear.

'I've got to get going,' I said.

They sat.

Then the big one got out of the car. The little one sat for a moment longer before getting out too.

'Sorry,' I said through the closed doors. Then I touched the gas and shot back into the thumping rain. A mile up Monument Road, I passed another car on the roadside, its hazards blinking. I turned on the radio. The Foo Fighters were playing 'All My Life.' More ripping guitar. More pounding drums.

I never did ask the little one's name.

'It was Steven,' the prosecutor would say. 'He was thirteen years old.'

I never did look the big one in the eyes.

They were blue. The jurors would hand his picture down the line. 'Fifteen,' the prosecutor would say. 'An innocent child.'

I never touched either of them, aside from the big one's T-shirt.

Steven wore flip-flops, orange shorts that looked brown in the dark and rain, and a gray T-shirt. His big brother, Duane, wore the red T-shirt, camouflage pants, and Nike tennis shoes. They both wore white jockey underwear – Steven's threadbare, as if they were hand-me-downs. The jurors would finger each piece of clothing, dry now and packaged in a plastic exhibit bag.

FIVE

And homicide detective Bill Higby, wearing a brown suit with a blue tie, would stare at the jurors from the witness box and say, 'Franky Dast raped and killed Steven Bronson and killed his brother Duane. Franky Dast's blood was on the T-shirt worn by Duane Bronson. Franky Dast's fingerprints and palm prints were on the car that Steven and Duane Bronson were driving. Steven and Duane Bronson's fingerprints also were in Franky Dast's car. Franky Dast confessed to me. Franky Dast persuaded these boys to get into his car on an empty road in the middle of the night. Or he abducted them with force. We'll never know. But we do know that he drove these two children to a closed Shell service station and brutalized them.'

The jurors would believe every word he said. When the judge sentenced me to death, he would call me an *outrage*.

And it would go downhill from there.

Eight years after that night on Monument Road – and just a week after another judge told the prison warden to unlock the gates and set me free – I woke up at the Cardinal Motel and turned on the TV to see the latest on Bill Higby and the man he shot. Morning sunlight shined through the cracks around the window shade. On the concrete walkway outside my room, a man and a woman were arguing. The woman sounded frenzied, the man angry – which meant he probably was her pimp. She called him names, and he threw her against the wall to my room. I knew the price of getting involved, so I turned up the volume on the TV. A blond anchor-woman smiled, fixed the neckline on her dress, and welcomed viewers to *The Good Morning Show*.

The shooting led the news. Overnight, Joshua Skooner had become Josh, the well-loved but troubled son of Chief Judge Eric Skooner. 'Josh,' the judge said, standing on a wide lawn in front of a big house near Black Creek, 'didn't deserve to die. He didn't *need* to die.' The judge's other son stood at his side. 'We trust that there will be a full investigation into what happened only feet from the safety of my home, and we trust that the responsible party will be held accountable.' He turned from the camera without taking questions. His son stared at the lens as if he might speak too but then followed the judge.

The on-site reporter said that yesterday evening the police received calls concerning an erratic driver and a possible hit-and-run in the Black Creek neighborhood. The officer who crashed into Josh Skooner was no regular patrolman. He was homicide detective Bill Higby, who was returning home after a fourteen-hour shift when he saw a yellow Ford Mustang blast toward him through a stop sign. He aimed his Pontiac at the car, but the Mustang kept coming. There were no skid marks leading to the collision. Josh Skooner never braked. Neither did Bill Higby.

The reporter said, 'Detective Higby claims that, after the crash, Josh Skooner shot a gun at him. Detective Higby shot back. Neighbors say they counted seven or eight gunshots.' The camera cut from the reporter's face to the crash site on Byron Road. A half-dozen uniformed men and women were scouring the road shoulder, the lawns, and the bushes. 'Evidence technicians are continuing to work the scene this morning. Officer Higby has been placed on paid administrative leave.'

The camera cut back to the anchorwoman. She said, 'Josh Skooner was twenty-six years old and had a record of drug arrests and one minor felony.' A picture of a thin, tan-faced man in his early twenties appeared on the screen. He had a three-day stubble and green eyes. He would have lasted about an hour at the state prison. 'This morning, he's being remembered by family and friends as a likeable, sociable man.'

The anchorwoman put on a thoughtful, tight-lipped face. She said, 'Byron Road, west of Henley, remains closed this—'

I switched off the TV, ran into the bathroom, and threw up in the toilet. But when I caught my breath, I grinned at the mirror. 'Jesus Christ!' I said, and I laughed. Bill Higby was 'claiming' Josh Skooner shot at him, the reporter said. *Claiming*. Already the doubt. 'He's screwed,' I told the mirror. A *much-decorated* cop could get away with putting an innocent kid on death row if the innocent kid came from a family like mine. That cop could even hold his head in the clouds after a court threw out my conviction. But shooting a judge's son? Even a judge's son with a record?

'Screwed,' I said.

I went back to the bedroom and got dressed. The man and woman out on the concrete walkway were still arguing – about money. I didn't want to hear it.

I opened my door and glared at them. The woman had stringy blond hair and a bruised eye. The man was meth skinny, and he wore an ankle sheath with a knife in it. He glared back at me.

I slammed and locked the door. They were still arguing ten minutes later, so I called the reception desk and talked to the motel owner, Bill Hopper.

'A guy with a knife is outside my room,' I said.

'Yeah?'

'So can you do something about him?'

'He with a pretty blonde?'

'I wouldn't call her pretty.'

'That's Jimmy and Susan. They live next door to you. They're good people.' He hung up.

I'd seen enough shanks in prison to never want another piece of metal shoved against my throat. But I could either walk out my door or hole up as if I still had bars around me. I walked out into the bright morning.

The man and the woman gave me looks that said *Don't fucking dare*, but I crossed the parking lot, and they went back to arguing and slapping each other.

The bus dropped me off a block from the Justice Now Initiative office at seven forty-five. When I climbed the stairs, Jane Foley and Hank Cury already sat at their desks. Jane stared at a computer screen, and Hank read the morning paper. They looked sad and tired. They must have returned late from Sammy Nines's execution.

'Good morning,' I said.

Jane kept reading the screen. Hank looked at me over the top of the paper.

'You see the news?' I said. 'Bill Higby is going down for a killing.'

'I just read the story,' he said. 'But why do you think he's going down? You, of all people, know it doesn't work that way. Not for a cop like him.'

But he couldn't wreck it. 'They already suspect him.'

He shook his head and came around his desk. 'In these first months, the *ups* can be as dangerous as the *downs*,' he said. 'Jane and I have seen it before. Don't get ahead of yourself. Don't expect the universe to realign and make things right that have been wrong for eight years or a hundred or a thousand. Men like Bill Higby don't get caught, or, if they do, they don't get punished. That principle is as powerful as gravity. If you ignore it, it will crush you.'

I looked at Jane. She was staring at me now too, concerned.

I grinned. 'Nah,' I said, 'he's going down.'

So they put me back to work on Thomas LaFlora, the man Judge Skooner had prosecuted for killing crackheads twenty-five years ago. Although LaFlora was on death row with me at Raiford, like a lot of the old timers he'd stopped talking with others, as if he was already dead. The woman I'd located in Callahan had been sleeping with one of the crackheads LaFlora supposedly murdered twenty-five years ago. Before we visited her, Jane wanted to know everything about her – her sympathies, her vulnerabilities to prosecution or probation revocation, her work history, whether her parents were alive – anything Jane and Hank could use to get her to come clean.

'You'll force her?' I asked.

'We want her to act according to her conscience,' Jane said.

'And if she has no conscience?'

'Then we'll force her – if we sense she's lying.'

That sounded a lot like what Bill Higby did to me, but I sat at the reception desk and made search after search. Criminal History Services at the Florida Department of Law Enforcement said the woman spent eighteen months in jail twenty years ago on cocaine possession charges and later was fined three hundred dollars for marijuana possession. I found nothing that said she belonged to a church or volunteered at charitable organizations. If she had a job, she kept it off the books.

I'd just started looking into family history at ten o'clock, when Thelma Friedman came in and needed the computer. So Jane asked me to file the records on Sammy Nines.

As I worked, I opened one of his folders. At the top, there was a picture of him. At twenty-three, wearing the blue pants and orange shirts we all wore on death row, he smiled at the camera with a gold crown on one of his front teeth as if he still hadn't fully figured out that the system bites back. As I looked at that photo of a man who, less than twelve hours earlier, had stopped breathing, my excitement over Bill Higby's troubles dissolved.

Under the photo were Sammy Nines's appeal records, each with the same stamp – DENIED – and each with the smell of sweat and courthouse rot. I crammed the records back into the folder and jammed the folder into a cabinet between files for other dead men. I slammed the drawer shut.

Jane looked up from her computer. 'Is everything all right?'

I gave her my best smile, as if the system hadn't bitten me too, but said, 'Why did you make me do that? I didn't need to see him again.'

She looked tired. 'No one can make you do anything, Franky. Not now. It's your choice. But the records needed to go into the cabinet. We have others to worry about.'

Hank said, 'If we don't move fast, everyone goes over the edge. It was like that when we started working with you too.'

I knew they were right, but by the end of the morning I was coming down hard. Again I wanted to crawl out of my skin, slough it off, glisten wet and new. I needed a boost.

So when Thelma got up to use the bathroom, I sat at her desk and searched for information on last night's shooting. The story was developing fast. According to the *Times-Union* website, investigators hadn't found the pistol that Bill Higby said Joshua Skooner shot at him. How hard could it be to find a gun in the tangle of metal that had once been the Mustang and Pontiac? *Screwed*, I thought, and I clicked on a link to a Fox News exclusive. According to the report, Bill Higby, who lived in a small house next door to the Skooners, had fought with the judge's family in the past. He'd showed up seven years ago on the night that the judge and his wife, Melody, were arrested for domestic battery. Although the judge and his wife had calmed down, Higby insisted that the reporting officers take them into custody. To the surprise of no one, the prosecutors dropped the charges. 'Detective Higby was combative,' the judge told the prosecutor's office. 'We worried for our safety.' More recently, when Josh Skooner held regular late-night parties, Higby ticketed him for noise violations. Only the intervention of the undersheriff kept Higby from arresting him.

I figured the reporter could have gotten the information only from Judge Skooner or from the Sheriff's Office. If the judge was powerful enough to spin the news so soon after the shooting, then Higby once again was screwed. If Higby had enemies in the Sheriff's Office willing to leak information that hurt him, then he was *doubly* screwed.

I realized Thelma had come back and was watching me only when she spoke. 'His suffering won't make you feel better,' she said.

'You sure about that?' I asked.

I left the JNI at three for an appointment with my reintegration counselor. Dr Patel had an office on the eleventh floor of the Baptist Hospital Medical Services Building on the south bank of the St Johns River. A floor-to-ceiling window looked out at the river, a railroad drawbridge, a scattering of skyscrapers, and, beyond them, a mix of neighborhoods, forest, and swamp. A successfully reintegrated man might look through the window and feel at home in the surrounding city. An unsuccessfully reintegrated man might step through the glass and plunge to the brick walkway below.

'It's a dissociative disorder,' Dr Patel said, when I told him about wanting to crawl out of my skin. 'Specifically, a depersonalization disorder. Quite common among people with PTSD, if that's any consolation. You feel detached from yourself? As if your body isn't your own?'

'Right,' I said.

'We can fix you up with medication and therapy.' He spoke cheerfully, as if I'd told him my turn signal had stopped blinking.

'Replace the spark plug?' I said.

'Not the metaphor I would use,' he said. 'Have you thought more about spending time with your brother' – he looked at his notepad – 'Jared?'

'No.'

'Being around those you know best – and who know you best – can sometimes help.'

He was getting tiresome. 'I saw a girl I might be interested in,' I said. 'She sold me popcorn at a movie theater.'

'You went out to the movies? That's good. Getting out of your room is good.'

'She's young. Maybe eighteen.'

'The same age you were when you were arrested?'

'Is that too young?'

'You aren't eighteen anymore. You can't pretend you are. But you missed eight years of your life, and you also can't pretend you didn't. Some exonerees come out and want to be kids again. It doesn't work. Some try to jump right into the future, as if they never went away. That doesn't work so well either. Most try to run their lives fast-forward – live all those missed years in a couple of months – and that's worst of all. You know what happens when you drive fast when you're used to standing still? You plow your car into a viaduct.'

'Thanks for cheering me up.'

'The trick is to keep a finger on your pulse,' he said. 'Experiment, but keep your experiments safe. Are you going to ask this girl out?'

'I haven't even talked with her. Except to ask for popcorn.'

He nodded. 'You should see your brother. You should visit the house where you grew up.'

'I would rather plow into a viaduct.'

When I came out of the appointment, thunderclouds hung heavy overhead. If I caught a bus soon enough, I could be locked inside in my room at the Cardinal Motel by the time that lightning cracked the sky and the first fat raindrops hit the ground. Instead, I boarded a bus to the Regency Mall and the AMC Cineplex.

I got off as the clouds broke open and rain pounded the dusty pavement. I ran across the parking lot, passed the department stores and another parking lot, and stepped into the Cineplex, soaking wet, twenty minutes after *Toy Story* started. Water ran from my hair and dripped from my clothes, but I went to the concession and looked for the popcorn girl.

A skinny boy with curly black hair and glasses worked alongside a heavier version of himself. No one else was there. The skinny boy asked what I wanted.

'More than you can give me,' I said.

I went to the *Toy Story* theater. Seven kids sat in the second row, two of them in birthday hats. I went to an end seat in a middle row.

I'd seen *Toy Story* when I was a kid myself. Now, Woody and Buzz Lightyear competed again for the love of the boy who owned them. Their fight got vicious – Buzz fell out of a window, and he and Woody tumbled from a car – though I remembered that, after all the battles and adventures, they would work together and love each other. The movie theater was cool and calm, and the sugar in the air smelled like a place far from my troubles, but I shivered in my wet clothes, and Dr Patel's voice rang in my head, telling me, *You should see your brother.* When a neighbor kid started torturing Buzz and Woody, I'd had enough. I went out to the hall and back to the concession.

The skinny boy eyed me as if he hoped I would go away. But I said to him, 'A girl was working here yesterday. Cynthia. Is she here again?'

He looked left and right, as if she might be hiding behind the counter. 'Haven't seen her.'

'What days does she work?'

He just frowned.

I turned away again, and he called after me, 'You want a Coke with that?'

When I went back to my seat, Buzz Lightyear, realizing how rotten his life was, jumped from a banister and broke off an arm. Who could blame him? Then the neighbor kid tied him to a rocket.

I went back out to the hall to catch my breath, glanced at the concession, and then returned to my seat to watch the happy ending.

Yes, Buzz and Woody became friends. *Yes*, Woody saved Buzz's life. *Yes*, they landed in the arms of the boy who loved them. Life might not work that way, but movies sometimes did, and that might get me through the afternoon.

As the credits ran up the screen, the birthday party kids filed from the theater, and I followed them out to the hall. I headed for the exit, eyeing the wet pavement through the glass doors.

Then a voice called to me from a corridor that led to other theaters. I turned and Cynthia smiled at me. She gave me the same fingertip wave she'd given me yesterday. 'Hi,' she said, and moved toward me.

I wanted to say *Hi* back. I wanted to go to her. But my stomach clenched. I stood for a moment, staring at her. Then I fled outside into the evening.

The bus tires hissed on the wet pavement as I rode back to the motel. The clouds were clearing, but I felt as if I was riding a nightmare bus that had left its route and plunged into holes that the city planners dug for people like me. I was falling toward places in my mind that I'd promised myself I would never revisit – toward the first night they put me into general population and three men came to my bunk, smelling like three men who come to a cell in the middle of the night. And then I was falling toward the infirmary, which smelled like an infirmary where you go after three men come to your cell in the middle of the night. And further falling – toward the solitary box that I entered a week after getting out of the infirmary.

How does one claw one's way up the sides of an oil-slick tunnel when one is falling, falling, falling?

I dug my fingernails into the skin of my upper arms until blood rose in crescent moons. That was a start. I forced myself to remember how – after that first night in my bunk and then the infirmary afterward – I learned to fight as if my life depended on it, which is to say, fight as if I was willing to die, ready to kill or be killed before I let three men come to my bunk again. Then I blinded one of them in the left eye with a spoon – which put me into solitary for seven months – but when I got out, no one came to me in my bunk anymore and the man with the eye patch stayed clear in the exercise yard. One of the others became my friend. His name was Stuart and all he'd done was hold me down for the others, and if you can't forgive a man who's done no more than that, who *are* you going to forgive?

Now, as the sun set outside my window at the Cardinal Motel, I lay naked in bed and watched the news.

Mostly, the reporters told the same story they'd told throughout the day. But they did add that all eight bullets from Higby's gun hit Josh Skooner – in the abdomen, the chest, and the head. A ballistics expert told an ABC reporter that, even at close range, Higby shot with exceptional accuracy.

The reporter asked, 'Does that suggest this was an execution?'

The expert said, 'It might indicate nothing more than Detective Higby's high degree of professionalism.'

They flashed a picture of Higby at a practice range, and I said, 'Give the man a cigar.'

CBS ran a short segment on Josh Skooner.

A male reporter said, 'Two stints in drug rehab. Kicked out of both for relapsing. Assault charges for a fight outside a bar.'

A female reporter said, 'His father says that while he was far from perfect, he was getting help. He was making an effort.'

The male reporter said, 'Police have confirmed that, just before the shooting, he was driving erratically – speeding, driving through stop signs, cutting across lawns.'

The female reporter said, 'The police have also said that the rumored hit-and-run never happened. Basically, this kid needed a traffic ticket.'

'Perhaps so,' the male reporter said.

I wondered again how much Judge Skooner could control what came out of the TV, the prosecutor's office, and the other big mouths in the city. He must have intimidated or coaxed powerful people to tell the story his way.

When the reporters flashed another picture of Higby on the screen, I said, 'It sure looks bad for you.'

Twenty minutes later, CNN brought the story to a national audience. 'Josh Skooner's father denies his son ever owned a gun,' the newscaster said, and then, 'Investigators canvassing the scene have failed to produce the gun that Officer Higby claims Josh Skooner shot at him.'

The news reports sang to me like a lullaby. By midnight, I was breathing calmly again, and I smiled to think of the popcorn girl saying *Hi*.

Then someone knocked on the door – three taps that sounded like the warden coming to tell me it was time.

I put on pants and yanked up the zipper. The warden had skipped my turn, moving on to Sammy Nines and the others, but when the fingers knocked again – three more taps – I felt like they were poking my chest.

I looked through the security peephole.

My brother stood outside. The peephole lens made his face clownish.

When I opened the door, Jared held one side of the doorframe. His eyes hung half closed. His lips looked like he'd heard a half-funny joke. 'You're up?' he said. He sounded drunk.

'Barely,' I said.

He looked past me to the flickering light of the TV. 'Can I come in?'

'What do you want?'

'I thought we could talk.'

I blocked the door. 'You know when I could've used someone to talk to? When I was locked up for eight years. You know where I would be happy to talk now? At your house, if you invited me to stay with you.'

'Right,' he said. 'So are you going to let me in?'

'It's midnight, Jared.'

'I know. I don't sleep so well.'

'I wasn't thinking about *your* sleep.'

'You don't look like you sleep so well either.'

'Go home, Jared.'

'Five minutes. That's all.'

I moved aside.

He came in, went to the TV and turned it off, walked to the bathroom and peered inside, then sat down on the bed.

'This place isn't so bad,' he said.

'It's a shithole.'

He laughed. 'Yeah, it's a shithole. How are you settling in? You adjusting?'

'Did my reintegration counselor ask you to come talk to me?'

He stared at me. 'Don't be that way.'

'What do we have to talk about?' I asked. 'I mean, really.'

'You know, we had good times together too.'

'I don't remember many,' I said.

He looked at me square. 'Are you making friends now that you're out?'

'I haven't been out long enough,' I said.

He stared some more. Then a grin broke across his lips. 'You know what we need to do? We need to get you laid. I mean, you're living on hooker alley, but the girls out here – they're not what you want, right? We'll go to a nice club, and I'll introduce you to some girls and—'

'Not interested,' I said.

'*Not interested*? You've been locked up with dudes for eight years, and you're *not interested*? They turn you while you were inside?'

'I already met someone,' I said. 'I don't need—'

His grin widened. 'You *met* someone? Good man. You banging her?'

'Jesus, Jared. It takes longer than that.'

'Why wait? You know what I did when Trina and I split? The afternoon that the papers came through, I bought a ticket to Thailand. Two days later, I was there. The night I got to Bangkok, I went straight to a sex show. They had a girl shooting ping-pong balls out of—'

'It's time for you to leave,' I said.

'No, *listen*,' he said. 'There was no passion in it. It left me cold. *But* – and this is what I'm telling you – I bought a hooker anyway, because either you're in the saddle or you're out, right?'

I went to the door and opened it. 'Great to see you again,' I said. 'You can tell Doctor Patel I'm doing fine.'

But Jared just sat there. 'Now I'm tired of porn,' he said. 'Bored. And I hate the soft-focus shit.' He stared hard at me. 'You know what I mean?'

'It's time for you to go,' I said.

His grin had fallen, and I felt a sadness coming from him like a fever. 'We did have good times too,' he said. 'A lot of good times.'

'Sure we did,' I said.

He stared. I stood with the door open, the smells and sounds of the highway leaking into the room.

He said, 'Do you remember that night Dad got drunk and—'

'I remember a lot of nights Dad got drunk.'

'OK,' he said, 'OK,' and he pushed himself to his feet and stumbled toward the door. 'I just thought we could talk.' I moved to let him pass. But he stopped in the door and forced the grin on to his face again. 'I mean, we were kids, Franky. Just kids.'

'Yeah,' I said, 'we were kids,' and I closed the door behind him.

SIX

Eight years ago, the news said the Shell station owner found the boys' bodies when he arrived at work. Said one was sexually assaulted. Quoted a police detective who reported that the assailant bit them both and shot them, once each, in the forehead. Said they were Duane Bronson, age fifteen, and his little brother, Steven Bronson, age thirteen, out for a joyride. Single mother. Minor juvenile records. Said anyone who'd seen anything should call the Sheriff's Office.

I'd seen something. Christ, I'd given them a ride to the station. I called the number.

Responsible one that I was. Answering the door when I didn't know who was knocking. Never afraid of the worm that might crawl into my ear when I picked up the phone. Fool that I was.

Officers would send a car to pick me up, the man said. No need to drive myself. A quick conversation, that was all. They appreciated my cooperation.

Sometime during the second night, *I didn't* became *I did.*

Dream logic.

The big, tall, white detective with black hair always knew it. The black detective with a moustache always knew. The woman cop who brought me coffee, though I didn't drink coffee, always knew it too.

I was the only one who doubted it.

Like I didn't get the joke.

Say it, goddamn it, the moustache said.

Say it, goddamn it, the black hair said.

Please say it, the woman cop said.

For thirty-eight hours I didn't say it. And then I did. I said it.

I knew it, the black hair said.

So I caught my breath and backtracked. *I didn't do it.*

You did, said the black hair.

I didn't, I said.

* * *

'Help us out,' the black-haired man said when I first sat down in the interview room. His name – Detective Bill Higby. He said, 'You were there. You had your dad's rifle in the trunk. Help us understand what happened.'

'I wasn't there. I gave them a ride. I left.'

'It was raining,' he said. 'It was dark. It was two in the morning.'

'Three.'

'Good,' he said. 'What happened next? Imagine what happened.'

'Nothing to imagine. They got out of the car. I drove away.'

'Imagine what happened to them after you left.'

'Should I have a lawyer?' I asked. Not *always* a fool.

'Sure. We'll get you one. But this first.'

'I imagine . . . they went to the pay phone. Tried to call someone for a ride.'

'But the pay phone was broken,' he said.

'I didn't know that.'

'Of course you didn't. What did they do next? What did you do?'

'I didn't do anything. I was gone.'

'Imagine what they did,' he said.

'They waited. What else was there to do?'

'Where? Where at the station did they wait?'

'Somewhere in the light?' I said. 'Maybe they sat by the door to the minimart? The overhang would keep them dry.'

'A couple of kids who snuck out while their mom was sleeping?' he asked. 'And stole her car? They would sit in the open where everyone could see them?'

'OK, so they would sit in the dark.'

'Where?'

'I don't know. Wherever it was dark. Behind the station.'

'That's right,' he said. 'That's very good. And what did they do while they sat there?'

'I don't know.' Then I remembered the smell of wet cigarette smoke as I drove them to the gas station. 'They would smoke. Talk and smoke and wait for morning.'

'Right again.' Broad smile under all that black hair. 'We found the cigarette butts,' he said. 'You're good. You could do my job for me. What next? What happened next?'

'I don't know.'

'Of course you do.'

'Someone came?'

'Or someone never left,' he said.

'I left,' I said.

'Of course you did. And tell me – imagine it – how did those boys die?'

And hours later, after the pinnings to the wall, after the proddings and pokings and the dream logic, when they told me again to talk, I talked and I talked and I talked – crazy responsible fool that I was – and I said, 'I did it.'

Funny thing – my teachers always called me smart. 'You're smarter than that,' they told me. And when they called Dad in for a conference, they said, 'Your son is smart. But his thinking lacks structure.'

Dad told them, 'He's school smart but world foolish. He's got no common sense. I tell him all the time—'

The teachers interrupted before he buried me too deep. 'We would be happy with academic improvement. With more application—'

'And a lot more common sense,' he said – this man who drank himself out of every job he ever held and chased his wife out of his arms.

'Do you have anything to add?' the teachers asked me.

I looked at Dad and said, 'It takes one to know—' until he raised his hand to hit me.

'Enough of that,' the teachers said.

'He's too smart for my liking,' Dad would say.

And that was that until the next time they called him in.

They kept me in the county lockup for seven months while the court scheduled, delayed, and rescheduled. My public defender, Lance Stoddard, came to see me when he could and assured me he had all the evidence lined up so he could knock down the prosecution. I should relax and stop asking to meet so often, because our meetings took time away from his building my defense. I wanted to believe him. I needed to. But each time he came to see me, he seemed to know *less* about my case.

So when they took me out of the county jail and into the courtroom, and Lance started his opening argument by sputtering and looking to the judge for help, I knew *I was screwed.* When the prosecution showed slides of my fingerprints on the car battery from Steven and Duane Bronson's Cavalier, and Lance failed to tell the jurors how I tried to help the boys with their radiator, I thought again, *I'm screwed*. When the prosecution showed slides of the boys' fingerprints from inside my car, and Lance argued that I should be praised for being a good Samaritan instead of accused of murder, I thought, *I'm still probably screwed*. When the prosecutor said that the boys each died from a single gunshot into the forehead, that the bullets were twenty-two caliber, that I had a .22 rifle in my car trunk, and that ballistics showed that my gun *could have* fired the bullets – and then Lance failed to argue that *could have* was insufficient in a murder trial – I thought, *Yep, screwed*. When the prosecution hung up two pairs of white Fruit of the Loom underwear, one of them threadbare and smeared with blood, and Lance failed to ask why the hell the other pair was even relevant, I thought, *Oh, no*. When the prosecution demonstrated that the blood on Duane Bronson's T-shirt matched my own, and then Lance tangled himself up in an explanation that confused even me, I thought, *Oh shit*. But when the prosecution showed pictures of Steven's and Duane's bodies with the bite marks on them and then introduced an expert who said the marks matched my dental alignment – and Lance looked at me as if this was the first he'd heard about the bites – I knew I should start thumping my veins for the lethal injection.

But all the way to the verdict, Lance said he expected the jury to rule against the state. And, after the guilty verdict, he said no jury would sentence an eighteen-year-old to death.

He lined up three character witnesses. Dad came in a gray suit but never looked at me from the witness stand. He had tears in his eyes, though, and he brought tears to mine as he explained the difficulty of raising two sons as a single parent and said he knew me only as a loving son. Jared wore a suit too, and he said we grew up side by side after the death of our mother. He told a story about a Christmas week when we were the ages of the Bronson boys and, along with Dad, we hiked and played in the snow around a rented cabin that backed up to the Cartecay River in the northern Georgia mountains. If the jury believed his version of that story, we'd lived a happy, wholesome life. Last, my freshman track coach, Ernie Kagen, came to the stand in a green sport coat, khakis, and loafers. He told the jurors that four years earlier he kicked me off the team a week before the season ended because I missed too many practices and seemed to lack commitment, but he'd never seen greater raw talent in a young long-distance runner. He regretted that I graduated from high school without ever returning to the team. 'What a waste,' he said, as he finished. 'What a waste of a life.'

Overall, I figured the testimony did me more good than harm, but I needed much more than that. The jurors came back after forty-five minutes and told the judge I should die.

On the night after the sentencing, although I knew a van would come the next day to take me to the state prison, I slept more soundly than I'd slept since I went to talk to Higby about what I saw when I picked up and dropped off the boys on Monument Road. I dreamed of the Christmas-week vacation that Jared had described on the stand.

At that time, Dad was trying, on and off, to break his drinking habit. One night, he stumbled in and looked at Jared and me as if he'd finally blown a fuse and his brain had just stopped. Flecks of spit hung on his chin. He said, 'That's *it*,' as if he'd made a big decision. Then he stumbled to the couch and passed out.

The next morning when I got up, he was cooking breakfast. He'd never before cooked us breakfast. I did remember him vomiting at the smell of scrambled eggs after a hard night. But this morning he chewed a piece of toast and laid strips of bacon in a skillet.

I stood in the doorway and watched. He hummed while he cooked. *Hummed*. He'd shaved and showered, and he'd slicked his wet hair back over his head.

When he saw me watching, he waved at the table for me to sit. 'Good, good, good,' he said. 'That's good.'

He brought a platter of eggs to the table and spooned some on to a plate. He jabbered about this and that and went to the toaster to put down the bread. 'That's right,' he said. 'I know what it is. I've been doing it all wrong. You've seen it, right?' He laughed to himself as if he'd figured out a puzzle that everyone else in the room had given up on. 'It's this stinking air,' he said. 'That's part of it. Standing water. Swamps. The damned paper mills pumping poison into the air. The damned Maxwell House plant. The damned brewery. You never thought you'd hear me say that, did you?' He laughed. 'The *damned* brewery. The goddamned brewery. Goddamned Anheuser-Busch.'

I asked, 'Did they fire you?' He'd worked for the past ten months as an electrician there.

He stared at me. 'Of course not. I'm just tired of this town. The fumes. The gasses on the ground in the morning. I'm sick of it.'

'You can't *not* breathe,' I said.

'Nope,' he said. 'You can't not breathe. And that's the problem. Part of it. That's why we're getting out of here.'

Jared stepped into the doorway, his hair messy, sleep in his eyes. 'What are you talking about?'

Dad's face gleamed. You hear about florid drunks, and he was like that – but this morning he was sober. 'Road trip,' he said. 'To the mountains. Northern Georgia. Clear air up in the mountains.'

'Did you get fired?' Jared asked.

'No, goddamn it, I did not get fired,' Dad said.

'Then, what's wrong with you?' Jared said.

I wanted to tell him to shut up before Dad changed his mind, but Dad said, 'For the first time in a long time, everything is *right*. I came in last night and I looked at the two of you, and do you know what I saw?'

'Child neglect?' Jared said.

If Dad had been drunk, that might've gotten Jared a black eye. But Dad just smiled. 'I saw two young *men*. My boys are growing up. And if you want to know the truth, that scared me. Made me think straight.'

'Nothing straight about you last night,' Jared said.

The toast popped up, and Dad buttered a piece for me and a piece for Jared. 'I got to thinking. This place has dragged on us. Ever since your mother died.'

'It took you until now to figure that out?' Jared said.

'You know what's been missing?' Dad said. '*Love*. I mean, I've loved you boys as well as I could. I've tried. But this is a bad place.'

'We know who made it this way,' Jared said.

'Sit down and eat,' Dad said. 'And then pack a bag. We're going to the mountains.'

*   *   *

So, after breakfast, we drove north into Georgia, up through Waycross and Tifton, then Macon and Atlanta. We headed toward the national forest that spanned the Georgia–Tennessee border. We rented an off-season cabin, and the air was cold and sharp on our lungs and smelled like pine and the frozen rot of fallen leaves. For three days we hiked the paths at the southern end of the Appalachian Trail, and at night we built log fires in the fireplace. When we woke on the fourth morning, the wind was blowing and snow was falling. Dad, who'd slept in pajama bottoms and nothing else, laughed and ran outside and danced like a mad man in the blizzard. Jared and I got dressed and went outside with him. We threw snowballs and stared up at the blinding white sky, and we were happy – so happy I almost forgot what sadness felt like.

When we went back inside, Dad's belly and back were pink and wet, and he'd bloodied the bottoms of his feet by dancing on the sharp mountain stones. But he still laughed and said, 'My feet are too frozen to feel the pain.'

We stayed in the cabin that day and the next because the hiking paths were slick with ice, and on the third day we cut our walk short, but in the car on our way back to the cabin, Dad said, 'You see what I mean now? The air is good.'

'I see,' I said.

'Sure,' Jared said, as if he was starting to hope it was true.

'It's good,' Dad said. 'Life is good.'

'The higher you fly, the farther you fall,' Jared said.

'Don't talk that way,' Dad said. 'Don't even think it.'

But Jared was right. Some infections get into the bone. You can take medicine and knock them down for a while. You can feel good enough to go out and dance. But the sickness roars back sooner or later. Dad's infection was like that. His life was.

On this trip, it came back in the shape of a waitress who served us at a diner on the morning before Christmas Eve.

Dad's face paled when she poured his coffee, and when she left our table, he said, 'Jesus Christ. Doesn't she look like your mother?'

'No,' Jared said, 'she doesn't.' There was fear in his voice because he knew what was coming.

'You don't know what you're talking about,' Dad said.

'I remember Mom a little,' he said. 'And I've seen pictures.'

'You were three years old,' Dad said, 'and pictures never catch the whole person. Not your mother, anyway.'

'Mom's whole person looked like a worn-out Georgia waitress?'

'I'm telling you, she looked like her.'

We spent an hour and a half at the diner, and when we left, Dad had the woman's phone number and her promise to meet him for a date that night.

'What do you all do around here for fun?' he asked her.

'Well,' she said, 'there's a bar called Pete's Haven where some of us hang out.'

'Oh, shit,' Jared said.

'I'll see you at eight,' Dad said.

Back at the cabin, he promised he wouldn't drink. But we knew he was lying – and knew that he knew it too – and when the snow started falling again in the afternoon and he glanced at Jared and me as if he was made of mischief, and took off his shirt and kicked off his shoes and ran to the door, Jared said he didn't feel like it and I said I didn't either.

And that was that.

In the county lockup on the night that the jury and judge sentenced me to death, I dreamed of the trip to northern Georgia, and when the van came to take me to the state prison in Raiford the next morning, I closed my eyes and pretended I was riding toward snow-covered mountains.

SEVEN

Five days after Bill Higby shot Josh Skooner, the sheriff, looking like a broken-hearted father, announced second-degree murder charges. The emerging details looked bad and worse for Higby. We learned that when Judge Skooner and his other son, Andrew, rushed from their house at the sound of the car crash, Higby threatened to shoot them too if they approached Josh, who was dying on the street. Two neighbors who also came from their houses said the detective ranted about crime scene integrity, but the fact was he denied Josh the last comfort of a father's or a brother's loving hands. Worse, he did nothing to keep Josh breathing or to resuscitate him when he stopped.

Although the police made three separate searches and kept an officer posted at the shooting site around the clock for seventy-two hours, Josh's supposed gun never appeared. Nor did a slug or shell casing from the bullet Josh supposedly fired.

Then the medical examiner announced that seven of the eight bullets that struck Josh were shot from close range. The eighth – which lodged in Josh's skull and probably killed him – was shot when Higby's pistol barrel was pressed against Josh's cheek. When asked whether the killing shot was necessary after Josh had already taken seven bullets to his chest and belly, the medical examiner said, 'I don't see how.'

The Sheriff's Office or Judge Skooner – or someone else who disliked Higby – had alerted the television stations about the arrest, and the news feed cut from the announcement to a video clip of him coming out of his house, his hands cuffed behind his back, a grim-faced plainclothes cop on either side of him. He stared at the cameras. I knew that stare – a proud stare, the stare of a man who would accuse but never tolerate being accused, a man who would never admit to being wrong. But in the hollow of his eyes, I saw something else I'd also seen in my own eyes looking back at me in a mirror and in the eyes of most of the men I'd known on death row. Fear.

Lying naked on my bed, I laughed as I watched the arrest. I laughed and laughed until I ran out of breath, and then I was crying, heaving from my chest and belly. I laughed and cried until I felt as if I would throw up. I imagined the owner of the Cardinal Motel finding me, my lungs collapsed, naked on my bed – surviving all those years in prison only to die at the good news that the man who railroaded me was going to jail for murder.

As the cops loaded Higby into the backseat of a squad car, though, he looked at the camera again, and I saw something else I recognized. I knew the look well. I'd felt it in my own eyes, and I'd wondered why no one else saw and believed it. The look said, *I didn't do it. Jesus Christ and swear to God, I didn't.*

I'd heard Higby lie too many times to ever believe him – heard him lie more than I'd heard him speak the truth. I'd listened to him tell a jury that I raped a boy and killed him and his brother. Now, watching his moment of shame and humiliation, I felt no sympathy for him. But I realized I was breathing again. And I wondered if the look in his eyes spoke the truth.

The next morning, Jane Foley, Hank Cury, and I drove to Callahan to talk to the woman who testified against Thomas LaFlora twenty-five years ago.

Her name was Kim Jenkins, and we found her in a garden that fronted a white-brick bungalow. She was almost fifty but had the clear face and eyes of a much younger woman. She wore a wide-brimmed hat, white shorts, and a flower-print blouse, and she had well-muscled arms. She looked like anything but a crackhead, and at first I thought we'd made a mistake.

But Hank walked across her lawn and said, 'Ms Jenkins? We're here to talk to you about Thomas LaFlora.'

She smiled at him, dangling a pair of sheers from one hand. 'I'm sorry,' she said. 'I don't know who you're talking about.'

Jane softened her voice. 'He'll almost certainly die in five weeks unless you help him.'

Kim Jenkins's smile hung on her lips. Again, she said, 'I'm sorry,' and turned back to the garden.

Jane said, 'This is Franky Dast. You've probably heard about him. He just got out of prison after eight years – three of them on death row, alongside Mr LaFlora. We believe that Mr LaFlora deserves to come off death row too. We think he's been unjustly incarcerated.'

'Your words put him in prison,' Hank said. 'Yours and your friends'. Now your words can make things right.'

The woman said nothing. She trimmed the underbranches of a boxwood hedge.

'Nothing can give him back the twenty-five years he's lost,' Hank said. 'But he can have the rest of his life. What remains of it.'

Kim Jenkins stopped trimming. The sheers shook.

Without thinking, I stepped forward and put a hand on her shoulder.

She sprang back – more wild cat than human – and spun toward me, holding the sheer blades toward my chest. But then something seemed to break inside her. She glanced at the house and whispered, 'I can't. Randy—'

'Your husband?' Jane said.

'We've been happy,' the woman said. 'I *won't* tell him. Not now.' She glanced from Jane to Hank to me. 'It's too late,' she said. She moved toward the front porch.

'You need to tell the truth,' Hank said.

'I can't.' She ran up the porch steps and disappeared into the house.

Jane picked up a pair of checkered gardening gloves from the lawn, carried them to the porch, and put them on the steps.

As we started back toward the city, she and Hank said nothing more about Kim Jenkins. They talked instead about a restaurant called The Pig Bar-B-Q, where they wanted to eat lunch.

'Why so cheerful?' I asked.

'She'll come around,' Jane said.

'Guilt is a powerful motivator,' Hank said.

I said, 'She's stayed silent for twenty-five years. Why talk now?'

'Because we asked her to,' Hank said, 'and because she knows someone is listening.'

'And because she saw *your* face,' Jane said. 'Now she can imagine Thomas LaFlora's face too.'

That afternoon, I waited for Thelma to leave, and then I hopped on to her computer. I looked into Josh Skooner's past. The earliest web pages I could find showed that, like me, he ran track as a freshman in high school, but as a sprinter instead of a long-distance runner. He had mediocre times in the hundred meters, and the absence of later meet records meant that, also like me, he stopped running after one year.

After that, up until the shooting, web coverage came from newspapers and television sites that told story after story about the delinquent son of the powerful Judge Skooner. At eighteen, he got pulled over for driving seventy-seven in a forty-five-mile-an-hour zone. He told the patrolman that his father would have him fired, and so the patrolman arrested him for resisting without violence. Prosecutors dropped the charges when he completed a diversionary program.

Three months later, the police arrested him again after a fight outside Mavericks Nightclub. He had a joint in his pocket, and they found a knife and a baggie with traces of cocaine while searching his car. The search was ruled inadmissible, and he got community service for the assault and marijuana charges.

On the evening that Bill Higby shot him, he was on probation for a disorderly intoxication and battery charge after he beat up a girlfriend. He'd asked the arresting officers to give him a break since his dad was a judge, but the break came at a higher level when the prosecutor gave him a plea deal that included no time in jail. The news story about that deal also compared him to his brother, Andrew, who succeeded every time Josh failed. The salutatorian at Episcopal High School, Andrew had just finished his junior year at Cornell. The photo of Andrew made him look like a younger version of the judge – big, square-faced, serious, handsome except for a scar across the bridge of his nose and another above his left eyebrow.

I Googled Andrew's name separately and came up with links to old articles about him on a high school crew team. Then I searched Judge Eric Skooner. The judge graduated from the University of Miami School of Law, then served as an assistant state attorney. As a prosecutor, he became notorious for pursuing death penalty convictions – including Thomas LaFlora's – sometimes against the wishes of the victims' families. Then he worked for three years in private practice before becoming a county judge. Later, the governor appointed him to the circuit court, where he eventually became chief appellate judge. Although he seemed to be best known for work he did on violent crimes, he also served for two years on the juvenile drug court where he sentenced fifteen- and sixteen-year-olds to max time. One website said, though, that when Josh stumbled into the arms of the cops with reefer in his pocket and coke in his nose, Judge Skooner cut deals to get other judges to go easy on him.

According to several websites, on the night that Higby arrested the judge and his wife on domestic battery charges, the couple were drinking heavily, and Melody Skooner was taking prescription medications for an unnamed psychological problem. She'd thrown her cell phone at him. He'd punched her in the mouth and gone after her with a bottle. She'd called 911 and said her husband was trying to kill her. Three patrol cars raced to their house, followed by Higby who, disturbed by the sirens while eating dinner, came over from next door. A week later, when dropping the charges, the prosecutor said simply that he was exercising his *discretion*. When pressed to explain, he added, 'Pursuing the matter further would be imprudent.' I heard fear in his evasions. Two websites also noted that Melody Skooner died five years ago – one said of a heart attack, the other kidney disease.

I read nothing that changed my mind about Higby or told me anything new about what happened on Byron Road after he and Josh Skooner slammed their cars into each other.

But the more I read, the more I saw the crash and shooting as a high-speed version of my own experience with Higby. This time, he skipped the interrogation and trial. He carried out the death penalty himself.

Nothing I could do would save Josh Skooner now.

And I still wondered if I was even managing to save myself. Or if I had a self to save.

Dr Patel seemed to think I did, though he had more optimism than I did. He seemed to think I could find my way back by seeing familiar people and places. A long shot, but I'd read and reread the websites on the Skooners, so I figured I would make searches for people *I* once knew.

I tried my old track coach.

After speaking at my trial as a character witness, Ernie Kagen visited me several times during my first four years in prison, and then he sent occasional notes. Until my last two years, he also sent Christmas cards that went heavy on Santa and the reindeer. I'd always wondered why he took interest in me after my arrest. In prison, I appreciated visits from anyone who lived outside, but even then I sensed that his interest in me came from a questionable source.

Online, I found an address for him on Nelson Street in the Murray Hill neighborhood – an hour by bus from the JNI office.

I sweated just thinking about making a visit. So I Googled the AMC Regency website. They were screening *Mrs Doubtfire* as part of the Afternoon Kids Classics Series.

'See you tomorrow,' I said to Jane and Hank, and I left the building, ran to the corner, and got on a bus. Forty-eight minutes later, it stopped at the Regency Mall. I kicked gravel across the parking lots again, then ran as light-footed as if I was skipping across tree roots in the woods behind the house where I grew up.

Inside, I went to the concession, where Cynthia stood behind
the counter filling a drink cup for a man in a gray hoodie.

Standing next to her, the skinny teenager I'd seen when I came
to watch *Toy Story* frowned. 'Yes?' he said.

'Get lost,' I said.

After Cynthia gave the man his change, she came over. She
did her little fingertip wave and said, 'Hi.'

'Hi,' I said, and asked, 'Would you like to go out with me some
time?'

She narrowed her eyes. 'Some guys just ask me for extra butter
on their popcorn.'

'I'll take popcorn too.'

'I don't know who you are,' she said. 'Why would I want to
go out with you?'

I stepped backward without realizing it.

She laughed. 'I'm kidding. Yeah, I would go out with you.'

'Yeah?'

'Yeah.'

I grinned through the movie and on the bus ride back to the motel.
That night, I dreamed I was running free through the back woods,
under the shade of pine trees and loblollies, cool even in the
summer heat, because a boy could feel cool if he created his own
wind. And then I floated on open water, the sunshine pricking the
tips of waves as a breeze crossed over them. There was nothing
more beautiful than sun sparkling on water.

I grinned again in the morning as I turned on the TV. But then
a reporter said Bill Higby would walk out of jail before noon, free
on his own recognizance. Higby had lied and lied. He would sooner
see me die than admit to lying. Hank's comment came back to
me – I of all people should know that the system would never
hold a cop like him accountable.

What goes up must come down. Hit the gas as hard as you like,
because there's a viaduct around every bend waiting to kiss you
and crush your teeth.

So I stopped grinning. But I didn't really fall, and I didn't crash.
Instead, I decided, when Higby got out, I would go to see him at
his house as he'd come to see me at the Cardinal Motel. Coach
Kagen could wait. Higby also was part of my past that needed

revisiting. An overfamiliar part. A part that Dr Patel might advise me to bury under the weight of better memories and a good future. But I sensed that Higby would refuse to be buried. He would kick at the soil I dumped on him. He would claw through truckloads of stone until I dealt with him. Like a bad spirit, he needed killing if not placating.

EIGHT

When the blue that lined the muscles in Dad's arms and neck receded into his skin, like a magic trick – when he broke the kitchen table, the clock radio, and the glass bowl that his mother gave him for a wedding gift, the last remnant – when he threatened to break Jared's neck and mine – I ran out the back door and into the woods. I broke through the bramble, the branches and thorns raking my arms and face. My feet sank into the cushioning soil. The roots tangled like broken spider legs, like a web that a scared boy would break through as he ran from a father who loved but might kill him. I skipped over those roots, as if I was flying. Fear moved me – and one should never underestimate what fear can make a boy do. Fly even. Skip across a tangled earth where gravity is the least of our problems.

I disappeared into the woods. Disappeared. Like a magic trick. I ran fast and faster. At a certain speed, a body becomes invisible even to itself. At that speed, fear dissipates, and all that remains – aside from the dry film that scums the dish – is joy. A boy needs to run far into the woods to get to it. A boy needs to run fast. But when he tumbles and lies on the forest floor, legs throbbing, chest billowing, eyes almost blinded by tears and sweat, he sees joy in a sky that burns through the spaces between the tree branches. He sees it in the bark of trees that sway in the breeze. If he's lying by a swamp, he sees it in the algae and the cypress trees that rise from the water like probings of life. If he digs into the soil with his fingers, he finds it in the worm. If night has fallen and he lies on the ground long enough, he sees it in the eyes of a long-toothed possum wandering toward the garbage that neighbors have put at the roadside for pickup.

'We're a family of extremes,' Dad said.

'What's that mean?' Jared asked. I couldn't have been older than twelve.

'I've told you how my father died?' Dad said.

He had – often. Along with working as a salesman at a used boat dealer, Dad's father played the French horn in a wedding band. One night, when Dad was sixteen years old, the van carrying the band from a Valentine's Day party in southern Georgia skidded on an icy bridge.

'The van burned,' Dad said. 'Everyone and everything inside it turned to ash – everyone but the girl who sang and everything but my father's horn. The girl went through the windshield, and except for some cracked ribs and cuts on her face, she was fine. My father's horn went through the windshield with her and landed on the roadside gravel. Everything else was twisted metal and cinders. The fire was so hot, they couldn't identify the teeth.' He looked at Jared and me to see if we understood the point. I didn't. 'Extremes,' he said. 'The police gave that horn to my mother, as if it would help us grieve. I always hated that horn.'

'Do you think it's strange that Mom also died in a car wreck?' Jared asked.

'It's to be expected,' Dad said. 'In a family like ours.'

Jared told me later that night something I'd never heard before – that Mom had been with another man when she died. They were driving in his car. He said, 'Who knows what they were doing when he veered into the truck.'

'Liar,' I said.

'Ask Dad,' he said.

'Never.'

Months later, I found the French horn in the attic. When I dusted it off, the tuning slides, the valve levers, and the leadpipe looked like parts of a marvelous machine. I put my lips to the mouthpiece and blew. My breath made no sound – at least nothing like music. I brought the horn down to my bedroom anyway and hid it in my closet. When Dad went out or was working, I tried to make the horn sing. Then the music teacher at school announced she was starting a concert band. I snuck the horn to her classroom where she taught me enough notes to play the *Star Wars* theme song, 'Across the Stars.' Twice a week in after-school practices, I rehearsed the song, and at night, when Dad was sleeping, I whistled it.

On the evening of the spring concert, I slipped out of the house. Sitting in the dark auditorium before the lights came up, next to other kids with their flutes and trombones, I felt the same joy I felt while running through the woods or lying on the ground staring up through the tree branches.

Then it was my turn. When I blew into, the French horn, I felt the music light up inside me.

I completed only four measures before I heard rumblings from the audience. But I focused on the mouthpiece and the valves and the brightness inside me. I played four more measures and then heard laughter – polite, uneasy, then unrestrained. I stopped playing, looked into the dark that hung over the audience, then played again. The laughter came harder. I stopped and started again. As I lurched through the notes, I strained to see beyond the lights that flooded the stage.

I saw him. Dad was dancing in the space between the stage and the front-row seats. I never learned how he found out about the concert. The audience thought he was hysterical. Their laughter seemed to energize him, and his dance became outlandish. Maybe the dancing and laughter would have broken another boy's focus, but my lips found the mouthpiece again and I finished the song, missing no more notes than I did in the best of my practice sessions. When the song ended, the audience clapped, and Dad bowed twice before going back to his seat.

He'd come to hear me play an instrument that hurt him.

And he'd humiliated me.

I never hated him more than I hated him that night.

I never loved him more.

I looked for him at the end of the concert, but he'd already gone. So I walked home alone, and when I got there, I looked into his bedroom. He was lying face down on his bed. The next morning, he was still sleeping when I left for school. In the days that followed, neither of us mentioned the concert.

Then, during the summer, the French horn disappeared from my closet, and when I checked the attic, it wasn't there either.

Maybe Dad pawned it for drinking money. Maybe he dropped it in a dumpster. Maybe he disassembled the marvelous machine and buried the parts in the backyard. I never saw it again.

But during my three years on death row, I sometimes heard that French horn playing – more softly and truly than I ever learned to play it, as if Dad's father was serenading me. The music might have come from my dissociative disorder, another version of the impulse that made me want to crawl out of my skin. But it gave me peace. Locked up between concrete walls for twenty-three hours a day, the other death row inmates and I existed apart from day and night and from time itself, except that every passing second rang like a bell reminding us that we'd moved a second closer to the needle that would kill us. Some of the men found religion, seeming to believe God cared more for sinners than saints, even sinners who'd raped and killed and would rape and kill again if they got the chance. Other men descended deep into the insanity that had put them on death row to begin with.

I clung to the edge. The weight of insanity tugged at me, and clouds of faith teased me. I was grateful when I heard the French horn soundtrack from *Star Wars*.

NINE

'I lied,' Cynthia said.

'Yeah?' We sat in front of Big Easy Cajun in the food court at the Regency Mall.

'When you first asked me out, I said I didn't know who you were. That wasn't true. I saw you on TV – at the courthouse when they let you go.'

'Does that scare you?' I asked.

'Should it? They say you didn't do those things.'

'It scares people anyway,' I said.

'Not me,' she said.

Somewhere in the mall, a machine started rattling, jackhammering a floor or laying down a new one.

'So, what do you want to do?' I asked.

She smiled as if I'd said something weird. 'Let's go someplace.' The way she looked at me, I thought she would let me take her anywhere. She said, 'Where do you *wish* you could go – if you could go anywhere right now?'

I could think only of the woods behind the house where I grew up. I said, 'I like movies.'

She rolled her eyes. 'If I could go anywhere, I would go someplace with ice. All ice. Walls of it. Nothing but ice.'

'Why?'

She touched her thumbnail to her teeth. 'I don't know you well enough to tell. And anyway, it's your turn. Where would you go if you could go anywhere?'

I would lie on a forest floor. Worms would crawl from the ground. The leaves on the branches above me would fold in the breeze. I said, 'I would go with you to that place with ice.'

'Nice one,' she said. She leaned across the table. 'Did they teach you to flirt in prison?'

'You're unusual,' I said.

'You are too.'

'But you knew that already,' I said. 'From seeing me on TV.'

So she told me she lived with her parents in a house a mile from the beach. And she'd taken three courses toward an associate's degree in respiratory care before deciding she needed a break. She'd worked full-time at the Cineplex for the past six months. A lot of guys asked her out while she was working – one or two a day at least. I was the first she said yes to.

'Oh,' I said.

'You should feel flattered.'

'I do.'

'I said yes because you're unusual,' she said, 'and I am too.'

Then we walked through the mall. It smelled of dust and plastic and whatever they sprayed through the vent system. The lights were dim, as if the mall managers were trying to save on electricity. A woman in exercise shorts and earphones speed-walked past us. Another woman, pushing a stroller with a crying baby, walked the other way. Then we were alone.

'I come here sometimes when I get off work,' Cynthia said.

It was a lonely place. 'Why?'

She said, 'Anything's possible.'

'More like a land of the dead.'

'Anything can happen,' she said again, and when we came to a brightly lighted jewelry store, she ducked inside. I followed her to a glass counter, where a man in a brown two-piece suit gave her an undertaker's smile and glanced at her hand for a ring. 'Yes?' he said.

Cynthia looked at the necklaces in the display case, then leaned toward him and said, 'I need a nipple ring. Something that hurts.' She nodded at me. 'So does he.'

If she was trying to shock the man, she failed. 'The Piercing Pagoda is on the other side of the mall,' he said. 'You might try them.'

'Thank you.' She reached to shake his hand. 'My name is Cynthia. Do you live here?'

He smiled. 'At the mall? Sometimes it seems like it.'

'Me too,' she said cheerfully, and she headed for the exit.

'Nice to meet you, Cynthia,' the man said.

'You see?' she said, when we were out on the walkway. 'When we're here, we can be anyone we want.'

'You were just making fun of him.'

She shook her head, skipped a few steps in front of me, and turned to face me. 'I was making a world and inviting him into it.' She turned and headed toward the JCPenney entrance. 'Come on,' she said.

She led me to the women's clothing section, went to a rack of jackets, and took one with a zebra print, another with a jungle pattern, and a third with leopard spots. 'Hold these.' She put them in my arms. Then she went to a rack of pants and took every pair with a flower or an animal print. 'These too,' she said, and piled them on to the jackets.

'What are you doing?' I said.

'If you don't like the past, you still can have a good time,' she said. 'Eventually.'

'Maybe we have different ideas of a good time.'

She picked up a leopard spotted hat with a black band and put it on my head. 'What's your idea of fun, Franky?' she asked.

Before I could work out an answer, a woman clerk and a security man rushed down an aisle. 'Uh-oh,' Cynthia said.

'No, no, no,' the woman clerk said to her. 'Not again.'

'Out,' the security guard said, and pointed back toward the mall. 'Now.'

A second clerk came from another aisle, as if she would tackle us.

Cynthia took the hat from my head and set it on a manikin. Then she ran for the exit. I dropped the clothes and ran after her. She was waiting for me outside the Piercing Pagoda.

'You've done this before?' I said.

'I told you, I come here sometimes after work. It's better than going home.'

I looked up and down the empty walkway. 'It's kid stuff,' I said. The dim light hung like a weight. 'I want to leave now.'

She stared at me as if I'd disappointed her.

So I said, 'I don't know what's the matter with you.'

'OK,' she said, and she headed toward the doors to the parking lot.

But as we passed the Vitamin World kiosk, she darted into it as if she couldn't help herself.

'Get the hell out of here,' the clerk said, even before Cynthia opened her mouth.

She picked up a box of Ultra Man daily multi-vitamins and said to me, 'This might be what you need.' Then she asked, 'Do you also have Ultra Woman? I've been feeling . . . what's the opposite of "ultra"?'

'You can leave, or I can call security,' the clerk said.

'Let's go,' I said.

She said, 'Who forgot to take his Ultra Man today?'

Then we were outside in the heat of the July afternoon, thunder-clouds piling on top of each other. As we walked across the empty lot to our bus stops, her hand brushed mine. I put my hands in my pockets.

She would need to cross the highway to get from my stop to hers. But she stood with me as cars and trucks rushed past. 'Are you going to take me home with you?' she asked.

I felt a shiver. Dread. Desire. Mostly fear. 'Do you want me to?'

'I don't know,' she said. 'Maybe.'

Jared thought I needed to get laid. But Dr Patel warned about going from zero to ninety. Viaducts and all that. 'I'm pretty much wrecked right now,' I said.

'I know,' she said, as if that added interest.

'When I get this way, I sometimes throw up.'

She nodded. 'Maybe we should wait until next time.'

'Yeah, maybe,' I said.

She stared at me as if wondering whether I was worth the bother. 'Tomorrow night?' she said.

'You think so?'

'Pick me up at the theater at eight,' she said. 'Find a car. We'll go someplace.' Then she stepped into the traffic.

TEN

B ack at the Cardinal, I stretched on my bed with the lamp off, thinking about Cynthia at home with her parents and how far away that seemed from me. The blue light from the TV flickered on the furniture and ceiling. My head spun. After a while, Bill Higby appeared on the TV screen in footage of him leaving county jail – clean-shaved, wearing khakis and a blue sport coat, two women at his side, one of them gripping his hand. With that look in his eyes, I figured his head was spinning too. I got down on the carpet and did a hundred forty pushups and three hundred sit-ups. But when I got back on my bed, my head still spun and spun until I fell asleep.

When I woke again in the middle of the night, staring at the flickering on the ceiling, I thought for a moment that I was breaking apart, shattering into shards of light. I watched the wavering and fluttering, and decided that if I did break, I would let myself smash into pieces without resisting. Then I slept again and woke the next morning only when my neighbors – Bill Hopper had called them Jimmy and Susan – started fighting outside my room. *Good people*, Hopper had called them. I looked through the window shades. Broken glass on the parking lot glinted in the early-morning sunlight. Jimmy wore black jeans and a black T-shirt, and Susan, both eyes bruised now, wore a short green dress, as if they'd just come from an all-night party, though I couldn't figure who would invite them.

I pulled on pants, opened the door, and said, 'Would you mind quieting down or taking it to your room?'

Susan glared at me. Jimmy said, 'What kind of sick-ass freak are you?'

I said, 'Huh?'

He gestured at my door.

A pair of white Fruit of the Loom boy's underwear hung from the handle. It was threadbare and streaked with blood or something that looked like it.

I yelled, 'Jesus!' and jumped away. My heart pounded. Sweat broke from my skin. I screamed at Jimmy, 'Get it off my door!'

'Freak,' he said, and walked toward the motel office.

'Who put them there?' I yelled at Susan.

'Don't know.'

'Get it off,' I said. 'Please.'

'Sorry, honey.' She followed Jimmy to the office.

I ran out to the highway and sat in the gravel along the shoulder. I stared at my door. It remained half open. I stared at the underwear hanging from the handle. It matched Steven Bronson's pair, as the prosecution presented it at my trial. The fumes of a passing truck washed over me. Bits of gravel – kicked up by a car – stung my back.

Jimmy and Susan left the motel office, glanced at me as if I was wrecking the neighborhood, and disappeared into their room.

So I went to a bush on the roadside and tore off a branch.

Then I went to my door and poked at the underwear until it hung from the end of the stick. I carried it to the office and dropped it on the counter.

I was shaking with anger. 'Someone left this on my door.'

'The other guests are complaining about you,' Hopper said.

'What are you talking about?'

'Playing your TV too loud last night. Yelling at them outside their room. You know I welcome all kinds, but—'

'I had my TV on quiet,' I said, 'and I yelled at them because *they* were yelling and' – I pointed at the underwear – 'because these were hanging on my door handle.'

'Why would Jimmy and Susan put those on your door?' he said.

'I didn't say they did.'

'Then why were you yelling at them? You can't be disturbing the other guests.'

'I *wasn't*.'

'They say you were,' he said.

'Do you have a security camera?' I asked.

'It broke four years ago.'

'This place sucks,' I said, and I turned to go.

'Hey!' he said. 'Take those with you.'

I carried the underwear out on the end of the stick. Like a flag of surrender. I took them to the trash bin and dropped them in. I chucked the stick in after them.

My mind raced and I sweated and stank on the bus downtown. The other passengers gave me space and eyed me as if they heard me ticking. First thing when I climbed the stairs to the Justice Now Initiative and went in, Jane looked at me and did a double take. She said, 'What happened?'

I told her and Hank about my morning.

'A nasty prank,' she said. 'At that place, I'm not surprised.'

I said, 'It was someone who knew the details. It was the same brand. Same everything.'

Hank looked skeptical.

'I remember,' I said. 'I remember everything.'

'You've got to get your mind off it,' Jane said. 'Put all of that bad energy into good work.'

'I'm staying at this motel because the people there have no right to judge me.'

Hank said, 'You've got to stop taking yourself down to the lowest common denominator.'

Now I turned my anger on him. 'I've been lower than the lowest. For eight years. This is a big step up.'

His face flushed.

'No one has a right to judge you,' Jane said. 'Least of all for what happened to the Bronson brothers.' She picked up a folder and carried it to Thelma's empty desk. 'Thelma comes in at ten today. In the meantime, take a look at this file. Maybe you can make something of it.'

I was still sweating. 'You know what? I can't handle this today.' I turned to leave.

Jane went back to her desk. 'I think the file will interest you.'

I kept going.

'It's on Bill Higby,' she said.

I stopped. 'What about him?'

She just stared at me, so I went to the desk and opened the folder.

The file was twelve pages long – a tightly formatted list of citizen complaints and commendations, reaching back to the beginning of Higby's career at the Sheriff's Office. There were thirty-one entries in all, and they appeared with columns marked *Dates*, *Complainant or Endorser*, *Actions*, and *Resolutions*. When I was in prison, I spent years tracking down information about Higby, but I'd come up with only about half of the list.

'Where did you get this?' I asked.

'Your case isn't over,' Jane said. 'The State Attorney might decide to try you again. And you still have your civil suit.'

'Right. But where did you get it?'

'Take a look at numbers eighteen, twenty-three, and twenty-seven.'

The three entries involved the Skooner family. I already knew about twenty-three and twenty-seven. The Skooners filed formal complaints after Higby came to their house to intercede in the fight between the judge and his wife, and again to stop Josh from playing loud music. According to the report for the first of those incidents, Higby wore a pistol on his belt, and though he never drew it, he kept touching it – 'caressing' was the word Melody Skooner used.

But entry eighteen – filed four years before the marital dispute – praised him for tracking down and returning Josh Skooner, who, at age eleven, ran away from home. The *Actions* column said Higby found him fifty miles away, east of the town of Bostwick along the St Johns River, on land owned by a company named Tomhanson Mill. The incident report ended with the notation *Fam prop. No charge.*

I figured *No charge* meant the Tomhanson Mill owners decided against prosecuting Josh for trespassing and whatever else he did.

I typed the letters *Fam prop* into Google, and the top hits came from real estate ads and records of last wills. In them, *Fam prop* meant *Family property*. Did the Skooners own Tomhanson Mill or a stake in the company? If they did, that would explain how an eleven-year-old knew to go to this place, fifty miles from home, though not how he got there. And it would explain why Higby knew to look for him there.

I searched the pairing 'Eric Skooner' and 'Tomhanson.' The names brought up three links to reunion events for alumni of Episcopal High School, where 'Eric Skooner' and 'Melody Tomhanson Skooner' graduated. They also brought up a funeral announcement for Melody Skooner's father, Geoffrey Tomhanson, a year after Josh ran away and another funeral announcement, for Melody Skooner, five years ago.

I looked at Jane and said, 'Done.'

She'd just gotten back to work. 'What do you mean?'

'Josh Skooner was camping out on his grandfather's land. Higby brought him back. That's all.'

'That was quick,' Hank said.

Jane said, 'The point is, he did bring him back. He knew the kid. And he helped the Skooners before everything went wrong between them.'

'Even a bad man does good now and then,' I said. 'Probably by accident.' I laid the file on her desk. 'I'm heading out.'

But then Hank's phone rang, and when he picked up, he said *uh-huh* a couple of times, listened for a moment, and held the phone to me. 'It's for you,' he said.

'You're kidding?'

He shrugged.

I took the phone.

Kim Jenkins, the witness in the crack house shooting, said, 'How well do you know Thomas LaFlora?' Before I could answer, she asked, 'What's he like now? Because I knew him. Back then, he *could've* killed those people, even if he didn't. He was capable of it. I saw him do as bad as that to others.'

'I can't say what he did or didn't do back then,' I said. 'I can only tell you what he was like on death row.'

'That's all I want.'

'He was broken,' I said. 'He said nothing to anyone. He looked away if you talked to him. I would've thought someone had torn out his vocal cords except I sometimes heard him talking to himself in his cell at night. If they execute him now, they'll just be finishing the job.'

Jane and Hank watched me as if my finger hovered over the switch that would inject the lethal drugs into Thomas LaFlora's body. On the phone, Kim Jenkins was quiet for a long time. Then she asked, 'Is it too late for him? If he got out now, would it be too late?'

I hadn't seen him in five years, ever since they moved me from death row into general population. But I guessed it was already too late even then. I said, 'If he didn't kill them, you've got to say so.'

'I don't know,' she said.

I felt a flash of anger. 'You don't know if he killed those people? Or you don't know if you can say it?'

She hung up.

When I handed the phone back to Hank, he and Jane were all smiles.

I shook my head. 'I got mad at her.'

'You did great,' Jane said.

'You have authority,' Hank said. 'She called to talk to you. She'll come around.'

Jane gave me a gentle look. 'You're doing good work. You've just got to go easy on yourself. Maybe you would do better to stay here today than to go back to the motel. Too much time to brood there.'

Hank said, 'Or if you need to take the day to yourself, do something you enjoy.' Dr Patel's advice too – as if they were in this together.

I looked at him. I looked at Jane. 'Fine,' I said. 'Give me something to do.'

I spent the rest of the morning at Thelma's desk, searching the internet for information on the lawyers who represented Thomas LaFlora in his original trial and his appeals, looking at transcripts of Eric Skooner's original prosecution of him, and digging through the electronic case files of the judge who sentenced him to death. Even after Thelma came in, Jane let me continue at the computer. There was peace in the work. I liked the case numbers. I liked the clean fonts in the depositions, the transcripts of testimony, and the court rulings. I liked the neatly squared bureaucracy. I knew that much of what I saw might lie to me and anyone else who saw it. The documents I'd researched in my own case had lied and lied and had dripped with hypocrisy. But I also knew that if I looked long and hard enough, I could detect the lies as lies and see the hypocrisy as hypocrisy. And that meant that even if the world was screwed up, order might remain under the chaos. I just needed to find it and show it to others, and maybe, if the right people saw it – people like Jane and Hank, or the judge who released me – we could sweep the chaos aside.

I worked through lunch, disappearing into the computer screen the way I sometimes did in prison, sweating again, working until Jane and Hank eyed each other, as if they smelled wires burning. At four o'clock, Jane said, 'You've done enough for today.'

'Plenty more to investigate,' Hank said. 'Can't do it all at once.'

'Fine,' I said again. 'Anyway, I have a date tonight.'

Jane smiled. 'You're full of surprises. That's what Hank was talking about. Go out and enjoy yourself.'

Hank looked more concerned. 'You're hanging on to a pendulum, aren't you?' he said. 'It's all or nothing? Swinging on a wrecking ball?'

I stared at him.

But Thelma came from behind me and ruffled my hair. 'Our own Lazarus.'

'One problem, though.' I glanced from Jane to Hank. 'I need to borrow a car.'

Jane looked at Hank. 'Can you give me a ride?'

He tipped his head, as if to say he could.

She reached for her purse but then asked, 'Have you gotten a driver's license?'

'Soon,' I said. 'I'll do it tomorrow.'

She put her purse on the desk. 'Well, you can borrow my car when you have it.'

'Sorry,' Hank said. 'Same goes for me.'

'For God's sake,' Thelma said, and she gave me the key to her car. 'Don't get pulled over or I'll deny I let you borrow it.'

So I drove her Nissan out of the parking garage. But instead of going back to the motel or straight to the Cineplex, I drove to the west side of the city, then south on the ring road. When I came to Blanding Boulevard, I exited and dropped past cinderblock carwashes, tire shops, credit unions, a cemetery, an IHOP, a pawnshop, and a Christian bookstore. Overhead, thunderclouds piled in the sky. My mind raced, and I wanted to pull over and close my eyes, but I kept driving, past dingy roadside businesses and then a scrappy patch of woods with vines that had killed the trees they grew on.

I turned on to Henley Road, crossed Black Creek, and cut on to Byron Road. Four news vans and two police cruisers stood in front of the house next door to the mansion where Judge Skooner, with his older son beside him, gave a TV interview on the morning after Josh died. The people by the vans now seemed to be waiting for Bill Higby to stick his head out of his front door. I figured the police were there to keep the reporters from storming his house when they ran out of patience.

Compared with the surrounding houses, Higby's single-story ranch was small, but he kept the yard neat and landscaped. Three flower gardens, bordered by railroad ties, dotted the front lawn, and purple-flowered bougainvillea grew up a trellised arch where a brick walkway met the road. Through the side yard, I saw the slow dark water of Black Creek.

I parked on the grass shoulder behind one of the news vans and walked toward the house. A man with a long-lensed camera said, 'Don't bother. He won't answer the door.' But I went up the two steps to the front porch and rang the doorbell.

I waited for almost a minute, then rang again.

A voice behind me on the driveway yelled, 'Hey,' and when I turned, the man with the camera took a picture. 'Thanks,' he said, and retreated to the road.

I turned back to the door and was about to knock when I heard movement inside. I put my face by the glass peephole. I wanted Higby to see me. When no one answered, I touched the doorbell again.

The door yanked open.

Higby, who'd appeared dressed neatly on the news last night, had turned into a rough-faced, barefoot man in cargo shorts and a yellow golf shirt that barely covered his belly. The way he stared reminded me of how he'd held me against the wall of an interview room.

I made myself grin and said, 'I wanted to see what you look like. Because I know what's going through your head right now. You're thinking, *This can't be happening. It isn't real.* And most of all, you're thinking that you're screwed. But the difference is, you deserve it. I came by to tell you that.'

He looked at me from my feet to my head and said, 'To me, you should be dead. They should've strapped you to a table and put a needle in your arm. I would've come and watched.'

The words punched me. But I managed to say, 'I'm alive. And do you know how I spent my day? I looked into all kinds of nastiness that people have accused you of. It's a long list. But I had time – because a judge said you messed up. The judge said to set me free. So now I can do whatever I want. Every day. You know what I think I'll do tomorrow? I'll dig up more dirt on you. Maybe I'll find something to help put you in prison for shooting your neighbor.'

I stared at him, waiting for an answer. His eyes had gone blank.

Again I said, 'I wanted to tell you that.' I turned and started down the steps.

'What makes you think you can come here?' he said.

I turned and faced him. 'What makes you think you can stop me? Look at yourself.'

If he said anything to that as I walked down the driveway to the Nissan, I didn't hear it. My head was buzzing too loud.

I drove back to the Cardinal Motel, did my pushups and sit-ups, and then stood in the shower. The stream from the showerhead went from weak to weaker, and currents of cold water flashed through the hot, but I soaped my body, rinsed, and soaped again. My sweat went down the drain, and though my stains ran too deep to ever wash away, I scrubbed and lathered and rinsed again as if I could clean myself to the bone.

I dressed afterward and ran my fingers through my hair, then squared the towel on the towel bar. I fixed the bed sheets. I balled up a strip of toilet paper and dusted the night table and the top of the TV. I carried the bathroom garbage outside to the bin.

Before leaving to pick up Cynthia, I looked at myself in the bathroom mirror. 'I know you,' I said to the face that stared at me, and then I closed my eyes and turned away before I could change my mind.

When I pulled up at the Cineplex, Cynthia ran to the car from the ticket booth. The clouds had blackened as the sun started to go down, and thunder rolled across the sky. As Cynthia climbed in, the first raindrops splattered on the windshield. She smiled at them, smiled at me, and gave me her fingertip wave. 'Hi.'

'Where to?' I asked.

'I'm starving,' she said. 'Take me out to eat.'

Now the rain came hard, pummeling the hood and roof, and she watched me as I drove toward downtown, then cut back again on Philips Highway.

When I pulled into the lot at Sahara Sandwiches, I said, 'It's close to where I live, and it's better than it looks.'

Inside, the fluorescent lights glared, and the air smelled of the deep fryer. Three stools, covered with orange vinyl, faced a white counter.

'Here or to go?' the grill man asked when we ordered gyros and fries.

'Here,' I said.

But Cynthia said, 'To go,' and then, to me, 'I want to take you somewhere.'

As we waited for the food, the old black prostitute who'd ducked under a bus shelter when I walked back to the Cardinal after my first trip to the Regency limped in, rainwater running from her hair. She winked at me and said, 'Hey, there.' She eyed Cynthia and then came to me. 'Give me a cigarette.'

The man behind the counter reached for a pot of coffee. 'Leave them alone, Felicity.' He poured a cup and set it on the counter for her.

'No need to be rude,' she told him.

Cynthia had me drive across the river and into the industrial area northwest of the city. An overpass took us across a big railroad yard. The rain came down hard, and lightning cracked the sky. After we passed the Nextran Truck Center and the White Wave Food Warehouses, she said, 'Turn at the next entrance.'

The sign said *Cardice Cold Storage*, the words draping over the image of an iceberg. At the back of the parking lot there was a gray warehouse with nine truck bays and a street door. Cynthia pointed at a spot next to a white van. 'Park there.'

When I turned off the car, she grabbed the food and darted through the rain and into the building. I got out and followed her.

The lobby had brown carpet, cheap wood paneling, and a metal desk. The air felt like an open refrigerator. An attendant, wearing yellow coveralls over a thermal T-shirt and a flannel shirt, sat on a metal chair behind the desk. A parka, a wool hat, and snow gloves lay on a table next to him.

Cynthia stood at the desk talking with him. She waved me over and said, 'Mr Tony, this is my friend, Franky. We'll be about a half hour.'

He considered me. 'This one don't look like he'll last that long.'

We went through a door into a small interior hall with a heavy door.

'You've brought other guys here?' I asked.

'Once or twice,' she said.

She opened the door, and we went inside. The walls and the high ceiling were fat with insulation. Heavy-duty metal racks, rising thirty feet from the concrete floor, stood in long rows. Ice crystals coated them and the plastic-wrapped boxes on the shelves. Vented machines with icicles hanging from their brackets blasted icy air from near the tops of the wall. Industrial fans, mounted on the ceiling, circulated a freezing wind. Toward the back of the warehouse, there was a separate metal shed, covered with extra insulation, which was coated with frost.

My pants and shirt stiffened as the rainwater froze.

'This is insane,' I said.

'Yeah,' Cynthia said happily. She took our bag to one of the racks and, using a box as a table, unpacked our food. She shivered as she handed me my gyros.

I looked around the space, from the metal shed to the wide interior loading docks. 'Why?'

'It's my favorite place. All ice.'

'Yeah, but *why*?'

She shrugged and bit into her pita.

'How did you find it?' I asked.

'I've been coming here since I was eight years old.'

We ate – shuddering in the cold, our clothes turning brittle with ice, the grease in our sandwiches congealing, soft as cheese. I ate an oil-crusted French fry and said, 'Tastes horrible.'

She ate one too. 'Yeah.' Then, eyeing me, she took another fry from the bag and fed it to me.

'I don't get this,' I said.

'You don't need to.'

My legs trembled with cold. She laughed as she watched me shake. Then she started trembling too. I looked at the ceiling and around at the rest of the wide room. I nodded at the separate metal shed. 'What's in there?' 'That's the deep freezer,' she said. 'They use dry ice. A hundred and ninety degrees below zero. You want to try it?' 'This is what – a test?' 'Maybe,' she said. 'Or maybe it's a gift. I don't know. You want to go in?' 'Another time,' I said. 'I'll hold you to that.' We left the warehouse after twenty-five minutes. I could hardly bend my fingers, and my feet were numb. Cynthia thanked the attendant, and, as we went back out into the rain, he said to her, 'I think this is a record. By ten minutes at least.' 'Feel better?' Cynthia asked when we got back into the Nissan. 'I feel cold,' I said. The car windows steamed as the chill radiated from our clothes. She leaned over and kissed me on the cheek. Her lips felt hot. 'So, what now?' she asked. 'Go for ice cream?' I said. She was quiet for a moment, then said, 'Why don't we go back to your room?' The idea scared me. 'I haven't been with anyone since I got out. I was barely with anyone before. There was one girl. At a party in high school.' 'So maybe it's time.' 'Maybe,' I said. We sat for a minute longer. Then she said, 'Start the car, Franky.' By the time we reached the river, the rain had eased, and when we merged onto Philips Highway, it turned to mist. Still, the water standing on the pavement slicked off the backs of the tires and hissed against the bottom of the car. Cynthia sat next to me, her eyes on the road, her hands crossed in her lap. When we pulled past the Cardinal Motel sign and into the parking lot, she looked at the shabby building and looked over her shoulder at the red neon bird. 'Nice place,' she said.

'It's complicated,' I said.

We went inside, and I locked the door behind us. She eyed the bed, the TV, the night table, and the dresser. 'It's not so bad,' she said.

'I needed a place to get started,' I said.

She walked to the bed, touched it, walked to the TV, touched it too. 'I live with my mom and dad,' she said.

'We do what we need to do,' I said.

She went to the window shade, looked under it into the parking lot, and let it fall back into place.

She faced me. 'Do you know that woman who asked you for a cigarette at the restaurant?'

'The hooker? I've never seen her before. Or I've seen her – out on the street – but I don't know her.'

'Because I wouldn't blame you if you did.'

'As I said, I've been with no one.'

'Good,' she said, and she came to me.

'Hold on,' I said, and I went to the lamp.

But she said, 'Leave it on.' Her voice seemed to catch in her throat. 'I need to show you something.'

She unsnapped the top of her pants, stared at me as if uncertain about what we were about to do, then unzipped and lowered the pants to her knees.

Her legs were scarred. Mottled red and gray. Shiny. Pitted. They looked like old sicknesses – leprosy or the plague. 'What is it?' I said.

'When I was little, we had a fire. I was sleeping in my bed.'

'Christ – I'm sorry.'

She smiled.

'What?' I said.

'You've been through it too, right?'

'I guess.'

'So we've got *that*.'

'Does it hurt?' I asked.

'Sometimes. And sometimes my throat does. I breathed a lot of smoke. Cold air feels good, especially on my legs. I like ice.'

I was afraid to go to her.

She slipped off her shoes and pulled her pants off the rest of the way.

She stared at me and said, 'Your turn.'

I took off my shoes and socks and pants. I unbuttoned my shirt and took it off too. I stood apart from her, and I shivered though I no longer felt cold. Then the shame of the pair of boy's underwear hanging on my door handle came back to me. But she took off her shirt, unhooked her bra, and let it fall.

I looked at her legs. I'd never seen anything uglier. 'Can I touch?'

'Please do.'

We did our best at sex. But images of the men who'd come to me during my first night in general population kept flashing in my memory. When I fought those memories down, images of the Bronson boys – the photographs Higby had shoved in my face in the interview room and the big slides that the prosecution had showed the jurors – replaced them.

'I'm sorry,' I said.

She put her hand between my legs and whispered, 'Never be sorry. Never.'

When she bit my neck, the bite marks on Steven and Duane Bronson flashed in my vision.

I tried lying on top of her, and she pretended to enjoy it, but I could see the pain.

'We're a mess,' she said, when I rolled off of her.

'Sorry,' I said again.

'But I don't mind being a mess,' she said. She kissed me and said, 'Lie on your back.'

She used her hands again and her mouth, and when I was ready or close to it, she said, 'Good enough.' She climbed on top of me and guided me inside her.

In a burst, I was done.

'Shit,' I said.

But she stayed on top of me, kissing my forehead, my lips, and my shoulders. And when she rolled off and lay on the bed beside me, she touched her hand to mine.

'Sorry,' I said.

But she said, 'That was great,' as if lying could make it true.

So I lied too. 'It was,' I said.

ELEVEN

Some nights on death row, I lay on my bunk and I thought I could taste the boys' blood on my lips. The salt. The copper. In solitary confinement, the dark has fingers. It plays you and plays you until you make cracked music like no French horn has ever made.

Some nights, I wondered if I did it.

With the lights back on in the morning, I knew I didn't. I shouted my innocence at the walls. I wrote letters. I whispered into the toilet pipes so the men in the other walled-in cells would hear me.

But some nights, I wondered if my memory lied.

Higby told the jurors I bit Steven and Duane Bronson *in the worst places imaginable*. He said the teeth that bit the boys were my teeth. He said the lips that sucked away their blood were mine. Some nights, with the fingers of dark playing me, I believed it.

I bit my arm. To taste the blood. To see if it was true. If it excited me. But it was my arm. My blood. Not theirs. I didn't fool myself. I tried.

Higby never showed Steven and Duane Bronson's mother pictures of their bodies. He showed her only their faces. She could identify them, say goodbye. But he showed *me*. He showed the jurors.

I told all this to the other inmates through the plumbing pipes. We were men suspended over stainless steel toilets, talking to ourselves until we heard echoes of our own voices. Or sitting under stainless steel sinks. Certain pipes resonated when others went silent. One man sang songs he'd learned twenty years ago, before he killed his wife and daughter. If I could have made the plumbing sing, I would have piped the *Star Wars* theme into the other cells. Instead, I whispered to the toilet, whispered to the sink, *I didn't I didn't I didn't*, even when I wondered, *Did I?* And the echoes came back—

I didn't either.

Me neither.

I was in a different town at the time.
A different state.
Out of the country.
Ask my mother, my brother, my sister, my lover.
Liars. Most of them.
Would I call any of them my friends?
More or less.
But the bar was low. When the people who bring you your food and allow you to bathe also plan to kill you with a needle, an inmate who flings his own shit at you if you get too close starts to seem neighborly.

When the court transferred me off death row, I listened to French horn recordings online in the prison library. Mark Taylor. Vincent Chancey. Old guys like Philip Farkas, who could have blown the hell out of *Star Wars*.

The thing about a French horn is you always know what you're listening to. It's like hearing a man singing with an accent. With a flute or a trumpet, the music gets so pure it seems to separate from the metal, lips, and fingers that make it. But with a French horn – with all those tubes turning the sound this way and that – you know you're hearing twists against perfection.

I had a lot of time to think about such things. I talked about them to my friend Stuart. He seemed to understand, or at least he nodded along as he often did, because he generally ran the way the current was flowing, no matter the direction. If I had talked to the other men about the French horn, I might have given them courage to come at me with shanks. *Them* I would lunge at in the yard and make sure they backed away, or they would lunge at me, testing, always testing for a soft spot.

To see Stuart, you would think others would victimize *him*. A big, heavy, yellow-skinned black man, he carried himself like a gallon jug of water, always more sideways than forward. He had gentle eyes and lazy lips that went with the eyes. If you watched him lift weights in the yard, you knew that muscles rippled under the fat, but he seemed always short of breath, and, with the way he spoke – his *T*s and *D*s crumbling between his tongue and his teeth – the hyenas should have eaten him for dinner.

But, after lights out, the worst of the predators recruited him to hold down their prey while they took turns, though – as far as I knew – he never took a turn himself. And yet, in spite of the night times, the prey hung near him whenever they could in the daylight, as if he would shelter them. And sometimes he did. As the predators circled, he would slosh into the middle of the action and speak with the intended victim, and the predators would pause and then break from the pack as if they forgot their hunger.

I never learned what Stuart did to get sent to Supermax. He wouldn't say, and no one else seemed to know. But we all knew he'd come for life plus thirty years. He laughed his gentle laugh and said, 'I'm gonna stink this prison to high hell for every one of those extra thirty years. A corpse like mine gonna rot for a long time.'

So I told him about the French horn, and I told him about the Bronson boys and the letters I was writing, though admitting that you'd gone down for raping a kid was like inviting others to hang you from a bar with a bed sheet.

Stuart would listen and he would say, 'You got to be strong, Franky.'

I couldn't figure out if he believed me. Belief seemed beside the point.

'If only I can get the government to test the rape kit,' I said. 'But they keep it locked in a box, like I'm asking for the key to their houses.'

Now and then, he asked a question like, 'If you didn't do those boys, who did? You got to have that.' But mostly he just took it in. He seemed to absorb it.

TWELVE

Dr Patel said, 'You need to accept that freedom is essentially transgressive.'

'I don't know what that means,' I said. My head was still full from my night with Cynthia.

He leaned toward me until he seemed about to hold my hand. 'To be free is to be unafraid of the law – to be *able* and *willing* to break it if moral conditions require that you do so.' Outside his window, the sky over the St Johns River looked brilliant and hot. Any moment, the water under it might start boiling.

'If you aren't raping and killing, you aren't free?' I said.

'Once upon a time in evolutionary history, that might have been true. For us now, it just means living without undue fear of the law.'

'Even if the law has tried to kill you?'

'Especially then.'

I thought about that. 'So it was OK to go to Higby's house?'

'You *should* confront your past,' he said, 'and you should ignore arbitrary boundaries.'

'But?'

'But beware of taking pleasure from others' misery. And beware of treating them unjustly.'

'Unjustly? Higby is a hypocrite. He lies. He tried to get me killed and still would like to see it happen. I'll cheer when a prosecutor buries him. I'll bring the shovel.'

Dr Patel leaned back in his chair. 'May I ask two questions?'

'I'd rather you didn't.'

'First,' he said, 'is it possible that Bill Higby sincerely *believes* you killed those boys?'

'No,' I said. 'He had the evidence. He only needed to check. He could've opened the rape kit, run the tests, and let me go. He wanted me to be guilty. He needed it. He still does.'

'He *and* the prosecutor *and* the judge *and* the jurors? They all wanted and needed it?'

'Yes,' I said. 'All of them.'

He just waited.

'It was their job to figure it out,' I said.

'Second,' he said, 'what if Higby is innocent? What if Josh Skooner really did have a gun and shot at him?'

I laughed at that. 'Higby executed that kid. He makes his own rules. He kills when he wants to. That's what he tried to do to me.'

Dr Patel folded his fingers and said, 'You seem pretty sure of yourself. Are you the police now? Are you the prosecutor, the judge, and the jury? Are you the law?'

'Don't screw with me,' I said.

'Do you just *want* him to be guilty? Do you *need* it?'

I stood up. 'I've had enough,' I said.

'I agree,' he said.

I went to the door.

He said, 'True freedom is also only possible for those who avoid imposing arbitrary laws on others.'

'Fuck off,' I said, and I went out.

'That's the spirit,' he called out.

I stopped by the DMV on my way to the Justice Now Initiative. After I waited forty-five minutes for my turn, the clerk said I needed to come back with a birth certificate or a passport and also tax records, pay stubs, and utility bills showing where I lived.

'What if I don't have any of that?' I asked.

The clerk looked impatient. 'You just landed on the planet?'

'More or less,' I said.

As I climbed the stairs to the JNI, I thought that even after a warden pops the lock on your cage, the hallway to the front door stretches a hundred miles and looks like a rat maze. In the office, Hank was talking to Jane about paperwork that might compel Kim Jenkins to testify in Thomas LaFlora's next hearing. And Thelma was tapping on her computer keyboard.

I put the keys to her Nissan on her desk and picked up her phone. I dialed my brother and, when he answered, asked if he still had papers from Dad's house.

'Boxes of them,' he said. 'Why? Do you want part of what I sold it for?'

'I need—'

'Because your half went to legal fees.'

'I had a public defender and volunteer aid,' I said. 'You never paid for a lawyer. You never even—'

He hung up.

I dialed again.

'What?' he said.

'I need my birth certificate. That's all. You can keep the money from the house. I just want to get a driver's license.'

He went silent for a moment. Then, 'I'll look.'

I said, 'Look soon, OK?'

'We're cool, then?' he said.

'When have we ever been cool?'

'About the money? For Dad's house?'

'Sure, Jared, we're cool.'

'Because the money's gone,' he said.

'Just the birth certificate.'

'Sure.'

I hung up. Hank was going on and on about writs and subpoenas. So I said, 'I thought we wanted Kim Jenkins to testify voluntarily.' He looked at me irritably. 'We do. But we'll compel her if we need to.'

'We did a lot of compelling for you,' Jane said.

'We're ready to do more,' Hank said. 'We'll make the state pay for the time it took from you.'

'But you need to do something to help your cause,' Jane said.

'Of course,' I said.

'You need to stay out of trouble,' she said. 'Avoid messes. Some people still think you belong in prison. They'll refuse to pay you what's due to you if they can. You've got to be a poster boy for innocence. If you need to fight, then fight for others who are innocent. Stay clean.'

'Did I do something wrong?' I asked.

Hank took a folded-out newspaper from his desktop and tossed it to me. My picture stared back at me. It was the shot that the photographer took yesterday afternoon on Higby's driveway. The caption said, *Released Convict Confronts Accused Officer*. The article under the photo said little more than the caption. *Recently released death row inmate Franklin 'Franky' Dast visited homicide detective Bill Higby, whose testimony helped convict him and who now faces second-degree murder charges. A heated exchange followed – the subject unknown.*

'Wow,' I said.

'People are watching,' Jane said. 'A lot of them are undecided about you. The governor and others who control the bank accounts will listen to them. Avoid unnecessary entanglements. Live your life, but live it clean.'

Dr Patel had just told me to stop fearing the law. Now Jane and Hank were telling me to be careful who I talked to. 'Got it,' I said.

Jane gave me a tight-lipped smile.

I turned to Thelma, looking for a friend.

She shook her head and said, 'Never lie to me again.'

'What?'

'Too many men in my life have lied,' she said. 'I won't tolerate it. If you say you want to borrow my car to go on a date, then go on a date.'

'I did. I went—'

'Right,' Hank said. 'Who are you dating? Higby's wife?'

'Where did you take this date?' Thelma asked.

If I told them that Cynthia and I froze ourselves half to death in a cold-storage warehouse, they would laugh at me. 'We hung out,' I said. 'That's all. We hung out.'

Hank just turned to his computer, Thelma started working on her keyboard again, and, after shaking her head at me, Jane asked me to run to the FedEx shop to pick up an order.

So I went back down the stairs. Two blocks away, the woman at the FedEx counter handed me a mailing tube, and when I took it back to the office, Hank popped the top and unrolled a poster-size picture of Thomas LaFlora's face – a recent shot of him, with a couple of days of beard stubble and eyes that I recognized from every long-term death row inmate I'd known.

Thelma taped the poster to the back of the office door. It would stare at us as we worked.

'The man of the hour,' Hank said. 'We do these when a case is heating up so that we stay focused on a flesh-and-blood person. We don't focus on the Bill Higbys of the world. We don't focus on ourselves. We focus on the man whose life is on the line.'

I asked, 'Did you also have a poster of me?'

'Sure,' Jane said. 'We still have it – in the cabinet, along with posters of eight other men. Would you like it?'

I was already spending enough time gazing at myself. 'I think I'll hang out in the cabinet with the other guys,' I said.

That afternoon, the thunderstorms came early, and the bus back to the Cardinal Motel moved through a sheathing downpour, gusts slapping the glass and metal. I planned to change clothes and head to the Regency Cineplex. A quick check on Thelma's computer had told me that the AMC had scheduled a three-day run of *Home Alone* in the Afternoon Kids Classics Series. If I never got past the concession stand, I would also be happy.

But when I ran across Philips Highway from the bus stop, a woman was standing under the concrete overhang outside my room. She had olive skin and a black ponytail. Even in the July heat, she wore heavy cotton pants and solid shoes. That made her a cop.

She stepped out into the downpour. 'Franklin Dast?' she said.

'Obviously.'

'I have a message for you,' she said.

'Who are you?' I asked.

'The message is simple. If you step on Bill Higby's property again—'

'I upset him that much?' I said. 'What does he have to fear from me?'

'He'll protect what's his. Stay away from his house.'

Thunder rolled across the sky.

'What's your name?' I asked.

'That's all I came to tell you,' she said. 'Ignore me, and whatever happens to you is your own fault.' She started across the parking lot toward a black Mercury Grand Marquis.

'I get it,' I called after her. 'I've been helping out at the Justice Now Initiative, and whenever they start worrying about me, they give me a little job to do. File papers. Run an errand. Make phone calls. It's like that for you too, right? Higby is worried. So he sends you out here.'

The woman turned and came back. She said, 'You don't get it at all. You crawl out of the ground like a locust, and you want to stretch your wings – you want to make some noise. But if you do, someone will stomp on you.' She was wearing heavy black shoes. Police issue. Good for stomping. But she started toward the car again.

I asked, 'Did he really ever think I killed the Bronson boys? Does he *really* still think so?'

Once more, she stared at me, the rain smearing her face. She said, 'That night on Monument Road, you might have had a friend with you. Your friend might have raped the younger boy. But your blood was still on the engine. Your fingerprints were everywhere. You haven't proved your innocence. You've only managed to give a judge some doubts. But the fact is you're out of prison now. So, does it matter what Detective Higby thinks?'

I said, '*I* really think he murdered Josh Skooner. No justifiable force.'

She said. 'From all I've heard, you're a pretty smart guy. But this time you're wrong.'

I went inside and stripped off my wet clothes. Outside, the rain drummed against the pavement and the hoods and roofs of cars. I punched the wallboard by the bed, bloodying my knuckles. Then I went into the bathroom and turned on the shower. As I stood under the hot stream, my anger at Bill Higby blossomed again. Why had he blamed *me* for the deaths of the Bronson boys? Why did he call me evil and act like a god who would destroy all he hated? And why did I let him cling to my thoughts? Why did he stick in my throat like the taste of vomit, like a pinched nerve that kept me from crying for help? Why did he rage after me when I got out of jail – a cancer in my mind – and then send a messenger to warn me away from him?

A man like that deserved to suffer.

Who was I to say so?

Was I the police now? The prosecutor, the judge, and the jury? Was I the law?

Sure. I could be all of that.

When I got out of the shower, my knuckles were throbbing. I dried myself, then wrapped my hand in a cold wet towel. As I worked my hand through the sleeve of my T-shirt, someone knocked on the door.

Maybe the woman had come back to threaten me again.

Maybe Higby had come to threaten me himself.

I yanked the door open.

The reporter who'd taken my picture outside of Higby's house – accompanied now by another man, with a camcorder perched on his shoulder – stood on the walkway. The reporter smiled, which meant that the camcorder was already running, and said, 'Just a few questions.'

'Uh-uh,' I said, and closed the door. He knocked and I yanked it open again. I asked, 'How did you find me?'

'Public records,' he said. 'You're everywhere.'

'If I'm on any lists,' I said, 'Higby put me on them. He's a liar and a criminal. He manipulates the system. He kills young men like Josh Skooner. He tried to kill me. He seems to get off on it. I can't explain it any other way. And then he hides behind the law. He's a coward.'

The reporter smiled bigger. I'd given him what he'd come for. Then he looked at me, straight-faced. 'Will the legal process treat Detective Higby as it has treated you?'

'Never,' I said. 'Did the State Attorney even consider capital murder charges against him? He shot an unarmed kid eight times. *Eight.* That's not second degree. Then a judge let him out on his own recognizance—'

The reporter asked, 'What did the two of you discuss at his house yesterday?'

But I kept going. 'What kind of legal team will the police union put together for him? How hard do you think the prosecutor will try to convict? Who will be on the jury?'

The reporter nodded, and, as he asked his next questions, I realized how fast even a sympathetic listener could turn against me. 'What happened to your hand? Did you punch someone?'

Jane had called me the smartest client the JNI ever represented, but I knew that, at core, I would always be my dad's senseless son who opened the door when he should leave it shut. 'Household accident,' I said.

When the reporter and his video man climbed into their van and drove away, I stood in the doorway and watched the rain. Before I could slow my racing thoughts, my brother's SUV pulled into the parking lot and slid into the spot outside my door. Jared got out, gazed at the sky, and shouldered past me into my room. He shook the rain from his arms, went into the bathroom to check his hair, and came back. 'You waiting at the door for me?' he said.

'I was heading out.'

'Just couldn't decide how to get your body out of the doorway, huh?' he said. He looked at my bare feet. 'Couldn't figure out how to put your shoes on either?'

I shut the door. 'Checking if it still was raining.'

'It is.' He dug into his pocket, pulled out his wallet, and fingered through the leather folds. 'This afternoon, a friend showed me your picture in the paper. Making a house call to the cop who arrested you is a little fucked up, if you don't mind my saying.'

He found what he was looking for – a laminated card, which he flipped toward me. It landed on the carpet. It was my old social security card. 'I figured you might need it for your license.'

'You also find my birth certificate?'

'Sure.' He dug into his pocket again. 'What were you doing at the cop's house?'

Getting myself in trouble, I thought. 'I'm working as an investigator for the Justice Now Initiative,' I said, as if that answered the question.

'An *investigator*?' He grinned, doubtfully. 'Let's see the badge.'

'They pay me to investigate. That's all.'

'Unless you get an ID, you're not an investigator,' he said. 'You're the guy who runs the copy machine and makes coffee. They have you doing the errands?'

'Don't be a fool.'

'They're humoring you,' he said.

I looked past him at the dent I'd put in the wall. I could hit him too. But I said, 'What did you ever do with Dad's car?'

'Still have it in my garage. No one would buy it. When they arrested you, the cops cut up the seats and tore out the interior lining looking for evidence.'

'Why did you keep it?'

'I figured someday it might be worth something.'

I thought about that. 'You mean after my execution?'

'Some collectors like that kind of thing. I looked into it.'

'I want the car.'

He laughed. 'I haven't started the engine in seven years. The gas has probably turned into varnish.'

'We'll get a siphon,' I said. 'We'll get a new battery.'

He shook his head. 'Engine's probably fried.'

We drove to Walmart and then to his house. Hours later, under the bright lights in his garage, as the rain fell outside, I turned the key in the ignition. The engine caught, coughed, and died.

I tried again.

Nothing.

'Hah,' Jared said.

I turned the key. The engine caught, sputtered, coughed, and caught. I gave it gas. It died.

'Fuck this,' Jared said. 'Let's go to a bar. I'll get you laid.'
I turned the key again. The engine caught, and I shoved the accelerator to the floor. For a moment, the engine made no sound. Then an oily black wad shot from the tailpipe. The engine roared.

THIRTEEN

The next morning, Jane, Hank, and I went back to Callahan to talk with Kim Jenkins. Channel 4 had aired my interview from the Cardinal Motel on the eleven o'clock news, and when I walked into the JNI office, everyone stared at me as if shocked I had the guts to come back after disregarding the slam-down they'd given me the day before.

Jane rubbed her chin and said, 'Be careful.'

Hank shook his head and said, 'I'd thought more highly of you.'

Thelma gave me a glimmer of a smile. 'You're burning it high, aren't you?'

'To get a driver's license, I need a letter saying I work here,' I told Jane. 'It needs to include the address of the Cardinal Motel.'

When we knocked on Kim Jenkins's door, a square-jawed, athletic man in his fifties answered. The rain had stopped in the early morning hours, and now the July sun beat against our backs. Jane and Hank introduced themselves, and the man said his name was Randall Haussen – Kim Jenkins's husband. Last time we came, Kim Jenkins had worried about telling him about her past. But Haussen looked like he could take it.

Jane asked if we could speak with his wife, and when she came, he stood beside her with an arm draped over her shoulder. Kim Jenkins seemed terrified. Her husband, though, showed no surprise when Hank told her that the JNI was filing papers requiring her to testify at an appellate court hearing.

'Of course, we'd prefer that you testify of your own accord,' Hank said. 'That would serve Thomas LaFlora's interests best – and yours.' He implied that we had evidence showing that she'd perjured herself in the first trial.

Jane touched my arm and spoke to the husband. 'This is Franky
Dast. He also was on death row. The courage of a couple of expert
witnesses set him free. We're asking your wife to show such
courage. We're asking you to support her.'

The husband's voice was deep and loving. He said, 'I support
Kim in any decision she makes. A hundred percent.' But I realized
he was digging his fingers into her shoulder.

Hank and Jane seemed only to hear his words. They smiled at
Kim Jenkins expectantly.

She forced a smile too. 'I'll do it,' she said. She glanced at her
husband for approval, but he kept digging.

Hank shook hands with both of them. Then the husband shook
Jane's hand. He reached for mine, but I turned and went to the
car.

As we drove back toward the city, Jane turned to me and said,
'Great work.' As if I'd done more than wag my tail when she
patted me on the head.

'The husband took that well,' Hank said.

I said, 'He already knew we were coming.'

They ignored that.

Hank glanced over the seat and offered his lesson of the day.
'In our experience, most people want to do the right thing.
Sometimes fear makes them lie or cheat. But if you show them
the hollowness of the fear, they come around. Jane and I have
seen it. *You* just saw it in Kim Jenkins.'

'She won't show up at the hearing,' I said. 'Or if she does,
she'll say Thomas LaFlora killed those people.'

Hank laughed at me. 'Why do you think that?'

'Who's the husband?' I asked. 'How long has she known him?'

'She married him fifteen years ago,' he said. 'That's what she
said last time we were here.'

'But who is he?' I asked.

'Seems like a pretty good guy,' Jane said. 'Considering where
Kim Jenkins started, she's come a long way.'

Back at the office, I hovered over Thelma's desk until she said,
'Fine,' and got up so I could use her computer. I typed *Randall
Haussen* and *Kim Jenkins* into Google and got nothing that inter-
ested me. So I typed in *Randall Haussen* alone and got over nine

hundred hits – too many to make sense of. I opened the Florida Department of Law Enforcement Criminal History Information site and typed his name again.

I hated to be right. From the time he was eighteen until he was twenty, Haussen had four drug arrests on charges ranging from simple possession to possession with intent to distribute. The first two involved marijuana, the last two cocaine. The first three charges were dismissed, and the last resulted in a sentence of probation. Then, twenty-three years ago – two years after Kim Jenkins's testimony put Thomas LaFlora on death row – the police arrested Haussen for shooting a crack dealer in the same neighborhood where LaFlora supposedly committed his killings.

I printed the arrest record and then opened the *Times-Union* website to search the archives. Two articles gave the details. The crack dealer, shot once in the leg and once in the arm, survived but refused to testify. Haussen took a plea deal – seven years, including time served.

I printed the articles too and put them and the arrest record on Jane's desk.

As she read them, her face flushed. But she said, 'So what? They both were in the life twenty-five years ago. We already knew that about her. What's the big deal?'

'Why did she lie when we first went to see her?' I said. 'Why did she imply that he had no idea about her past?'

'She wants to forget. She wants her past to stop haunting her. She wants his past to go away too.'

I said, 'She's afraid of him.'

'Nonsense.'

'She'll skip out on the appeal hearing,' I said. 'If you scared her enough, she'll run. Maybe Haussen will buy her a ticket and put her on the bus.'

'Nonsense,' Jane said again. She looked at me, worried. 'Is it possible you're projecting your own circumstances with all the betrayals against you on to others? You shouldn't blur the lines. Work out your own problems, and let other people have theirs. Randall Haussen isn't Bill Higby. Deal with your issues, but separate them from the rest of us.'

So I did as she told me. I went back to the computer, but now I searched for details on Higby's shooting of Josh Skooner. Sure,

I had issues with Higby. Even when I was looking into Kim Jenkins' and Randall Haussen's pasts, Dr Patel's words had needled me. *What if Josh Skooner really did have a gun and shot at Higby?* And I still could hear the words of the woman who came to threaten me at the motel, answering me when I said Higby killed Josh Skooner without just cause. *You're wrong.*

I needed to prove I was right.

I reread the articles that discussed the hunt for the pistol Higby said Josh shot at him. They all told the same story. The police had pulled apart the wreckage of Josh's and Higby's cars . . . and found no gun. The police had searched the bushes and lawns near the crash . . . and found no gun. They'd all but dug into the asphalt and put ladders up into the tree branches . . . and found no gun.

Then I read about the moments after the shooting. As I'd known from before, Josh's father and older brother rushed to the scene, as did their neighbors. Higby threatened them against getting close to Josh's body. He failed to try to save Josh's life himself.

But an online publication called *Metro Jacksonville*, which had the most comprehensive report, included two details I hadn't seen before. One of the neighbors, angry at Higby for killing 'a neighborhood boy,' told the reporter that Josh's brother, Andrew, bloodied himself while trying to staunch Josh's wounds before Higby pulled him away. Another neighbor, also angry, described the horror on Andrew's face as he walked up the driveway to his house after paramedics loaded his brother into the back of an ambulance.

My stomach turned. Maybe those details changed nothing. But they contradicted the reports that said Higby kept Andrew and the judge entirely away from the shooting scene. And they gave Andrew a chance to carry away a pistol.

I closed the site and said, 'You know what? I don't care.'

Jane looked up from her computer. Hank turned from a document he was reading.

'About what?' Jane said.

'I just don't give a damn,' I said. 'It all comes down the same way anyway.'

Hank said, 'What are you talking about?'

I stood up and started toward the stairs. 'I'm going to get my driver's license.'

Jane said, 'We were hoping you might record a statement supporting Thomas LaFlora's appeal.'

But I was gone.

Two hours later, with a new license in my pocket, I drove my dad's car – its seat cushions sliced with X-ACTO knives, the few remaining strips of fabric hanging from the roof – on Byron Road and parked on the shoulder fifty feet before Bill Higby's house. A Channel 4 News van idled by the driveway. The other vans must have left for another story, though they would come back as soon as the reporters smelled meat. I sat in the car, watching the house. Shades hung over the windows. The front door looked wedged tight against the gleaming sun. Beyond the side of the house, Black Creek bent toward the St Johns River. A man floating on it on a raft or a jon boat might imagine that nothing in the world mattered but the slow, warm current of his life.

I got out of the car. I felt none of the bravery or foolishness that I'd felt two days earlier when I'd gone to Higby's door. I scuffed over the front lawn, passed the bougainvillea trellis, went up the brick steps, and rang the doorbell.

No one answered.

I looked back at the news van. It idled, pulsing, its tinted windows reflecting the sun. I glanced at the neighboring houses – Judge Skooner's, another big house on the other side. They looked as tightly closed as Higby's. I seemed to be the only one alive.

I rang the doorbell again.

When footsteps approached from inside, I fought off the impulse to run. Then the door opened, and a woman's face appeared instead of Higby's.

She frowned. 'Yes?' She had short, tightly curling blond hair.

'Is Detective Higby here?' I managed to ask.

'No' – as if I'd asked a question that she'd long ago tired of answering – 'Detective Higby is *not* here.'

'You're his wife?' I asked.

'I wish you people would leave us alone,' she said.

'I'm not *you people*,' I said, and when she just stared at me, I said, 'My name is Franky Dast. Will you tell him I came by to talk to him? I need to ask him some questions.'

'*You're* Franky Dast?' She looked at me without fear or disgust or any emotion at all. 'Well, Franky Dast,' she said, 'you don't belong here, and you'd do well never to come back.' She started to close the door.

'The problem is, ma'am, I don't belong anywhere. And so here seems as good of a place as any.'

For a moment, she stared at me again. Then she closed the door the rest of the way and snapped the bolt lock.

Early that evening, I drove to the Cineplex and bought a ticket to *Home Alone*.

'It started an hour ago,' the ticket clerk said.

'All the good stuff is in the second half.'

I went straight to the concession stand. A line of customers waited at the counter, but Cynthia came to me and said, 'I'll be off in ten minutes.'

I told her I would be watching the movie.

'Wait,' she said, and she went to the drink machine and filled a cup with crushed ice. She handed it to me.

'For what?' I asked.

But she turned back to the customer line.

Fifteen minutes later, she settled into the seat next to mine. She'd changed out of her work clothes and into a dark dress that fell to her knees. She touched her hand to mine, and as Macaulay Culkin sprang booby traps on the robbers and tormented them with his brother's pet tarantula, the hours, days, weeks, and years that led to this moment crumbled into pieces of darkness that felt less real than the light flickering on the screen. As the robbers threatened to burn Macaulay's head with a blowtorch and bite off his little fingers *one by one*, Cynthia pulled my fingers to her lips and kissed them. Then she guided my hand into the cup of crushed ice. As the police arrested the robbers, she took my cold fingers, pulled her dress up her thighs, and set my hand on her scarred skin. She whispered, 'That's nice.'

I touched her, and she sank low in her seat, exposing more of her legs. I pinched crushed ice from the cup and held it to her skin, drawing circles. When I inched up her thigh and under her dress, she whispered, 'No,' and so I inched back down, and she whispered, 'Yes.'

Someone on the screen was saying, *Kids are resilient like that.* Someone was saying, *It's cool that you didn't burn the place down.*

And soon the credits appeared, and, after the credits, the lights in the theater came up.

Cynthia straightened her dress over the wetness on her legs.

I said, 'I love movies.'

She said, 'Let's go back to your room.'

We drove to the motel. The sun was setting outside, and golden light glowed at the edge of my window shade. Cynthia unbuttoned her dress and let it fall to the carpet. I took off my shirt and unzipped my pants.

She said, 'If you could go anywhere tonight – anywhere at all – where would you go?'

'Right here,' I said. 'Right here and right now.'

'Nice one,' she said, and came to me.

When the sun dropped below the horizon and only the glimmering light of passing cars and trucks broke the dark, we lay together on my bed, legs touching, arms and shoulders too.

'That was better than last time,' Cynthia said. Then a minute later – 'Not that I minded last time.' She rolled over, facing me. 'But this was better.'

'It was good,' I said.

'Kind of great,' she said.

'Yeah,' I said. 'Kind of great.'

Outside, the tires of cars and trucks swished over the dry pavement on the highway.

'I saw you on TV last night,' she said. 'Talking about the detective.'

'Yeah,' I said. 'Strange, right?'

'Are you going to hurt him?' she said.

'Higby?'

'Because I would understand it,' she said. 'It would make sense, I mean. To want to hurt him. After what he did to you.'

I said nothing for a while. Then, 'I don't know what I'm going to do. I'm still figuring it out.'

We were quiet, and I slept – I *think* I did, because, like a man dreaming that he's dreaming, I thought, *This is the way real people sleep.* For the longest time – eight years – I'd felt unreal, felt that way so long that now that I lay in a real bed, touching real skin, cooling in the real sweat of the night, I could only think of myself with astonishment. The goodness of the night seemed as undeserved as all the bad I'd suffered. Asleep or awake, I looked at Cynthia and asked, 'Why?'

And, asleep or awake, she answered, 'Why not?'

FOURTEEN

Walk into a prison to visit an inmate, and you need to shower afterward to get the smell off. Spend a night in a prison, and the place holds to you for a time like fat under your skin. Spend a month or a year, and you're stained deep. Strangers see it on you. They hear it in your voice. Eight years in prison *turns* a person. You are what you eat. You are where you sleep.

On the third day of my trial, my public defender attacked the victims. 'Were the Bronson boys drunk at the time of their deaths?' Lance asked the blood expert, as if drunkenness would excuse rape and murder. 'Were they high?'

I was feeling so screwed by that point that I welcomed the attack as a glint of hope.

But the blood expert put out that flicker. 'No, Mr Stoddard,' he said. 'There's no evidence of alcohol or drugs. Not even aspirin.' He added, to reinforce his point, 'The boys *did* have elevated levels of mercury.'

'Aha,' Lance said, as if he'd caught him up.

The expert all but rolled his eyes. 'Any of a dozen common causes could lead to such levels. The boys might have played with a broken thermometer or spent time near a coal-burning power plant,' he said. 'Or they might have eaten too much tuna fish.'

The jurors laughed.

Lance turned from the expert and looked at me, wide-eyed. As he sat down, I felt an itching and crawling in my bones.

The itching and crawling never went away. They deepened and spread until, after a year passed in prison – and then two – if a surgeon had cut into me with a scalpel, or if another inmate had cut into me with a shank, the gasses that came out would've smelled like a rat that died behind a wall.

And with that knowledge, I felt the rotting inside me speed its work.

Some of the other men gave themselves to that rot, accepted it as they accepted the sweat we breathed in our prison cells and the gristle and rice we ate. Stuart did – fat, sideways-moving, lazy-lipped, go-with-the-flow Stuart. How he managed to turn diabetic on the food they fed us, I never figured out. Sometimes he breathed hard even after the smallest exertion. Supermax tore him apart even faster than the rest of us.

'Sit down,' I would say, and I would get off my bunk so that he had a place. 'Catch your breath.'

'My breath ain't going anywhere,' he would say. 'Not behind these bars.' And he would laugh his breathless laugh.

Another inmate would tell him, 'You got to go to the RMC' – which was the Raiford Medical Center.

'What for?' Stuart would say. 'RMC is just like here. They put you in a different bed is all, and tell you you're sick when you already know it.'

So he held down the new prisoners for the predators and protected the old prey if they asked him to, and he rotted from the inside out, and he never complained. After a while, his uncomplaining acceptance led the rest of us in Supermax to love him.

FIFTEEN

At two in the morning, a boot kicked a hole through my door at the Cardinal Motel. The wood by the bolt lock shattered. I jerked from my sleep and turned on the lamp. In the bright light, Cynthia, terrified, naked on the bed beside me, stared at the crumbling door.

The boot came through again. A man's hand reached into the

hole and fumbled with the handle. I froze – in a nightmare of men coming in the night to attack me in my cell.

The broken wood jammed in the frame. Outside, the man swore, pulled his hand from the hole, and kicked again. The door flew into the room.

The man came – followed by another man, and a third.

They were in their early twenties. The kicker wore black cargo pants and a black sleeveless T-shirt. The others wore blue jeans, gym shoes, and untucked golf shirts.

Strangers.

But they knew me.

'Franky Dast?' the kicker said – asking but also saying.

I saw no weapons. They must have thought three-on-one would give them all the advantage they needed.

I looked for something to defend Cynthia and myself. The car key, on the night table, would take out a man's eye. I grabbed for it.

But one of the men in blue jeans – with military-cut blond hair and a couple of days of beard – reached under his golf shirt and took out a pistol. He eyed me, then Cynthia. He seemed no more interested in her nakedness than mine, gazing only at her scarred legs.

The man in boots stepped close to the bed. I grabbed the key. He grinned. 'What? You're going to run us over with a car?'

I slashed the key at him.

His friend aimed the gun. 'Don't,' he said.

But the reflex after eight years is to never back down. My head felt clearer than it had since I walked out of prison, where danger from other men was constant. The man in boots reached for me, and I slashed again. The key raked across his arm, and he jumped back as if I'd touched him with a hot electric wire. He yelled as a crease of blood rose on his forearm.

Cynthia made a high wailing unlike any sound I'd ever heard.

The man with the gun shouted at her, 'Shut up.'

The one I'd wounded shook his bleeding arm. He said, 'Shoot him.'

'Be quiet,' said the man with the gun. He aimed at my head. 'Get up.'

I eased myself out of bed, gripping the key in case the man in boots came at me again.

The one with the gun said to the third man, 'Lock him up.'

The third man pulled out a set of handcuffs and approached me, then stopped, eyeing the key.

'Drop it,' the man with the gun said. 'And if you touch my friend, I'll kill you right here.'

Cynthia watched, as if curious about what I would do. I handed her the key. 'Let me put on pants,' I said.

'Fuck you,' said the man I'd hurt.

'Put your hands behind your back,' said the man with the gun.

'Who are you?' I asked.

'Hands,' he said.

I put them behind my back. 'You're not cops,' I said.

The man with the cuffs came to me. I smelled his nervous sweat. He locked my wrists.

'Why are you doing this?' I asked.

'Why did you kill Steve and Duane?' the man in boots said. 'Why do you think you can—'

'Were you their friends?' I asked. The ages seemed about right.

The man with the gun said to Cynthia, 'Do you know who you're sleeping with? Do you know what he's done? Do you know what that makes *you*?'

She surprised me. 'If he did it, that might make me a lot of things,' she said. 'I've thought about it, yeah. But that's *if* he did it. I don't think he did. I know what *you're* doing, though. And you know it too. What does that make *you*?'

He stared at her scarred legs. 'Figures,' he said. Then he said to the man in boots, 'Let's do it.'

He came to me, cautious, as if I might be hiding another key. But then he got brave and shoved me toward the door.

'Where are you taking me?' I asked.

'Where you can't hurt anyone else,' he said.

I looked out the door. A gray van stood in the closest parking spot. If I got into it, I might never come back.

My legs locked. I'd promised myself after my first night off death row that I would never again beg. 'The court threw out the conviction,' I said.

'Technically,' said the man who'd handcuffed me.

The man in boots shoved me again.

The one with the gun stepped outside on to the walkway.

Then my neighbor Jimmy stepped into the light from behind the wall outside my door. He also held a pistol, and he pressed it against the other man's head. He took that man's gun, shoved him back into my room, and came in after him. He looked at Cynthia, naked on the bed. He looked at me, naked and handcuffed. He pointed his pistol at the man in boots. 'What the fuck?' he said.

'This is none of your business,' the man said.

'No,' Jimmy said, 'I mean *really*, what the fuck? You can't come around kicking down doors. People live here. This is our home.' He aimed his gun at the other two men before pointing it at the man in boots again. 'If you don't respect our home, what do we have left?' He glanced at the others and said, 'Uncuff him.'

Neither of them moved.

'Do I look patient?' he said.

The man who'd locked my wrists came and freed me.

Jimmy said, 'If you have a problem, take care of it somewhere else. Don't come here.' He looked from one man to the next, as if he expected an answer.

None of them said anything.

Jimmy said, 'Get your asses out.'

The men left, climbing into the van and spitting gravel from the tires as they drove from the parking lot.

Jimmy watched through the broken doorway.

'Thanks,' I said. I was sweating, cold.

He shrugged. 'Hopper asked me to keep an eye on you, take care of you when he was out of the front office – be neighborly and all. Neighborhood Watch, right?' He offered me the other man's gun.

My head buzzed as I reached for it.

But he pulled it away. 'Nah, you're still a sick-ass freak.' He went back out into the night.

I stood naked in the doorway. Now and then a car or truck passed on the highway. The air stank like the exhaust of the day. At one end of the parking lot, a streetlight hummed.

Cynthia came up behind me. She had put back on her dress. 'Take me home,' she said – tired, sad, scared.

'Sure,' I said.

She turned away as I sat on the bed and pulled on my pants and shirt.

'Sorry,' I said.

'I need to think about all this,' she said.

'I know.'

The broken door would invite thieves. So, as she watched, I loaded my clothes and belongings into the car trunk.

Then, without speaking, we drove out past the Regency. As we went up the long stretch of highway that passed over the Intracoastal Waterway, I fought an impulse to jerk the steering wheel and send us over the railing into black air. The quiet between us pounded in my ears.

'Here,' she said, when we came to Penman Road. I turned. 'Here,' she said again, when we came to Coral Way. We drove past houses on sandy lots with brown lawns until we came to a yellow two-story house with a short, narrow driveway. 'Here,' she said.

A lamp burned by the front window, a beacon of some kind. I pulled into the driveway, turned off the car, and looked at her.

'It's not your fault,' she said.

'Whose is it?' I asked.

She got out.

After she went inside and turned off the lamp, I eased the car out of the driveway, drove a half block down the street, and stopped again.

I saw no reason not to drive to an all-night Walgreens and buy a box cutter. I saw no reason not to drive to the house where I grew up and push through the backyard bramble into the woods. I saw no reason not to break past the pine and loblolly branches until I found a clearing. I saw no reason not to strip off my clothes and lie on the ground. I saw no reason not to thumb the blade from the box cutter until it extended a half inch. I saw no reason not to cut a line from my forehead, over my nose and lips, down my neck and chest, across the top of my belly, and down, splitting my balls. I saw no reason. I could imagine none.

Then fingers tapped on my window. I turned, wondering whose mask death would wear tonight.

But Cynthia – ghostly in the glass – looked back at me.

'What?' I said.

She motioned for me to roll down the window.

I did.

'Hey,' she said.

'Hey.'

'I'm sorry,' she said. 'Those men scared me.'

'Yeah. Me too.'

She touched her fingers to my face. I wished she would dig them into my skin the way Kim Jenkins's husband dug into her shoulder at their house in Callahan.

'Where are you going to stay tonight?' she asked.

I have a date with a box cutter, I thought. 'I'll drive around for a while,' I said.

'You can't come into my house. My parents would freak out. But you can sleep in your car in the driveway.'

I took her fingers from my cheek and kissed them.

Then she leaned into the window and kissed me on the lips. 'I get off at eight tomorrow,' she said then. 'Will you pick me up?'

'Yeah,' I said, and I rolled up the window and started the car. I didn't really know what I would do. But as I drove back toward the city and came to the Walgreens, I accelerated past.

Instead, I drove straight to the house where I grew up. When I'd lived there, the house had been white, with black shutters, but the people who lived there now had painted it a color that looked olive green under the headlights and had stripped the shutters from the walls. A boy's bicycle lay on its side by the front steps. I wondered if the parents of the boy knew that I once lived there too – and if they gave him the bedroom of a convicted rapist and murderer. Dr Patel had told me to revisit the house and other places that gave me pleasure before my arrest. At four in the morning, the house seemed to squeeze its eyes shut, refusing to see me. If I knocked on the door, would the people who lived there call the cops, and would the cops fly with sirens screaming to rescue them from a man who also once had claims on this place?

Next, I drove to the development where Jared owned his house, pulled into his driveway, and cut the engine. The lights in the house were off. I could kick through his door as the man in boots had kicked through mine. By the time Jared padded down his carpeted stairs, I could be lying on his living room couch. I could refuse to leave. I could demand a brother's shelter.

I leaned the front seat back as far as it would go and stared through the windshield at the dark upstairs windows. I closed my eyes. Best to sleep where I was.

But I couldn't sleep. I sat in the car and stared at Jared's windows, waiting for him to wake. But when the sun rose, his lights remained off. So I started the car, pulled from the driveway, and left him to live his life.

At seven in the morning, I got coffee and a bagel from a Dunkin' Donuts. Then I drove back to Philips Highway and pulled into the Cardinal Motel parking lot. Bill Hopper was hanging a new door to my room as I got out of the car. I thought he would kick me off the property, but he looked happy to see me.

'Hey,' he said, 'you're alive.'

'Yeah.'

He nodded into my room. 'There's blood on the carpet.'

'Yeah.'

'Glad it's not yours,' he said. 'Bad all around when a guest gets hurt.'

'Right.'

He eyed me closely. 'We get a lot of break-ins like this. They scare most of the guests away. Why didn't you call the cops?'

I saw no reason to correct his mistake. 'What good would the cops do?'

'Exactly,' he said. 'They just hassle me. You know, they've tried to shut me down. Thanks for keeping it in-house. I like loyalty.' He tapped in a hinge pin with a hammer. 'You know I take care of the lost.' He tapped in the second pin. 'I'll always keep a place for you. You know, you could have pounded on my door.'

'Why wake you in the middle of the night?'

'I like how you handled this,' he said. I watched as he tapped in the third hinge pin. He eased the door closed, opened it again, and closed it. It fit. He took a key from a key ring and handed it to me. 'I hope you'll stick around.'

'Where else would I go?' I said.

'Exactly,' he said.

When I climbed the stairs to the JNI office an hour later, Hank drew in his breath sharply and said, 'You're looking bad, Franky.'

'Tired,' Jane said.

'I had a hard night,' I said.

They stared as if they expected me to explain, but I went to Thelma's desk and sat at the computer. My neighbor Jimmy had warned the men to stay away, but I needed to give them a personal message.

If I was right that they'd been Steven and Duane Bronson's friends, I knew where to start. During my trial, the Bronson boys' mother had testified, and I searched for her now. The pictures that popped up on Facebook made her look about twenty years older than during the trial. According to her postings, she took in rescue dogs and nursed injured ones back to health. Anything to fill the hole. She mentioned no family members, no love life. Her Facebook friends mostly seemed to share her interest in dogs.

Three months ago, another woman, who owned a German shepherd with a broken leg, asked for help, and Felicia Bronson posted her address.

I turned off the computer and headed for the stairs.

'We need to make that video for Thomas LaFlora,' Jane said. 'We want the judge to have it before the hearing.'

'Later,' I said.

'The hearing is in three days,' Hank said.

'I'll be back this afternoon.'

'We also need to see Kim Jenkins again,' he said.

'This afternoon.'

Jane said, 'We need to be able to count on you.'

I stopped on the top stair. 'I can't even count on myself.'

Felicia Bronson lived on Prospect Creek Drive, south of the airport, in a blue stucco house in a strip of other blue stucco houses. The front yards had little palms or no trees at all.

When I knocked, a half-dozen dogs erupted inside. Felicia Bronson opened the door, glancing behind me as if she expected me to bring another dog to the party.

I said, 'My name is—' I stopped, thinking she would recognize me, especially since my face had appeared so often in the news since my release. But she didn't seem to know who I was. I said, 'Last night, some men came to where I'm living. I think they were friends of—' Again, I stopped. Her eyes were flat. I could almost believe I'd come to the wrong house. 'I think they were friends of your sons,' I said.

Just then, a black standard poodle and a terrier mix escaped around her. She grabbed the terrier's collar with a nervous laugh. I caught the poodle and shoved it back into the house. 'My babies,' she said. She meant the dogs, not Steven and Duane.

'The men broke down my door last night,' I said. 'They were going to—'

The woman held back the other animals. 'Please, come in.'

I stepped inside.

Although the day was already hot, she used no air conditioner. The windows were closed, and, with the raw animal scent, the house smelled like a filthy kennel.

'Come,' she said, and she led me through a hall to the kitchen. 'Please sit.' She cleared a space at a kitchen table. 'Now, what is this about?' she asked.

'These men think I killed your boys, Ms Bronson.'

'I'm sure I don't know what you're talking about,' she said.

I looked around the kitchen. Pictures of dogs hung on the cabinets. A giant bag of dog food lay on the counter. A dog crate stood by the door to the backyard. Magnets held feeding schedules and reminders of vet appointments to the refrigerator. Old photographs of Steven and Duane peeked from behind the papers.

'Steven and Duane's friends broke into my room last night,' I said. 'I need to get in touch with them. I didn't do what they think I did.'

'I'm sorry . . .' She seemed perplexed.

'My name is Franky Dast,' I said. 'Franklin Dast. But I didn't do it. I didn't kill your sons.'

She looked dazed. 'I know that.'

She seemed to have lost her mind, but a wave of relief rolled through my chest anyway. 'You do?'

'I've always known.'

'I don't understand.'

'He threatened them.'

'Who?'

'Duane and Steve often found trouble.' She smiled at the memory. 'And they *made* trouble when they couldn't find it.'

'I still don't understand.'

'Sometimes, at night, they snuck out and went driving,' she said. 'Sometimes they broke into houses. They would steal money and watches while people were sleeping. Liquor from the cabinets. They did it for the excitement after their dad moved away. When Duane was fourteen, the police arrested him after he sold the watches to a pawnshop. The pawnshop gave him twenty-three dollars. For that, he got a record and—'

'What does this have to do—'

'I learned about the man during your trial. Duane had a girl-friend. He told her about him, and later she told me. She said Duane and Steve broke into his house. I don't know what they took, and I don't know how the man figured out it was them. I don't know how he tracked them down once he knew. He wanted whatever they'd stolen. Duane told his girlfriend the man said he would hurt them if they didn't give it to him.'

I looked at Felicia Bronson's blank eyes. I wondered if she'd made up this story to help her sleep when she learned about my release from prison. 'Why didn't the girlfriend tell you this earlier?' I asked. 'Why didn't she tell the police?'

'She was scared. And sometimes Duane told lies or exaggerated. She might've convinced herself this was one of those times, until the man came into the courtroom and sat by her during the trial. He knew who she was. He asked if Duane gave her a present before he died. He told her he wanted it. He told her that if she refused to give it to him, he would hurt her the way he'd hurt my boys.'

'What was it?'

She laughed again. 'I don't have any idea.'

I thought about what she'd just said. 'So, you know I didn't kill your sons. And you knew it eight years ago, *before* I went to prison.'

'I thought at first you might be with that man. But I couldn't see how or why.'

'Did you . . .' I fought to get my thoughts straight. 'You could have talked to the police. You could have testified. Eight years ago, you could have—'

'Could I? What makes you think I would have escaped him if I'd talked?'

'I went to prison—'

'I'm sorry,' she said, but she seemed to be beyond regret.

Then, across the house, the front door opened, and footsteps approached through the hallway.

'Who was Duane's girlfriend?' I asked.

She smiled again. 'She's married now and has two babies of her own.'

'What's her name?'

'Lynn Melsyn,' she said. 'She was a pretty girl.'

A man, carrying grocery bags, appeared in the doorway. He stopped hard when he saw me. I knew him – he had locked my wrists in handcuffs last night.

He glanced from me to Felicia Bronson and back to me. Then he dropped the grocery bags and ran.

I took off after him. I caught him outside on the driveway as he reached for the door to his van. I slammed him against a side panel. He fell to the pavement and raised his hands.

I kicked him in the ribs. Last night, I would have kicked him again and again until I heard bone breaking. I would have gouged him with the car key.

Now, I just felt sick. 'Why?' I said.

He gazed at me, scared, in pain.

I said, 'Their mother says someone else did it. She—'

'She's messed up,' he said. 'She knows nothing. Most of the time, she can't tell if it's morning or night.'

I stared at him. 'Give me your wallet.'

'Why?'

'Give me your goddamned wallet.'

He pulled it from his pocket. I took out the driver's license and read it. His name was Cory Nussbaum. He lived a block away, on Mission Creek Drive. I put the license back and threw the wallet at him.

'OK, Cory, what are your friends' names?'

He stared up at me.

'I don't want to kick you again. And the last thing I want to do is knock down your door the way you knocked down mine. But you're begging for a kick, and now I know where you live.'

'Phil Middleton and Darrell Nesbit,' he said.

'Which one is which?'

'Darrell wore the black T-shirt and boots. He was Duane's friend.'

'And Phil Middleton?'

'We knew Steve,' he said.

'And now you do their mother's grocery shopping?'

'I've helped out ever since you killed Steve.'

'I didn't kill anyone.'

'I've cut her lawn. I've painted her house. Every couple weeks, when the inside gets bad, I clean out the garbage. They put you in jail for killing Steve and Duane, but you killed her too. You saw what's left.'

'So now you and your friends think you should kill *me*?'

'You've had it coming for eight years.'

'Have you been paying attention? The court says someone else did it. Someone else's DNA—'

'We know what we know,' he said.

'Yeah, but what's that?'

'You confessed to the police. We *saw* the videotape.'

If kicking him would have put sense into his head, I would have done it. 'No more middle-of-the-night visits. Do you understand?'

He glared.

'If you or your friends come after me, I'll hunt *you* down.' I learned in prison that if I talked hard enough, I might convince myself. 'Do Phil and Darrell live in the neighborhood too?'

'I'm not telling you how to find them.'

'Then you can give them my message. And you can tell them I also don't want any more bloody underwear hanging from my door handle. If I find another pair, I'll cram it down your throat.'

His eyes lost some of the anger. 'What are you talking about?'

'Underwear – like Steven was wearing that night.' He looked confused. 'Hanging on my door handle at the motel? Stained with blood?'

He shook his head.

'You didn't do that?'

'Uh-uh.'

I read his face for a lie. 'Your friends?'

A mean smile cracked at his lips as if he saw that he had – and always would have – the upper hand. He said, 'You have a lot of enemies.'

SIXTEEN

That afternoon, I made the video for Thomas LaFlora. I said, 'The judge who sentenced me to death committed an act as brutal as the rape and murder of Steven and Duane Bronson,' but I was thinking, *Who is Lynn Melsyn? Was she really Duane Bronson's girlfriend or is she just a creation of Felicia Bronson's grief? Who is this mysterious man – real or fantasy? What did Duane and Steven steal from him, if anything?*

Then I said, 'The judges, who for eight years refused to listen to my appeals with an open mind and a willingness to correct an injustice, treated me with less humane concern than they would show an already dead man,' but I was thinking, *If the guy at Felicia Bronson's house really didn't hang the underwear from my door handle, then who did?*

I said, 'Any judge who fails to listen to Thomas LaFlora's appeals with the respect for his life that four judges failed to show for mine – five, if you count the judge who first sentenced me—'

Hank sighed and said, 'I'll edit together the best parts.'

First, though, we needed to go back to Callahan to talk to Kim Jenkins about the testimony she would give at the hearing. Jane and Hank believed we'd convinced her to tell the judge that LaFlora didn't kill the two crackheads. Now, they said, we needed to do the hard work. We needed to convince her to name the real killer. If she refused to offer an alternative to LaFlora, the judge would laugh at her for changing her testimony.

'She'll never do it,' I said.

'You've earned that cynicism,' Jane said, loading papers into a briefcase, 'but, as you know better than anyone, if we stopped every time we faced bad odds, you would still be in prison.'

'Kim Jenkins *wants* to do it,' I said. 'But she can't.'

Hank looked at me for an explanation.

But downstairs, the street door banged open. Footsteps came up, and a woman barged into the office – the same woman who'd come to the Cardinal Motel and warned me to stay away from

Bill Higby's property, threatening to stomp me like a locust if I ignored her. Again, she wore the heavy cotton pants and solid shoes of a cop. But now, she also wore a hip holster.

She stared at each of us and said, 'Jesus Christ!' – as if we all disgusted her equally – and then came at me. She was eight or ten inches shorter than I was, but I backed away. 'What the hell are you thinking?' she said. 'You go back to Detective Higby's house. And now you go to Felicia Bronson's. You're out of your fucking mind.'

Jane got in front of her. 'Ma'am, you need to leave. This is a private office.'

Keeping her eyes on me, the woman reached for a badge and flashed it.

But the badge meant little to Jane. 'If you don't have a warrant to arrest Mr Dast or to be in this office, then I respectfully ask you to go back down—'

But I said to the woman, 'Who are you?'

'Lieutenant Detective Deborah Holt,' she said. 'I'm Bill Higby's goddamned partner. And you – *you* are—' She decided against whatever she planned to call me and instead said, 'I'm arresting you for assaulting Cory Nussbaum.'

'Who is Cory Nussbaum?' Jane asked.

'He's a young man who helps Felicia Bronson with housework,' the cop said.

'Does Cory Nussbaum say I assaulted him?' I asked.

'A neighbor saw you beat him up.'

'But does Cory Nussbaum say I did it?'

Hank stepped into the mix. 'I think there's been a misunderstanding, Detective Holt.'

'You're damn right,' she said, and she pointed at me as if she would jab a hole in my chest. 'This man misunderstands where he belongs.' Then, to me, 'We never did arrest anyone else, did we? That's because we arrested the right man the first time. You're like an insect. You leave a trail wherever you go.'

'Are you speaking for yourself or for Higby?' I asked.

'A misunderstanding,' Hank said again.

'I understand a lot too,' I said. 'When all of the guards and half of the other men want to kill you, you understand what a killer looks like and how he behaves. For instance, I can look at Higby and—'

'Watch it,' the cop said. 'You leave him alone.' She glared as if I might challenge her. When I didn't, she added, 'And if you ever hassle Felicia Bronson again, I'll—'

Jane asked, 'Are you making an arrest?'

'I'm giving a warning,' the cop said. 'A *last* warning.'

Jane moved close to her. 'If you aren't arresting Mr Dast, you need to leave. We understand your concerns and we've heard your warning. In turn, we need to warn you against harassing a man the court has released with no supervision or legal obligations.'

The cop stared at me a moment longer, as if thinking through her options. 'No more warnings,' she said, and she turned and went down the stairs.

We listened to the street door as it opened and then closed. When we heard only silence, Hank spun on me. 'You went to Felicia Bronson's house?'

'Sort of.'

'Why?'

'Unfinished business.'

He exchanged a look with Jane. 'The detective is right,' he said. 'You're out of your mind.'

Jane said, 'You do know you're walking a line here, don't you? If the State Attorney's Office sees you threatening the mother of the victims, they'll absolutely refile charges.'

'You're out of control,' Hank said. He picked up his briefcase. 'Jane and I will talk to Kim Jenkins on our own. You stay here. I recommend that you avoid acting on whatever idiotic impulse occurs to you next.'

Jane must have agreed. 'I'm sorry,' she said.

'It's fine,' I said. 'You're wasting your time with Kim Jenkins.'

Hank said, 'You might want to rethink your sense of what's worthy of your time. You lost a lot of it in prison. Don't blow the rest of it now.'

I felt like punching him in the throat.

Jane said, 'Hank has your best interests at heart.'

'*Your* interests and *others*',' he said. 'Thomas LaFlora needs you. Others do too. Your selfishness—'

He stopped when I lunged at him. He never flinched, though. He would fight me if I kept coming.

I said, 'In prison, my friends and my enemies wore the same uniforms. Seems like the same thing here.'

Jane said, 'Careful now.'

Hank gathered a pile of papers from his desk and stuffed them into his briefcase, keeping an eye on me. 'You've got to decide what really matters,' he said, and he and Jane went down the stairs to the street.

So I did decide. After they left, I drove back to Higby's house. Going places I didn't belong – and demanding to be heard by people who'd stopped listening – had gotten me out of prison. If I stopped now, I was afraid I would lose myself.

The last of the news vans was gone. There were two cars in the driveway. Next door, in front of Judge Skooner's house, two men on lawn tractors cut the grass. Overhead, heavy clouds were stacking toward the sun.

I parked behind the cars in Higby's driveway, crossed to the front porch, and knocked on the door.

Higby answered before I could knock a second time. He'd shaved and combed his hair, and he wore gray slacks and a white buttoned shirt, as if he'd just come from church or court. He said, 'You've got to be kidding.'

I said, 'I'm sorry for bothering you again.'

'But here you are.'

I asked, 'Can I come inside and talk to you?'

'No, sir,' he said. 'No, you cannot.'

'Because I'm confused,' I said. 'Really messed-up. Just a few minutes? I have some questions—'

I guessed he wanted to hit me as badly as I'd wanted to hit Hank Cury. But then his wife appeared beside him, resting her fingers on his big arm. He said, 'I've got this, Jenny,' but if he meant his words to send her away, the attempt failed. She stared at me with cold, unmoving eyes.

'Just five minutes,' I said.

'I can't touch you,' he said. 'Not right now. I regret that. But I'm going to call some officers who can. I suggest that you put yourself as far away from my house as you can before they show up.'

Then he shut the door.

I went down the front path. The air smelled of newly cut grass. Although wedges of blue sky remained between the stacks of clouds, a raindrop spattered on my shoulder.

Instead of getting into my car, I walked back to Higby's house and around the side to the backyard. A fishing dock stuck out into Black Creek. An American flag hung from a length of PVC bracketed to the gray wood at the end of the dock. The lawn rose to a little patio made of concrete pavers and decorated with pots of geraniums. A sliding glass door led from the patio into the house. I walked to the patio and tried the handle. The door glided open.

I went through a family room, where a TV was on, and through a short hallway. Higby and his wife were talking in the kitchen.

They jumped when I stepped into the doorway.

'I really want to talk with you,' I said.

Higby said, 'What's *wrong* with you? You've got to be out of your head—'

'Everyone keeps saying that,' I said. 'But I'm feeling a little more *in* it every day. I have setbacks, but I'm making progress.'

'If I shot you right here, I would be completely within my rights. You know that, don't you?'

'Of course,' I said. 'But going places I haven't belonged and—'

'Shut up,' he said. 'I don't want to hear it.'

'Talking to people who—'

'Get out,' he said.

'I have two questions.'

'Out.'

I said, 'Felicia Bronson says a man threatened her sons before they died.'

'Out!' But he stood still.

'She says she only learned about this man during my trial. But you're smart. You knew about him before, didn't you? I need to know who the man was. You owe me that much.'

'I owe you nothing.'

I went to the kitchen table and sat down.

That did it. He jerked toward me as if he would crush me. But I'd promised myself never to back away or beg, and so I stared up at him as he came. 'Go ahead,' I said. 'Add my blood to Josh Skooner's.'

He grabbed my shirt and pulled me to my feet. He was a huge man, and he dragged me up the front hall to the door. He yanked it open and threw me out on to the porch.

I sat there, sheltered by an overhang, as the clouds closed over the sky and a hard rain started to slap the ground. A wind blew through, bending the trees, cooling the air, and then it was gone, and the air was all thunder and water. I leaned against a wall and waited.

If Higby and his wife looked out the front window, they would see my car still in the driveway. If they looked through the door peephole, they would see me sitting – patiently. If Higby called his cop friends, reporters would also come in vans, and then we would dance together on the evening news.

After ten minutes, the door opened. Higby stepped outside and closed it behind him.

'Why are you doing this?' he asked.

'What do I have to lose?'

He seemed ready to laugh. 'Everything you've gained. Your freedom.'

'I'm not free,' I said. 'Not yet. I don't feel it. I don't know if I ever will.'

He scuffed the toes of his shoes on the porch tile, as if he might boot me on to the lawn. 'You would rather be dead or in jail?'

'No.'

'Because those are real possibilities for you.'

'I know.'

He considered me. Then he looked out at the rain. 'We heard about this man you're talking about,' he said. 'We checked into him. He was nothing.'

'How hard did you check?'

'We checked,' he said. 'Hard enough.'

I stared at him.

'We didn't need to,' he said. 'We had you.'

'What was his name?'

'No name,' he said. 'He wasn't real.' When I said nothing, he asked, 'Is that all?'

I shook my head. 'Do you really think I did it?'

He looked at me straight. 'Yes.'

His confidence chipped at me. 'You've always been convinced of it?'

'Never a doubt.' He reached for the front door, as if we were done.

But I said, 'Your partner – Deborah Holt – came to talk to me. Twice. She says you're telling the truth about Josh Skooner.'

'Deborah is a good cop,' he said. 'And a good friend.'

I nodded at the street. 'What really happened out there? Did Josh Skooner have a gun? Did he really shoot at you?'

'You've seen the news,' he said. 'You must have read the stories. Make up your own mind.'

'I want to hear it from you.'

'Sorry,' he said, and anger tinged his voice. 'I'm never going to put myself where you've been. Never.'

'I'm not asking you to,' I said.

'Yes, you are,' he said, and again he reached for the door.

I said, 'One news report – only one – said Josh's brother, Andrew, got close enough to him to get bloody. The same report said Andrew went back to his house when the paramedics put Josh in the ambulance. I'm guessing no one searched him for Josh's gun.'

Higby screwed his eyes. 'I still don't get it.'

'What?'

'Why do you care?'

I said, 'I hate you more than I've ever hated anyone. I guess that's why I need to know.'

Again he stared down at me. 'I can't help you there. But I'll tell you this. What you did to the Bronson boys has nothing to do with what I did to Josh Skooner. Whatever you've gone through in the past – and whatever you're going through now – has nothing to do with what I'm going through. I see nothing of myself in you and nothing of you in me.' Then he went back inside.

Three hours later, I drove to the Cineplex. All day, I'd loaded and overloaded myself, and the buzzing in my head had turned into a sharp headache. I probably should've stayed in my room.

Cynthia stood behind the concession counter when I went in, and I waved to her from beyond the cordon where a kid was taking tickets. Ten minutes later, she joined me. Her eyes were tired and the smile she gave me as she gripped my hand seemed forced. She probably should've stayed home too.

We walked across the parking lot and got into my car, then drove back to the Cardinal Motel and went into my room. As I unbuttoned her shirt, I felt that I was doing more than stripping off her clothes – that I was peeling back layers of skin – and when she pulled my T-shirt over my head, her fingers felt hot and electric. I had filled and overfilled, and as she unzipped my pants I wondered if I would get sick, but I clenched my stomach and I unzipped her pants too. Her fire-scarred legs glistened in the light from the window shade – like living marble, mottled, congealing fat, shining ice. Although I knew that her nerves remained raw and that pleasure fell hard into pain, I touched her scars, lifted her to me, and carried her to the bed.

Tears stung my eyes that night, and blood pounded in my aching head. If I had exploded – body and soul – the doctors would have said, *No wonder.*

Sometime late, after we'd slept and awakened and slept again, Cynthia looked in my eyes and said, 'I love you.'

SEVENTEEN

The next morning when I went into the JNI office, Jane handed me a key to the office and a plastic bag with a telephone in it. 'Hank and I talked on our way to Callahan,' she said. 'We think we might have overreacted. We know you're adjusting. You need to work things out for yourself.'

Thelma had come in early, and she watched me like a paid witness.

'What did Kim Jenkins tell you yesterday?' I asked.

'She'd gone out,' Jane said. 'We didn't see her.'

'Her husband?' I asked.

'Out too.'

I eyed her.

'What?' she said.

'You see any moving vans?'

'People go out,' she said. 'It's what people do.'

'Sure,' I said, and I held up the key. 'So, what's this about?'

'We trust you,' she said. 'And sometimes we may need you to open the office.'

'Fair enough.' I took the phone from the bag. 'And this?'

'We thought that by now you would've gotten one for yourself. We want to respect your need for privacy. But we also want you to be answerable. To yourself and to the world around you.'

'And to you?' I asked.

'If you allow us to be part of your world, yes.'

I thought about that. 'Then I want a desk and computer for myself.'

Hank said, 'We're working on a tight budget.'

'Am I part of that work?'

He glanced at Jane.

'Of course, you are,' she said.

Then, as if to tell me what part I played, she handed me a stack of papers and folders to sort and put into the file cabinets. I spent an hour thumbing through unsuccessful appeals arguing that, as prosecutor, Eric Skooner reduced or dismissed criminal charges against the three witnesses in the LaFlora case and that he suppressed evidence placing LaFlora at his mother's house when the shooting happened. The judges ruled, one after another, that, while troubling, none of the new information should overturn the initial verdict and sentence. They cited statutes, precedents, and common sense, but in their language I sensed the fear of being wrong – the fear of cracks in the paint that, once acknowledged, would spread and deepen until whole buildings crumbled.

By the time I finished filing the records, Hank had left for a meeting, Jane was talking on the phone, and Thelma was typing madly on her keyboard. So I opened the drawer marked A–D, which had just two sets of files – a thin one for a man named Manford Dewey and a thick one for me. I removed my papers. I'd either written or helped write many of the pleas and petitions, and I'd given information and sometimes sworn testimony that appeared in many of the other documents. I'd at least glanced at most of the rest.

I looked through the transcript from the first trial, searching for any hint that a man had threatened Steven and Duane Bronson before they died – or any reason to think that such a man might have killed them at the Shell station after I left them there during a midnight rainstorm. I remembered the car that slowed for the boys before speeding off in front of me. I remembered another car – or the same – that was parked on the shoulder, its hazard lights flashing, after the Shell station. But I had no idea if the boys' killer was driving so close to me on Monument Road that night.

I saw again now that, as part of a bungled defense, Lance Stoddard mentioned the boys' burglary arrests, insinuating that they were responsible for their own deaths, but the judge said the arrests were irrelevant. If Lance had planned to name any of the burglary victims, the judge cut him off before he could do it. Mostly, the prosecutor laid out a damning case, and Lance hemmed and apologized and all but agreed that I'd killed the boys.

Then I read the transcripts of the sentencing hearing. Steven and Duane's family and friends spoke about how much their deaths hurt them, and my dad, Jared, and my old running coach tried to defend me against the indefensible. I read the words of Felicia Bronson and Duane's girlfriend, Lynn Melsyn, closely. If they felt any fear of a man who'd appeared at the trial to threaten them with violence, their tears washed the fear away before they stepped into the witness box.

I reread Coach Kagen's testimony. He bumbled through a couple of minutes of clichés, calling me a *great kid*, a *great runner*, a *good-looking boy*. I had *great potential but was maybe too clever for my own good*. It was all a *great, great shame*.

I closed the file and then used Hank's computer to look up the phone number of the office of the Clerk of the Circuit and County Courts.

I called and asked, 'If I want to see old juvenile trial records, how do I do that?'

'Is the juvenile eighteen or older now?' said the woman on the other end.

'*Two* juveniles,' I said, 'and they're dead.'

'Oh.'

'But they would have been in their early twenties now.'

'We destroy most records on the day that children turn eighteen. In the cases in which we keep records, you would need a court order.'

'Could you check if you still have anything for a Steven or a Duane Bronson?'

She put me on hold. When she came back, she said the records system erased Duane Bronson's file five years ago and Steven's two years after that.

I hung up and typed Lance Stoddard's name into Google. His name popped up now on a site for his criminal defense and personal injury law firm and on a bunch of consumer advocacy sites. The client reviews on Lawyer.com gave most of the other lawyers four or five stars out of five. They gave Lance two. The reviews said he failed to return phone calls. They accused him of settling for whatever the prosecutors and insurance companies offered instead of fighting for clients. They called him a scam artist.

His own website offered *Free Consultations* and *Thorough Investigations*. I called the number.

I'd last talked with Lance shortly after the end of the trial. Then I'd started writing letters to others, pointing out the mistakes he'd made.

Now, a secretary put me straight through without asking who was calling, and the sound of his voice made me sweat.

He caught his breath at my name, but said, 'Hey, hey, Franky – how've you been?' as if we'd last seen each other at a football game or a bar.

'Bad, Lance. Real bad. But I'm out now – so, better.'

'Right – I saw you on TV,' he said. 'I knew we would get you out, sooner or later.'

'*We* didn't get me out, Lance. You had nothing to do with it. You got me *in*.'

He had the balls to laugh.

I added, 'And now you owe me.'

'I was young,' he said. 'Still learning the game.'

'But now you've learned it?'

'I'm the best in town,' he said, and – without pause – 'Are you in trouble again?'

'I need to know something about my trial.'

'It was a long time ago—'

'At one point, you tried to introduce the Bronson boys' arrest record, but the judge shut you down.'

He said, 'I remember that – the bastard.'

'Do you remember the details?' I asked. 'The names of the people the boys burglarized? Addresses? Anything unusual in the burglary cases?'

'Hell,' he said, 'I'd forgotten that the arrests were for burglary. I thought they were shoplifting or reefer.'

'How about your notes? Can you check them?' I said. 'Or anything that you got from the State Attorney?'

'I never work from notes,' he said. 'It looks bad to a jury. The prosecutor's office sent me a shitload of papers. It always does. But I chucked all of that a long time ago.'

'You didn't put it in storage?'

Again he laughed. 'You know how much that costs?'

'OK, look,' I said. 'I've heard that some guy – maybe someone the boys burglarized – was threatening them. He was hanging around before and after they died, even during my trial.'

'What's this about, Franky? You're out now, right? What's it matter to you?'

'Do you or don't you know anything about him?'

'Sure,' he said. 'I might remember the girlfriend saying something like that.'

'Did you look into it?'

'I'm only one man,' he said. 'I couldn't do everything.'

I felt sour in my own sweat. 'You've got nothing for me?' I said.

'It was a long time ago. We've moved on, right?'

'You failed me, Lance. You get that, don't you?'

'I understand that perspective,' he said. 'And I respect it. But—'

I hung up on him and stared at Hank's desk until Jane said, 'Are you OK?'

'No worse than I was an hour ago,' I said.

Then I typed the name of Duane Bronson's girlfriend into Google. Aside from the court records, *Lynn Melsyn* brought up exactly zero links. So she'd gotten married and changed her name. Or she'd changed her name before she got married and left no electronic trace of the girl she'd once been.

Just two *Melsyns* lived in the city – a man named Rick, who posted pictures of himself surfing and drinking with friends and who looked young enough to have a sister the age of Lynn Melsyn, and a sixty-three-year-old woman named Jean-Ann without online pictures. After a short search, I found addresses for both of them

– Rick in an apartment building at the Beach, Jean-Ann in a development off of Pecan Park Road, near the airport. I had a one o'clock appointment with Dr Patel. Afterward, maybe I would drive out to the Beach.

In the meantime, in Thomas LaFlora's case, Kim Jenkins's husband, Randall Haussen, interested me. I Googled his name and started reading. After his arrests in his early twenties and then his seven years in jail for shooting a drug dealer, he seemed to have lived clean. As far as I could tell from online business records, he'd owned a car repair shop called AJ's in Callahan and then sold it and opened an auto parts franchise a half mile from AJ's. For a while in his first years out of jail, he'd also worked at a drug and alcohol addiction hotline. I found only three pictures of him, all recent, all on a motorboat with friends – shirtless, muscled, tanned. His friends held cans of beer, toasting the camera. He held a can of Diet Pepsi. Property records showed that he owned the house where he and Kim Jenkins lived. Her name wasn't on the deed.

I made search after search until lunch, and then I left the JNI office. Twenty minutes later, I was sitting across from Dr Patel in his office.

'Bear with me,' he was saying. 'You say you and your brother lost all faith in your dad. You say he stopped believing in you too.' The afternoon sun came through his office window and caressed the carpet, the overstuffed chairs, his desk. 'You say you would have stayed home on the night the Bronson brothers died if you all had believed in each other. Instead of seeing the strike of lightning that hit you for the chance event that it was – instead of seeing an arbitrariness that could never happen again – you see everything as cause-and-effect. Just deserts. Karma. Your dad was a failure and you were a failure, and therefore you were on Monument Road at three in the morning, and therefore you went to jail for killing the boys. But your thinking is faulty. Being a father is itself an act of incredible faith. After your mother's death, for him to come home to you and Jared – drunk or sober – must have meant he believed in you deeply. He must have had faith in who you already were and who you would become. After that, the rest of your logic falls apart.'

'Sorry, but that's the stupidest thing I've ever heard.'

He said, 'We need to work on understanding the boundaries between reality and perception.'

'You're the one who said I should ignore them if they're arbitrary.'

'Who says that this one is arbitrary?'

I considered that, then said, 'I went back to see Bill Higby yesterday.'

He sucked on his bottom lip. 'I'm concerned about your impulse control.'

'I've had sex with Cynthia four times in the last three nights.'

He sighed.

'I'm feeling pretty good. Overall. I asked Jane and Hank for a desk and computer. Demanded, really.'

'Don't get your hopes too high.'

'They gave me a phone.'

'You're in danger of crashing,' he said. 'You don't see it yet. You don't feel it. But the sparks are flying.'

Screw that, I thought.

After my appointment, I drove out to the Beach and parked on the street outside the Sun Reach Apartments, where Rick Melsyn lived. Someone had propped open the lobby door, and so I ignored the intercom box, went to the elevator, and rode to the seventh floor.

Dubstep music played loud in Apartment 706. I knocked and, when no one came, pounded. The music turned off, but still no one came. I knocked again.

Then the man I'd seen online while searching for relatives of Duane Bronson's girlfriend opened the door. He was short and wore faded shorts and a faded red sleeveless T-shirt. Marijuana smoke wafted into the hall from behind him.

'Yeah?' he said.

'Are you Lynn Melsyn's brother?' I said.

His eyes went wide for only a moment. 'Who?'

'Liar.' I stepped past him into the apartment.

He lived on the cheap side of the building, facing away from the ocean. Double doors to a little balcony stood open, and two surfboards leaned against the railing.

Rick Melsyn didn't seem to know whether to run or fight. He yelled at a closed door at the other end of the apartment – 'Darrell!' – and then moved so that a couch stood between us.

'Who are you?'

'Really?' I said. 'You're the only one in town who hasn't seen me on the news?'

He yelled at the door again. 'Darrell – get out here.'

'Where's your sister, Rick?' I asked.

'Darrell!'

The door opened, and one of the men who'd broken into my room at the Cardinal Motel came out. Then, he'd worn black boots. Now, he wore green boxers and nothing else. A thin line of hair grew down the middle of his skinny chest. His legs were pale. When he saw me, he said, 'Oh, shit,' and ran for the kitchen.

I said to Rick Melsyn, 'I just want to ask your sister some questions. I don't want to hurt her – or you.'

His roommate came back, holding a steak knife, watching for an angle.

I said to him, 'Where I lived for the last eight years, in situations like this, you would want to be sure of yourself. I've seen men lose an eye – or all of their teeth – and keep fighting. So if you decide to do this, you better go all the way because I've been here before, and if you start it, I'll finish it.'

For a moment more, he looked ready to fight. Then he lowered the knife and, as if the handle suddenly got oily, dropped it. But he told his roommate, 'He killed Duane and Steve.'

Melsyn said, 'She won't talk to you. Someone threatened to hurt her. Bad. She won't talk to anyone.'

'I know,' I said. 'The man who came to her during my trial?'

'She won't talk.'

'What name does she use now?'

Still, he shook his head.

'Tell her I need to see her,' I said. 'Tell her it's for Duane and Steven. Tell her we all got hurt.'

He shook his head.

I went to the door to the hallway and opened it. Then I said to the roommate, Darrell, 'And *you*. Think it through. If I did what you think I did, would I come here? Would I be that crazy?'

He followed me into the hall and watched while I waited for the elevator. We both jumped a little when the bell rang. 'Think it through,' I said again, and got in.

EIGHTEEN

I once had faith. I ran through the night-time woods, fleshy leaves licking my face, my arms, my legs – tonguing my neck. A stick or branch jabbed me in the mouth, drawing blood. But still I ran. Like a child of faith.

Or of fear.

Fear is the *F* of *Faith*.

I also ran on a sunny beach. Barefoot. Skimming the wave-slicked sand. Floating almost. This world was *my* world once. Moments like this told me so – I could run for miles. And miles. If I could have run forever, the wet sand kicking up on my sweating back, the world could have been mine still. Trouble came only when my calf muscles cramped and the salt air raked my lungs. Trouble came when I stopped – my knees bending, my body lowering to the earth.

And, for one season, I ran on a track. The shock of the starter pistol stunning the air. The flesh of eight runners. The stinging sweat. Never sure whether we ran away from the pistol or toward the finish line. The pistol shot, a blank. The finish line, a blank too.

Then running *in place*. In my cell. In knotting loops around the prison yard. A caged cat – pacing for hours. And hours. And getting nowhere. Neither *from* nor *to*. Already and forever in the blank space where life is already and forever death. The muscles remembered, but what? A false memory? A memory of running in the woods, on a beach, around a track – none of which really existed, not from the perspective of a prison where starter pistol caps turned into live rounds in rifles in high guard towers.

Rifles sighted on the rabbitman who ran knotted loops around the prison yard. They aimed at the spot between my shoulder blades, where a bullet could make a heartbeat sound like silence – and at other men lifting weights at a bench press, as if they would ever use their muscle strength to do more than defend against other men like themselves. And at my friend Stuart who – short of breath, sugar spiking in his diabetic veins, sweating from every pore, helpless in his own enormity – collapsed one afternoon on the dirt in the yard. As if he could escape the prison walls only underground.

Did he call for help?

No one admitted to hearing him if he did.

I saw him from across the yard.

The guards aimed their rifles at him. Any strange act between these walls might lead to a riot, and, God knows, dropping to the dirt under an August sun – all three hundred pounds of a man – broke some rule somehow. Better to put a bullet through him if he twitched than to see him rise and roar and rage.

But Stuart never twitched. He was only sick. Heart and kidney. Lungs. Whatever shouldn't crawl through a stomach but does.

I ran across the yard, and the other men left their weights and basketballs and circled him as if he was a dying dog – enough to pity but dangerous and likely to bite, as all dying dogs of a certain breed are – and the guards let their fingers slide from the triggers and turned away.

Stuart gripped my hand and whispered something. I got in close to hear. He said, 'I pissed myself.' A dark, sad laugh rumbled in his chest. 'Like a goddamned child. I'd whip myself if I could.'

I yelled at the closest tower. 'Get the nurse.'

The guard looked at his wristwatch, as if considering whether he could wait it out and go off duty.

'Call the goddamned nurse,' I yelled.

He looked down at me. I knew that each of my eyes looked like a concentric target to him – pupil, iris, white. Then he reached for the radio on his belt.

The ambling, shambling nurse – carrying his bag of magic tools across the prison yard – saved Stuart that time. He seemed to resent the duty. As he stared down at Stuart, his eyes said, *Such a waste of my medicine. Such a waste of my magic.* When he looked up at me, they asked, *Who am I saving this man for? Will you carry his weight through the world?*

'He's still a man,' I said. 'Whatever else he is, he's a man.'

The nurse opened his mouth. He had yellow teeth. 'Move away,' he said. 'Stand over by the other inmates.' I held Stuart's hand. 'That's an order,' he said. 'Do it *now*.'

Then the guards came into the yard and cleared us back to our cells.

That night, lying on my bunk, I dreamed of a red kayak that my dad won in an Anheuser-Busch company picnic when I was twelve. It was only seven feet long and about a foot and a half wide and had the word *Budweiser* decaled on the front. It would flip in the smallest waves even when a hundred-pound boy sat low in the cockpit. But in my dream, I floated in it far out on the ocean. No wind blew. No ripples crossed the water. Land was a fading memory. I floated, hardly breathing, as the sun held in the sky above. In the dream, I was happy and knew I would always be happy.

NINETEEN

Three days after I visited Rick Melsyn at his apartment, Judge Laura Hendricks heard Thomas LaFlora's appeal. That morning, as I came into the office, Jane, Hank, and Thelma stood next to a metal-and-glass computer cart on casters. A black plastic folding chair leaned against the cart, and a laptop computer and a box from Dillard's department store lay on top.

'Surprise,' they said together.

Jane said, 'It's not much.'

Hank said, 'It's what we can afford.'

'Congratulations,' Thelma said.

I knew I should feel only gratitude instead of a mix of appreciation and dread, so I hugged them and laughed with them when they laughed, and then I opened the Dillard's box. Inside was a coal-gray button-up shirt and a navy blue tie.

Jane took the tie from the box, held it in front of me like a noose, and said, 'If you're going to be part of this.'

'I don't know what to say,' I said.

'How about *Thanks*?' Hank said, and they all laughed.

So I buttoned the gray shirt over my T-shirt and, with some help from Hank, tied the tie, and then we walked to the courthouse, all but holding hands.

At eight forty-five, as we stood on the courthouse steps, Hank looked up and down the sidewalk. 'Kim Jenkins should be here,' he said.

'I told her *nine*,' Jane said.

'That's cutting it close,' he said.

Jane gave me and Thelma a knowing smile. 'Less time for her to get nervous.'

At nine, as the morning sun came over the tops of the surrounding buildings, Hank glared at Jane and said, 'Call her.'

She said, 'Give her five minutes.'

At a quarter after nine, Hank said, 'The hearing starts in fifteen minutes.'

Jane pulled out her phone, dialed a stored number, and handed the phone to me. 'Why don't you make sure everything's OK?'

The phone rang four times, and a man with an unfamiliar voice answered.

'Can I talk to Kim Jenkins?' I asked.

He hesitated and said, 'She's unavailable.'

I hung up.

'Unavailable,' I said, and gave Jane her phone.

'She's on her way,' she said to Hank.

At twenty after nine, he said, 'Goddamn it,' and went up the steps and into the courthouse.

Jane told Thelma, 'Go with him,' then dialed her phone again. 'I need to talk to Kim Jenkins,' she said to whoever picked up. 'It's urgent.'

She listened, and whatever the person said made her turn from me and walk toward the street, where she talked some more but mostly listened, and as she listened, her whole body seemed to shrink into itself. My head buzzed as I watched, because this was the way it always was, and no matter how many times it happened and no matter how much I'd come to expect it, it twisted at my belly and sucked the breath from my lungs.

Jane hung up her phone and came back to me, and though she put each foot where it belonged, she seemed to stagger, and all of her happiness at giving me a desk and a computer and a tie

– and all the hope she'd held for LaFlora – all of that had gone pale. She opened her mouth and said – nothing. Then, as if she knew she had to say it, 'She's dead.'

I know, I thought. 'Her husband do it?' I asked.

She shook her head. 'She killed herself.' She looked around frantically. 'Excuse me – I'm going to be sick.' She ran back down the steps to the curb.

The hearing lasted eight minutes. LaFlora came in from the back, his wrists cuffed and his ankles shackled, escorted by two deputies. His eyes touched mine as he passed, and he showed no more recognition than an already dead man would show of an old neighbor.

Jane explained to the judge that the witness whose testimony formed the basis of LaFlora's appeal had committed suicide last night, and she asked for a postponement.

The judge, who seemed to have heard such things before, asked whether a new appeal would be possible now that the witness was deceased.

Jane said, 'I don't know, Your Honor.'

The judge looked impatient. 'Can you explain why I should postpone then?'

'No,' Jane said, 'I can't.'

The judge glanced at LaFlora, at the prosecutor, and then at Hank, Thelma, and me.

'Denied.'

When we went back to the office, Jane tore LaFlora's poster from the door. Hank went to his desk, yanked the phone from the cradle, and called a contact at the Callahan Police Department. He demanded to know what had happened and demanded again – until the contact hung up. Then he called again and demanded some more. Thelma, tears in her eyes, sat at her desk, staring at a blank computer screen.

I went to the computer cart, unpacked the cords for the laptop, and plugged them in. As the computer booted up, I whistled the theme from *Star Wars*.

Jane stared at me and said, 'Don't.' She went to her desk and sank into her chair as if she would never get up again.

I whistled anyway. As much as Kim Jenkins's death unsettled me, it also confirmed a world I'd come to know – bloody and out of balance. I felt hooked tight to that world. As I tilted and swayed with its tiltings and swayings, my parts stopped shaking.

I whistled until Hank, phone to his ear, glared at me.

I said to him, 'Ask how she killed herself.'

He made his hand into a pistol and pointed it at his temple. His contact apparently had already told him.

That started me whistling again.

When the laptop screen brightened, I brought up the internet. For a half hour, I Googled information about female suicides and homicides. Then I emailed three links to Jane, Hank, and Thelma. The National Center for Biotechnology Information said what we all knew – that *women who commit suicide use less violent methods, such as drugs and carbon monoxide poisoning, than do men, who often use violent methods, such as guns and hanging.* The FBI's 'Expanded Homicide Data' site said, *of female murder victims, thirty-seven percent are murdered by their husbands or boyfriends.* The Bureau of Justice Statistics at the U.S. Department of Justice said forty-eight percent of female homicide victims are killed by firearms.

When my message dinged on to Jane's computer screen, she read it and said, 'So what?'

'So we've got a chance,' I said.

'You're fooling yourself. *Some* women who kill themselves use guns.'

'And *half* of the women who get killed by others die from them.'

'That's nothing to work with,' she said. 'It's less than nothing.'

'What if Randall Haussen killed those crackheads twenty-five years ago? What if he worried about what his wife would say at the hearing – even if she promised to keep lying?'

'You have absolutely no reason to think so,' she said.

None but the way Randall Haussen had clawed into Kim Jenkins's shoulder with his fingers when we talked to them at their house. None but his plea agreement after he shot a drug dealer. None but my eight years of reading other men for danger. None but a lifetime of seeing innocent-faced men lie.

'This was Thomas LaFlora's last chance,' Jane said, 'and it's gone.'

I went to the poster of him and picked it up. I stretched it over the computer cart top, and smoothed the creases. I borrowed a roll of tape from Thelma and patched a rip across his left eye, then hung the poster on the door again. When I gave the tape back, Thelma smiled at me, and I wondered if she approved or pitied me.

'You want to go for a ride?' I asked her.

We drove to Callahan in my car. As we waited at a stoplight, her fingers found the slices in the seat where the police used X-ACTO knives as they searched for evidence in the deaths of the Bronson brothers. Then she looked at the strips of fabric that hung from the roof and started picking at them, pulling them away, collecting them in her lap, as if she needed to stay busy.

She said, 'Hank and Jane – they mean well.'

'They saved my life,' I said.

'No, you saved your own life. They just threw you a rope when you asked for it.'

'I would have died without that rope,' I said.

A half mile beyond AJ's, we pulled into the lot at Aardo Auto Parts. A white pickup had parked in the disabled space, and a green one in a regular spot next to it. We parked next to the green truck and went inside.

Two men stood behind the counter. Through an open door behind them, a woman sat at a desk. All of them wore black pants and red golf shirts with yellow Aardo logos.

One of the men gave us a big-toothed grin. 'What can I do for you?' he said.

'We need to see Randall Haussen,' Thelma said.

'Randy's out today,' the man said, grinning. 'Family emergency.'

Thelma said, 'Is that what you call his wife putting a gun to her head?'

The man's grin fell, and the other one spoke. 'Who are you?'

'We knew his wife,' I said. 'Where can we find him?'

'At the hospital?' he said. 'At the police station? At home?' Check around.'

'This must be hard on him,' I said.

'That's right.' As if he took it personally.

'When did you last see him?' I asked.

'Yesterday afternoon,' the big-toothed man said. 'He left early. Something—'

'Shut up, Tom,' the other one said.

'Why should he shut up?' Thelma asked. 'There's nothing wrong with a man leaving his place of business.'

'Randy can tell you what he does with his time if he wants,' the man said. 'Talk to him. Try him at home.'

'Why did he leave early?' I asked the man with the teeth.

'We're done talking,' the other man said.

Thelma said, 'If he comes in, tell him that people from the Justice Now Initiative stopped by to offer their sympathies.'

'Whatever,' he said.

As we left the store, the man with big teeth called after us, 'Randy's an all-right guy.'

We drove to the brick bungalow where I'd first seen Kim Jenkins in the garden. The driveway was empty. The police had *X*-ed crime scene tape over the front door. The flowers in the garden strained toward the sun as if they wanted the heat to scorch them. On the front sidewalk, two girls sat on little bikes and stared at the house. When Thelma and I got out of the car and started up the path, one of them said, 'You can't go in there,' and the other said, 'She's dead.'

I rang the bell and, when no one came, rang again.

Then Thelma rang.

Sunlight glinted off the front windows.

I reached to ring the bell once more, but Thelma shook her head. We walked back to the car.

The girls watched us drive away as if they'd told us so.

The police station was just outside of town on Highway 1. It shared a squat brown building with the mayor's office and town hall. Except for a sago palm in a planter in front of the Hardee's across the street and a pair of stunted evergreens in pots on either side of the station door, the strip of highway was dry and dusty.

When we stopped in front, Thelma said, 'You OK going into a police station? After what you've gone through, I could see never wanting to step inside one again.'

The buzzing in my head had started again, but I said, 'I'm fine.'

'I'm friends with the woman Hank called when we got back from the hearing,' she said. 'She'll talk to me.'

'That's good.'

'Because if you want to stay in the car—'

'Do I look like I'm going to pass out if I go in there or something?'

'Uh-huh.'

I got out of the car, and we went into the station together.

A thick-boned woman with tightly braided hair sat at the front desk. She wore a forest-green uniform that would have looked better fighting forest fires than doing police work. She stared at me the way you stare at a man with a bad fever – with sympathy but also worry that he might have something catching. Then she looked at Thelma, and her face lit up.

She gave her a hug and said, 'I talked with your boss on the phone this morning. He gave me an earful, then filled the other one too.'

'He's upset.'

'It's been an upsetting morning,' the cop said. She turned to two middle-aged men who sat at desks in a deeper part of the room. 'I'm stepping out for a cigarette,' she said.

Neither of them acknowledged her, and we went outside into the parking lot.

Thelma introduced me then, and the cop said, 'Yeah, I've seen you on TV.' Clearly, she disliked what she'd seen. She said to Thelma, 'I've told it all to Hank. What else do you need to know?'

'Where's the husband?' Thelma asked.

The cop glanced at the station door, as if the men might leave their desks to eavesdrop. 'Gone,' she said. 'He's got family in Georgia. He left late last night. Couldn't bear to stay in the same house.'

'Any chance he did it?' Thelma asked.

'Killed Kim Jenkins? No. That lady had troubles. In the last six months, she had her stomach pumped twice.'

'She was still using?' Thelma asked.

The cop said, 'It was more like life became too heavy. She would go to a CVS, buy up everything on the shelves, and give herself a going-away party.'

'What about Randall Haussen?' I asked.

'What about him?' she said. Talking to me looked like it tasted bad in her mouth.

'He spent seven years in jail for shooting a man,' I said.

'He's stayed clean since his release,' she said. 'And he's stayed sane, which is more than Kim Jenkins could say.' She glanced at Thelma. 'My guess is your bosses pushed too hard trying to get her to testify. She broke. That's all. It happens.'

'Whose gun did she use to kill herself?' I asked.

'Why are you asking this?' she said.

'You make mistakes if you accept the easy answers. Mistakes can kill a person.'

'Sometimes the answers *are* easy,' she said. 'You don't have to like them. But they are what they are. If you dig in the ground, you'll always find dirt. But there's sad dirt and there's bad dirt. This is just sad dirt.'

'It's the dirt they'll bury Thomas LaFlora in,' I said.

TWENTY

I f you're walking through the woods and you cross a flooded river and the water rises over the stepping stone you're on, what do you do?

Step to the next stone.

Takes no cleverness to work out that one.

And when that stone goes under, step to the next.

I learned that lesson when the first appellate judge said, *Get back in line and march toward the needle with the rest of the men.* After that, I spent a month beating my head against a cell wall. Then I stepped to the next stone. When the second judge moved me from the row into general population, I stepped to the one after that. And then the next and the next until the warden opened the gate, shook my hand, and said, *Be seeing you.*

As if.

So I dropped Thelma off at the Justice Now Initiative office, and when she asked, 'Aren't you coming up?' I said, 'Either I keep moving or I drown.'

She said, 'Huh?'

'I have another lead to check out,' I said.

'You want company?'

'I need to check this one on my own.'

'Maybe my friend is right,' she said. 'Maybe it's simple. Maybe Kim Jenkins did it.'

I said, 'The other times when she tried to kill herself she used drugs from a CVS, but this time she used a gun?'

'Maybe this time she meant it.'

In truth, I had no lead – at least none that would help LaFlora. But while I saw little I could do to keep him from drowning in the rapids, I knew some paths that might keep my own head above water. So I zigged instead of zagged, the stone to the left looking as good as the one to the right. That path took me to see my old running coach, Ernie Kagen.

Kagen lived in a white, single-story house with a dormered attic in the Murray Hill neighborhood. The paint was flaking, and the front porch had turned gray. Two cats lounged on the porch. Holly bushes scratched the walls, and the grass needed mowing.

When I was on the freshman boys track team, and still when Coach Kagen visited me in prison, he walked with the leggy bounce of a long-distance runner. But now, as he opened his door, he'd grown fat in the belly, though his legs and arms remained thin. His skin, tan from the sun when I last saw him, had a yellow tinge. A sour smell leaked from the inside hallway.

He blinked as if seeing sunlight for the first time, and then a broad smile broke across his face. 'Franky!' he said, and he stepped on to the porch. He pulled me into a sour hug. 'Look at you,' he said. 'A free man.' He put a hand on my shoulder and guided me to the other end of the porch, where there were two lawn chairs. 'I've watched you on the news. You're getting out and about. That's good.' His movements were nervous. He sat on one of the chairs. 'What brings you here?'

I said, 'Early on, when no one else believed me, and even my dad and brother stayed away, you came. That probably saved me. I was falling, and when you showed up, you reached a hand down to me.'

He smiled – uncomfortable – and looked at me as if I had failed to answer his question.

'My reintegration counselor told me to visit the people and places that have given me pleasure. I liked seeing you when you came. I appreciated the cards you sent.'

'That was nothing,' he said.

I said, 'When I was in high school, how well did we know each other?'

'You had talent,' he said. 'The first time I saw you run, I thought, *This kid is a winner.* You had a look I've seen only in the fastest boys. When you ran, you seemed almost to leave the ground. It was beautiful to watch.'

'But you kicked me off the team, and I barely talked to you for the next three years. And then you showed up at my trial and came to see me in prison. Why?'

He looked out across the front yard. A pickup truck, loaded with landscaping equipment, drove by, and then the street was empty, the air still, the midday sunlight glinting on the pavement. 'I missed a chance with you,' he said. 'I thought maybe if I had worked with you instead of kicking you off the team, your life would have turned out different. The things you did to those boys—'

'I did *nothing* to them,' I said. 'I did nothing.'

'I know that now,' he said.

'What did you think when you testified and visited me?'

'I didn't know what to think,' he said.

We sat for a while, quiet, and then I said, 'About two years ago, you stopped coming and sending cards. Had you worked out your guilt for kicking me off?' I wondered why I felt angry. In the early days, he'd stood by me closer than anyone else.

'I hit a rough patch,' he said. Nervous again.

I stared at him the way so many others had stared at me during the trial.

'You're no longer coaching?' I asked.

'No.'

'You quit?'

He said nothing. From his nervousness and the stink on him, I imagined a problem with drugs, or some kind of breakdown.

'What happened?' I asked.

'Nothing I care to talk about.'

I had no reason to harass him, except for my general anger and his infectious unease. 'There will be a public record,' I said. 'I can find it. Or you can tell me.'

He shook his head.

'Everything is accessible now, more or less,' I said. 'I can find out about things that didn't even happen. *My* name appears in hundreds of databases. You can find all the terrible things the police and prosecutor said I did. You can find details about my childhood that *I'd* forgotten until I read about them online. I'm good at finding these kinds of things. Give me a computer and an hour or two, and I'll know all of your secrets.'

'Why would you want to know them?' he asked. In the still air, I smelled him. 'It seems mean-spirited.'

'Your visits and cards may have saved me,' I said, 'but your interest also always confused me. I wondered why you cared. I want to know what motivated you. If that's mean-spirited, I'm sorry.'

He spoke then with a voice that echoed one I'd heard in my own ears as I talked to prison guards, lawyers, and judges – the voice of a man pressed hard against a wall. 'Look it up on your computer. Do what you've got to do.'

I stood up and said, 'I've also learned that, with all those databases and stories about me, I still can tell my own story. Sometimes that's all I've been able to do. Maybe no one listened. Maybe no one believed me even if they heard. For a long time, that's the way it was. But telling my own story felt better than listening to others talk about me.' He held his lips tight, closing against himself. So I said, 'Good to see you again, Coach,' and I went to the porch steps.

'They fired me,' he said.

I stayed where I was, letting him have distance.

'A few of the kids have posted about it online,' he said. 'You can find it. But the only truth you'll see is that I took the team to Tallahassee, and when the Holiday Inn was overbooked, I shared a room with one of the runners. The rest is lies.'

I felt a rushing in my head.

'The boy had troubles,' he said. 'He shouldn't have come to the meet.'

'But you let him come. And you roomed with him?'

'Who else would? You think he would've made it through the night with the other boys? I tried to help.'

'What exactly happened?'

'I coached for twenty-one years,' he said. 'In all that time, only this boy accused me. Why should anyone believe him?'

'What did you do?' Now I heard Higby's voice in my head, saying, *You did it.*

'They asked me to resign,' he said. 'I told them I wouldn't. They threatened to go to the police. The boy's family ruled that out. Instead, they fired me.' He gazed at me as if asking for something – forgiveness maybe, or sympathy.

But I still heard only Higby's *You did it.* I wondered what desire or guilt drew Kagen to come to my trial, visit me behind bars, and send cards. Maybe the charges against me sparked something that had kindled low and whatever happened in the Holiday Inn six years later flamed inevitably after he watched me and wondered what it would be like. Or maybe he already knew what it would be like.

I tried to stop that train of thought. Maybe he'd taken the runner into his hotel room to help a child in need – and he'd visited and written to me following the same impulse – and then the boy accused him falsely. I knew plenty about getting punished for good deeds.

But his nervousness and the sour stink made me think a nightmare became flesh in that Tallahassee hotel room.

I realized he was staring at me. He said, 'If anyone can understand, you should.'

But the rushing still came in my head, and I wondered if Higby heard the same wind as he grabbed me by the throat and held me against the wall of the interview room.

I managed to say, 'Sure, Coach,' but then I fled down the porch steps to my car.

Behind me, he said, 'You've got to understand.'

I drove to the Jacksonville Sheriff's Office – a concrete slab of a building with slit windows, sunlight baking the gray walls. The last time I'd come to the building, Higby breathed fire in my face until I told him I killed the Bronson brothers. Exhausted, frightened, broken, I'd half believed I did it.

People and places that gave me pleasure? Visiting the Sheriff's Office felt like a blade in the belly.

I went up the steps anyway, my insides turning liquid. At the information desk by the security checkpoint, I asked for Higby's partner, Detective Deborah Holt.

'Who's asking?' the deskman said.

'My name's Franky Dast,' I said. 'She knows who I am.'

The man's eyes lit up at my name. 'Yeah, we *all* know who you are.' He dialed his phone. Then he pointed at a concrete pillar by a garbage can and a table covered with street-safety brochures. 'Wait over there.'

That's where Deborah Holt found me five minutes later.

'What the hell?' she said.

'Can we talk?' I asked.

'Go ahead.'

'Inside?'

'No. What do you want?'

I already sensed I was wasting my time, but I asked, 'What do you know about a man named Ernie Kagen? Used to coach track at Sandalwood High School.'

'Never heard of him.' She turned as if we'd finished.

'He was fired two years ago for getting too close to one of the boys who ran on the team.'

'Sounds like a friend of yours,' she said.

'That's the thing. After Higby arrested me, Kagen started showing up. I ran track for a year at Sandalwood, but I thought Kagen had forgotten me until he came to my trial. Then he visited me in prison. For a while, he *was* my friend. My only friend. But I just found out about the thing with the runner.'

'Congratulations. Now you have something to bond over.'

'Don't be an idiot,' I said.

She looked at me with low rage and, without another word, walked away.

I called after her, 'Did you know about him before? Did Higby? Where was Kagen when the Bronson boys died?'

Holt turned and came back. 'Shut up,' she said quietly. 'You're out of prison. Be happy with that. But now you're real close to getting back into something that you want to stay far away from. You understand that? Be grateful you're out. Let that be enough.'

*   *   *

That night, I saw Cynthia for only a half hour. My stomach was churning and felt as sour as the smell that came off Coach Kagen. She and I sat in my car in the Cineplex parking lot, and she rested her hand on my thigh.

'Tell me,' she said.

'I wish I could,' I said. 'But I don't know. I don't.'

'Tell me anyway,' she said.

TWENTY-ONE

Over the next week, with LaFlora's execution ticking closer, Jane and Hank had me hunt for records that would prove that, along with receiving reduced or dropped charges, Kim Jenkins and the other witnesses were paid to testify against an innocent man.

But a bank long ago destroyed any records that would show even a small deposit into the account owned by the first of the witnesses. The second witness never *had* an account. And we would need a court order to see the financial records of the newly dead Kim Jenkins – impossible without the consent of her husband.

Each morning, Jane came in grimacing. Hank stared blankly at the poster of LaFlora. Thelma danced her fingers across the computer keyboard to a fast-forwarded soundtrack only she could hear. I drove back to Callahan three times, but Kim Jenkins's house remained empty and the employees at Aardo Auto Parts said Randall Haussen had stayed in Georgia even after the coroner released his wife's body and a dozen friends and neighbors sat in pews at her funeral.

When I wasn't looking into the police handling of LaFlora's case, I tried to find out more about Coach Kagen and his night at the Holiday Inn. I searched a dozen social media sites and found two mentions of him and a kid named Jacob. Contradicting what Kagen told me, the first postings said the Tallahassee police went to the Holiday Inn on the night of the track meet after one of Jacob's teammates called 911.

So I searched for a list of sexual predators on the city website.

Two lived within a quarter mile of Kagen's house, but his street and the streets on both sides of it were clean. Next, I looked at the house where I grew up. Again, no red flag appeared. Then I looked at the section of Philips Highway where I'd lived since getting out of prison. 'Goddamn it,' I said.

Thelma's fingers stopped dancing on the keyboard.

'They've got me down as a predator at the Cardinal Motel.'

'Let it go for now,' Jane said.

Hank said, 'Once you've got your apology and money from the state, you can sue to get off the list.'

In the evenings, Cynthia and I went to my room or watched movies at the Cineplex. One night, we went back to Cardice Cold Storage, and when the watchman left us alone, Cynthia unzipped her pants and I unzipped mine in the shivering cold.

Then Bill Higby hit the news again. As one of the conditions of his release, he'd signed an agreement to stay away from the Skooners, but according to the morning news, he crossed the property line, pounded on the Skooners' door, and confronted the judge. One report said that he punched the judge's son, Andrew, though the Sheriff's Office spokesman confirmed only that an altercation occurred shortly after midnight and the police now had one of their own in custody.

Whatever happened, Higby was back in jail.

A thrill passed down my back as the anchorman and reporter mulled over the dangers of rogue officers.

In a live interview on Channel 4, Higby's lawyer said, 'The circumstances of this incident have been misrepresented,' but when asked to explain, said only, 'The time will come for explanations.'

As for the Skooners, the judge said, 'We're installing a new security system at my house this afternoon. I would be sorry to lose confidence in our city's law enforcement.'

I floated – like a running boy – from my room out to my car and gripped the steering wheel with both hands so I would stay on the road while driving to the JNI office.

Thelma had just come in and was waiting for her computer to boot up. Hank had pulled his chair to the side of Jane's desk, and they were reviewing pretrial depositions from Kim Jenkins and the other two witnesses. Hank said, 'The lawyer asked straight out, "What incentives did you receive for agreeing to testify?" and the witness said, "Don't know what you're talking about." He evaded the question.'

Jane shook her head. 'Maybe he didn't know the word "incentive."'

Hank jabbed the deposition. 'They goddamned did it.' It was just eight, but Hank already had a sheen of sweat on his forehead.

'I hear it,' Jane said, 'but where does he say it?'

I turned on my laptop and said, 'It's too little. You know that.'

Hank glared at me. But when he turned back to Jane, he all but admitted it. 'I'm sinking,' he said. 'Give me something.'

She looked at another page of the deposition. 'The lawyer asked, "Why are you testifying?" And he said, "I've got kids to take care of." It's suggestive.'

'Still sinking,' Hank said.

'Who bailed them out?' I asked.

Hank and Jane looked at me. I said, 'The dealer got killed while the witnesses were smoking crack. Even with the reduced charges, they had to pay a lot to stay out of jail before the trial. Who paid the bail? Crackheads are poor, and most poor people have poor friends and family. Maybe the payoff went to them.'

Hank still looked as if he was sinking, but he said, 'Check it out.'

I spent an hour trying to identify Kim Jenkins's family members and the families of the other witnesses, but, like a lot of addicts, they'd cut themselves off from their loved ones or their loved ones had done the cutting. I had no doubt that I would find names if I searched long enough, but after another ten minutes with no hits, I checked the latest news on Higby.

Now, three stories said he'd punched Andrew Skooner, cutting him badly enough for stitches. The Skooner family lawyer was demanding that the District Attorney charge Higby with assault. Higby's lawyer now said no quarrel occurred.

I closed the internet connection, slapped the laptop shut, and got up.

'What?' Hank said.

'No luck,' I said. 'Not yet.' I headed for the stairs.

'Where are you going?' he asked.

'I'm trying another approach. Maybe faster.'

'What's that?'

'I'm going to talk to LaFlora's prosecutor.'

'Eric Skooner? You can't do that.'

'Watch me,' I said.

Hank got up and followed me down the stairs. 'You can't afford to stick a wrench into this right now,' he said. 'Thomas LaFlora can't afford it. The JNI can't. Eric Skooner is feared on the bench, and—'

He was still talking as I got into my car and pulled from the curb.

When I rang the bell at the judge's house, Andrew Skooner opened the door. Behind him in the hallway, as the judge promised, security technicians were mounting a video camera near the ceiling.

Andrew Skooner stared at me. He was big and square and muscled. Under normal circumstances, people would have called him handsome. But along with old scars on his nose and forehead, he had a stitched-up cut over his upper lip. Dry blood crusted the bottom of his nostrils. His left cheek was swollen.

'What?' he said.

'Hi,' I said, 'I work for the Justice Now Initiative.'

He started to close the door.

'Higby did a job on your face,' I said.

He closed the door the rest of the way, and a lock clicked into place.

I talked to the closed door. 'He did a job on me too – eight years ago. You can't see the stitches, but inside I'm sewed up like a rag doll. Higby seemed brutal when I first met him, but I've met others like him since then. It seems like their hands are made of scissors and knives—'

The door swung open again. 'What do you want?'

'When he cut me, he was incredibly precise,' I said. 'It was like brain surgery, or open heart. He knew what he wanted, and he went inside and got it. If you saw me then, you would have said he was a professional – top of his field. But look at *you*. He swung wildly, didn't he? From all I've seen, you and your family bring out the beast in him.'

The security techs stopped working and listened.

Andrew Skooner said, 'Who are you and what are you talking about?'

'My name's Franky Dast. He sent me away for eight years for—'

'Yeah, I know about you,' he said.

'Then you know how he carved me up. Or if you still think I did the things he said I did, he carved me up even better than you know.'

'Why are you here?' he said.

'What happened last night?' I asked. 'What made him go after you like that?'

'Why would I tell you?'

'Shared experiences?' I said.

From somewhere in the house behind him, a man said, 'Who is it, Andy?' I recognized Judge Skooner's voice from the TV interviews after Joshua died.

His son stepped outside and pulled the door closed behind him. 'You should leave,' he said.

'Why did Higby hit you?' I asked.

'Why does anyone hit someone?' he said. 'We argued. He got mad.'

'What did you argue about?'

'It doesn't matter now,' he said. 'It's over.'

'It's never over,' I said. 'Why won't you tell me what happened?'

He stared at me, as if gauging my strength as a man he might need to fight. 'I know you've had it hard,' he said. 'I get that. But, believe it or not, I've had it harder. I might not look it, but I have.'

The door opened, and Judge Skooner peered out and said, 'Andy, what are you doing?' Then he stared at me and added, 'I know who you are.'

'With respect, sir,' I said, 'you only *think* you do. I'm working for the Justice Now Initiative, and I need to ask you some questions about the case you prosecuted against Thomas LaFlora.'

The judge said, 'Get inside, Andy.' His son stared at him with cold eyes before obeying. The judge turned back to me. 'I've dealt with Hank Cury and Jane Foley before. They should know better than to send a man like you to harass me at home.' He closed the door, and again the lock clicked.

I knew men in prison who would bang on the bars if the guards ignored them – and others who would collect their piss and throw it at the guards until the guards tasered, pepper sprayed, and beat them, then dragged them to solitary where they could wallow for ninety days or a year or more. Me? I saved my energy for the law library, and except for the times when I pounded my head on the walls and rattled my cage after judges rejected my appeals, I left as light of a print on the prison as I could manage.

Now, in the heat of the July afternoon, I had two options. I could kick the judge's door. Or I could walk to my car.

I walked to my car.

And then I drove next door to Higby's house.

Shades covered the front windows. The outdoor furniture was shoved to one corner of the front porch. The little house looked like a clenched fist.

I guessed Higby's wife had gone to stay with friends or family, but when I rang the bell, footsteps approached, stopped, and then went away. I rang the bell again, and the footsteps came back.

The door opened. Higby's wife stood in front of me, her hair wet. She held a black pistol in her hand, but she aimed it at the floor.

I said, 'If someone took eight years of your life – and tried to take the rest – wouldn't you want to know everything you could about him?'

She gave me a tight frown. 'I think I would want to stay as far away from him as I could.'

'See, that's impossible,' I said. 'Your husband is with me everywhere I go. Sometimes I think he's as much a part of me as I am of myself.'

She held the pistol steady. I guessed she had practice shooting it, though I also guessed that, like most people, she would never shoot at a living man unless her own life was in danger. 'What do you want?' she asked.

'That's a long list,' I said. 'Most of it I can't have. But you can tell me why your husband hit Andrew Skooner last night.'

'He didn't,' she said.

'At the time he arrested me, he wouldn't do something like that,' I said. 'He calculated every move. He figured out every pressure point in my head and on my body, and he worked them all, one after another, until he had me where I would say and do anything he told me to. But the man who hit Andrew Skooner – and shot his brother – has lost control. He's acting out of fear or something like it. Your husband twisted me into all kinds of shapes, but someone else is making *him* jump now. That's what I think.'

She eyed me doubtfully. 'And who do you think that is?'

'The Skooners would make sense. But so far, he's battering them more than they're hurting him.'

Again, the tight frown. 'It would be best if you got back in your car and left,' she said.

'I really need to talk with him. But since he's in jail, I'll settle for you.'

'I have nothing to tell you,' she said.

I stepped toward her.

She raised the pistol so it pointed at my chest.

'I know everything you've done,' she said. 'My husband has told me.'

'You know what he *says* I've done. But do you believe it?'

'Every word.'

'Then you'd better call your cop friends,' I said, and I stepped past her into the house. Higby had locked me behind doors for eight years, and I was tired of his barriers.

The front hall reached straight back to the kitchen, where windows faced the dark water of Black Creek. I walked through the hall, with her close behind me, and sat at the kitchen table.

'Does your husband keep copies of case files at home?' I asked.

'Of course not.' She stood a few feet away, with the gun pointing at me.

'Would you mind if I look?'

'Yes, I would mind very much,' she said.

'Then tell me what he and Andrew Skooner fought about last night.'

'You understand, don't you, that you're the last person he would want me to talk to?'

I said, 'Unlike just about anyone else in this city, I think he might have been justified in shooting Joshua Skooner. I think Joshua had a gun. And I think your husband probably had a good reason, if not legal justification, to hit Andrew Skooner last night.'

'Then you must be happy about the injustice,' she said.

I said, 'I have mixed feelings.'

I thought your opinion mattered, I wouldn't tell you

I'm the only one who can help him?'
'Why would you be? And if you were, why in the world would you do it?'
In truth, if I helped him – *if* – I would do so only because I could show power over his life as he'd had power over mine. He would live every day knowing I had that power. 'I hate what happened to me,' I said. 'I never want to see it happen again. To anyone. I'll do anything to stop it.'
She considered me. Maybe she put my words into balance with all her husband had told her about me and whatever faith she had in him. She said, 'No. Just no. You need to leave my house. You need to never come back.'
So I got up from the table. But instead of walking back out through the front hall, I crossed to a door that led into a home office. Inside, a coffee table was covered with magazines. The desk was bare except for an electric bill and a car insurance renewal notice. I went to the file cabinet next to the desk and opened the top drawer.
Higby's wife said, 'I can't let you do that.'
'It seems to me that you and your husband have enough troubles without you shooting me.' I felt her heavy presence as I leafed through a file of travel brochures for Jamaica and Key West, another of credit card receipts, and a third of statements from Higby's police pension.
I closed the drawer and opened the second.
Higby's wife said, 'I told you, he brings none of his work home.'
The first folder in the drawer contained an old photograph showing Higby in his mid-twenties, standing on a fishing dock with a rod and reel, another photograph showing him when he was still younger, alongside two other teenage boys, and a third showing him and his wife at their wedding ceremony. The next folder – thicker than the others – contained medical records. Folder after folder held only his personal and financial records. When I looked up again, the pistol was quivering in his wife's hand.
'Satisfied?'
'Hardly,' I said, but I went back through the kitchen to the hallway, with her following close behind me. I glanced into the living room.

Then I headed for the front door. 'I'm sorry I had to do that,' I said.

She aimed the gun at my back. 'Get the hell out of my house.'

'Tell your husband I came by,' I said. 'Tell him I offered to help.'

She said, 'If I told him I even saw you, he would destroy you.' She slammed the door.

I smiled as I walked to my car. I would count her silence as a betrayal of Bill Higby.

When I got back to the JNI office, Jane and Hank were gone, though Thelma still drummed her fingers on her computer keyboard. She'd tracked down the brother of one of the witnesses against Thomas LaFlora, and Jane and Hank had gone to surprise him at the Long Oaks Apartments on the northwest side of the city.

Now, she peeled a Post-it note from her desk and gave it to me. 'For you. Andrew Skooner just called. But he left no return number.'

'Huh,' I said.

'What did the judge have to say?'

'He told me to go to hell.'

'You expected anything different?'

'I hoped.'

'You should know better by now.' And she drummed and she drummed.

I dialed directory assistance and got the Skooner's home phone number. When I dialed again, Andrew answered, and I said, 'It's Franky Dast.'

'It doesn't matter,' he said.

'What doesn't?'

'Thanks,' he said, and hung up.

I stared at the phone. 'Screwy boy.'

I left the office at four o'clock. Cynthia was working at the Cineplex until midnight, and so I drove back to the Cardinal Motel. As I approached, I saw a squad car parked by my room. Once again, my door was gone – kicked or knocked off. The motel owner, Bill Hopper, stood inside the doorframe, blocking two cops who seemed to want to get inside. I started to drive past, fought the impulse, turned into the lot, and parked next to the squad car. When I got out, Hopper was yelling at the cops, and the cops were trying to peer around him.

'What the hell!' Hopper said to them. 'What're you thinking?'

One of the cops leaned in, his hand at his holster. 'We got a call that he was—'

'You broke my fucking door,' Hopper said.

'We thought—'

'It was a new door!'

'Sir,' the other cop said, 'you need to calm down.' His fingers brushed against gun metal.

Hopper said, '*I* need to calm down? *You* kicked down my fucking door. *I* get along with the police. You just had to come to my office—'

'We believed an assault was in progress,' the first cop said.

'"In progress"? How the hell?' And now Hopper saw me. 'He wasn't even home. How could he *in progress* anyone? Jesus Christ – look at my door.'

The second cop asked me, 'Are you Franklin Dast?'

And the first cop said, 'We got a call—'

The second cop said, 'Show him.'

The first cop gestured at a pair of boy's underwear on the concrete walkway a few feet from my doorway. They looked bloody – like the pair I found hanging from my doorknob shortly after I moved in.

The second cop said, 'Why'd you put those on your door?'

'I wasn't here,' I said. 'It's an ugly prank.'

The cops exchanged a glance. One said, 'We still got to check the room.'

Hopper said, 'If you don't have a warrant, you sure as hell don't.'

'Sir,' the cop said, 'you need to step aside.'

Hopper said, 'Unless a crime is happening, you can't go in.' He reached into my room and hit the light switch. 'You see a kid in there? You see an assault?'

The cop started toward him, as if he would go in anyway, but the other one pulled him aside. They went to the squad car and talked for a minute, and then the first one came back and, ignoring Hopper, talked to me. 'Do we have permission to look inside your room?'

I had nothing to hide. I'd never had anything to hide. But that hadn't kept me off death row. 'Get a warrant,' I said.

The second cop came at me, as if I'd given the wrong answer. But then a black Mercury Grand Marquis drove on to the parking lot and stopped next to the squad car. Higby's partner, Deborah Holt, opened the car door, flashed her badge at the patrolmen, and said, 'Get out of here.'

The first cop looked confused, the second angry.

The first said, 'Ma'am?'

'Go on,' she said. 'It's a misunderstanding. You're done here.'

'No, ma'am,' the second cop said, and he seemed about to take a stand, but she got in close to him and mumbled a word or two, and then he backed down and slunk toward his squad car.

'What about the door?' Hopper said. 'Who's going to pay for it?'

Holt turned to him and said, 'I'm betting if we kicked down a couple more doors, we'd find meth or coke. Then we could take legal possession of the motel and put your scumbag flock on the street. Do you really want to worry about this one?'

He said weakly, 'It was a new door.'

'Go back to your office and let me talk to Mr Dast.'

He said to me, 'You cover my ass, and I cover yours.'

As he walked away, she said, 'Make sure Mr Dast has a stronger door this evening.'

Then we were alone. I stared at her. The beginning of a smile hung on her lips. Suddenly, everyone was trying to be my friend. I said, 'Why did you do that?'

'You wanted to talk to the street cops?'

'But why?'

'Can we go inside?'

I wondered if she was setting a trap. I stared at my broken door. She said, 'We can talk in my car instead if you want.'

I stepped over the pieces of my door and she came in after me.

'Sit, if you want,' I said, but she stayed standing and so did I.

'I'll deny I ever told you this,' she said, 'but Higby is responsible for the underwear. He has a few friends in the department who are glad to help.'

A wave of nausea passed through me. 'He can get to me from jail?'

'You deserved it,' she said. 'He talked on the phone with his wife this afternoon. You scared the hell out of her.'

'Oh,' I said.

'I thought I told you to stay away. I warned you.'

'Eight years ago, when I did what *he* told me to do, I ended up on death row. I mostly try to do the opposite of what cops tell me to do now. It seems safer.'

'Safer unless you like having a door on your room,' she said. 'And you know from experience that there are a lot of worse things that can happen than losing a door. Plenty of people would be happy to make those things happen for you. Why risk it?'

My stomach turned as I realized how close I'd come to having cops tear through my room – how easy it would be to set me up with more than a couple of pairs of bloody underwear.

'Hold on,' I said. I went into the bathroom and closed the door. I turned on the cold water in the sink, ran it over my hands and wrists, and splashed it on my face. I looked in the mirror. The water dotted my pale skin like a death-sweat. I splashed my face again and again until I figured my legs would hold under me.

When I went back into the room, Holt was sitting on the side of my bed. She stared at me curiously. I said, 'Why did you wreck Higby's plan to set me up? I thought you guys worked together.'

'You know what?' she said. 'You've wormed into *my* head. I see why he wanted to put you away.'

'Why did you wreck his plan?'

Again, she stared. 'I'll deny I ever told you this.'

She waited for a response, so I said, 'OK.'

'After I came to talk to you last time, I was looking through his old files,' she said. 'We share a caseload. You had a fascinating case. I've spent the last few days reading about it – and about you. I know you now, Franky. I could write a book. I think if I'd seen the same evidence Higby saw, I would've done exactly what he did. And, by the way, that track coach of yours – Ernie Kagen – he *is* a predator. We'll bust him sooner or later. But he had nothing to do with the deaths of the Bronson boys.'

'How do you—'

'The night they died, he was in jail in New Orleans, charged with soliciting an underage prostitute. He used a phony name, and the connection came out only after the Gainesville incident. So you would still look good for the Bronson killings, except for one thing. Five years before the Bronson boys died, another boy got killed in a way that looked a lot like them but in a state park down in Putnam County. A fourteen-year-old runaway. Raped. Bite marks. A single twenty-two-caliber bullet in the forehead. DNA recovered but untested. Higby date-marked the report when it came in. He had it in his hands before you went to trial. He either read it or should have.'

'I was thirteen when that one happened?' I said.

She nodded. 'And the Putnam investigator put notes at the bottom about similarities to still another killing. A ten-year-old boy went missing from a family campsite three years earlier. No rape, but he had the bite marks and bullet wound.'

'*I* was ten.'

'Yes.'

'Jesus Christ.'

'Everything else in the case file tells me *you* did the Bronson brothers,' she said. 'Or maybe you and someone else who left the DNA, but definitely you.'

'Did the bullets match the ones that killed the Bronson boys?'

She gave me a pained smile. 'They're missing from the evidence file. The guys in Putnam—'

'Missing? How?'

'I don't know,' she said. 'It happens more often than it should.'

I thought about what she'd told me. 'But you know I didn't do it.'

'Yes.'

No other cop had ever believed me.

'Detective Higby made a terrible mistake when he withheld that report,' she said. 'He's a good investigator, and I believe he *thinks* you're guilty. I can't see how he gets there, but I believe it.'

'Believing him can cause a lot of pain,' I said.

'That's why I broke up his racket today. He means well—'

'No, he doesn't,' I said. 'He means to hurt me.'

'For him, that's the same as meaning well.'

Hot air and highway fumes breathed in through the broken door. 'I need the files on the other boys,' I said.

'I know,' she said. 'You deserve to see them.'

'Thank you.' It hurt to say that to a cop, but I said it.

'I'll deny I gave them to you. But if anyone investigates, they'll know. If you can, I would appreciate your keeping quiet about how you got them. My job's on the line.' When I said nothing, she added, 'I'm trying to do right by you.'

'It's too late to do right.'

'I know that too.' And she brought in the files from her trunk.

When she left, I spread the report about the earlier killings on my bed. The first kid, whose name was Jeremy Ballat, had just turned fourteen when he died. He'd been dead for forty-eight to seventy-two hours when a park ranger found his naked body in a ditch in the Etoniah Creek State Forest. Insects had torn into his eyes and mouth, though the medical examiner said the bite marks on his legs were human. Swabs showed that he'd been raped – tissue analysis suggested, repeatedly. The killer had shot him through his tender forehead, probably pointblank, but the skin had deteriorated too much for the examiner to say more.

Jeremy Ballat had run away from home in Atlanta two weeks before he died. He'd hitchhiked to Macon and then to Savannah, where he had hung out with a pack of teenagers for eight days before continuing down the coast and crossing the Florida border to Jacksonville. At that point, he seemingly decided to play Huck Finn. Only a handful of barges work the St Johns River beyond the Buckman Bridge at the southern end of the city, but he talked his way on to one of them that was carrying used tires. He got into an argument with the barge captain and jumped into the river near the western bank about ten miles before the Palatka dock.

Investigators looked hard at the captain, but he'd arrived on time in Palatka and his schedule back downriver gave him no time for a side trip to the state forest. Nothing in his background suggested he might commit this kind of crime.

The report included two maps. A straight shot from the riverbank to the park measured about twenty miles through swamps and timberland south of Bostwick. The paths by road, or a mix of roads and hiking trails, would have taken the boy through Bostwick – or else the slightly smaller town of Bardin – where someone most likely would have seen him. Those paths measured over twenty-five miles. The Putnam investigators speculated that whoever killed the boy had picked him up or abducted him shortly after he came to shore from the barge and that the killer went to the park only to dump the body. The police never found the jeans, T-shirt, or gym shoes that the barge captain said the boy was wearing.

The note about the earlier killing that one of the investigators had added to the bottom of the report said a ten-year-old – a Mexican boy named Luis Gonzalez – was camping with his illegal immigrant parents and sister in woods behind the Mount Zion Baptist Church on the other side of the river from the point where Jeremy Ballat waded ashore. The area, called Federal Point, consisted mostly of large farms. The parents would come in winter to pick strawberries and return in early summer for the blueberry crop. One day, while they were working, their son disappeared. Fearing the cops, they didn't report his absence. When, a week later, a fisherman found a body floating in shallow water just downriver and the police tracked the boy back to the encampment, the parents said their son often played on the riverbank. Everyone at first thought he'd gone swimming and drowned. But when his sister said a man had come to the camp and taken the boy, the medical examiner looked more closely at the decomposed corpse and found the bite marks and the twenty-two-caliber bullet lodged in the skull. Then the parents and daughter disappeared.

And, I thought, sometime in the months or years that followed, so did the bullet.

I read and reread the note and the report, looking for any details that linked the Mexican boy and the Atlanta runaway to the Bronson brothers.

Along with the matching wounds, they all were between ten and fifteen years old, all living at the edge of legal systems that should have protected them. Steven and Duane Bronson lived in Jacksonville, and Jeremy Ballat came through the city on his way south, but Luis Gonzalez seemingly had no reason to travel off the rural farm circuit that his parents worked.

I started again at the beginning of the report and reread it for anything I'd missed. Like the Bronson brothers but unlike Luis Gonzalez, Jeremy Ballat lived with a single mother. Again like the Bronsons but, as far as I knew, unlike the Mexican boy, he had a record of minor arrests – for truancy, stealing a bottle of vodka from a neighbor's house, and attempting another burglary.

As was the case with the Bronson brothers, although the investigators never tested the rape kit, they did bloodwork and other
toxicology analysis on him. They found trace THC metabolites,
which meant he'd smoked marijuana in the days or weeks before
he died. Otherwise, the analysis came out normal – except for
highly elevated mercury.

I felt another punch in the belly. I remembered my public
defender stumbling through my first trial. *Were the Bronson
brothers high when they died?* he asked. The prosecution expert
answered, *No, sir, no alcohol or drugs*, though *the boys did have
elevated levels of mercury*. Of course, the expert then said that
any of a dozen common causes could have led to the high mercury,
including eating tuna fish sandwiches.

Even if a lot of kids had high mercury, it linked these particular
ones. I figured the medical examiner who overturned the finding
of accidental drowning after Luis Gonzalez's death would also
have done blood and toxicology. I should see if I could get that
report when I went back to my computer at the JNI office.

I paged through the rest of the report, glanced again at the
maps of Jeremy Ballat's possible routes from the St Johns River
to Etoniah Creek State Forest, and reread the note about Luis
Gonzalez.

When I finished, I felt I was still missing something – another
link, a pattern of the kind that I trained myself to see while fighting
to get off death row and out of prison. So I started at the beginning again, reading more slowly, pausing after each sentence,
thinking about each word.

As I looked at Jeremy Ballat's route maps, I saw what I'd
missed. But the realization disappointed me more than it punched
me with either pain or exhilaration. The link – the little town of
Bostwick – didn't connect Jeremy Ballat with any of the other
three boys, and so it almost definitely didn't matter. As the map
showed, his routes would have taken him either through or just
to the south of the town. And, on one of my first days at the
JNI, after I sweated through a bus ride from my motel room,
Jane, as a welcoming gift, gave me a report of complaints and
commendations that Bill Higby had received at the Sheriff's
Office. Along with filing two of the complaints, the Skooner

family also had commended him for returning Josh who, at age eleven, ran away to a plot of mill land, owned by his mother's family, just east of Bostwick. But I saw no deeper connection to the murdered boys.

Still, when I went back to the JNI office in the morning, I would also see if I could get my hands on Josh Skooner's toxicology report. It couldn't hurt to check. Maybe he'd eaten a lot of tuna fish too.

For now, I called the Skooners' house. The last time I'd called, returning a call from Andrew Skooner, he'd all but hung up on me, but I was glad when he answered. I asked, 'Why did your brother run away?'

'Huh?'

'When he was eleven,' I said. 'And Higby brought him back.'

'With my dad, you either perform or run away. Josh didn't perform.'

'Must be hard growing up the son of a judge.'

He said, 'You can't imagine.'

A little before ten p.m., a man came to build a new doorframe and put up a door. Bill Hopper walked over when the truck pulled up. As the man unloaded the door and his tools, Hopper told me, 'This one's got steel. No one's coming through without a battering ram.'

'Like the doors they used in solitary confinement,' I said.

He looked uneasy. 'But this time, keeping the animals *out*, right?'

After listening to the banging hammer and the rip of an electric saw for ten minutes, I went out to my car and pulled on to Philips Highway. I had time to answer a couple of questions before I picked up Cynthia.

I wondered, if Jeremy Ballat died fifty miles upriver of Jacksonville and Luis Gonzalez died just across the river from him, did Duane and Steven Bronson also spend time in that area? Their mother would know, but the last time I visited her in her dog-filled house was a disaster. Duane Bronson's girlfriend Lynn Melsyn also might know, but she was still hiding eight years after his death.

So I drove back toward the mother's house. The airport was

directing planes right over the neighborhood, and every minute or so a roar tore through the air.

When I knocked, no dogs barked and no one came. I could break a window pane and go inside, but what would I find in the mess of dog dishes and the disintegrated life of grief?

I went back to my car. In an hour and a half, I would pick up Cynthia. Too little time, really, to drive to the Beach and talk with Lynn Melsyn's brother Rick and his roommate Darrell Nesbit. But too much time to hang out in the Cineplex parking lot.

I shifted into gear and hit the accelerator.

A few minutes after eleven, I rode the elevator up to the seventh floor at the Sun Reach Apartments. The corridor was hot and smelled of cigarette smoke. Dubstep and techno music played behind three of the apartment doors. No noise came from Apartment 706, but the door stood open a crack.

I opened it further and called into the apartment. 'Rick?'

I stepped inside and closed the door. The air smelled of salt and burned metal.

'Rick?' I said again – quietly, though I didn't know who I would disturb. 'Darrell?'

I went to the balcony door, opened it, and stepped out into the dark. The sound of the ocean washed around the sides of the building – unseen waves breaking – and somewhere close by, out in the dark or clinging to the side of the building, an electrical circuit hummed. In the distance, a siren moved through the night.

I went back inside and walked into the kitchen. An empty bottle of Absolut vodka, its cap off, stood on the counter next to a half-gallon carton of grapefruit juice. Dirty glasses were scattered on a kitchen table and in the sink.

I went back into the main room. Music came through the walls from other apartments. Waves crashed and washed from outside as if water was rising. The siren droned.

I went to one of the bedroom doors. It was closed tight. I tapped it. Then I turned the knob.

This time, the punch hit so low and hard that I doubled over, and before I could catch my breath, bile rose in my throat. I spat on the floor. When I stood, the sight punched me again.

Rick Melsyn lay naked on his bed, a gunshot wound in his forehead, blood splintering across his skin. I couldn't go close. If he'd held the only key that would get me out of the apartment, I couldn't. But from the doorway, I saw other wounds – bites, deep and bloody, on his neck and thighs. His left nipple had been ripped away, by teeth or another jagged instrument.

I backed from the doorway. Tears and sweat heaved from me. In my ears, I heard a rushing. I moved toward the hall door, to escape – but the other bedroom door remained, and against every nerve, against every pulsing and pounding of my heart, against the throbbing in my veins, I needed to know. I crossed the room, touched the doorknob, and shoved.

Darrell Nesbit – his black boots set side by side on the floor, his black jeans and black T-shirt folded and set next to the boots – lay naked too. A bullet wound in his forehead. Bites on his neck and thighs. His left nipple, ripped and bloody.

Darkness clouded my vision, and I knew I was going to pass out. But then Darrell Nesbit's hand moved – I would swear it did. And, against every nerve and pulsing and pounding and throbbing – against my father's dead voice murmuring that I was *always picking up the phone when I didn't know who was calling* – I stepped into the room and went to the man and touched his bloody forehead to see if it remained warm and touched his bloody chest to see if his heart was beating and held my blood-wet fingers by his mouth to see if he was breathing.

He was dead.

My tears and sweat heaved. My insides wanted out.

I ran then. Out. Out of the bedroom. Out of the apartment. Slapping the seventh-floor elevator doors when the elevator didn't come. Pasting the first-floor button when it did.

In the lobby, I knew what I looked like. What I had done again – *picking up the phone when . . .*

But who had heard my voice when I'd answered?

No one?

No one at the other end of the line?

But I'd signed my name in blood on the elevator doors and elevator button. I'd signed it in the apartment and – what else had I touched? I'd spat bile on the floor. Some things never come clean.

I looked back at the elevator. I looked at the door leading out to my car. I looked around the lobby. A video camera, mounted near the ceiling, stared back. I went to it and we stared at each other. A set of wires ran through a back wall to a remote recorder – in a separate room or maybe another building miles away.

I jumped and smashed the camera with my fist, then jumped again and pulled it from the mount. My act of destruction would do no good. Video of me coming and going was already elsewhere, ready for processing by crime technicians, ready for a prosecutor, ready for a judge and jury. I crushed the camera housing under my heel.

When I looked up from the pieces, two women were watching me from the lobby door. They saw my eyes, and they fled back outside. Ready to talk to the police, to a prosecutor, to a judge and jury.

The sirens would come, and cops would run through the lobby and ride the elevator to Apartment 706.

And then they would come for me.

And then the doors would shut on me the way they'd shut before – as if all of earth's energy focused on shutting them, burying me behind them.

I drove from the Sun Reach Apartments, the dark pressing against the cones that stuck into the night from the headlights.

At the Cineplex, Cynthia would be waiting for me, a curious smile on her lips, her beautiful scarred legs ready for me.

But I should run. Into the woods. Into the ocean.

I barely felt the strength to keep my foot on the gas.

The darkness in the car darker than the darkness outside.

I inched along the beachfront road. The car engine ticking. A clock against time.

I turned inland. Past closed restaurants and surf shops. Over the Intracoastal Waterway, the ebb and tide that promised everything – a cleansing, a transforming – but changed nothing. Past wetlands and gated subdivisions.

One light beckoned.

Walgreens.

Church of pharmaceuticals.

White lab coats.

Plastic and chemical smells.

I parked in disabled, went inside, and brushed past all that goodness. In the Home and Tool aisle, I found a plastic-wrapped two-pack of box cutters. When the white-coated clerk rang me up, I tore off the cellophane and laid one of the box cutters on the counter.

'I need only one,' I said.

The white coat gave me an ugly smile. 'Save the other for next time?'

'What next time?' I said.

A thousand cuts.

My naked pulsing body, lying on my bed at the Cardinal Motel.

My new steel door protecting me from the world, the world from me.

Starting at my toes – the softness between – the arch, the heel, the ankle bones, the stretch of skin rising to the knees. The knees – the caps and the softness behind.

Licking the blade clean. Salt of my salt. Self-communion. *I could taste the boys' blood.* Copper. Blood of my blood.

Thighs. The tenderness that rises from the thighs to the hips. The belly. The underbelly. The belly crying tears of blood. The chest. Oh, that bone.

The neck. Careful around the carotid, the jugular – too quick. Nicks and notches. Chipping at the marble of life. The whole body crying. The bed sheet wet, clinging – and the joy of releasing myself from prison bars.

My face. Hardly necessary. The cheeks. The forehead. Splinters of wound.

And when the sirens came, I sang with them. French-horning the *Star Wars* theme song from deep in my bleeding throat. And when the emergency lights flashed outside, piercing the window shade, and voices spoke through megaphones as if from a farther mountain to a man who was no longer me – making demands I no longer understood, telling me the way the world worked though the world had stopped working – I blacked out.

TWENTY-TWO

In solitary confinement, the sounds in your head, echoing in your belly and coming up your throat and out of your mouth, are the sounds that you hear.

Even in general population, you have too much time to think.

Six weeks after my sideways-moving, lazy-lipped, go-with-the-flow friend Stuart collapsed in the exercise yard, he came back from the medical center. He came like a jug of water – half empty now. 'They wanted to cut off my leg,' he said. 'The diabetes. They say I'm dying.' He laughed. A huge, low rumble of a laugh. The laugh you would expect from a volcano if a volcano could laugh.

'What's the joke?' I asked.

'I'm escaping this goddamned place,' he said.

On good nights in prison, I dreamed I ran through the woods, on a beach, on a track. From myself. Toward myself.

'Play the horn for me,' Stuart said. Stinking already.

'I don't have a horn,' I said.

'Play it anyway,' he said.

Love is possible even in a desert.

We told lies in prison. Sometimes we told *only* lies. Lies about the girls we'd fucked. Lies about the families waiting for us on the other side. Lies about the superhuman acts of strength, cleverness, and daring we'd performed. But mostly lies of omission.

Once, early on, at the county jail, Coach Kagen brought me cookies. As if I'd gone to sleep-away camp.

For a long time, when I closed my eyes I imagined myself encased in a shell. A full-body aluminum jacket. A cowry with the gap sealed with a steel door. In general population, nothing can protect your sleep except your imagination. And, during the night, when dreams of running tumble off ledges into nightmares, the imagination is a traitor.

When a guard said, *Hey asswipe*, the proper answer was *Yes, sir.*

When another inmate said, *Hey asswipe*, the proper answer was a fork in the eye.

The night before Stuart collapsed again – and this time no ambling shambling nurse could save him – he said, 'Beating up on your past won't do you no good, Franky.'

I said, 'The problem is, I don't think my past is done beating up on me.'

He said, 'Ain't that the truth.'

Love is possible.

TWENTY-THREE

With my thousand cuts and an imaginary box cutter still clutched in my hand, the doctors sedated me – and then words came out of my mouth, sounds that *sounded* like words, until the doctors sedated me some more. They rolled in and out of the room, checking boxes on charts, glaring down their noses. Nurses greased me with antiseptic salve, laying bandages over the salve and then peeling back the bandages to let the wounds breathe. When they left the room, a key turned in the lock.

The window at the top of the door was embedded with wire mesh.

I tried to ask, *Jail or psychiatric ward?*

The words that came out of my mouth were *Fuck you, motherfuckers.*

Either way – jail or nut house – I was a recidivist.

Dr Patel visited. A nurse told him about me, as if I'd already left the room for whatever heaven or hell a man like me ultimately chooses.

'Flesh wounds,' the nurse told him. 'Only a pint or so. You could do as much damage at a Bloodmobile. In a week, you won't see the scars.'

'Has he said anything?' Dr Patel asked.

The nurse laughed. 'This one has a mouth.'

'Has he explained?'

She handed him a chart, covered with checked boxes and doctors' notes. 'Can you make sense of it?'

'Oh, Franky,' Dr Patel said, as he read. 'Franky, Franky, Franky.'
I opened my mouth, and more sounds that sounded like words
came out.

The punch line? The police knew within twenty-four hours that
someone else had killed Rick Melsyn and Darrell Nesbit. The
medical examiner put the time of death at six to eight hours before
discovery. I had alibi witnesses. Higby's wife. Thelma. Deborah
Holt and a couple of street cops.

Of course, if I'd skipped Walgreens and my thousand self-
lacerations, the cops who raced to the Cardinal Motel from the
Sun Reach Apartments might've opened my body with a thousand
rounds instead of recoiling at the sight of me. In that sense, I did
them and myself a favor with the box cutter. Less paperwork for
them. A hospital bed and another lap on earth for me.

After four days, the nurses stopped bandaging me, and the doctors
dosed down the sedatives.

After six days, my thousand cuts had closed, and except for
little pink spots here and little brown scabs there, you could've
believed that I'd steered clear of disease-ridden lands for all of
my adult life.

On the seventh day, Dr Patel returned and said, 'How's tricks?'
'Can I see Cynthia?' I said.

He gave that some thought. He said, 'Before you lean on others,
you should stand on your own.'

I gave that some thought too. I said, 'Fuck you, motherfucker.'
'Pardon me?'

'I stood on my own for eight years,' I said. 'Almost everyone
tried to knock me down, but I stood. When the JNI took up with
me, the news told stories about the crusading lawyers – on *their*
feet – and they showed my mug shot as if I was already on the
slab. And now that I'm out, everyone says I need to stand on my
own, but then they tell me to sit down and be patient – wait for
my check from the state, get my meds right, let others do the
standing for me. But I've been standing on my own for a long
time. So, fuck them and fuck you.'

'It's good to let the anger out,' he said.
'Fuck you.'

'Good.'

'Fuck you again.'

'I'll see what I can do,' he said.

The next morning, Cynthia came. She stared at my little pink spots and little brown scabs and then sat on the side of my bed. 'And I always thought *I* was the problem child,' she said.

We stayed quiet like that for a while, but we both knew where the quiet needed to take us if we wanted to get out of this alive. So I asked, 'Why would you want to be with me? I mean, you have choices . . .'

'Do I?' she said.

'Sure. The first time I saw you, I knew. And you told me that every time you work at the movie theater, guys hit on you. You could take your pick.'

'I pick you,' she said.

'Why?'

She touched one of the pink spots on my face, as if prodding for sensitivity. She said, 'Even the first time you saw my legs, you never asked about me beyond the basics. You seemed to know that fires happen. You accepted it – and me.'

'That makes no sense,' I said.

'My dad lit the fire,' she said. 'An accident, he said. A cigarette. It *could* happen and it did. Now, I live in the same house with him, but he can't look me in the eyes and he can hardly talk to me. He pretends. He pretends all the time. But you know how that goes. Once, he saw me wearing shorts, and I thought he would kick me out. He'll never forgive me for getting burned. By sleeping in my own bed in my own bedroom, I wrecked his life. And then you came along. You feel like the home that my home is supposed to be.'

I shook my head. 'With me, you're jumping out of one fire and into another.'

'No,' she said. 'You're all ice.'

'I don't know what that means.'

'It means you make me feel good.'

I reached for her hand. It was sweaty. 'I like being with you,' I said.

She leaned and kissed me on the mouth. 'I know.'

* * *

Jane and Hank never visited, though on the tenth morning Thelma came with a bouquet and a *Get Well* balloon. The marks on my face, neck, and arms were fading, but her eyes lingered on them, with more anger than pity. She clutched the flowers and the balloon ribbon and stayed a few feet from my bed.

'Jane and Hank send their wishes,' she said.

'That's something,' I said.

'If you're looking for someone to feel sorry for you, you've come to the wrong people,' she said. 'But you know that already. They'll fight alongside you, but if you're done, they're done with you.'

'So this is the *come-to-your-senses* visit?'

'No,' she said, 'you're long past that.'

'So, what then? *Kick Franky in the butt*? Get him to *buck up*?'

'You don't get it,' she said. 'You're betraying Jane and Hank and all they've done for you – and, worse, all they're doing for others.'

'With my meds, I'm a little slow. But I get it now. This is the guilt trip.'

She threw the flowers on my bed and let the balloon float to the ceiling. 'I try to be civil,' she said. 'I try to hold myself to a standard. But fuck you. That's what this is. It's the *fuck-you* visit.'

For the first time since I shredded my skin, I laughed.

'I mean it,' she said. 'Fuck you. If you want to play the who's-had-it-hardest game, you win. No contest. You can stand on the podium all alone, and we'll clap and cheer. *Hooray for Franky Dast! He's had it hardest!* But then, you know what we'll do? We'll go home. And you can stay there all alone, knowing you've had it hardest. So you can come down off your goddamned podium and join the rest of us, or you can stay there.'

'I wish I could come down,' I said. 'I wish I could.'

She shook her head, but her anger was melting. 'I *should* kick you in the butt. I swear, the men I've known. The world throws a hammer at you, and you smack yourself on the head with it.'

I picked up the bouquet and set it on the bedside table. 'You're a good person,' I said. 'Even better than Jane and Hank.'

Two days later, she visited again. I had the flowers she'd brought last time in a vase. Next to the vase was a single greeting card, which Coach Kagen had sent. In big print, it said, *When the world rubs hard against you . . . Shine.* The last of my brown scabs were flaking off my skin, and the pink spots were paling.

'You're looking good as new,' one of the nurses had said when she brought breakfast.

'New didn't look so good on me either,' I'd said.

But when the nurse left, I did my sit-ups and pushups and running in place.

Now my healing seemed to ease Thelma's mind. She sat in a chair by my bed and said,

'A young man like you. All that life to live. I don't know why you're lying around here day and night.'

As I'd felt better, I'd started to wonder the same thing.

'I've needed time to think,' I said. 'Everything moved so fast when I got out.'

'The world keeps turning, with you on it or without,' she said.

So I asked, 'Who killed Rick Melsyn and Darrell Nesbit? What are the cops saying?'

'Mostly they're keeping their mouths shut,' she said. 'But they're hinting at a bad drug deal.'

That kind of thinking could make a man give himself a thousand cuts. 'They died the same way Duane and Steven Bronson did,' I said. 'They had bite marks—'

'I don't know anything about that,' she said, 'but the police are playing it funny. In one of the pictures that ran in the paper a few days ago, Bill Higby was at the Sun Reach Apartments with the homicide unit.'

'Higby is out of jail?'

'For the past week,' she said. 'Wearing an ankle monitor and mortgaging his house, but out.'

'And he's back working?'

'Not that I've heard of. But they had him at the apartment just the same.'

'I need to get out of here,' I said.

'Unless you like lock and key now, you do,' she said. 'The world keeps turning. You know, the governor signed Thomas LaFlora's death warrant. He's scheduled for next week.'

'Shit.'

'Shit for him. And for the rest of us too.'

*   *   *

On the fourteenth morning, Dr Patel came back, carrying my discharge papers. He stood by my bed and gripped them as if he might decide against giving them to me. He said, 'Why did you cut yourself, Franky?'

'When I was on death row, I knew men who'd done things that more than earned them their death sentences,' I said. 'After a while, it seemed like I'd earned death too. It was like I was in a machine that carried me toward the needle. The only question was how fast. When I saw Rick Melsyn and Darrell Nesbit in their apartment, the machine seemed to switch on again.'

'We all die,' he said. 'But nobody deserves to.'

'Some of the men I knew did.'

'*You* deserve to live.' He handed me the papers. 'I expect you in my office tomorrow afternoon and every afternoon after that until we straighten out your thinking.'

I rode the bus back to the Cardinal Motel, and as we drove down Philips Highway, the car and truck fumes smelled like home. But when I opened the door to my room, the mattress was gone from the bed frame. The cops, or maybe Bill Hopper, had dragged it away. Too bloody from my thousand cuts. Sweet for flies and roaches.

So I went in, closed the door, lay down on the carpet, and did sit-ups. A hundred. Two hundred. Four hundred. I did sit-ups until my stomach muscles burned and cramped and I thought that even one more would rip ligaments and tendons.

Then I flipped on to my stomach and did pushups.

Afterward I showered and then stood naked, facing the bathroom mirror. Only eyes that knew to look for the evidence would see the blemishes from my night with the box cutter. Otherwise, as the nurse said, I looked good as new. But *my* eyes knew better, and so did my memory. I remembered the release and relief I felt with each of the thousand incisions. And I remembered the words of the Walgreen's clerk who'd bagged the second box cutter from the two-pack. *For next time.*

Early in the afternoon, I drove back downtown and parked in the garage by the Justice Now Initiative office. When I climbed the stairs, Jane and Hank stared at me as if shocked that I lived. Thelma let her eyes close, as if she knew it would come to this.

I went to my computer cart, flipped on the laptop, and sat. As the laptop booted up, Jane left her desk and came to me. Her eyes looked moist.

I offered a smile. 'Hi.'

She said, 'You've ignored every rule. Common sense as well as legal.' There was no accusation, just sadness.

'Doctor's orders,' I said. 'My reintegration counselor says that freedom is—'

'You've broken into people's houses,' she said.

'Never,' I said. 'Whose?'

'Bill Higby's. Twice. Rick Melsyn and Darrell Nesbit's apartment.'

'No. I walked in uninvited. That's all. That's different from breaking in.'

'According to what law?'

I said, 'Higby withheld evidence from my public defender. He should—'

'Yeah, that's right, he *should* have done a lot,' she said. 'And you should have stayed away from his house and wife.'

'The hell I should have,' I said.

Hank left his desk then and stood by Jane's side. 'I'm sorry,' he said. 'But you can't work here anymore.'

I stared. 'Really?'

'Really.'

Jane said, 'I'm sorry. But there's too much at stake. Other people's lives.'

I stared at her now. 'Thelma said the governor signed Thomas LaFlora's death warrant – for next week. You need my help now.'

'Not next week,' Jane said. 'Four days from now. It's too late.'

'You've got to talk to Kim Jenkins's husband,' I said. 'He—'

'Even if it weren't too late, you would just get in the way,' she said. 'I'm sorry.' She went to her desk, got an envelope, and gave it to me. It held a couple of hundred dollars in cash. 'This covers your unpaid hours. I wish we could do more.'

'Who killed Kim Jenkins?' I said. '*That's* LaFlora's last chance. Talk to Randall Haussen.'

'Kim Jenkins killed herself,' Hank said.

'She was scared of Haussen,' I said.

'I'm sorry,' Jane said.

I stared at her. I stared at Hank.

'That's fucking great,' I said. 'Just fucking great.' I went to the stairs, went halfway down to the street door, and yelled back up, 'Fucking great.' Then I charged back up the stairs. Jane and Hank stood by their desks. Thelma sat at hers, tears tracking her cheeks. I grabbed the laptop. 'I'm taking this,' I said. Then I went back down the stairs.

Hank yelled after me, 'We need the office key.'

I kept going.

Outside, the sun blasted the roofs of the cars parked at the curb. It glinted off the building windows. A squad car passed, its emergency lights flashing, its siren piercing the air. It rounded the corner and disappeared into silence.

I climbed the stairs to the third level of the parking garage and got into my car. I was sweating and my skin was crawling, but I had no desire to cut it away. I knew I was wrong to blame Jane and Hank. They'd done their best with what I'd given them. But they expected me to act free, and at heart I remained a prisoner.

But prisoners, the ones who survive, make use of the tools that we're given, and we fashion the tools that we need but are denied. We fight to keep these tools as if our lives depend on them because our lives do depend on them.

I would fight to keep the laptop.

And I would use the phone Jane and Hank gave me until they cut off the service.

I fished it out and called Aardo Auto Parts. When a man answered, I said, 'I need to talk to Randy Haussen.'

'Not here,' he said.

'Is he still in Atlanta?'

'Sure.'

'I need his phone and address,' I said.

'Sorry,' he said.

'Let me talk to whoever's in charge there right now.'

'I guess that's me. I've got the shop to myself right now.'

Fool, I thought. *Answering the phone when he doesn't know who's calling.* I hung up on him.

A half hour later, I drove into Callahan, pulled on to the auto parts parking lot, and took the spot in front of the door. Only one other car was on the lot, parked at the far end – the car of an employee leaving the good spaces for customers. When I went into the store, the clerk grinned and welcomed me to Aardo. He'd been working when Thelma and I came a little over two weeks earlier, and he said, 'Hey, you were—'

'Yeah,' I said, 'I was here, and then I called a little while ago.'

His grin slipped. 'You wanted Randy's—'

'I need an address. Or at least a phone number.'

'I'm sorry,' he said, 'but Randy told us no one—'

'You seem like a nice guy,' I said. 'And I'm nice too. I swear I am. But I really need to see him.'

'I'm sorry,' he said.

'No,' I said, '*I'm* sorry,' and I looked around for a tool.

He moved toward the checkout counter.

'You see, this isn't who I really am or what I do,' I said. On the counter, a plastic carousel displayed tire pressure gauges, and another displayed sunglasses. A third displayed screwdrivers. Anything with a sharp or narrow end would gouge. So I grabbed a screwdriver and lunged at the man.

He made a high-pitched sound when I held the tool end against his cheek. I said, 'I'm sorry. But I'll hurt you unless you give me an address. And if you call Haussen and tell him you gave me the address, I'll come back for you, and I swear—'

'OK,' he said. 'OK, OK.'

I loosened my grip.

He had the look of an animal in the clutches of another's teeth. 'Why?' he said.

'Believe it or not, I'm trying to save someone's life.'

'OK,' he said. He picked up a pen, seemed to look for a pad of paper, and opened a counter drawer. Instead of paper, he pulled out a black pistol. He aimed it at me and tugged the trigger.

Nothing happened.

He thumbed at the safety lever.

'Goddamn it,' I said, and I slashed the screwdriver at him.

The gun clattered to the floor.

I moved in hard against him and held the tool to his face. 'I told you, I *don't* want to hurt you.'

'Jesus,' he said. 'Don't—'

I let him go. 'Don't make me.'

Panting, he reached into the drawer again and pulled out a pad of yellow paper with numbers and names scribbled on the front. He flipped through three pages until he found an Atlanta address. 'It's his sister's house,' he said.

I took the pad from him and ripped out the sheet. 'I won't tell him you told me,' I said. 'But if you tell him I'm coming—'

'I won't,' he said, backing away again. 'I won't.'

I picked up the pistol and stuck it in my belt. 'I'm sorry,' I told him again, and I left him to his humiliation.

I drove north toward the Georgia border. The pistol – a nine-millimeter – lay on the passenger seat. I went up past the Okefenokee Swamp, where a happier man might float on the tangled flood until the heat sucked him dry. In Waycross, I cut over to I-75, then hit the gas and sped alongside semis and cars.

Five hours after leaving Callahan, I slowed with the late-evening Atlanta traffic. An hour later, with the sun lowering in the west, I turned from Memorial Drive on to the broken asphalt of Berean Avenue.

The houses on the street were wood, single story, and small, and most of the yards were rough with weeds and long grass. But the address on the yellow sheet took me to a place with a new coat of green paint and a freshly cut lawn. A white pickup truck with a Florida license plate was parked in the driveway.

I pulled past and drove back out of the neighborhood. I hung out in my car until the sky became dark, and I drove to Home Depot, where I bought two rolls of duct tape and a plastic-wrapped coil of pre-stretched nylon rope. I drove back to the house where Randall Haussen was staying and parked at the curb.

For a long time, lights stayed on inside, and, when they went off, the blue flicker of a television still showed through the front windows. Then the flicker stopped and the house was dark.

I got out of my car, stuck the barrel of the pistol back into the top of my pants, and went to the front door. I stood, listening. In one of the neighboring houses, a woman laughed. Somewhere, on a farther street, a car horn honked. I considered the front door. Like the house, it was freshly painted but in a darker shade of green. A wreath of summer flowers hung on a nail at chest height. The doorbell glowed. I could knock, or I could ring the doorbell.

But I'd learned a few lessons since getting out of prison. I raised my foot and kicked.

The door ripped from the frame, and I pushed it aside and stepped into a living room.

A light went on, and Randall Haussen sat up on a couch, where he'd stretched out to sleep. He wore underwear and a white T-shirt. He started to speak, but I yanked the pistol from my belt and said, 'Time to go home.'

A bedroom door opened, and a woman in a nightgown peeked out. She had the same strong chin as Haussen, but she also had bruises around her mouth.

I pointed the pistol at her and said, 'Go back to bed.'

But she stared, wordless, as I went to Haussen and made him get up. He reached for a pair of pants, but I prodded him toward the front door with the gun. 'We need to talk,' I said. 'Outside.'

'About what?'

'About what happened to your wife. And about what happened to a couple of crackheads twenty-five years ago.'

The woman at the bedroom door said, 'You bastard.' I turned to her, wondering if she meant Haussen or me. It seemed either of us would do.

I gestured at her bruised mouth. 'How did that happen?'

'Not a word,' Haussen said to her.

She glared at him, glared at me, and then ducked behind the bedroom door and closed it.

So I turned back to Haussen and said, 'Go.'

I took him to my car, and I bound his wrists and ankles with duct tape and tied him with the nylon rope. 'Trunk or backseat?' I said.

'Whatever you think I'll tell you, you're wrong.'

'The trunk it is,' I said.

At four the next morning, I drove through the dark streets of downtown Jacksonville and parked outside the JNI office. When I popped the trunk, Haussen's underwear had pulled halfway off, and he'd worked his bare feet free of the rope and duct tape, but his wrists remained bound. He looked ready to fight.

'Am I wrong about your wife and the crackheads?' I said.

'You're dead,' he said.

'I've heard that before,' I said.

'Never from me.'

'So you killed them?'

He spat at me.

'I'll take that as a yes,' I said.

'LaFlora dies in three days,' he said. 'Kim's in the ground. Do you think anyone cares? They've got their answers.'

'I care,' I said.

'But you don't matter, do you?'

I pointed the pistol at his head. 'Get out. I'll introduce you to a couple of other people who care.'

He swung his legs out of the trunk, and I yanked the rope around his wrists so that he could sit. He said, 'If I don't kill you – and I *will* – you'll go back to jail. I see it on you. Guys like me, we're born to stay out of jail. Guys like you, you're born to die there.'

I touched the pistol barrel to his head. 'Let's go.'

I unlocked the street door and took him upstairs to the office. Outside the window, a streetlight glowed orange in the dark. Inside, the desks, chairs, and file cabinets threw shadows on the floor and walls. I left the office lights off, made Haussen go to Hank's desk chair, and bound him with more duct tape and rope.

At four thirty, I sat on the floor next to my computer cart. I rested the pistol on my belly, draped my hand over it, and closed my eyes. I stayed awake, though, and when I heard Haussen shifting on Hank's chair, I opened my eyes and stared at him staring at me, until he turned away and settled down.

At seven thirty, with the morning sun brightening and warming, another key turned in the lock downstairs, and Hank came up into the office. He looked at Haussen strapped to the desk chair. He looked at me lying on the floor with the pistol beside me. He said, 'What the hell?'

'It's as bad as it looks,' I said. 'But he admitted killing Kim Jenkins and the crackheads – or all but.'

Hank repeated himself. '*What* the hell!'

'You and Jane seemed to have given up on LaFlora,' I said. 'Thelma told me something the other day, though. She said the two of you would fight alongside me, but if I was done, you would be done too. Yesterday you told me you were done with me. And you seemed to be done with LaFlora. But, you see, I'm not done with you. And I'm still fighting.'

More footsteps came up the stairs.

I said, 'I've been telling you for weeks that Haussen's the answer. So last night, I got him.'

Jane stepped into the office behind Hank. She looked at me, looked at Haussen, and also said, 'What the hell?'

I said, 'The first time I saw him, he was digging his fingers into his wife. Last night, I saw his sister. She took a beating too.'

Jane shook her head and said, 'Jesus Christ, Franky, *no*.' She went to Haussen. 'No, no, no.' She sounded like she would cry. She pulled at the duct tape and said, 'I'm so sorry, Mr Haussen. It wasn't our intent.' She started to untie the rope around his chest and arms.

I clicked off the pistol safety and said, 'Don't do that.'

She stared at me, unafraid, and said, 'You're going back to prison. You know that, don't you?'

'Maybe I am,' I said. 'But leave the rope. Leave the tape. Listen to what he has to say.' I said to him, 'Tell them what you told me about no one caring how your wife died – or the crackheads twenty-five years ago. Tell them what happened.'

He just said to Jane, 'Do me a favor. Call the police.'

'Yes,' she said. 'Yes, of course.' She went to her desk and picked up the phone.

I pointed the pistol at him. 'Tell them what you did.'

He stared at Hank. 'I loved my wife. I love everyone. I would never hurt another person.'

That seemed to be too much for Jane. She stopped dialing and looked at him. 'How about the drug dealer you went to prison for shooting? Would he agree?'

'He never testified against me,' Haussen said.

'But you took a plea agreement. Seven years. That's a big commitment for a man you would never hurt.'

'Maybe he had it coming to him.'

Jane set down the phone. 'How about your wife?' she asked. 'Did Kim also have it coming to her?'

'Maybe,' he said. 'I wouldn't know. I was at work when she died. Two of my employees have told the police.'

'Good to have friends,' I said.

'Yes, it is,' he said.

Jane eyed me as if to tell me to shut up, then asked Haussen, 'Did any customers see you at work that afternoon? Anyone off your payroll?'

'A slow day,' he said. 'July and August get that way.'

'And did the crackheads have it coming to them twenty-five years ago?' she said.

'I'm sure they did,' he said. 'Why else would Thomas LaFlora shoot them? You can count on crackheads to mess up. They smoke a rock and forget to pay their bill. They break into your house and steal your stash. For brain-dead people, they're very determined.'

Jane glanced at Hank, uncertain. She glanced at me. Then she asked Haussen, 'Did you—' but she caught herself. She said to him, 'I've decided not to call the police. If you want to call them and bring attention to yourself, you can do so. We keep some pants and shirts here in case our clients have court hearings and need to change out of their prison uniforms. You may borrow some clothes. In fact, you may keep them.' Then she glanced at me. 'And now Mr Dast will untie and release you. What happens after that is up to you.'

Haussen shook his head. 'He's another boy that's got it coming to him.'

Jane nodded at me. 'Franky?'

I stayed where I was. 'He did it, and you know it.'

Jane asked him, 'Are you admitting you had anything to do with your wife's death or the deaths twenty-five years ago?'

'No, ma'am,' he said.

I pointed the pistol at him. 'I could shoot you now.'

Jane said, 'But you won't.'

'No, you won't,' he said. 'Because you aren't a killer. I see that too. You're just a boy who goes to jail.'

'Enough,' Jane said, and then to me, 'We can't hold him. We can't make him say anything he's unwilling to say. That's not who we are. It's not who *you* are.'

I aimed the gun at his forehead. 'If we let him go, Thomas LaFlora dies.'

'We'll get a subpoena,' she said. 'We'll try. We have three days.'

'It's too little, and you know it,' I said.

'Let him go,' Jane said.

'LaFlora will die.'

'Let him go,' she said again.

Hank spoke now. 'It's the only way.'

When I untied the ropes and ripped the duct tape from his skin, Haussen kept his hands to himself. He put on the pants and shirt Jane brought him. He folded the cab money she gave him and stuffed it in a pocket. He sat back in Hank's chair and slipped on a pair of socks and tied a pair of dress shoes.

Then Jane offered him her telephone and said, 'Do you want to call the police?'

He looked at me, then Hank, then her. 'I'm going to think on that a while.' Then he looked at me again and winked. 'Be seeing you.' He went down the stairs and out the door.

I looked at Hank and Jane. They were sweating, and I was too. I said, 'He did it. You heard that, didn't you?'

Jane walked to her desk. Slowly. As if the floorboards had come unglued. 'Get out,' she said.

I stared at her.

'Please,' she said. 'Get out.'

'You're going to subpoena him?'

Hank stepped toward me. 'She said to leave.'

I looked at the gun in my hand. I could do anything with it. I said, 'I brought Haussen here. I did my part. You let him go. That's on you.'

'Go,' Jane said. She looked exhausted.

I went to the stairs, but turned back. I wanted to shake them. I wanted to make them rush out to the street and drag Haussen back into the office. I wanted them to throw him against a wall and say, *You did it.*

I said, 'You can't let him—'

'Leave the gun here,' Hank said. 'Nothing good can come of it.'

I wanted to shoot at the ceiling and rattle them out of their stupor. But I stuck the pistol barrel into the top of my pants and went downstairs and out to the street.

TWENTY-FOUR

I drove to the Sheriff's Office, parked my car at a meter, and stuffed the pistol under the front seat. Last time, when I told the information desk attendant that I needed to talk to Deborah Holt, he told me to wait outside the security checkpoint. This time, he made a call and then handed me a pass with directions to the Homicide Room.

Eight years ago, after spending thirty-six hours in that room, I left in handcuffs – the first step on my path to death row. Now I felt a tremor in my belly as I pushed through the door.

Holt leaned against a reception desk, waiting for me.

She looked me over. 'I thought they had you in the hospital.'

'They kicked me out.'

'When they took you in, they said maybe this time you'd gone down for good.'

'Apparently not even close.'

'You look OK now,' she said. 'Tired.'

'A long night,' I said.

'Come on, then.' She led me back through the room to a double cubicle she shared with Bill Higby. She sat at one of the desks and gestured at the other. 'Have a seat.' I took Higby's chair. 'What's up?' she asked.

I said, 'A man is scheduled to die at Raiford in three days. Thomas LaFlora.'

'Right,' she said, as if she knew.

'You've got to help me stop it. I'm pretty sure someone else did the killings.'

The glimmer of a sad smile showed on her lips. 'You're pretty sure, huh?'

'Another guy who was dealing cocaine back then. His name's Randall Haussen. Kim Jenkins's husband.'

'Kim Jenkins, the suicide?'

'I think he killed her too,' I said.

Again, the sad smile. 'What makes you think so?'

I couldn't tell her about pulling Haussen out of his sister's house. 'I talked to him. He's hiding it, but he teases with what he knows.'

'Did he tell you he's responsible for any of the deaths?'

'Basically.'

'Explicitly?'

'He didn't need to.'

'Do you have proof?' When I said nothing, she said, 'I know you've had bad breaks, Franky. But LaFlora will die because he killed two people. Witnesses saw him kill them. You can't undo that.'

'Haussen went to jail for shooting another dealer,' I said. 'Thomas LaFlora had a drug record but that's all. Nothing violent until this.'

She shook her head.

'Kim Jenkins OD'ed a couple of times on over-the-counter drugs,' I said. 'She never used a gun.'

'I wish I could help you,' Holt said. 'What do your friends at the JNI say? They're the ones who know how to do this.'

I stood up. 'The JNI can't do anything. I can't do anything. You at least could pull in Haussen and talk to him.'

'I'm sorry,' she said. 'But once we break the rules, bad things happen. Detective Higby broke the rules with you. You know how that turned out.'

'Bad things happen with the rules or without them,' I said, and I started to leave. But first, I said, 'Why was Higby at Rick Melsyn and Darrell Nesbit's apartment?'

She looked at me as if I was missing the obvious. 'He's a homicide investigator—'

'On leave.'

'The higher-ups called him back for this one.'

'Because the killings look like the ones he railroaded me on?'

'Among other reasons.'

'And also like the killings of the boys up the St Johns River?'

'In some respects.'

'What respects?'

She pointed at Higby's chair again, and I sat. She spoke quietly. 'There was no sexual assault this time.'

'Rick Melsyn and Darrell Nesbit weren't as pretty as the boys.'

'And the wounds on the upper torso are new,' she said.

'The ripped-up chests.'

'Yes. We might have a different killer. Or the same killer might have changed his behavior. Either way, we've learned things we didn't learn from the earlier killings.'

'Like what?'

She frowned. 'I'm telling you this for only two reasons. First, as I said at your motel, you deserve to know. You're a victim too. Second, you've worked on this harder than anyone else, and while we all still thought you killed the Bronson boys, you were out ahead of us. I want to hear your thinking.'

'So what have you learned?'

She sighed. 'Telling you any of this could get me fired.'

'OK,' I said.

'Right,' she said. 'Except for the man who supposedly threatened the Bronson boys and Lynn Melsyn – a man Detective Higby thought and still thinks was a fiction – the earlier killings, including the Bronsons, seemed to be crimes of opportunity – kids who crossed random paths with a predator. But the deaths of Melsyn and Nesbit, which link directly to the deaths of the Bronson brothers, turn the murders into motivated crimes. The killer is a sexual deviant, but he also had another reason to kill Rick Melsyn and Darrell Nesbit. Maybe they knew something about him. Maybe they angered him. Whatever the reason, the killer chose to kill these particular men. So maybe he also targeted the Bronson brothers and the other boys. Maybe they also knew something about him or angered him.'

'Sure,' I said.

'You'd already figured that out?' she said. 'What else do you know?'

I thought about the file she brought me at the Cardinal Motel. The runaway Jeremy Ballat and the Mexican kid Luis Gonzalez were last seen alive on the same stretch of the St Johns River but had little in common otherwise, and less in common with Steven and Duane Bronson.

'Almost nothing,' I said.

'Tell me.'

I said, 'The Bronson brothers and one of the other kids – the runaway – were thieves. They had juvenile records for breaking into neighbors' houses. Small-scale stuff, though Felicia Bronson thinks the man who was threatening her sons was one of the robbery victims.'

'What else?'

I said, 'Mercury.'

'Huh?'

'The blood expert said the Bronson brothers had elevated levels of mercury. The report on Jeremy Ballat, the runaway, said he did too.'

'Weird,' she said. 'What do you think it means?'

'Probably nothing. All kinds of things can cause it. I haven't checked the Mexican boy.'

'I'll look into it,' she said. 'What else?'

I'd seen nothing that directly connected the four boys. But I thought again of the upriver town of Bostwick that Jeremy Ballat seemed to have passed on his way to being dumped in Etoniah Creek State Forest and near where Higby retrieved Josh Skooner when Josh ran away from home. Since Higby charged me with killing Steven and Duane Bronson, Bostwick also made *him* a kind of connection. I said, 'You say Higby's a good investigator.'

'One of the best.'

'Well, you figured out the connection between the Bronson brothers, the runaway, and the Mexican kid. And I figured it out. Why didn't he?'

'What are you saying?'

'I'm wondering is all,' I said. 'Does he still think I killed the Bronsons?'

'He has a hard time admitting he's wrong.'

'Seems like a pretty bad investigator to me, then.'

'He's complicated,' she said.

I got up to leave again. 'One more thing,' I said. 'The lobby camera at the Sun Reach Apartments caught me coming and going. Who else did it catch?'

'That's the thing. No one of interest. There's a service entrance and an elevator at the back of the building. We think the killer must have gone up that way.'

'Which means he knew about the lobby camera.'

'Maybe, maybe not.'

'And that would mean he'd gone to Rick Melsyn and Darrell Nesbit's apartment before.'

'Maybe. Only maybe.'

'So the killer knew them.'

'Maybe.'

In the afternoon, I went to Dr Patel's office. When the receptionist sent me in, Dr Patel was sitting behind his desk, paging through a book.

I sat on his couch, and after a minute he put the book down, came over, and sat in a chair facing me. 'I've been reading,' he said.

'I see that.'

'About the bewilderment of the self,' he said. 'And the making and remaking of traumatized minds. Sometimes, it seems, even with radical therapies—' He stopped himself and focused on me. 'Are you all right? You look exhausted.'

'A long night.'

He suppressed a smile. 'With Cynthia?'

'I wish,' I said.

'Trouble sleeping? I can prescribe—'

'I kidnapped a man I thought was responsible for a murder. A few murders, really.'

His smile fell.

'I picked him up in Atlanta and took him back to Jane and Hank at the JNI. They made me let him go.'

He paled.

'I tell you this for a couple of reasons,' I said. 'One, he might call the cops on me. He's guilty and scared, so I don't think he'll call them, but if he does, I'll miss tomorrow's appointment. And two, he threatened to kill me.'

'Oh, Franky,' he said, 'you crashed two weeks ago – you came within an inch of killing yourself – and the moment you get out of the hospital you shove the gas to the floor. I can't help you if you're unwilling to help yourself.'

So, following doctor's orders, I took the evening off. I left the pistol deep under the front seat of my car where I could get to it if I needed it, but it would stay out of reach – mine or anyone else's – if I didn't. Then, at seven thirty, I picked up Cynthia at the Cineplex, and we went out for pizza. Afterward, we drove to the beach and sat on the sand and talked as waves ripped and rushed and then pulled back with a hushing. The sun set, and the moon – huge and yellow – rose over the ocean. Cynthia and I sat and watched, touching hands because we needed nothing more from each other when a moon that huge and yellow was rising.

The next morning, after sleeping on the carpet, I woke early. I turned on the TV as I did my pushups. The news led with a story about an overnight fire that burned most of a condominium complex on the Westside, and followed with a feel-good story about how kids were spending the last month of their summer vacation. During the commercial, I flipped on to my back and started my sit-ups.

When the news came back on, a serious-faced Asian reporter stood in front of the county courthouse and said a controversy was brewing over the execution of a local man convicted of double homicide twenty-five years ago. I stopped exercising and watched. With forty-eight hours remaining before the scheduled execution, the man's lawyer was calling for a delay after discovering new evidence. The camera cut to an interview the reporter had taped with Jane yesterday afternoon. Jane said that a man had emerged who had knowledge of the events of twenty-five years ago and possibly an active role in them. This man's knowledge might exonerate Thomas LaFlora. The reporter asked why Jane was introducing this man only now. The urgency of the moment had made wheels turn that were stuck for more than two decades, Jane said. Then she named Randall Haussen.

'Shit,' I said. 'Good for you.'

When I called the JNI office at nine, though, Thelma said Jane wouldn't talk to me.

'How about Hank?' I said.

'Uh-uh,' she said.

'Tell them Haussen will run now that they've named him. He did it before and no one even suspected him.'

'They know that,' she said.

'Then why did Jane go public with his name?'

'LaFlora has two days. Unless something happens now, nothing happens.'

'Ask if I can help,' I said.

'You already know their answer,' she said. 'Straighten your own mess. Until you get yourself together, they can't depend on you.'

'What if I never get myself together?' I said.

'Then it's been good knowing you.'

Last time I'd tried to get myself together – to resolve the circumstances that had torn me apart – I'd gone to the Sun Reach Apartments and found Rick Melsyn and Darrell Nesbit dead. And then I'd slashed myself with a box cutter.

But the dead men must have known more about the circumstances that led to the Bronson brothers' deaths than they told me – maybe even more than they realized they knew. Why else would the killer visit them in their apartment, exposing himself to attention that had mostly disappeared with my arrest eight years ago? Maybe I'd gone to bed with the box cutter just when I was finding my way back to myself, or at least to what happened to me and the Bronson brothers.

Who else would know the same things Rick Melsyn and Darrell Nesbit knew? Rick's sister Lynn. But she was still hiding. Darrell Nesbit's two friends who kicked down my motel room door with him might also know. So might the Bronson boys' mother.

I decided to try the mother again. I would ask if her boys ever went to Bostwick. I would ask about the man who threatened them. I would ask for Lynn Melsyn's address.

But as I left my room, Deborah Holt's black Grand Marquis pulled on to the parking lot and stopped behind my car. The detective got out, holding a black vinyl portfolio. She said, 'Good news. Or interesting, at least.'

We went back into my room. 'I drove down to Putnam County yesterday afternoon,' she said. 'They still have records for the Mexican boy.' She unclipped the portfolio and pulled out a file. 'He also had high mercury. Way high. Like if he was a thermometer he would have geysered.'

'Huh.'

'My reaction exactly. But get this.' She leafed through the pages. 'The kid had a seven-year-old sister, right? After he died, the sister told their mom and dad about the man who came to their campsite. The lead investigator sat the girl down with a sketch artist.' Holt handed me a photocopy. 'This is what they came up with.'

The sketch showed a square-faced white man. Handsome and

serious. Familiar too. If you averaged the features of Judge Skooner and his son Andrew, the face would look a little like the one in the sketch. 'That's screwed-up,' I said. 'Who do you think?' She shook her head. 'You say it.'

'Eric Skooner sixteen years ago?' I said.

'Looks like him. But I expect it looks like hundreds of other men around here. Maybe thousands.'

The resemblance was strong, and the judge and his family were always brushing against trouble even as he collected awards for his toughness as a prosecutor and rigor on the bench, but the idea that he could have anything to do with the death of even one child, much less four boys – and with the killings of Rick Melsyn and Darrell Nesbit too – was outrageous. But I said, 'His family owns property across the river from where the Mexican kid's family was camping.'

She nodded. 'Tomhanson Mill.'

'That's where the runaway kid – Jeremy Ballat – swam to shore from the barge.'

She held the sketch so it caught light from the window and adjusted its angle as if that would change the picture. 'I'm sure plenty of men in the area look like this,' she said.

'Sure,' I said. 'Did you check to see if Tomhanson Mill uses mercury?'

She nodded grimly. 'Fourteen years ago and then again three years ago, the Department of Environmental Protection fined them for dumping waste into a creek that empties into the river. In the settlement, Tomhanson admitted to regularly piping out what the DEP called "effluent with chronic toxicity." The suit never mentioned mercury, but I made some calls. The mill uses it in its machine parts – the gauges and switches. It's also in the chemical compounds. And it's in the incinerator ash. So, yeah, there'd be a lot of mercury.'

'Enough to show up in the boys' blood after they died?'

'Maybe – if the kids had close contact with the waste,' she said. 'The lawyers for Tomhanson Mill argued against the DEP, saying that once the waste spread into the river water it would become harmless, but the DEP showed that this kind of waste concentrates in pools.'

I thought about all she'd told me. 'One problem,' I said. 'Steven and Duane Bronson also had high mercury. Were they ever near the mill? If they weren't, then the Tomhanson mercury might have nothing to do with any of the deaths. And if that's true, maybe the sketch isn't Eric Skooner.'

'Could be,' she said. But she stared some more at the picture. 'You know what happens if this is him? Everything collapses. Hundreds of verdicts. All the work that people like me have done to send him the cases. All the trust that people have—'

'Then it can't be him?'

'If it's him, if he's involved in even the slightest way, it all falls down.'

'Sure,' I said.

She shrugged. 'His accusations against Bill Higby would collapse with everything else.'

I thought about that. 'No,' I said. 'Higby has also spent time at Tomhanson Mill.'

Now I'd surprised her.

So I told her about Higby's commendation for bringing Josh Skooner back to his family when, as an eleven-year-old, he ran away to the mill. 'He went from rescuing Josh Skooner to shooting him. In between, he arrested me for killing two boys who might have died because of some connection to Eric Skooner. Higby rammed me on to death row even though he had evidence of earlier killings that I couldn't have committed – killings that happened around mill land owned by the Skooners. His next-door neighbors.'

'Oh,' she said.

TWENTY-FIVE

When Holt left, I got in my car and followed her on to Philips Highway. She exited into downtown, and I headed north toward the airport and Felicia Bronson's house. I parked in the driveway, and as I went up the front path, her dogs barked at me from the windows. The air was still and hot and smelled of swamp water and jet fumes. I knocked, and the dogs went wild.

Felicia Bronson opened the door, wearing cut-off shorts and an orange T-shirt. Her dogs danced around her, and she held her overexcited terrier by the collar. Her eyes looked flat, but she recognized me and said, 'I'll call the police.'

'Ask to talk to Detective Holt,' I said. 'She'll tell you I'm more of a danger to myself than to you.'

'I want you away from my house,' she said, and she started to close the door.

But two mutts, one with a diseased left eye, broke free and dodged outside. I caught the one with the bad eye, but the other ran across the yard and into the street. I shoved the first dog back into the house and went after the other.

It let me get close, then bore down to the ground as if it would attack. I reached for it, and it darted away. We repeated that game three times, moving farther up the block and then back toward the house.

Then from the front lawn, Felicia Bronson said, 'You're an idiot, aren't you?'

She stood by the driveway, cradling her terrier in her arms.

The dog I was chasing bore down again and barked, daring me. I reached, and it darted away.

'You're letting him call the shots,' Felicia Bronson said. 'Walk away. Make him come to you.' She went to the front porch.

I looked at the dog. It barked. I followed Felicia Bronson to the house. The dog barked again and fell in behind me.

Felicia Bronson held the front door open, keeping the other animals back. I stepped inside, and the dog came in after me.

The house smelled terrible. Garbage lay on the hall floor, and a stain from dried dog urine marked the doorway to the living room. Felicia Bronson closed the door and scolded the dogs.

'Should I leave?' I asked.

She looked at me with those flat eyes and asked, 'What do you want?'

I said, 'There's a little town called Bostwick, about fifty miles upriver from here. Were you ever there with your boys?'

She frowned. 'I've never heard of it.'

'How about Tomhanson Mill?' I asked. 'It's near Bostwick.'

She shook her head. 'What's this about?'

'Could Steven and Duane have gone there without you knowing?'

She said, 'In the last year before they were killed – after their father left – they snuck out at night. They would take my car and drive. In the final months, it became an every-night thing. They could have gone anywhere between midnight and morning if they had enough gas. But I've never heard of these places.'

'You never heard them talk about driving that way? There's a park there too – Etoniah Creek State Forest.'

'I'll tell you something,' she said. 'I've forgotten *nothing* about Steve and Duane, especially in those last months when they stayed up all night and started acting crazy. I take care of these dogs so I won't hear their voices in my head or smell their sweet skin in the air. I remember every word they spoke. Every time they laughed. Every time they cried. In the last month before they died, they talked all the time, and I remember it all. I thought it was drugs, but they swore it wasn't. I remember every promise, every lie. If they went to that town, they never mentioned it in this house.'

So I tried to place them near the judge on Byron Road. 'How about Black Creek?'

'Sure,' she said. 'We all spent time over there. When their dad and I first separated and before he moved to the Southside and then to Miami, he rented a place on Orangewood. Why?'

'I'm trying to put the pieces together,' I said.

But she said, 'The pieces don't go together. They never did. You'll drive yourself crazy trying.'

'Did they get caught for any burglaries in the Black Creek area?'

She shook her head. 'They mostly broke into big houses out at the Beach. They liked the mansions.'

'Is it possible they also did places by Black Creek?'

'I suppose so,' she said. 'They have some big houses there too. Duane and Steve got caught for pawning watches and jewelry from the Beach, but after they died, I found other things. Bracelets. Coins.'

'I'd like to see anything you still have,' I said.

She said, 'I gave it all to Duane's girlfriend. That wasn't the part I wanted to remember.'

'Can I see what's left?'

'Why?'

I figured that if Duane or Steven had stolen something that got them killed, it probably was more than a watch or jewelry or coins.

Felicia Bronson might not know what she had. 'I told you,' I said, 'I'm trying to put together the pieces.'

'And I told you the pieces don't go together.' But she considered me, and I thought I saw life behind the flatness of her eyes. 'You can't touch anything,' she said, and she walked into the hallway.

Before the kitchen, there was a closed door with a child-safety gate stretched across the frame, probably to keep the dogs out when the door was open. She touched the doorknob as if she feared it was hot – and pushed the door open.

Although the cops must have searched the house after Steven and Duane died, the room looked as if Felicia Bronson had closed the door when she'd heard about their murders and never gone in again. The covers on the bunk bed were pulled back, the sheet on the top bunk hanging down like a curtain over the bottom bunk. Dirty clothes – T-shirts, a pair of shorts, a pair of jeans, socks turned inside out – lay on the floor. On a table where one or both of the brothers had been taking apart a little television, a set of screwdrivers rested on top of a pile of electronic parts. A pair of pliers lay on the floor. Two school backpacks leaned against the table legs. A closet door was closed. Pen and pencil drawings of fighter jets hung on the walls. A blanket of dust covered everything.

The backpacks and the closet interested me. I started to step over the gate.

But Felicia Bronson grabbed my arm. 'No.'

I said, 'I need to see—'

'No,' she said again.

'Did anyone ever go through their things? Someone must have. The police? Bill Higby?'

She looked at me, and the life had sucked back out of her eyes. 'This is mine,' she said, and she steered me down the hall.

I could have shoved her aside and gone into the bedroom. I could have poured her dead sons' backpacks on to the floor and rooted through their closet. But I just said, 'I need to talk to Duane's girlfriend.'

'No,' she said.

'I need to know more about the man who threatened her and your boys.'

'She has two babies of her own now. She's hiding but she's also living.'

'I need to talk to her.'

Felicia Bronson pushed her dogs away from the front door and opened it.

But I pushed it closed again. I said, 'The man who killed Steven and Duane also killed two other boys – down near Bostwick.'

Her hands trembled.

I said, 'That man, or someone connected to him, just killed Rick Melsyn and your son's old friend, Darrell Nesbit. Lynn Melsyn can help.'

She closed her flat eyes, as if to make me go away, then opened them again. Her whole body shook. 'No,' she said.

'Who will be next? Can you carry that weight too?'

Again she closed her eyes. Again she opened them. '*I'll* call her,' she said finally. 'I'll ask if she'll talk to you.'

I knew I would get no more than that. 'Thank you,' I said.

She shuddered, and the dogs quieted around her as if they sensed her distress. She said,

'I'll tell her I think she shouldn't talk. She should keep her mouth shut and live.'

That afternoon, as thunderclouds stacked over the river, I went back to Dr Patel's office. I sat on his couch, and he sat on his chair, and I asked, 'What do you know about mercury poisoning?'

'Are you thinking of trading in the box cutter?' he said.

'What are the symptoms?'

He set down his notepad. 'Do you know about mad hatters?'

'In *Alice in Wonderland*?'

'No, the real story. Back when Lewis Carroll was writing, hat makers often went insane. True story. They used mercury to make felt for hats. It gave them muscle spasms. Caused brain damage. They hallucinated, had mood swings. They stopped sleeping.'

I thought about Steven and Duane Bronson driving through the city night after night in their mom's car.

'Probably good for business at first,' he said. 'They worked while others slept, but that just meant putting more mercury into their systems and a faster decline. Before hat makers, alchemists used mercury when they tried to turn lead into gold. Instead, they turned their brains into paste. Psychiatric journals are full

of case studies reaching back more than three thousand years.'
He picked up the notebook again and readied his pen. 'Why the
interest?'

I gave him a short version of what I'd learned about Jeremy
Ballat, Luis Gonzalez, and the Bronson brothers. I left out the
connection to Judge Skooner but mentioned Tomhanson Mill.

'A place like that could do a lot of damage,' he said. 'The most
famous case happened in Japan in the nineteen-fifties. A fertilizer
company pumped mercury waste into a bay near a fishing village.
More than a thousand people died.'

After we finished talking about ways that chemicals could
wreck the mind and body, he taught me a slow breathing technique
that, he said, might stop my head from buzzing and my skin from
crawling. Each time I breathed in, I should ask myself if the
source of my tension was real. Then, as I emptied my lungs, I
should assure myself that it was an illusion.

'But what if the source *is* real?' I asked.

'Breathe some more until you convince yourself it isn't,' he said.
'Never underestimate the power of false belief. If it keeps you on
the right side of sanity, go for it.'

A hard rain fell as I drove out of the Medical Services Building
parking garage. The tires hissed on the wet pavement as if prac-
ticing Dr Patel's technique. When I passed Sahara Sandwiches,
the black hooker was sitting outside at one of the picnic tables,
letting the rain drench her. Maybe she was denying that the source
of her misery was real.

At the Cardinal Motel, I pulled into the spot by my room.
Sheltered from the rain by the overhang, a new mattress, wrapped
in clear plastic, leaned against the outside wall. Next to the mattress,
my old running coach Ernie Kagen also leaned against the wall.
He wore exercise shorts, a sleeveless T-shirt, and flip-flops. He
looked almost as wet as the hooker.

'Hey,' he said with a nervous smile as I got out.

'Hey,' I said.

I unlocked my door, and he stepped inside, his odor swelling
around him.

As he stood by the TV, I lugged the mattress inside and dropped
it on the bedframe.

'I told you a lie when you came to my house,' he said. 'At least, I was less than honest.'

'I know,' I said.

'The truth is you scared me, showing up like that. I should have been prepared.'

'That's all right,' I said.

He stepped toward me, then stopped. 'I haven't been well,' he said.

'Sorry to hear it,' I said.

'I should've lived different,' he said. 'I guess I've been a hypocrite.'

'Sorry,' I said again.

'Don't be,' he said. 'It won't help. But I want to come clean with you. Of all people.'

'You don't need to,' I said. 'Not to me.'

But he said, 'That kid on the track team in Gainesville? I did it. It was a one-time thing. An accident. But I wanted to tell you the whole truth.'

The whole truth. I could've pressed him about his arrest for soliciting a kid in New Orleans. I could've told him that in my eight years in prison, I'd never met a one-time abuser. I could've told him to get the hell out of my room. I said, 'Thanks for telling me.'

'I'm sorry,' he said.

'You have nothing to be sorry to me for,' I said. 'Your visits did me good when I was inside.'

'Yeah, but what I was thinking about you when I came – you know what I wanted.'

'Don't worry about it,' I said.

He stepped toward me again. He smelled like old milk. I wondered if desire could curdle like that.

'It's time for you to go home,' I said.

He screwed up his lips, as if he would beg me, or curse me, or weep.

But he said nothing.

He went out through the door into the rain. I watched as he got into his car and started it. He pulled on to Philips Highway – slowly, so slowly it seemed he must think that when he reached his home he would find the windows covered with bars.

I locked the door. I pulled the window shade closed. I stripped the plastic wrap from the mattress, and the smell of new fabric tangled with Kagen's odor. I stripped off my clothes and lay naked on the mattress.

I breathed in deep, sucking the smells into my lungs.

I breathed out, denying the world's evil.

I breathed in, thinking, *Is every person – my dad in his drunkenness, Jared in his selfishness, Bill Higby in his self-righteous injustice, Felicia Bronson in her confused despair, Coach Kagen in his rot – a disease?*

I breathed out. *No, Cynthia is fire-hardened and beautiful, and there are others like her – Thelma Friedman, Deborah Holt maybe, Hank and Jane at their best.*

I breathed in. *Can I vent the badness from inside me with a box cutter? Can I shoot it out from between my ears with a pistol?*

I breathed out and started laughing. I laughed at Coach Kagen, at all the abused boys and girls, at my father, at Felicia Bronson, and at Bill Higby. I laughed at myself. I punched the new mattress with my fists and elbows and laughed. My neighbors, Jimmy and Susan, pounded on the wall separating our rooms and yelled at me to *Shutthefuckup.*

So I dug my fingers into my arms and held the laughter in until tears streamed from my eyes. I looked through the tears to see if I was cracking from the inside out. Who needed a box cutter? Who needed a pistol in the ear? Insects ripped free of their shells. Birds molted. Snakes shed their skins. Why shouldn't I?

When I stopped crying, I had sweated a stain into the new mattress.

I got up and walked around my room, looking at the TV and furniture as if they were objects new to the world, or *I* was new and seeing the world for the first time. I showered then and put on pants. I turned on the TV and lay back down and waited for the five o'clock news. When it came on, the follow-up to the story of Jane's plea for a delay on Thomas LaFlora's execution got only thirty seconds. The reporter said the State Attorney and the Governor's Office believed the execution should go forward as scheduled. The reporter also had tried to contact Randall Haussen for a comment on Jane's insinuations, but Haussen hadn't returned phone calls. The story ended with a clip of an assistant state attorney for the Fourth Judicial District saying, 'The time for delay was twenty-five years ago, when Thomas LaFlora shot his victims to death. His execution is long overdue.'

The news ended with a teaser. On the eleven o'clock broadcast, the anchor promised, they would give fresh details about the shooting deaths of Rick Melsyn and Darrell Nesbit.

I turned off the TV. I had five and a half hours until the news came on again and six and a half hours until midnight, when I'd told Cynthia I would pick her up.

Time – my enemy and friend.

I finished dressing, grabbed my keys, and went out through the rain to my car, thinking that, if nothing else, I would get dinner. Then my phone rang. Caller ID said Felicia Bronson was calling.

When I answered, she said, 'Lynn Melsyn will talk to you.'

TWENTY-SIX

Lynn Melsyn – now married and named Lynn Pritchard – lived in an enormous house near the ocean in the suburb of Ponte Vedra. People in Jacksonville moved to Ponte Vedra for the schools, the golf courses, and the private beach clubs. The houses were newer than in the city, the lawns greener, the streets cleaner, the nights quieter. Outside of Lynn Pritchard's house, the air smelled of rain and the fertilizer and mulch that a landscaping crew had spread around the palm trees and on the gardens.

We stood in a two-story foyer, a cut-glass chandelier above us, polished, white, marble tiles under our feet. An antique wooden table with an arrangement of flowers stood in the middle of the entryway. In a room visible through an open double doorway, a nanny talked in a babyish voice to twin girls in side-by-side cribs.

Lynn Pritchard wore a red dress that stretched to her thighs. Her black hair fell halfway down her back. Her skin was pale, and her fingernail polish matched her dress. She wore bright red lipstick like a mask. It was the kind that still looks wet hours after a woman puts it on.

'I'm sorry about your brother,' I said.

'The police said you found him and Darrell,' she said.

I nodded.

She glanced at the flowers on the table, as if my presence pained her, and said, 'I heard they put you in the hospital afterward.'

'For a while.'

She looked at me again, said, 'Let's sit,' and led me into a hallway that took us away from her daughters.

I guessed that, like Duane Bronson and me, she came from a poor part of town, but she looked comfortable in wealth. We went through a large living room with a white carpet, draped windows, and a brass-screened fireplace, and crossed into a sitting room. Tinted glass doors looked out at a screened-in pool, lighted by flood lamps from above and submerged lighting below.

She gestured at an upholstered chair and said, 'Please.'

I sat, and she settled on to a matching couch, slipping off her shoes and tucking her legs under her. I looked at bookshelves lined with glass figurines, a little fireplace that matched the big one in the other room, and all the fine furniture.

I said, 'Do you mind if I ask—'

Apparently used to such questions, she said, 'The man I married – a year and a half ago, when I got pregnant – owned car dealerships in Alabama before retiring here. I thought he would try to pay me to get rid of the twins. Instead, he asked me to marry him.' She stared at me. 'Is that more than you were asking?'

'No – that was fine.'

She frowned and smoothed her dress over her thighs. 'I can already tell that you ask a lot. Probably too much.'

'For eight years, I had very little,' I said, 'and I didn't have much beforehand. I lost what I had.'

'Others lost more.'

'Duane and Steven,' I said.

'They lost the most.'

'And you went into hiding.'

She nodded.

So I said, 'Tell me what you're scared of.'

She frowned again. 'I'm scared of the man who killed my brother,' she said. 'I'm scared of the man who killed Duane. I'm scared that the police said they'd worked out Duane's murder eight years ago, but I knew they hadn't. The man who killed him could get to me and no one would stop him. I'm scared that before my brother died he might have told the man where to find me.'

I said, 'Tell me about him.'

She moved a strand of hair from her cheek. 'He sat next to me during your trial. He said I had something of his and he wanted it back. He said Duane must have given it to me.'

'Did he tell you what it was?'

She hesitated. 'A briefcase. Papers. But I told him, if Duane stole papers, he would have thrown them away or burned them. If it didn't shine, Duane didn't want it.'

'If it didn't shine?'

She allowed herself a little smile. 'Duane was kind of crazy. He broke into houses for the thrill and because of the way they shined – that was his word. He didn't care about the money so much, and he only got in trouble when he tried to sell the things he stole. But he liked fancy houses. He liked to pretend he belonged in them.' She looked out toward the pool. 'He always said he would live in a house like *this* someday. That was his dream. The closest he got was breaking into them. If he took a briefcase from the man, he took it to carry the things he found in the house.'

'How about Steven?'

'He did what Duane told him to do.'

'Do you have the jewelry that Duane's mom gave you?'

She shook her head. 'I threw it out a long time ago. I only kept this' – she pulled a chained pendant from inside the top of her dress. It was a golden star with a diamond chip at each of its points. 'It's stolen, but everything about Duane broke the rules, so it's a good remembrance.' She stared at me. 'You're scared too.'

Instead of answering, I said, 'What did the man look like?'

But she said, '*I'm* alone with my girls most of the time. Sometimes I have Jen – their nanny. She's sweet. It's like having a third baby to watch over.'

'Where's your husband?' I asked.

'He goes places with his friends. Hunting. Rafting in Argentina. Drinking and cigar trips. He travels with guys he's known since high school.'

'You say he's retired?'

'He's sixty-four.'

'Huh,' I said.

'I know,' she said, 'but I love him as much as I love anyone. Ever since Duane, I've had a hard time loving. I lost something too.'

'Tell me about the man who came to you at my trial. How often did you see him after that?'

'As I said, you ask a lot.'

'You agreed to talk with me.'

'Because I wanted to ask *you* questions.'

Across the house, one of her babies started crying.

'Fine,' I said. 'Ask anything.'

She untucked her legs, crossed them, and uncrossed them. 'When you found my brother in his apartment,' she said, 'what did he look like?'

'The police didn't tell you?'

'They only showed me a picture of his face.'

'Then you saw. The killer shot him in the forehead.'

'What else?' Her eyes were steely but I heard the fear.

'Why do you want to know?'

'What did he look like?' she said.

'He looked like Duane when he died. The killer bit him. On the legs. Around—'

'Exactly like Duane? No difference?'

'Little differences,' I said. 'That's all.' She looked incapable of asking, so I told her. 'The killer ripped away part of his chest. One of his nipples. That didn't happen to Duane.'

Pinpoints of sweat broke from her pale skin. She said, 'That's what he said he would do to me if I talked. So I hid. My aunt lives in Orlando. I finished high school there. When I moved back, I used my mother's maiden name. Then I met my husband.'

'Who's the man who threatened you?' I said.

She shook her head – unwilling, unable.

'But you know who he is?' I asked. 'You know his name?'

Still she shook her head. She said, 'For eight years, I hid. I was safe. Then you got out and went to see my brother, and now he's dead.'

'What did you tell him about the man?'

'You've asked enough,' she said.

'If he got to him, he can get to you.'

'Not if I keep my promise,' she said.

'Your brother kept his promise. He told me nothing. Now he's dead.'

She shook her head.

If she could identify Judge Skooner, I wanted her to do it on her own, without my naming him. But I gave her as much as I could. 'If this man has power – if he has the kind of connections that got him to your brother – he'll get to you.'

'I told the police,' she said. 'Eight years ago. They did nothing.'

'*Who* did you tell?'

'The detective who investigated Duane and Steve's deaths.'

'Bill Higby?' I could hardly breathe.

'He called me a liar. He said he knew who killed them. You.'

I couldn't help myself. 'Did Eric Skooner threaten you,' I asked. 'The judge?'

'I'll disappear,' she said. 'I'll leave—'

I knew the danger of dictating someone else's story, insisting on the details of another person's experience. But I said, 'I need to hear you say it. Did the judge threaten you?'

'I'm here alone,' she said.

The baby cried more loudly now. But Lynn Pritchard didn't seem to hear.

'Tell me who threatened you.'

Again, she shook her head.

The nanny called across the house, 'Mrs Pritchard? Lynn?'

'Did Duane and Steven break into Eric Skooner's house?' I asked. 'Did they steal his papers?'

The nanny came through the living room and into the sitting room, carrying the crying baby. The girl's face was bright red, and the nanny looked almost as stricken. 'I'm sorry,' she said. 'She won't stop.'

Lynn Pritchard took her daughter, pulling her to her shoulder. The baby stopped crying as if she'd been falling and flailing through space and had come to a soft landing.

'I'm sorry,' the nanny said again and left to get the baby's sister.

'I need to know,' I said.

Lynn Pritchard gazed at the baby, soothing her, and said, 'I told Duane's mom I would talk to you for another reason too. She said you're working as an investigator for a prisoner rights group.'

I stared at her and her child. 'Something like that. The Justice Now Initiative. But they fired me.'

'Do you mind telling me why?'

'Too much enthusiasm on my part,' I said. 'Too aggressive. I go into places I shouldn't go. At least they thought so.'

She turned her eyes from the baby to me. 'Do you have a gun?'

I shrugged.

'Are you willing to use it?'

'If necessary.'

'I watched the stories about you on TV. You got yourself out of prison. You must have done something right.'

'I had a lot of time and very few distractions.'

She said, 'So my question is, will you work for me? Will you protect me and my girls? I have money. I'll pay whatever you ask.'

I hadn't expected that. 'Why me? You should hire people who do this. An agency.'

'*You* believe me. You know it's true. We've both been locked up for the last eight years.'

'How about your husband? Can't you pack up your family and leave?'

'I can't tell him. I won't. He has an idea of me. He goes out on his adventures with his friends, and he thinks he leaves me happy and safe. If he knew, he'd be more scared than I am. Can't you see what I am for him?'

'What are you for yourself?' I said.

'You don't want me to answer that,' she said. She went to a credenza and opened a drawer. She took a stack of fifty-dollar bills and brought it to me.

'I can't do this,' I said. 'I'm driving all around, trying to figure things out.'

'So drive by here too,' she said. 'Check on us. Make sure we're OK.'

'I can do that without you paying me.'

She almost smiled. 'The money's nothing to me. Maybe it's something to you.'

I said, 'My head's all over the place. You can't count on me.'

'Who else am I going to count on?'

I looked at the money. Then I counted out a thousand dollars.

'This will keep me going for a couple of weeks. It'll give me time.' I gave her back the rest. 'But I need you to tell me who threatened you. When Bill Higby arrested me, he put words in my mouth. I won't do that to you. But if I'm going to protect you from this man, I need to know for sure who he is.'

She looked at her baby again, then at me, and she made her decision. 'Eric Skooner.'

'He sat next to you at my trial?'

'Yes.'

'Tell me what happened.'

'He sat by me and my mom. After a while, he let his hand fall between his leg and mine, against my thigh. My mom didn't see. I slid away, but he kept his fingers against me, the way you touch something to show that it's yours. Then, during a break, while my mom was in the bathroom, he followed me into the hall. He told me I was brave for coming to the trial. Such a young girl, he said, and so *willing*. He said it like I was the dirtiest thing he'd ever seen. Then he told me he could do anything he wanted in the city. He could go into other people's houses more easily than a teenage thief. He could read people's histories. He could get into their lives. He told me I had something that was his. When my mom came out of the bathroom, he introduced himself and said he was a judge and had been sitting in on the trial. He told my mom she should be proud of me – such a young girl and so brave.'

The baby squirmed in her arms.

'He had no fear,' she said. 'That scared me more than anything else. He *knew* he could get away with anything, and I knew it too.'

'Did he say he killed Duane and Steven?' I asked.

Her baby made a sound as if she would cry. Lynn Pritchard rocked her in her arms. She touched her tongue to her lipstick. 'I've never felt as dirty as when he touched me.' The baby started crying, and she hushed it and said, 'He never quite told me he killed them. He said Duane and Steve took a briefcase. He said he was sorry, very sorry, about what happened to them, but it had to happen to boys who broke into a judge's house and stole his briefcase. Didn't I see that? He would be sorry, very sorry if something like that happened to me – that or something worse, something special for me since I was so young and so pretty and so brave and so *willing*.'

She hushed her daughter again and rocked her, but now the girl cried as if nothing would console her.

When we walked to the front door, the nanny came into the entryway with the other baby, who also started crying. Lynn Pritchard, in her red dress and her matching lipstick and fingernail polish, took her second daughter and held one on each shoulder. With the cut-glass chandelier hanging above her from the high ceiling, she looked small and vulnerable. But she'd lasted eight years since the murder of the Bronson brothers, as alone and unsure of her life as I'd been in my prison cell, and I thought she must be stronger than she admitted. I wondered if she saw in me a kindred spirit, one who would understand how she had lived. I wondered if she'd decided that since she couldn't deny that life entirely, she was willing to pay me to keep me close.

I stepped out into the rain.

'Come by tomorrow,' she said. 'Check on us.'

I ran to my car. But before getting in, I turned back and went to the front porch. 'One more thing,' I said. 'Do you know if Duane and his brother ever went to a town called Bostwick – about fifty miles south of here?'

Again, she almost smiled. 'I did too. That was our best night together. Ever.'

'Tell me.'

'Two months before he died, Duane told me he'd found a new place on one of his night-time drives. I'd snuck out once before with him and Steve and once with just him. My mom caught me the second time, and I'd promised never to do it again, but he made this place sound magical. So one night we drove down through Bostwick and over toward the river. We parked by some buildings that looked like a factory, though the smell that came out was sweet. We climbed over a fence and went down a grassy area and behind some trees, away from the lights. Duane told me to take off my clothes. I wouldn't. He and I hadn't gone that far, and now Steve was with us. But they stripped and waded into a pond. They were laughing, and Duane told me to come in – the pond was the best ever. So I thought, *what the hell* – it was dark, and I'd already snuck out. So I took off my clothes and went in. The water was hot – like an amazing bath. For the first time, I understood what Duane meant when he said a place was shining. Whatever was in the water was beautiful. That pond shined.'

TWENTY-SEVEN

A few minutes after midnight, Cynthia ran from the Cineplex and climbed into my car. The rain came hard and, when she closed the door, layered over the windows and shelled us from the world. She kissed me and I tasted rain on her lips.

We drove to a park along the Intracoastal Waterway, a couple of miles from her house. Before I went to prison, I would fish from the dock there or set my dad's red kayak into the tidal water. Now the boat ramp disappeared in the storm and dark. I stopped at the top, and the headlights shined on needles and threads of rain.

I told Cynthia about my visit with Lynn Pritchard and my conversations with Coach Kagen and Deborah Holt. I said, 'Eric Skooner must have killed Steven and Duane Bronson. Before them, he killed Jeremy Ballat and Luis Gonzalez. He probably did the first two kids when he found them near his mill. He could do anything to them and get away with it. Just another dead runaway. Just another dead Mexican.'

I felt Cynthia staring at me in the dark.

I said, 'Maybe he stopped for a while then. Or maybe he found other boys we don't know about. There was a guy who came to prison at Raiford just before I got out – a seventy-year-old who'd molested his granddaughter. He'd spent just three years in prison before, also for molesting a girl, but that was thirty years ago. One night, some guys were beating him up, and they asked him about the thirty years. He spat out a tooth and laughed at them and said, *Oh, he'd always had girlfriends, but most of them had been discreet.*

'Maybe Skooner kept it quiet like that guy, or maybe he fought the urge, but when the Bronson boys broke into his house, they stirred him up. He had access to juvenile records – he'd even done juvenile drug court for a while – and he could track down a couple of teenage thieves easily enough. He would think these kids had it coming to them. Jeremy Ballat and Luis Gonzalez bothered him at the mill land, but the Bronsons stole papers that might have showed something bad about the place. How else would they have known enough about it to drive there and climb over the fence with Lynn Pritchard?'

'So, what are you going to do?' Cynthia asked.

'Tomorrow I'll go to talk to the judge,' I said.

'With Deborah Holt?'

'Unless Lynn Pritchard will tell her that the judge threatened her, that won't happen – and Lynn Pritchard distrusts the cops as much as I do. More, if that's possible. She barely could get herself to tell me. She'll never tell Holt. And unless Holt has more reason than she has right now, she'll never accuse the judge. He has too much power.'

'So you'll just knock on Skooner's door alone?' Cynthia said.

'I've done it before.'

'That would be idiotic,' she said.

I figured telling her about the pistol under the seat wouldn't help, so I said nothing.

She kissed me then anyway.

'I thought I was an idiot,' I said.

'You are,' she said, and a gust of wind slapped rain against the side of the car. She kissed my neck, then said, 'The world might be fucked up, but why would I want to be anywhere else? I want to be fucked up with you.'

Two hours later, I drove back toward my room. Rainwater pooled on the shoulder of Beach Boulevard, and the stoplights, set for late-night traffic, blinked and blurred yellow. The rain battered the roof of my car, and I slowed and drove alongside a delivery truck. A car in the oncoming lanes shot past, water rooster-tailing from its tires.

When I reached Philips Highway, the lights were off at most of the roadside businesses.

I pulled on to the parking lot at the Cardinal Motel. A pickup truck had taken the spot by my room, and other cars filled the spaces along the walkway. The motel windows were black, and the streetlight over the highway shined dismal orange light on the wet pavement. I parked in the middle of the lot and ran to my door. As a car whished by on the highway, I fumbled my key into the lock.

The rain and wind knocked down the sound of footsteps behind me. Or maybe Randall Haussen knew how to move without making sound. Maybe he'd also gone into a crack house twenty-five years ago and shot two addicts without anyone hearing him coming. Maybe he'd come up behind his wife as she stood at their kitchen counter and he'd crammed his gun into her mouth before she could scream.

Now, a pistol barrel touched the back of my head, boring into my skin.

I tried to turn.

'No,' Haussen said. He patted me down and laughed scornfully, as if I was a fool for going unarmed. 'Come on,' he said, and turned me back out into the rain.

I said, 'What—'

The pistol barrel lifted from my skin, and the butt smashed the back of my head. 'Not a goddamned word,' he said.

The blow stunned me. Fear flooded my belly. So did rage.

I spun and struck out at him, catching his chin with my fist.

He stumbled back, and his gun fired.

I wondered if the wet on my skin was rainwater or blood. When no pain came, I stepped toward him.

He fired again – wide – and yelled, 'Goddamn it,' then steadied the gun, aiming at my chest.

I showed my palms.

'What *are* you?' he said, and I thought he would shoot again.

Lights went on in two of the motel rooms.

'Come on,' he said, and he gestured at my car.

When the first motel room door opened, I was in the driver's seat, and he was sitting next to me.

'Go,' he said, and I pulled on to Philips Highway.

'Where to?' I asked again.

'Do you know what you did to me?' he said. 'Do you have any idea?'

'I think so. But no one has charged you.'

'I can't go home,' he said. 'I can't go to my goddamned

business. I can't go back to Atlanta – my sister's got a protective order. I can't—'

'Then turn yourself in,' I said.

For a moment, he looked as if he would shoot me, but he said, 'You're a goddamned whore.'

'You shot those crackheads twenty-five years ago. You killed your wife.'

'Who the fuck cares?' he said.

'The crackheads might.'

'No one cares about crackheads,' he said. 'They don't even care about themselves. I've been there. I know.'

'Your wife?'

'Not *my* fault. She would've talked – and that's on you.'

'Thomas LaFlora? He's about twenty-four hours from the needle. *He* cares.'

'He's a thug,' Haussen said. 'If he hadn't gone down for the crackheads, he would've gone down for someone else.'

'How about me? I care.'

'But *you* don't matter,' he said. 'Anyway, you're dead now too. And if no one cares about a crackhead, from all I've seen they'll care less about you.'

The rain whipped across the intersection at Emerson Street and came down hard again as we passed a Walmart.

'But you're in the news,' he said. 'They'll want to know who killed you. Better for you to disappear, don't you think? Better for me. Better for everyone.'

So I cut the steering wheel.

As easy as digging a spoon into a man's eye.

The tires slid on the wet pavement, and the car left the road, bounced down through a rain-filled ditch, and rose on the other side. Haussen fell against the passenger door. *If he died*, I thought, *I might live.* I straightened the wheel, and the tires found the asphalt on a driveway leading to a Chinese restaurant. We careened toward the front wall of the building. *If he lived, I would die.* I yanked the wheel, and the car skidded. Haussen tumbled into me, and his pistol fell on the floor. I straightened the wheel again, and we flew past the side of the restaurant. Haussen grabbed for the gun. I hit the brakes, and he slammed into the dashboard. Still he groped for his gun.

I reached under my seat and found my pistol. I brought it up and saw the end of the asphalt coming at the car. I crushed the brake to the floor.

The car slid.

Stopped.

Haussen came up with his gun.

I aimed the pistol and said, 'No.'

He aimed at me.

I pulled the trigger and shot him in the head.

TWENTY-EIGHT

Haussen's head flew back.

Crashed against the passenger window.

Bounced.

He fell across the seat.

On to my lap.

On a night when I expected nothing.

Nothing.

I shoved him and opened my door.

Shouldn't have. The interior light went on. Some things best unseen. Abandoned to nature. Sunk in saltwater. Dumped in a swamp.

Wind gusted through the open door, raining mist and light.

Blood spatter. Fishhooks for nightmares.

Haussen's eggshell head.

I tipped out of the car, on to my hands and knees. On the flooding pavement. Under the slamming rain.

And vomited.

I had killed a man.

After eight years. Writing appeals on scraps. Whispering into the plumbing. Gripping the bars when lawyers visited. Saying, *I'm an innocent fool who picks up the phone when he should let it ring, who answers the door when he should hide in the attic, who stops on Monument Road to help two boys when he should drive drive drive.*

I'd killed a man.

I pushed myself to my feet. Stumbled from my car. Stared at the sky. The rain burning my eyes. I stumbled past the Chinese restaurant. The sign said *Chopstick Charley's*. As if that was possible.

I walked to the side of Philips Highway. Empty except for a pair of headlights blasting through the blasting rain. Tunnel of light. To take me from here to there. If I stepped into it.

As every dying man must.

The rushing tires in the wind and rain. A last denying of the real that is here and not there. If I stepped into it.

As every dying man must.

I closed my eyes. Held my breath. Stepped into the highway.

Wheels, metal, light shot past.

The driver as unconscious as a brass bullet.

I opened my eyes. I opened my mouth.

Double tail lights.

Red.

Snake eyes.

I'd missed my bus, my train, my flight.

I stood in the highway.

Five minutes.

Ten.

Couldn't catch a . . .

Fifteen.

I stood until despair met futility, cleansing in a dirty rain, because what more could I lose?

What does a man do when pounding his head on a prison wall fails to kill him and he gasps through the bed sheet he has wrapped around his neck?

He writes another appeal.

He whispers into the plumbing.

He rattles the bars.

He lives because when he looks in the rearview mirror, death has quit the chase.

What does a man do when he stands on a highway waiting for a car or truck that never comes?

He stumbles back across the restaurant parking lot.

If only Randall Haussen had let himself out of the passenger door.

But his head lay against the dashboard, blood jagging through the vinyl. Yellow fluid pooling in his ear.

Again, I bent to vomit. Couldn't.

So I dragged him from the seat and hoisted his body into the trash dumpster. I chucked his gun in after.

My hands – black with rain and blood and the dark night.

I wiped them on my shirt.

Realized what I'd done.

Stripped off the shirt and threw it into the dumpster.

Realized.

Always a step behind.

I climbed into the dumpster with the rats and the rancid Kung Pao chicken and Haussen's body. I wiped down his gun with my shirt. I threw the shirt toward my car. I tumbled out and lay on the pavement, wishing the rain would wash me downriver.

Scared boy that I was.

Foolish boy, answering the door, picking up the phone, shooting a man in the head.

I'd killed a man.

Self-defense being only self-justification. Dead being dead.

I drove toward the Cardinal Motel but turned at Emerson and, after the railroad tracks, pulled into an open-air, self-service car wash. Open all night, but lights off except the business sign, which said, *CAR WASH.*

I put my pistol in the trunk, opened all four doors, and sprayed the inside of the car with the pressure hose. The water tore chunks from the vinyl, soaked the seats, ripped the last fabric threads from the inside roof. Flakes of paint and dirt floated in the footwells and cascaded from the car and into the car wash drain. The passenger window had cracked where Haussen's head hit it. His hair and blood stuck to the fracture. I punched out the glass with the hose nozzle.

I wet vac'd the water out of the footwells and off the seats. I scrubbed the stains with my shirt, hosed the car again, and vacuumed again.

Sometime during the early hours, the rain weakened to a drizzle and then, as the first sunlight grayed the clouds, stopped entirely. I dug in a garbage can for a plastic bag and stretched it over the punched-out window. I dug for another bag, wrapped the pistol in it, and stuck it under the front seat.

Then I drove to the motel, let myself into my room, and locked the door. I lay on the mattress and stared at the ceiling. *I'd killed a man.* That was a fact, final and irreversible. Did that fact – that act – make my story of myself – as a man who would fight for himself with laws or a sharpened spoon but would never take another human life – a nasty fiction? I'd had a choice – to kill or be killed – and I had killed. Too easily, it seemed to me. Too automatically. With the instincts of a natural killer, the deadly reflexes that Higby said he saw in me.

What did that make me?

A fist knocked on my door. My heart pounded. Outside, my neighbor Jimmy talked to his girlfriend Susan, saying something about me. The fist knocked again, and Jimmy spoke. 'You all right?' After a while, they went away.

I peeled myself from the bed and climbed into the shower with my clothes on. Haussen's blood and the filth from the Chopstick Charley's parking lot ran from my shirt and pants and runneled into the drain. I stripped then and cranked the water to cold and stood until I shivered.

As I put on dry clothes, Jimmy and Susan came back with Bill Hopper. The fist knocked. The fist knocked again. I went to the door and listened to them.

Hopper's pass key rattled in the lock.

I yanked the door open.

They stared at me.

'Jesus Christ,' Jimmy said. 'We thought you were dead.'

'*I* did,' Susan said.

'No,' I managed to say. 'Not me.'

'A guy shot you last night,' Jimmy said. 'In the parking lot. I watched—'

'Shot *at*,' I said. 'Missed.' I asked what I had to ask. 'Did you call nine-one-one?'

''Course not,' he said.

'But someone did,' Hopper said. 'The cops came. I had to let them check your room.'

Susan glanced at my car with its bagged-up window and steamed windshield. 'What happened?'

'Nothing,' I said. 'Nothing happened.' I tried to close the door.

'You all right?' Hopper asked. 'You look like someone—'

'I'm all right,' I said. 'Tired.' I closed the door.

Sweating.

I couldn't stop sweating. I lay on my bed. I paced from my door to the bathroom, and I couldn't stop sweating.

Voices spoke to me.

Sounds spoke.

The trigger snapping, the gun shell exploding, Haussen crashing into the glass. The pleasure of it. Only a fool would deny it.

Be that kind of fool. No one saw the bullet boring into Haussen's head. No one knows.

Jimmy and Susan know. Bill Hopper knows.

The cops came.

But only to the motel.

If no one saw and no one knows, it didn't happen.

It happened. It's in my sweat.

At seven thirty in the morning, I called Jane's cell phone. It rang four times and bounced to voicemail. 'Christ,' I said to the recorder, hung up, and tried again. Again, it rang four times and bounced to voicemail. I hung up and tried Hank's phone.

He picked up on the third ring. Still sleeping, mostly. My call, a waking nightmare.

I said, 'Haussen came last night. I—'

'Franky?' – my words not yet penetrating.

'Randall Haussen,' I said.

'What? What about him?'

'He came to the motel last night. I—'

'What the hell are—'

'I did. I—'

'Look,' he said. 'Jane and I spent most of last night filing emergency appeals for Thomas LaFlora. The courts will ignore them.

The governor will. At four this afternoon, we're driving to Raiford. We'll stand with the others at the vigil. We'll be there when the announcement comes out that LaFlora is dead.'

'I—'

'The last thing we need today is more of your bullshit.' He hung up.

I lay on my bed and closed my eyes.

My mind raced. I thought I would never sleep again.

Then, as if a hammer smashed me, I slept.

I dreamed of the day my sideways-moving friend Stuart died in the exercise yard.

He'd gone back to the bench press for the first time since he returned from the medical center where the doctors wanted to cut off his diabetic leg. He'd sometimes done sets with three hundred pounds before he got sick, but now he did two-fifty and just five reps before he let out a chestful of steam, dropped the bar on the support, and laughed. 'Hell,' he said, and shoved himself up from the bench. He took two steps, swayed to the side, and crashed to the ground.

When I got to him, his eyes were already stone, and white froth came from his mouth. I thought he'd had a heart attack, and I yelled at the guards to get the nurse. They pointed their guns at me. They pointed them at Stuart on the ground. They pointed them at the other men in the yard. They told us to line up, backs against a wall, as if they were a firing squad.

Then they called the nurse. He ambled and shambled across the yard and stood looking at Stuart's big body.

One of the men yelled, 'He ain't breathing.'

So the nurse ambled and shambled back to the medical center and got an oxygen tank. By the time he came back, ten minutes had passed. He fidgeted with the valve and the mask, and something was wrong with the mask, so he threw it on the ground and started back to the medical center to get a new one.

I stepped out from the wall and said, 'Let me.'

The guards aimed their guns. The other men stared as if I'd yanked down my pants.

But the nurse spat on the ground and said, 'You want to put your lips on that motherfucker, have at it.'

I took off my shirt and wiped Stuart's face. I gave him mouth-to-mouth.

After a minute, something rattled in his chest. His eyes got a kind of soft focus, and he looked at me – then up at the sky – with the gentlest expression I ever saw.

His eyes went white then, and his chest let out another load of steam. He died on the ground by the bench press. The nurse checked his pulse and found none. The guards ordered us back to our cells. I never saw Stuart again.

But in the dream, he turned his gentle eyes to me and said, 'It's all right. It's all right because it's the way it's got to be. You beat yourself up and all you do is give yourself bruises and a black eye, and then the girls don't love you. It's all right. You man enough.'

'Enough for what?' I asked.

'It's all right,' he said. 'You cry all those tears for what? You making an ocean of your own now? What you going to do with that ocean except drown?'

'I'm not crying,' I said. 'I wish I could cry.'

That afternoon, I skipped my appointment with Dr Patel.

That evening, I didn't pick up Cynthia from the Cineplex.

That night, the executioners threaded a needle into a vein on Thomas LaFlora's left leg, and, as Jane and Hank chanted and prayed outside the gates at Raiford, an innocent man died.

TWENTY-NINE

At seven the next morning, another fist – a little one – knocked on my door. Cynthia's voice said, 'Franky?'

I lay on my bed, staring at the ceiling. Sweating.

She knocked again. 'Franky?'

I thought, *No one home.*

'Franky?'

I rolled over. Sweating.

She knocked and knocked. 'Franky?'

No one.

'If you don't answer, I'm calling the cops.'

No.

'Because I'll know you're dead. If you don't answer.'

I got up, my vision draping and darkening from the sides.

When I opened the door, Cynthia said, 'Christ, Franky. What the hell?' She pushed past me into the room.

Then she smelled my hours of sweat, the fumes of my rot. 'Jesus Christ!' She came back to the door and fanned it open and shut. She slammed it, raised the blinds, and slid open the window. She stared at me. 'What the fuck, Franky?' She looked at my bed, as if I'd hidden a dead rat, then shoved me into the bathroom. 'You're pathetic,' she said. 'Gross.' She tugged my shirt to my chin, and I lifted my arms and let her take it. She undid my pants. She pushed me into the shower and turned it on. She squirted a snake of shampoo from my shoulder down my left leg. She slathered the shampoo over my body, said, 'Turn,' and slathered my back. 'Stay,' she said, and went into the bedroom, as if she couldn't bear it.

When she came back, she saw the pile of clothes I'd worn when Haussen snatched me. She picked up the shirt, held it to her nose, and threw it into the trashcan. She picked up the underwear and threw it in on top of the shirt. She picked up the pants and put them in the sink.

She turned off the shower then, gave me my towel, and took the bathroom garbage outside to the bin.

She returned as I was threading my belt through a clean pair of jeans.

She said, 'Now, what the fuck?'

I told her. All of it.

By the time I finished, she was sitting on the side of my sweated-up bed. 'You had to do it,' she said, her anger gone.

'I know.'

'But you've got to report it.'

'No.'

'Self-defense. They'll—'

'No!' Sweating.

As if I'd broken something inside her, she said, 'All right.'

'Don't you see?' I said. 'Eight years ago—'

'I see,' she said. 'I understand.'

'I can't.'

'OK.'

But she insisted that we drive past Chopstick Charley's to see
if the cops had found Haussen's body. When I said I couldn't
do it, she said, 'You've got to. Or else you won't know what's
coming at you.'

So we stretched my bath towel over the damp seats in my car
and went down past the Walmart to the restaurant. Tire trenches
remained in the grass where I'd swerved from the highway, but
a day of sunshine followed by a rainless night had dried the storm
water. An old white Chrysler New Yorker was parked near the
front door. There were no police cars or evidence vans, no crime
scene tape.

'Turn in,' Cynthia said.

'No—'

'*Turn.*'

I turned on to the driveway.

'We need to see him,' she said.

'No.' But I drove along the side of the restaurant to the dumpster. As Cynthia got out, I said, 'Why?'

She lifted the dumpster lid.

Bile rose in my throat. I got out. The sun, rising over the highway,
already had heated the morning. I peered into the dumpster.

It was empty.

I stared as if I'd watched a magic trick.

Cynthia asked, 'Are you sure?'

The look I gave her.

'OK, OK,' she said.

We went back to my car. As we pulled on to the highway, she
said, 'A garbage truck must've picked it up. Haussen's probably in
a dump by now.'

I just drove.

When we got to the stoplight at Emerson, she asked, 'So,
you're OK?'

I would never be OK. I said, 'You should go home.'

She gazed at me, concerned. 'I think I'll hang out with you this
morning.'

The light turned.

She said, 'Are you still going to talk to Eric Skooner?'

'I don't think so.'

I drove us back to the Cardinal Motel and pulled into the parking spot by my door.

She said, 'I was scared when you said you were going to talk to him. I'm more scared now when you say you aren't.'

I got out of the car and let myself into my room. She followed me in.

She said, 'If he killed the Bronsons and the others, he's also taken eight years of your life. He's made you what you are. You wouldn't even have known about Haussen except for the situation he put you in. He set your life up to make that happen. If you let him go, you'll be giving yourself to him. Can you live with that?'

I said, '*Your* dad burned you. You're scarred forever. You live with him. *You* live with it.' I meant my words to anger her – to send her away so I could lock my door.

But she said, 'Don't talk to the judge for yourself. Do it for Steven and Duane Bronson. Do it for their mom. Do it for that runaway and the Mexican kid. Do it for Rick Melsyn and his roommate. Do it for Lynn Pritchard.'

I said nothing.

'Do it for Thomas LaFlora,' she said.

I glared at her.

She said, 'Do it for me.'

I still said nothing.

'Fuck it then,' she said, and she went out the door into the sunlight.

I looked at the bed. I looked at the door. I wanted to close my eyes and sleep. I wanted to forget and keep forgetting. I wanted the fishhooks of blood that were tearing at my mind to disintegrate.

But Cynthia's appearance at my door – and her words to me before she left – had sharpened and barbed those hooks. There was no escaping.

I went out the door and got into my car. Cynthia was crossing Philips Highway toward the bus stop when I pulled alongside her. I ripped away the plastic bag that covered the passenger window and said, 'Get in.'

She kept walking.

I drove alongside her on the shoulder.

'I'm going to talk to the judge,' I said.

She kept walking.

'I love you,' I said.

She came to the window. 'What's that supposed to mean? What's it supposed to do?'

'I don't know,' I said.

'You kick me out, and then you come after me. I don't know what that even is.'

'I don't either.'

She shook her head.

'Get in,' I said. 'Please.'

She did.

The county court would open at nine, which meant we should have time to catch Eric Skooner at home or as he left his house. I drove to Byron Road with Cynthia staring out of the broken window, pulled past Higby's house, and turned through the gate on to the Skooners' driveway.

Cynthia and I went to the front porch, and I rang the bell.

A minute passed before footsteps approached.

Andrew Skooner opened the door, wearing only a pair of pajama shorts. He looked as if we'd awakened him. The bruises where Higby punched him were gone. Only a red blemish remained over his upper lip from the stitches. But along with his old scars, he had new dime-sized welts on his chest, as if someone had poked him with a stick. 'What do you want?' he said.

'I need to talk to your dad,' I said.

'You missed him,' he said. 'Early meeting.'

'I'll look for him at the courthouse,' I said, and I turned to go.

But Cynthia eyed his welts and said, 'What's it like to live in a house like this?' Her voice had the same combative boldness as when she teased the jewelry store salesman and vitamin kiosk clerk on our first afternoon together – but now there was an edge to it.

Andrew Skooner just stared at her.

She said, 'What we really want to know is, what's it like to live with your dad? My own dad is a challenge. Some people think he's kind of a bastard. I could show you the scars. I don't mean emotional or psychological. I mean the real thing. How about your dad? Would you say he's a good man? You've got scars too.'

Andrew Skooner looked at me, as if I might rein her in or explain her behavior. When I didn't, he said, 'I know girls like you. They're brash and talkative and in-your-face. But it's just an act they put on to hide their insecurity.' Then he closed the door.

'He's messed up,' Cynthia said, and rang the doorbell again. The door opened. '*What?*'

Cynthia said to me, 'Your turn.'

I frowned at her but I did have a question. I said, 'Last time we talked, you told me that, as hard as my life has been, you've had it harder. What did you mean by that?'

He started to close the door again.

'I know what your dad did,' I said. 'I know about the boys.'

He opened again. His cheeks flushed.

I said, 'I know about Tomhanson Mill. I know about Jeremy Ballat. I know about Luis Gonzalez. I know about Steven and Duane Bronson.'

He looked like he would hit me. Then he looked like he would throw up. Or cry. But he spoke with quiet anger. 'Do you know what you're saying?'

'I think so,' I said.

He closed the door.

We waited.

When he opened it again, he said, 'Do you realize what he can do to *you*?'

'I know what he's already done,' I said. 'I spent eight years learning it.'

He seemed unable to speak or move. He barely breathed.

Cynthia said, 'What I want to know is—'

He said, 'Shut up.' Then to me, 'You too. Both of you, shut up. You've seen what happens. You don't want this – you *can't*. Whatever you know or think you know, just shut up.'

Neither of us said anything, but he acted as if we did.

'You don't get it,' he said. 'No one will care what you say. I've tried. My mom did. Josh did. He shut us all down. He starts talking and everyone believes—'

'Bullshit,' Cynthia said.

'Yeah?' He touched the blemish above his lip. 'Everyone believed him about this. The sheriff dragged *Higby* out of his house—'

I almost laughed. 'Higby *didn't* hit you?'

'It doesn't matter what *I* say. It doesn't matter what *you* say. It only matters what *he* says.'

Cynthia looked unsure. 'Your dad did it and then blamed a cop?'

'If someone becomes a problem, he takes care of it. Higby became a problem.'

'But he's out of jail again,' I said.

'For now. Only as long as my dad lets that happen. You know he's coming after you too. He'll take anything that's left of you.'

'He'll just get scraps,' I said. 'Others have been there before him.'

'No one like him.'

'Bullshit,' Cynthia said again.

He glared at her. But then he did an amazing thing. Leaving the door open, he turned and walked into the house.

Cynthia glanced at me and stepped inside.

The front hall was cool and dark. We followed him back to a large sunroom with broad windows looking over a swimming pool, a back lawn, and a dock that tongued into Black Creek. He went to a cabinet and opened the bottom drawer. He hesitated, then removed a small piece of metal. 'Nothing will change,' he said. 'You can shout in their faces. No one will believe you. Why should they? Who the hell are you? A guy with nothing left to lose?'

'What are you talking about?' Cynthia said.

He said, 'One of the first things my dad taught me was that this is an old town built on old friendships. He says, if your old friends are the right friends and if you keep those friends close, you have nothing to worry about. *His* old friends are the right friends.' He looked at the piece of metal.

'What's that?' I said.

'It *should* be everything, especially to someone with nothing to lose,' he said, 'but if I give it to you, it will almost definitely disappear. You'll disappear too. But you deserve to have it if anyone does.' He handed it to me.

It was a bullet slug from a small-caliber gun.

'What?' I said.

'It's the bullet my brother shot at Higby,' he said.

I stared at it. If what he was saying was true . . .

'Your brother *had* a gun?' I asked. 'Higby shot in self-defense?'
'I don't know who shot first, him or Josh,' he said, 'but Josh did shoot.'
'Where's the gun now?'
'My dad has it. He thinks I got rid of the bullet.'
'How did you find it? The cops looked for it for days.'
'It was never missing,' he said. 'It was on the road when we went out to the crash. I picked it up. My dad picked up the gun. There was nothing left to find when the cops roped off the area.'
Cynthia looked suspicious. 'Why are you giving it to Franky?'
'It's your only chance,' he said to me. 'Maybe my only chance too. It probably won't do any good. My dad has warned you. He always warns. But then he acts.'
I said, 'If I turn it in to the cops, will you admit you gave it to me?'
'You haven't been listening,' he said. 'If you give it to the cops, it will disappear. Even if the cops start looking at my dad, he'll talk to the sheriff or one of his other friends, and then the cops will look at someone else.'
Cynthia said, 'No one has that kind of—'
'If I turn it in,' I asked again, 'will you admit it?'
'No,' he said.
'Why?' I asked.
'You're still not listening.'
'I hear you. I just don't like your answers.'
He said, 'Ever since I can remember, my dad has beat up on the world and claimed he's doing it for everyone's good. He beat up Josh. He beats me up. He beat up my mom. He beats up everyone in the city, and then the mayor and the city council give him awards. He hangs the plaques in his courthouse office. And so now you think you'll call him out for what he's done to you and others, and you think everything will be OK. Give it a try, but he already knows how to beat you up again. Unless you figure out how to take him down first, this time you won't get out of prison – you'll be gone – and as you're lying in a swamp or in the woods or wherever he puts you, someone will be thinking of another award to give him.'
I turned the bullet in my fingers. The blast had peeled back the copper jacket in strips and melted the lead. 'Where did your brother get the gun?' I asked.

'He stole it from my dad. My dad has carried it since he was a prosecutor. He makes enemies.'

My skin crawled, and Cynthia gave me a sharp look, as if she felt it too.

'Does he have a lot of guns?' I asked.

He looked at me as if he knew what he was admitting. 'Just the one. He says if a man can't do his business with one, it's time for him to get a new weapon.'

'Sounds like a thought to live and die by,' I said, and I closed my fist on the bullet.

Cynthia and I drove out from Byron Road. The bullet Andrew Skooner gave me rattled in the cup holder. It weighed only a few grams. Almost nothing. But if Andrew Skooner was telling the truth, it could blast apart the world I'd been living in for eight years. If Eric Skooner owned only one gun, the ballistic markings on the bullet should show that he committed the killings that sent me to death row. And Andrew Skooner's testimony, if he ever felt safe enough to give it, would exonerate Higby, the man who sent me there. The bullet would shake the courthouse and the Sheriff's Office, and who knew where the beams would fall?

Cynthia fished it out of the cup holder and turned it between her fingers.

As if she also knew it was a bomb.

She said, 'Even if this is what he says it is, you need more. You need the gun. And you've got to put the gun in Eric Skooner's hand.'

We drove to the courthouse and parked in the lot across the street. When a woman at the information desk said we could find the judge in Hearing Room 781, we rode the elevator and walked to the end of a wide hallway. The doors at 781 were open, the room empty. We went back toward the elevator and took a hall that led behind the hearing rooms.

Eric Skooner's chambers were in a suite of offices served by a shared secretary, a red-haired woman in her fifties. I told her I had information about Bill Higby, and I needed to see Judge Skooner.

She dialed his office, and a moment later the door to his office opened. He stepped out in a charcoal gray suit with a starched white shirt and a gold tie. 'What's this about?' he asked.

Cynthia stayed with the secretary, and I walked past the judge into his office.

As Andrew Skooner said, the judge's walls were lined with framed certificates and awards honoring him for his accomplishments and good acts. In the middle of the room, there was a big wooden desk with a high-backed black-leather office chair and, on the other side, three small chairs for lawyers and their clients.

The judge went around the desk. 'You have information about Bill Higby?'

'You and I share bad relations with him,' I said. 'He arrested me for crimes I didn't commit. He's hassled your family for years. He tried to put me to death. He killed Joshua.'

'This is true.'

'But I'm curious. You used to get along with him. I mean, you wrote a letter praising him when he brought Josh home after he ran away. So, what went wrong?'

'I thought you said you have information about him.'

'As far as I can tell, he started bothering you and your family around the same time he arrested me for killing the Bronson brothers.'

'Perhaps,' he said, 'but I fail to see either a connection or the relevance—'

'It's probably nothing,' I said. 'But when I was in prison, I learned to see connections really well. Well enough to get myself released. I'll tell you something I've told very few people, though. Sometimes I saw connections where they didn't exist. I had to be careful. Especially early on, when I was in solitary confinement, I needed to learn how to tell the real connections from the imaginary ones.'

He was getting impatient. 'I still fail to—'

'Except for the bedroll, which was green, and the sink and toilet, which were stainless steel, everything was white. The floor, the walls, the ceiling – all white. I had no TV or radio, so when I wasn't exercising or writing appeals, I stared at the white. And after a while, I started to notice specks and spots in it, and then I saw connections and whole patterns between the spots and specks. I saw a horse and a fish and a bicycle frame. Crazy stuff. I was like a man thousands of years ago looking at stars in the sky and connecting the dots. I made up pictures where there were none.'

'I'm afraid your point escapes me,' he said.

'Maybe Higby's treatment of your family and his treatment of me are like one of those pictures I saw on my cell wall. No real connection. All in my imagination.'

'I'm sure that's the case,' he said.

'No constellation in the night sky.'

'Right,' he said.

'And I've just been an idiot lying in the dark, looking for meaning.'

'Is this all you came to tell me?' he asked.

I said, 'I see that a man you prosecuted twenty-five years ago was executed last night.'

He offered a thin smile. 'Yes, Thomas LaFlora. A man particularly worthy of his fate.'

'He was innocent,' I said.

'I'm sorry?'

'Innocent. But the difference between innocence and guilt doesn't mean a lot in this city. Especially with men like you and Higby. In Higby's case, people mostly seem to think he's trying to do good but gets confused in his thinking. But with you, the message is clear. I keep meeting people who are scared of you.'

He kept the smile. 'Are these men who've spent time in prison with you? I expect I would be unpopular among them.'

I shook my head. 'They're mostly people who've never harmed anyone as far as I know.'

'I would like to know who feels this way.'

'Mostly people who've gone quiet now. A couple of boys upriver near Bostwick – you scared the hell out of them.'

His eyes showed no recognition. He said, 'I spend little time there.'

'By Tomhanson Mill?'

He nodded. 'My wife's property, not mine until after her death. Her great-grandfather started the mill. When her father passed away, it went to her. Beautiful land.'

'Lynn Melsyn? Scared too.'

'Should I know the name?'

'She goes by a different one now. She was Duane Bronson's

girlfriend. And she's the sister of Rick Melsyn, one of two guys killed a couple of weeks ago in their apartment at the beach.'

'I saw the story. But again your point is escaping me.'

'The point is she's scared of you. Scared enough to change her name and hide. Frightened almost to death.'

'That would be very strange,' he said, 'inasmuch as I don't know her.'

'She knows *you*. You sat next to her during my trial.'

'I did stop in on your trial periodically,' he said. 'I sat next to several people, all of them unfamiliar to me.'

'Did you threaten them all?'

For a moment he gave me a look that made me understand the fear others felt in his presence. Then he glanced at his desk and said, 'Well, I'm sorry for this young lady if she's frightened. I can't imagine why she would be.' When he raised his eyes again, he appeared tranquil, and that change was even scarier. He said, 'At any rate, you seem to have come here under false premises. I'm interested in Bill Higby for obvious reasons. But you've told me nothing. I need to ask you to leave.'

I said, 'Did the Bronson boys break into your house and steal some papers? Maybe papers showing something going on at Tomhanson Mill?'

He shook his head. 'Whatever connections you think you see aren't there,' he said. 'At least, I don't see them. I expect no one else will either.'

'Maybe you've just convinced people to close their eyes.'

He forced the thin smile. 'Do you or don't you have anything relevant to tell me about Bill Higby?'

'Yeah,' I said. 'I hate to say it – because I hate Higby and he's guilty of a lot of other things – but he shot your son in self-defense. But you know that already.'

Again, his eyes flashed with fury. Again, he controlled his voice. 'It's time for you to leave.'

'OK,' I said. 'But I'll come back.'

As I walked to the door, he said, 'I'll cause a great deal of trouble for you, you know – a great deal of discomfort.'

'I've heard that about you.'

'I'll pick up my phone. The city will close around you. You'll wish you were back in your prison cell.'

I said, 'That sounds hands-off. But people say you like to do the nasty stuff yourself. The stuff that's personal. The stuff that excites you.'

'I'm sure I don't know what you're talking about.'

After leaving the courthouse, Cynthia and I drove ten blocks to the Sheriff's Office.

Inside, the deskman called the Homicide Room. When he hung up, he said that Deborah Holt was out on a call. I told him we'd come back and turned to go.

But Cynthia said, 'How about Bill Higby?'

'Don't—' I said.

And the deskman said, 'He's on administrative leave.'

Cynthia said, 'If he's in today, Franky Dast would like to talk to him.'

The deskman looked at me.

Cynthia did too. 'You've got to do this,' she said. 'One way or another, you've got to deal with it.'

I wanted to deal with it my way, not hers, but I said to the deskman, 'Ok – if he's in.'

Five minutes later, Higby, wearing jeans and an untucked yellow T-shirt, came out past the security check and said, 'Every time I see you, I hope it'll be the last. Either someone will stick a knife in you or you'll cut yourself and bleed out.'

My words caught in my throat.

Cynthia said to him, 'That's a shitty way to treat a guy who brings you good news.'

He stared at her. 'Who are you?'

'Franky's girlfriend,' she said.

'God help you,' he said.

She seemed to think that was funny. 'Ask Franky for his news.'

He looked at me. 'Are you planning to do it right next time? Because, if you are, I've got advice. Go for the arteries. Here' – he touched his neck – 'and here' – he touched his wrist. 'It's fast, it's effective, and it would be great news.'

'You're an asshole,' Cynthia said.

I said, 'The news is that I know the Skooners are lying. The shooting charges against you are bad.'

He just shook his head. 'I told you before, I don't care what you think, and I don't care what you know. So, how does that make it good news?'

I said, 'Because I've got witnesses and evidence.'

He didn't believe it. 'You've got someone who saw the shooting?'

'Someone who saw what happened afterward.'

He said, 'Only the Skooners and I were there.'

'I have evidence of what they did.'

He said, 'Give it to the lawyers. Mine or the prosecutor's office.'

'No,' I said, 'I'll hold on to it for now.'

He gave me a long look. 'OK, I'll bite. What's the evidence?'

It rested in the cup holder in my car. I said, 'When are you going to come clean?'

'What are you talking about?'

'When are you going to admit that I had nothing to do with the Bronson killings?'

Something happened with his face. 'Why would I?'

'I think you've always known I was innocent. Everyone says you're a good investigator, but you screwed up with me. You knew about the killings of Jeremy Ballat and Luis Gonzalez up by Bostwick, and you knew I couldn't have done them. I was a kid myself when they died. So, what made you want to blame the Bronson killings on me?'

'You were on Monument Road,' he said. 'You picked up Duane and Steve. Your blood was on their car. You took them to the gas station. The logic was clear eight years ago. It's still clear.'

'The logic should have fallen apart as soon as you thought about it. Unless you had a reason to go after me – or avoid going after someone else – you should've known I couldn't have killed them.'

'I knew enough to convict you,' he said.

'And that wasn't enough.'

He turned to go into the station, but then he turned back.

He said, 'Just so you know I still think about you, *I* have a question for *you*. What do you know about Randall Haussen?'

He could've held me by the throat against a wall. I fought for words. 'The people at the JNI talked to him a couple of times. I went with them.'

'That's all?'

'Thomas LaFlora got executed last night,' I said. 'We thought Haussen did the crimes.'

'Right. When did you see him last?'

'It's been a while,' I said.

'Because he's gone missing. You know that, don't you?'

'Maybe he ran,' I said.

'Maybe.' He moved in close the way he moved in close eight years ago in the interview room. 'A couple of nights ago, we got a report of shots fired over by the motel where you're living. Middle of the night. Pretty common in your neighborhood. But this time the people who glanced out their windows said they saw you with a man who looked like Haussen. What do you know about that?'

'The people must be mistaken,' I said.

'I hate it when that happens.' He touched my collar, as if he was straightening it out. 'Seems to be the story of your life. Mistaken identity. You say you're an angel but you look like the devil.'

THIRTY

'Fuck!' I shouted when Cynthia and I got outside. 'Fuck!' Two cops in uniform eyed me as they came up the steps from the sidewalk.

'Calm down,' Cynthia said.

'Fuck!'

One of the cops stepped toward me. 'Sir?'

Cynthia moved between him and me. 'It's all right.'

The cop considered us. 'Get him off the street,' he told her.

As we drove from the Sheriff's Office, she said, 'Higby doesn't know.'

'Someone saw me,' I said, and hit the gas.

'Someone saw someone who *looked like* you and someone who *looked like* Haussen. That's different from seeing you. If Higby knew, he wouldn't have let you walk out of the station.'

'Fuck,' I said.

'Calm down. You're going to get us in a wreck.'

I breathed in deep and turned to cross the river on the Main Street Bridge.

I breathed out.

In deep.

Out long.

Reality.

Denial.

The sun glinted through the windshield, blinding me to the traffic at the end of the bridge. A hot river-wind blew through the broken passenger window.

Cynthia said, 'I actually thought that went pretty well – until you panicked.' When I said nothing, she added, 'He doesn't know what happened with Haussen, but you told him that you know what happened between him and the Skooners and also what happened to Duane and Steven Bronson and the others.'

My mind spun, turning from Higby's insinuations about Haussen to his insistence that I killed the Bronson boys and then to Judge Skooner, smug with his dirty honors. I glanced at Cynthia as she picked up the bullet from the cup holder. The tiny gravity in the lump of metal seemed all that held me together. If the bullet flew from her hand, out the window – if it disappeared – then what would become of me?

'Put it down,' I said.

She looked at me.

'*Put* it down.'

She dropped it back in the cup holder, reached over, and steadied the steering wheel. 'Don't lose yourself now,' she said.

She wanted to call in sick and stay with me, but at noon I dropped her off at the Cineplex. 'I'll be all right,' I said. 'I'll do better alone for a few hours.'

'You can't even drive straight,' she said.

'I made it for eight years on my own,' I said.

She looked doubtful. 'Are you going to lock yourself in your room again?'

A tempting idea. 'I told Lynn Pritchard I would check on her,' I said. 'And I've got to meet with my reintegration therapist.'

'Pick me up at eight?'

'Sure,' I said.

'You really are crazy,' she said, though I heard no criticism. She kissed me long, as if she could radiate life and love into me.

I drove to Lynn Pritchard's house in Ponte Vedra, watching my hands on the steering wheel like a drunk determined to thread a highway without getting pulled over or drifting across the yellow line.

I glanced at the bullet in the cup holder, back at the road, and at the bullet again. It needed a vault with armored walls. I pinched it out of the cup holder. It felt hot from the sun through the windows. Like a man standing on the edge of a roof, tugged toward open air by invisible forces, I worried that I would drop it into a void. I clenched it in my fist.

You really are crazy.

I touched the bullet to my lips – my tongue. It tasted of salt and mineral. A drop of blood. Blood of the earth. Blood of the Bronson boys – and Jeremy Ballat and Luis Gonzalez and Rick Melsyn and Darrell Nesbit.

Don't lose yourself now.

For the rest of the drive to Lynn Pritchard's house, I held the metal in my sweating fist. After pulling up her driveway, I dried it on my shirt and put it in my wallet.

Lynn Pritchard came to the door when I rang. She wore tight, low-riding, bleach-white pants and a bleach-white T-shirt that showed her belly. Her nails gleamed with red polish again, and her lips shined wet with red lipstick. She looked past me toward the road as if afraid someone might have followed me to her house, then ushered me inside and locked the door.

'Are you all right?' I asked.

She nodded toward the room where her twin daughters had cribs and said, 'They're sleeping.'

We went to the living room. She'd pulled the drapes, and even in the early afternoon she needed to turn on the table lamps.

'What happened?' I said.

'I think, nothing,' she said. 'Someone called last night. First around midnight. Then after two in the morning and again an hour later.'

'What did they say?'

'They just hung up.'

'Wrong number?' I said.

'Maybe.' She glanced at the drapes. I expected that she glanced at them a lot. Her husband may have built a house to protect her, but he couldn't save her from her own fear.

I said, 'I talked to the judge. He knows that I know.'

She shook her head. 'He'll come after you. He has to.'

'I feel like he's been coming after me for the last eight years. Now I'm going after *him*.'

'It doesn't work that way.'

'I can almost prove what he did. If you'll tell your story, that might be enough.'

'No one listens,' she said, echoing Andrew Skooner. 'When you talked to the judge, did you mention me?'

'I asked about the boys who were killed near Tomhanson Mill. I asked if Duane and Steven broke into his house.'

'Yeah, he'll come after you,' she said.

'I also talked to Higby. He gave me nothing. As you said, no one listens. But if you talked to him—'

'No.'

I understood her fear, but it also infuriated me. I said, 'If you—'

'*No.*'

I could yell at her and shake her until I broke through. I said, 'I'll come by to check on you again tomorrow morning. If the phone rings tonight, don't answer it.'

'Can you stay for a while? I'm alone with my girls.'

'Where's the nanny?'

'She left this morning.'

'When's she coming back?'

'She isn't. This house freaks her out. Or I do. The whole thing does.'

'How about your husband?'

'He comes back tomorrow before lunch. Then he leaves again next week. He's going hunting in New Hampshire.'

'Then I'll swing by again tonight.'

'You can sleep here,' she said. 'We have extra rooms. I'll pay you.'

'You've paid me enough.'

* * *

On my way back to the city, I stopped at Lupido's Auto Glass. Lupido looked at the broken-out passenger-side window, looked at the torn interior of the car, and said, 'I'll put in a new one, but it won't make you any prettier.'

Then I drove to the Sheriff's Office. If I could have split the bullet in two – dividing the part that, according to Andrew Skooner, would match the ballistic markings on the bullets that killed the Bronson brothers from the part that, also according to him, his brother Josh had fired at Higby – would I have done it? Would I exonerate myself but not Higby?

I had no answer when I asked the deskman to call Deborah Holt's desk, and I had none when she came through security and said, 'What did you say to Higby to piss him off this time? He's been ranting about you all afternoon.'

'Can we take a walk?' I asked.

We went up the block to the Bay Street Café and got coffee. When we sat at a table, I said, 'If I give you something that my life depends on, what will you do with it?'

'What is it?' she said.

'Not just my life either,' I said, and, with my head buzzing, I took the bullet from my wallet and set it on the table between us.

She picked it up, studied it. 'Twenty-two caliber,' she said. 'Jacketed. I see them all the time. Go to a gun range, and you can sweep up a hundred pounds of them at the end of the day.'

'Get it tested.'

She rubbed the roughness of the bullet with her thumb. 'You say your life depends on it? And you're putting your life in my hands?'

'Yeah, I suppose so.'

'Where did you get it?'

I shook my head.

She put the bullet on the table and stood up. 'I don't play games.' She started toward the door.

'It'll clear Higby,' I said.

She stopped.

I picked up the bullet and offered it to her. 'When Higby arrested me,' I said, 'he ran tests on the gun I had in my trunk – my dad's gun. He wanted it to match the bullets that shot Steven and Duane Bronson. Everyone else seemed to want it to match too. So at my trial the ballistics expert said the gun "could have" shot the bullets. I don't know enough about ballistics to tell the difference between "could have" and "must have," but I know that my dad's gun *didn't* shoot those bullets.'

'So, what will a ballistics test tell me that I don't already know?' she asked.

'Do the test and find out.'

She stared at me, then snatched the bullet from my hand. 'I don't play games,' she said, and she walked out of the café.

THIRTY-ONE

At eight, I picked up Cynthia at the Cineplex. We went to a Texaco Food Mart and bought hot dogs off the roller grill and bags of pretzels and Cheetos. Cynthia filled a big plastic cup with crushed ice and topped it with Coke. As we ate in my car, I told her about my visit to Lynn Pritchard, and we agreed that fear can rip up the inside of a body, leaving the outside bleach-white and pretty. I told her I'd given Deborah Holt the bullet, and she looked relieved. 'If the police have it,' she said, 'Eric Skooner has no reason to hurt you.'

I figured the judge still had plenty of reason, but I said, 'You might be right.'

Her parents would be out past midnight, and so, for the first time, we went back to her house instead of my room. We stepped inside like thieves and climbed halfway up the stairs, where she stopped and unbuttoned my shirt. I started to take off her shirt too, but she said, 'Uh-uh,' and ran up to the landing.

Her bedroom was furnished as if for a twelve-year-old. The childhood toys were gone, but a pink duvet covered a twin bed, and daisy decals were pasted on the sides of a set of pressboard bookshelves. A green teddy bear watched over the room from a night table. A mobile made of cut-out construction-paper stars – dusty, bent, childish – hung in the corner.

'This is the first time I've had a guy up here,' she said.

I took off my pants, and nodded at the mobile. 'What's that?'

'I made it when I was seven,' she said, and she unzipped hers. I went to her and lifted her shirt off. 'Why do you keep it?'

'I made it before the fire.' She unhooked her bra and let it fall to the floor. 'The paint peeled on the ceiling around it. The firemen sprayed the room with water. I don't know how it survived.' We stood together, naked, in her childhood room and looked at the paper-star mobile. 'It seems like it would be bad luck to take it down,' she said.

She pulled the duvet off the bed. The bed sheets were yellow, with a flower pattern that had faded from years in the wash. She pulled off the top sheet. The mattress with the remaining sheet looked like a slab or an altar.

Cynthia said, 'I want you to do things to me.' Then she put her body on the mattress.

I left her, sleeping, at one in the morning. In the light of the bedside lamp, the skin on her breasts glistened with sweat. Her burned legs shined. I covered her with the top sheet and kissed her on the lips.

I spent the rest of the night on Lynn Pritchard's couch. I meant to stop by, make sure she and her daughters had had a quiet evening, and go back to my room at the Cardinal Motel. But when she answered the door, still dressed in the pants and T-shirt she'd worn that afternoon, she said she'd gotten more phone calls. She'd ignored the first two but picked up the third. A man who didn't identify himself said he was calling to see if she was home and then hung up. She thought she recognized the judge's voice.

She looked terrified. *Couldn't I come in?* she asked. *Couldn't I answer the phone when it rang again? Couldn't I let the caller know there were two of us in the house?* One of her babies started crying while we stood at the door, and when she went to soothe her, I walked to my car, got the pistol, and returned.

She fed her daughter, put her back in her crib, and joined me in the living room. I sat on the couch with the gun on my lap. She sat in an upholstered chair and stared at the gun as if she hated it but appreciated my having it.

The phone never rang, and, after a while, she slept. With her white pants and T-shirt, and her pale skin, she would look little different if the judge broke into the house and shot her, except her blood-red nail polish and lipstick would have a matching blood-red bullet wound. I looked down at the pistol, which could shoot as blood-red as any gun the judge carried.

As if she sensed my thoughts, she jerked awake. I told her to go upstairs and sleep in her bed.

'But—' she said.

'I'll stay,' I said. 'I'll stay.'

When she left, I closed my eyes and slept too. I dreamed of a man standing on an icy bridge. At first it was daytime in the dream, and then it was night. And at first the man stared over the bridge rail at an icy river, and then he played the French horn. The instrument gleamed like a tangle of engine pipes. As the man played, a van burned on the bridge behind him – my grandfather's van – and a girl crawled from the burning wreckage. At first the girl was the singer in my grandfather's band – the one who survived the southern Georgia crash along with my grandfather's horn – and then she was Cynthia with her legs burning, flaring like logs soaked in kerosene. The man playing the French horn shifted tempo and tone, and soon he played screaming jazz.

I jerked awake to the sound of Lynn Pritchard's babies wailing.

Although she soothed them again and the house became quiet, I stayed awake the rest of the night. I thumbed the safety on the pistol. I probed the barrel with the tips of my fingers. I tried to recall the tunes the man in my dream played as the world around him turned to fire and ice. A little before seven, I got up and opened one of the window curtains. The sun was rising, and points of dew glowed on the grass, brighter than the brass gleam on the horn I'd seen in my unconscious. The van-spinning ice had melted in southern Georgia. The fires that burned my grandfather and Cynthia had extinguished. The world was a beautiful place, temperate and pointed with dew. From behind Lynn Pritchard's window, it looked like a place where one could live happily and peacefully. Except that the world still had Judge Skooner in it.

For the next three days, little happened.

I stopped by to see Deborah Holt each morning and afternoon. I wondered whether the bullet that Andrew Skooner had given me really would show the ballistic marks he said it would. 'No news,' she said, and 'Still no news. These tests take a while.'

I wondered when the judge would make a move. Most of the time, my mind spun. I woke up four or five times each night, sweating, and I had to fight off the fear that poked and prodded at my thoughts before I could sleep again.

Cynthia and I hung out when we could. We went back to Cardice Cold Storage, but a new guy was manning the desk and he looked confused when Cynthia explained that she was a regular. So, we lay on my bed and watched TV, and, one morning, got in my car and drove the length of the 295 ring road around the city, because much of the road hadn't existed before I went to prison and I was curious and driving sometimes helped with the knives of anxiety.

I met with Dr Patel once a day. He asked if I was feeling suicidal and if my relationship with Cynthia was going well. I told him I'd bought into the value of denial – and so, no new suicidal thoughts. I said Cynthia and I were swimming along like fish.

'Are you having sex?' he asked, 'and, if so, are you suffering any dysfunction? Many men in your circumstances do.'

'We're great,' I said, and he seemed perplexed.

He said, 'I ask all this because, honestly, you don't look so good. Are you losing weight?'

'Not that I know of.'

'Are you sleeping well?'

'Not particularly.'

'I can write new prescriptions if you need them.'

'I'm good,' I said.

'Are you? Because you don't look it.'

Each day, I stopped by Lynn Pritchard's house and phoned between visits. The late-night calls stopped, she said, and her husband – a heavy-set man who grinned whenever he glanced around his big house and at his young wife – returned from Argentina and hadn't started packing for New Hampshire. But whenever he left the room, she looked like she was falling apart. She said she had Xanax and Ambien in her medicine cabinet but was afraid to take them. What would she do if the judge arrived? I wondered what she would do even if she was totally conscious, but kept that thought to myself.

*   *   *

Deborah Holt called late on the third afternoon.

'What did you find out?' I asked.

'You asshole,' she said.

'What?'

'Meet me at the Bay Street Café,' she said.

An hour later, I did.

She was sitting at a table when I came in, and she said, 'Where the hell did you get that bullet?'

'What did you find out about it?' I asked.

'You *know* what I found out. I ran it through the Ballistic Information Network. The marks on it match the bullets from the Bronson boys. Also the marks on the bullets from Rick Melsyn and Darrell Nesbit.'

I shook my head. 'At my trial, the ballistics expert said the bullets matched the gun I had in my trunk.'

'How close?'

'He said seventy percent. And a margin of error.'

'This one is ninety-eight percent. Where did you get it?'

So I told her about my visit to the Skooners' house. I told her about Andrew Skooner giving me the bullet and his vow never to name his father to the police or a jury.

Her face looked flushed. 'The bullet is still it, though,' she said. 'It's enough.'

'No. Think of what the judge will say. Think of the defense. Unless Andrew Skooner testifies that he gave me the bullet, all we have is my story. A lot of people still think *I* killed the Bronsons. So, now I give you a bullet that matches the ones in the killings even better than the tests of the gun from my trunk. It makes me look guilty, and it makes my story about the Skooners look like a lie. We need the gun,' I said. 'Or we need Andrew Skooner to talk.'

She thought about it. 'I'll get Andrew Skooner.'

'How do you plan to do that?'

'I'll say it's time for this to stop.'

'It won't work,' I said.

'Then I'll crush him.'

THIRTY-TWO

B ut when Deborah Holt went to the Skooners' house to talk to Andrew, no one answered the door. She tried twice more and then persuaded a court clerk to ask the judge – casually – about his son. Word came back that Andrew had returned to Cornell for his senior year. Holt booked a flight to upstate New York and went to the apartment Andrew was renting with three friends. The friends said that, despite promises, Andrew hadn't arrived. She waited twenty-four hours and flew back. Two days later, the judge filed a missing person report for his son. According to the report, Andrew disappeared from the house more than a week earlier – *before* he gave me the bullet. No one had accused the judge of anything, but he was already screwing with the timeline.

The next day, when I returned to the Cardinal Motel after visiting Lynn Pritchard, Holt was waiting for me in the parking lot. I climbed out of my car and into hers.

'We need to find the gun,' she said. 'Andrew Skooner has gone rabbit. Or else the judge has put him somewhere we can't find him. When you talked with Andrew, did he have any idea where the judge might be keeping the weapon?'

'He just said his father had it. Before Josh died, the judge kept it somewhere his sons could get to it – probably in the house. But I think Andrew would have given it to me along with the bullet if he could have. So the judge has hidden it somewhere Andrew doesn't know about or can't reach.'

'He wants quick access to it,' she said. 'He should have dumped it a long time ago – after killing the Bronson boys. But he must get off on using it. He even kept it after Josh died. Then he killed Rick Melsyn and Darrell Nesbit with it. He keeps it close.'

'So, it's at the courthouse,' I said. 'Or in his car. Or he's carrying it. Or he has it somewhere else we don't know about.'

'Where?' she said.

'Did you search the office?' I asked.

She shrugged. 'Nothing there.'

'So, it's in his car, or he's carrying it.'

'Or it's somewhere else.'

'Where?' I said.

'We need to go into the places where he might have it.' She gave me a long look. 'You could do that.'

I shook my head. 'Get a warrant.'

'You're kidding, right? I ask for a warrant, and you know what they do? They call Skooner and say, *We've got a detective asking to search your car and house. Should we let her?* And Skooner says, *Why, certainly. I have nothing to hide.* And by the time we look at his house and car, he's right. He has nothing to hide because he's hidden it somewhere else.'

'*I'm* not searching for it,' I said.

'We need the gun,' she said.

'Yeah, you said.' I started to get out of the car.

But she said, 'I hate to do this, but I've got another question. What do you know about Randall Haussen?'

Higby had already hit me with that question, so I'd prepared for it. 'What's to know? Jane Foley and Hank Cury at the JNI thought he might be involved in the killings that got Thomas LaFlora executed. LaFlora's dead now, so even if Haussen was involved, no one will admit the mistake.'

'That's right,' she said. 'And Haussen would know that too. He's safe now. And he has a house and a business to take care of. So why doesn't he come out of hiding?'

'You would have to ask him.'

'I wish I could,' she said. 'An interesting thing that Bill Higby pointed out to me – the last witness report has you climbing into a car with him.'

I thought she must see that I was faking it. 'Who was the witness?'

'That's what makes it especially interesting. The call was anonymous, and the phone was disposable, but we got the number and worked out that the caller bought the phone locally. While I was in New York, I had one of our new detectives go to the store. They had video of the purchase.'

'You recognized the buyer?'

'Sure,' she said. 'It was Eric Skooner.'

I caught my breath. 'First,' I said, 'that would mean that the judge was outside the motel, watching me.'

'And that should scare the hell out of you,' she said.

'But second,' I said, 'you know he's a liar. So why believe him if he says I was with Haussen?'

'I doubt every word he says. But that doesn't mean he lied about you and Haussen. He took a risk calling this in. He must have seen a big payoff.'

'I don't know what that would have been.'

'Maybe he could take you off the street the way he did Higby,' she said. 'If he's as sick-headed as he seems to be, he probably would have preferred to kill you, but you're big news since you got out of jail. If he saw a good opportunity, he might want to point out one of your bad mistakes and avoid the risk of all the publicity that would come if you died.'

'Or maybe he's telling lies about me, the way he did with Higby. Maybe he's trying to set me up.'

'Maybe.'

'I have enough worries with my own life without wasting my time with Haussen,' I said.

'I would think so,' she said. 'But I've talked with your old bosses at the JNI. I heard about you bringing him back from Atlanta.'

She was dancing me into a corner. 'What are you accusing me of?'

'Nothing at all,' she said. 'As far as I know, Haussen is just missing, and we have an unreliable report that you were with him. I'm just asking you questions.'

'Well, don't ask them,' I said.

'There's one other way to get Skooner,' she said. 'Other than finding his gun.'

'What? Have Higby grab him by the throat?'

She said, 'We could catch him doing it again.'

'Sure,' I said. 'Do you have any boys you want raped, bitten, and murdered?'

'I can think of only one person who interests the judge enough for him to do that right now.'

For a moment I thought she must mean Lynn Pritchard. But I'd left her out of our conversations. Besides, Holt had never mentioned her. 'Me?'

'You've unsettled him,' she said. 'He killed Rick Melsyn and Darrell Nesbit because you rocked him out of complacency with all of your running around and questioning people. Wherever Andrew Skooner is, he's there because you were pressuring the judge. And the night that the judge saw you with Haussen—'

I started to object, but she waved me quiet.

'That night, the judge was coming to kill you or to see what it would take to do it. You know it's true. He wouldn't have hung out in your neighborhood unless he had business to do. You were that business. Whatever you were doing with Haussen, that man saved your life. You've pushed the judge, and he's reacting. Push him harder, and he'll come after you again. But this time we'll be waiting.'

'You want me to set myself up for him?'

'I want you to make yourself irresistible to him. Break into his home when he's at the courthouse,' she said. 'If you find the gun, take it, and that's all you'll need to do. We'll fingerprint it and trace it. If that doesn't put it in the judge's hands, we'll find another way to put it there. But if you can't find the gun, let him know you were there. Piss on his couch. Piss on his bed. Sign your name. Make him mad.'

'What if I say no?'

'First, the judge will probably come after you anyway. You've already pushed him hard. Second, he will get away with it. When he's done things his own way, no one has been able to stop him.'

'Why can't a cop break in to search for the gun?'

'A hundred good reasons,' she said, 'but mostly the judge needs to know it was you. The house has a new security system, inside and out. We can take care of the outside, so that you don't set off alarms when you go in. But there's a camera in the front hall and another on the stairway. You need to be on the cameras. No one else can be.'

'Why won't the judge just take the video to the cops?'

'Do you really think there's any chance of that?' she said.

'No.' I had to admit it. 'If he sees me in his house, he'll want to tear me apart.'

That afternoon, instead of keeping my appointment with Dr Patel, I drove to Lynn Pritchard's house. Her husband had gone shopping

for new hunting boots and a fleece jacket. He would leave for
New Hampshire that evening. She set her babies on their bellies
on the living room rug and sat down with them.

She said, 'The man called again last night. Twice.'

'Was it the judge?'

She held her palm to one of her daughters the way you do to
an anxious dog that might either sniff or bite you. The baby gripped
a finger with her whole hand. 'I don't know,' she said. 'I'm tired.
Really tired. He said he could hardly wait to see me. He said he
would come by.'

'Your husband was here?'

'I guess,' she said. 'He slept through the first call. He woke when
the phone rang again. I told him no one was on the other end.' She
drew her finger from the baby's hand, touched it to her lipstick, and
then touched the smeared fingertip to the baby's tiny lips.

'Just hold on for another day or two,' I said. 'I'll get him.'

'No, you won't. He'll do the same things to you that he did to
my brother and Duane.'

'He won't hurt you, and he won't hurt me.'

'You're sweet to say that,' she said.

'Hold on for a couple of days. If I don't get him, then you
should hide until someone else catches him.'

'No one will catch him.' She got up from the rug and came to
me. She touched her lipstick again. I thought for a moment that
she would dab my lips with her finger, as she'd dabbed her baby's.
I thought that, worn down by fear, she might even ask me to climb
the stairs with her to her bed. But she just said, 'You should run.
That would be the smart thing to do.'

I picked up Cynthia from the Cineplex at eight. After we ate dinner
at Woody's Bar-B-Q, I told her I felt ill and needed to take her
home. She eyed me as if she knew that I'd signed on for another
ride that I should stay off. As I drove out Atlantic Boulevard and
then south toward her house, she sat with her hands folded in her
lap and, before getting out of the car, asked, 'What are you going
to do?'

'I wish I knew,' I said.

She stared at me. I'd come to love those hard eyes. She said,
'See you tomorrow?'

'I need a couple of days,' I said.

She said, 'Whatever you're doing, I need to do it with you.'

'I know.'

'Then, why not?'

I wanted her with me always. I forced a smile. 'I've only got one ticket.'

'You're a fool,' she said.

'I know.'

We sat on her driveway, and the night was all around us. She said, 'Don't hurt yourself again.'

'I won't.'

'If someone else hurts you, I won't forgive you.'

That night, I went to bed early and slept badly, waking up every twenty or thirty minutes. At midnight, I got up, shaking and nauseous. Outside on the parking lot, three men were arguing loudly. Somewhere, a room or two away, a woman was laughing. I went into the bathroom and turned on the shower. I stood in the stream until the water subdued the anxiety and I no longer felt like retching.

When I came out, I turned on the TV to knock down the noises of my neighbors. I lay on my bed and watched *Nightline* and then *Family Guy* and *King of the Hill*. I turned on TMZ and got the latest on people whose lives held little interest for me. At four thirty, I started flipping between *Action News* and *First Coast News* and learned that I would have sunny and hot weather when I burglarized Judge Skooner's house. They had no stories on Higby's legal troubles or the murders of Rick Melsyn and Darrell Nesbit or the execution of Thomas LaFlora or the disappearance of Randall Haussen. Those men were last week's news. At six, I changed the channel again. *Caillou* was starting on PBS – an episode in which the kid catches chickenpox – and in my exhaustion I felt tears in my eyes. I turned off the TV, did fifty sit-ups, and got back into the shower.

Holt showed up at seven along with four plainclothes cops and explained where she would post them so they could watch my room after I came back from the judge's house. She took a bag from her trunk and we went into my room. She gave me a GPS tracker and told me to strap it to my ankle. She gave me a phone that she'd already keyed in to one she would carry and said, 'For if you need me. This way, no one will trace calls to our regular phones. Use it if you've got an emergency or need us to come in and take you out.'

She gave me an adjustable crescent wrench and a flathead screwdriver. 'Some thieves carry fancy tool kits,' she said. 'Most keep it simple. Let's keep it simple here. The dirtier the entry, the better. It will anger the judge. But make it quick. Get in and get out.'

'How about a gun?' I had the pistol under the front seat of my car, and I planned to keep it with me. But I wanted to know her thoughts on the matter.

'You'll be safer without a weapon,' she said. 'He could turn it against you.'

I said, 'In other words, you won't give me anything to protect myself?'

'We'll have armed officers watching you. When the judge comes, we'll have him covered.'

'You won't give me a gun?'

'No, we won't.'

'Fine,' I said.

She looked skeptical, but said, 'I'm glad you feel that way.' She gave me a shoulder pack for the wrench and screwdriver and anything I needed to carry from the house. 'Be smart,' she said. 'We're breaking about twenty laws and a thousand rules. The guys we've got doing this will save your life, but if you screw up, they'll deny they ever knew about it. Every man for himself.'

'How about you? Will you deny me?'

'Just be smart,' she said.

At ten, another cop called Holt and said the judge had arrived at the courthouse and started a hearing. So I drove from the Cardinal Motel toward his house. The morning sky was hot and cloudless. Rush-hour traffic had cleared, and I crossed the city faster than I wanted to.

As I turned from Henley Road on to Byron, I passed a man in a black Chevy Impala. According to Holt, a black Tahoe would be parked up the street on the other side of the judge's house. If anyone approached, the men would contact her, and she would call me and tell me to run.

I pulled into the Skooners' driveway. As I got out, a locust was whining in one of the hedges, and, far off, in another yard, a lawnmower hummed. I glanced next door. Higby stood on his front porch.

His eyes had always accused me. His presence made me want to turn around and call off the break-in. I wondered then if he and Holt had set a trap for me. I wondered if they would get me inside the judge's house and spring the steel jaws. I wondered if my release from prison and my struggle toward freedom were only a dream that would end when I broke through the judge's door and stepped into the front hall.

I flipped my middle finger at Higby and went to the door. A security camera that the technicians had installed to point at the front porch hung broken. I stepped on the pieces of glass and plastic and ground them into the brick.

I rang the doorbell – just in case.

No one came.

I rang it again.

Then I kicked the door.

It was solid.

I kicked a second time.

It was still solid.

I looked across the yard at Higby, and he shook his head.

So I went to work on the door with the screwdriver, hacking and gouging the wood around the lock. After a couple of minutes, I'd dug through a layer of plywood into a hollow core. I pried and twisted, spraying the porch with splinters and shards of wood. *The dirtier the entry, the better.* The muscle and mental work felt good. Better than taking out the eye of the man who attacked me in prison.

I jammed the screwdriver through the plywood on the inside of the door and turned the shaft, widening a hole. Then I punched at the hole with the head of the crescent wrench. Soon, I'd widened it enough to stick my hand through and open the lock.

I stepped inside, closed the door, and went down the cool, dark hall to the sunroom where Andrew Skooner had given me the bullet. I knocked over a wicker recliner and a wrought-iron table. I went to the cabinet, opened the bottom drawer, and poured it on to the floor. There were pieces from a Monopoly game, two packs of playing cards, and a bunch of dusty checkers. There were paperclips, a bottle of Elmer's glue, and a hundred other pieces of junk. But no gun. I pulled out the other three drawers and emptied them on to the floor. More junk. No gun. I tipped over the cabinet, then went to one of the broad windows and looked out over the pool, the lawn, and the dock. The sky above Black Creek remained cloudless, and heat radiated from the glass. If I tapped on the window with the crescent wrench, it would shatter, and the heat would rush in.

I turned away and walked into the hall, but then came back. I picked up one of the wrought-iron tables and heaved it through the glass. The heat rushed in.

If that didn't piss off the judge enough to make him want to kill me . . .

I went into the living room and tipped over the couches and chairs. I walked along the walls, taking paintings from hooks and chucking them into a pile. In one corner, a grandfather clock ticked at the seconds as if it was chopping time into pieces. I let the clock stand.

I circled to the back of the house and went into the kitchen. I swiped cans and bags of food on to the counters from the cabinets. No gun. I poured the silverware from a drawer on to the floor. No gun. I opened the oven, the dishwasher, and the refrigerator. No gun.

Breathe, I told myself. *Deep in, hard out.*

I went back to the front door and opened it. The sky was blue and hot. The lawn was green. A locust whined. A lawn-mower hummed in another yard. My car waited for me where I'd parked it.

I closed the door and climbed the stairs to the second floor. There were five bedrooms. The Skooners had fitted out the one closest to the stairs with a recumbent bicycle, a step machine, free weights, and exercise mats. They had bolted a large-screen TV to the wall. I went in, glanced around, and left.

A linen closet separated that room from the next. I pulled the sheets, blankets, and towels off the shelves. No gun.

The next room, I guessed, had been Josh's. On a bookshelf, there were framed pictures of him – grinning into a camera with groups of friends, holding a redfish on a little motorboat when he was about sixteen and had long hair. I opened his dresser drawers, lifted his clothes, and set them back in place. I opened his closet and checked the shoe boxes that he'd stacked in the back. I went into the attached bathroom and checked the drawers and cabinets. I returned to the bedroom, lifted the mattress, and lowered it on to the springs. No gun.

Andrew's bedroom was across from Josh's. The bed was unmade. A pair of jeans lay on the floor. The window shade was down. I opened the drawers and stirred the clothes with my hands. No gun. I checked the closet and under the mattress. In the bathroom, a deodorant stick and a toothbrush lay on the counter. A shampoo bottle stood open in the shower. No gun.

At the other end of the hall, the judge had set up one room as a home office and another as a bedroom. I went into the office. He'd decorated the walls with awards and certificates of the kind that also hung in his courthouse chambers. Behind his office chair, he had a framed picture of himself as a young man shaking the hand of the first President Bush. I emptied the desk drawers on to the desktop. I took the folders from the file cabinets, threw them into the air, and watched the paper snow. I pulled the cushion from a daybed. No gun, no gun, no gun. I threw the desk chair against one of the file cabinets, and it rang like a bell.

In the judge's bedroom, a dark-wood headboard on a sleigh bed was upholstered with gray leather. A large photograph of the judge and his late wife hung on the wall on one side of the bed. A large photograph of the whole family – when Andrew and Josh were smiling toddlers – hung on the other side. A dresser with side-by-side drawers stood by a closet door. A large mirror topped the dresser. A chest, with five vertical drawers, stood by a window that faced out to the pool, the backyard, and the creek. A nightstand with two more drawers stood next to the bed.

All those drawers.

All those possibilities.

I emptied the dresser first, dumping clothes on to the bed. Undershirts. Underwear. Pairs of socks.

Then the chest. Shorts, brightly colored and creased. Golf shirts, the same. Swimsuits. Unopened packages of underwear and socks. A metal box full of old watches, pocket knives, and British and Jamaican coins.

The nightstand last. A strip of condoms. A flashlight. A bottle of Advil. An elastic-banded sleeping mask. A book of art photography called *Boys of Summer*. Nail clippers.

And – I grinned – a pistol. Black metal. With a rough, brown plastic grip.

But my stomach dropped. The pistol also had a lanyard that passed through an eye at the bottom of the grip, as if you might hang the gun around your neck. And the barrel was as wide as a twelve-gauge shotgun shell.

It was the wrong pistol. Not even a *real* pistol. A marine flare gun. Why would the judge keep it in a bedside drawer – unless to substitute for a pistol he no longer felt safe keeping there?

I picked it up and threw it at the mirror. It missed, bounced off the wall, and clattered across the floor. I picked up the photography book to throw it too – it was one of those glossy art books that weighed two or three pounds, and if I couldn't break a mirror with it, what good was it? But I stopped when the pages fell open. *Boys of Summer* was full of softcore, black-and-white pictures of boys in swimsuits from the 1930s and 1940s. The swimsuits hung loose over the boys' hips. In group pictures, some of the boys looked as if they had erections. They draped their arms over each other's shoulders, or their hands fell casually on each other's thighs in the unaware way that some men might see as an unconscious or even conscious invitation to sex. The boys were skinny, and you could see the ribs through their skin. Several of them flexed muscles for the camera. The book spine was soft, the pages well thumbed. The judge must have spent many nights leafing through the pictures, looking for the incarnation of his dreams.

The book was more evidence.

And still not enough.

It was erotic art photography. No court would call it child porn.

I shouted, 'Goddamn it,' and threw it. The pages opened like a bird's wings, and it fell to the floor.

So I yanked the lamp off the nightstand and flung it across the room. The light bulb exploded against the wall.

I stood, panting. I wanted to tear down the house.

Then the phone in my pocket rang. I dug it out and answered. 'What?'

'What's taking so long?' Holt asked. 'Are you all right?'

'I thought we weren't supposed to call unless we had an emergency,' I said, and hung up.

I went to the window and opened it. I sucked in the hot air and blew out hard. I stared at the sky. I stared at the creek water, slowly passing the backyard. I sucked in more air. An egret had perched on a piling at the end of dock, looking into the creek water for fish. Now it craned its neck toward the house and seemed to stare at me.

So I went back and got the photography book. I threw it out the window toward the egret. It soared over a strip of lawn – and into the pool water.

I left the room and went downstairs to the kitchen.

The phone rang in my pocket.

I looked in the refrigerator and found a carton of eggs, a half-full bottle of wine, plastic-wrapped lettuce, broccoli, and celery, cartons of orange juice and milk, cheese. The door rack held ketchup, a jar of pickles, Sriracha, and a squeeze bottle of mustard.

The phone rang.

I took the mustard and went back up to the judge's bedroom. I lifted the mattress and spilled the contents of the drawers on to the floor. I stripped off the bedcover and sheets, leaving a quilted white mattress pad. *Piss on the judge's couch*, Holt had said. *Piss on his bed. Sign your name. Make him mad.*

I opened the mustard bottle and squirted. I wrote words that echoed in my memory – *You did it.* I wrote names of people I believed the judge had killed – *Jeremy Ballat. Luis Gonzalez. Steven Bronson. Duane Bronson. Rick Melsyn. Darrell Nesbit.* I added *Thomas LaFlora* since Skooner prosecuted him and got him sentenced to death. I wrote, *With love, Lynn.* Lynn Pritchard deserved to have a voice in this too. The words recorded a history of pain. They played in my head like a song. When I was done, I needed to sign it. So, across the bottom of the mattress pad, I wrote in big letters, *Franky Dast.* I knew that those words would also make the judge want to kill me.

As I admired my work, the phone rang in my pocket again. I let it ring, and I went down the stairs and out the front door. I glanced at Higby's house. He was gone.

The inside of my car was hot from the sun. As I pulled from

the driveway on to Byron Road, sweat rippled on my skin and fell into my stinging eyes.

As I approached Henley Road, I waved at the man in the Chevy Impala. He kept his hands below the dashboard and his eyes to himself.

The phone rang again, and this time I answered.

Holt sounded relieved. She asked, 'Did you find the gun?'

'Hardly.'

'OK.' No surprise. 'Why didn't you answer when I called?'

'I was busy.'

'What took so long?'

'I left the judge a detailed message.'

I saw no stake-out when I pulled back on to the parking lot at the motel. Maybe that should have reassured me – the undercover cops were doing their job. I crammed the barrel of the pistol into my belt and went to my door. Although I knew that the judge must be completing his morning hearings, snug on his bench, and that he remained ignorant of my break-in, I fumbled the key in the lock and peered into my room before going inside.

The room was quiet and dark and looked exactly as I'd left it. I kept the shades closed but turned up the air conditioner and turned on the TV. I sat on my bed and the images from an episode of *Law and Order: Special Victims Unit* swam past. Whatever the characters said became background noise to voices in my head that whispered and argued. I switched the channel to a show called *I Will Bless the Lord at All Times*, then to *Divorce Court*, then to the noon news, and back to *Law and Order*. It was all the same to me. Then I realized I stank of sweat, so I turned on the shower. As the water cascaded over me, I thought, *This will bury me*. I fought off that idea, but it came around the back side and stung me.

Through the afternoon, I watched *Jerry Springer*, *The Love Boat*, *Judge Judy*, *Dr Phil*, and *People's Court*, and I couldn't have repeated a word any of the hosts, guests, or characters said a minute after they spoke.

At five thirty, Holt called and told me the judge was leaving the courthouse, apparently heading home. 'You're safe,' she said. 'We've got you locked down.'

'Bad metaphor,' I said, 'but thanks.'

'We'll be with you,' she said.

When we hung up, I stepped outside on to the concrete walkway. Jimmy and Susan were smoking by their room, watching cars and trucks pass on Philips Highway.

Jimmy nodded toward the road and asked, 'What the hell is going on?'

Maybe the cops weren't staying as undercover as I thought. 'What?' I said.

Susan said, 'Drug bust, maybe. They're fixing to nail someone.'

I went back inside and called Holt. 'You're too visible,' I said. 'Everyone sees you.'

'No one sees us,' she said, like a baby hiding behind her hands.

I used her words back to her. 'Be smart.'

I left the lights off, kept the TV playing, and sat on the carpet. I set the pistol by my leg. If the judge came through my door, I could shoot him in the chest before his eyes adjusted.

But the judge didn't come through the door.

I watched the evening news and then prime time, and it was all a wash of faces and voices. Holt and I had agreed that the judge might come anytime from the moment he saw the damage I'd done to his house to the middle of the night, or he might wait for a day or two or even more, in which case we would need to change our plans.

I'd known I needed to be ready for a long night, but as the sun set, my nerves acted up. Holt's must have too, because at nine she called and said, 'Anything going on?'

I said, 'I hope you would know if it was.'

'I'll send a car past the judge's house to see if he's there,' she said.

A little before ten, she called again and said, 'We can't tell for sure, but he seems to be out. Could be he's getting ready. Could be he's on the way. Could be he's already near the motel and waiting.'

'That's a lot of different possibilities,' I said.

'We're ready for them all.'

Midnight came and went without the judge.

I did pushups and sit-ups. I ran in place. I paced the room, from the door to the bathroom. I did more pushups. The TV said what it always said, but I kept it on for the noises of the living. At one in the morning, I called Holt and asked, 'What's happening?'

'I sent another car by the judge's house,' she said. 'No lights. No movement. He's out.'

'Then, where is he?'

'Be patient.'

'I've never been patient,' I said. 'Even when I had nothing to do but be patient, I wasn't patient.'

We hung up, and I dialed Lynn Pritchard. At least I could talk with someone who was as full of fear as I was.

Her phone rang and rang.

That worried me. As far as I'd known, she always stayed in her house at night.

I tried again. The phone rang eight times before I hung up. No answering machine. No voicemail.

Something curled in my skin. I dialed a third time.

After two rings, the phone clicked, and silence followed.

'Lynn?' I said.

The phone clicked again.

I yelled, 'Shit,' and dialed.

The phone rang three times, and a man's voice answered. 'We're busy right now.'

Hearing a voice relieved me. Lynn Pritchard's husband must have canceled his New Hampshire hunting trip.

But the relief lasted only a moment.

Because I recognized the voice on the other end of the line.

It wasn't the husband's.

Judge Skooner had picked up Lynn Pritchard's phone.

THIRTY-THREE

I ran from my room to my car.

Except for the streetlights, the night was dark and empty. The windless air smelled of exhaust and oil. I saw no cops or unmarked police cars, but as I turned the key in the ignition, two men, shouldering black rifles, emerged from behind the ends of the motel. I hit the gas and sped out on to the highway. Two more armed men came from behind buildings on the other side of the road, one of them yelling into a radio.

I charged south, passing two pickup trucks and a delivery van. Two women in skin-tight yellow skirts stood on the highway shoulder, giving me big obscene smiles, and a hundred yards farther their pimp watched and waited.

Then the phone that Holt gave me rang.

I answered, 'He's at Lynn Pritchard's house.'

Holt had no idea what I was talking about.

'Rick Melsyn's sister,' I said. 'Duane Bronson's old girlfriend. The judge is—'

'What are you—'

'I called her,' I said. 'The judge answered.'

'Where?' Holt said.

A stoplight in front of me turned yellow and then red, and I punched the accelerator and hoped.

I gave Holt the name of the Ponte Vedra street where Lynn Pritchard lived and described the house.

'I'll call it in,' she said. 'We're heading there too.'

'He'll kill her.'

Streetlights streaked the windshield like brilliant whips.

'You've got to pull over,' Holt said. 'You've got to stop. If you walk in on the judge, what'll you do? He'll kill you too.'

I could've answered. I could've told her that the judge was mine. I could've told her that there would be no *me* if I stopped now, that the possibility of my existence rested on my going to Lynn Pritchard's house. Instead, I hung up. And I shoved the gas to the floor.

Except for a single front porch light at the end of the block, the neighborhood around Lynn Pritchard's house was dark. There were no streetlights, no landscape spotlights shining up at the fronds of the palm trees or the Spanish moss that hung from oak branches, no low pathway lights along the walks from the street to the front doors. The moon had set or hadn't risen. If stars burned somewhere in the heavens, I couldn't see them.

I slowed and turned on to Lynn Pritchard's driveway. A bright light showed inside a second-story window. A warning and welcoming beacon. I stopped when my headlights shined on a gray SUV.

I got out. Sirens were coming from somewhere, cutting the night. Lynn Pritchard's babies wailed inside the house. But the yard outside was silent.

I went to the front door – a slab of hardwood. I threw my weight against it.

Nothing.

I stepped to the edge of the porch by the concrete planters so I could build momentum. I ran at the door, hit it.

Nothing.

Then Lynn Pritchard screamed inside.

I went down to the walkway and stared at the house. The light in the second-floor room seemed to flicker as if a fire was burning. The babies cried. Over the roof of the house, the night hung black and heavy. The curtained first-floor windows faced me like blind eyes. I pulled out the pistol and shot at one of them. The bullet made a hollow sound, as if the glass sucked the metal into it. I went to the window, ran my hand over it. A dimple sank in where the bullet had gone through.

I ran back to the front porch. The concrete planters were full of soil and flowers.

I put my foot on one of them, tried to budge it.

Heavy.

I tried to lift it anyway.

Too heavy.

Lynn Pritchard screamed. The sirens came closer.

I tipped the planter so the soil and flowers tumbled out. I tried lifting it again.

Too heavy.

I lifted it anyway.

I stepped off the porch, cradling it. I stumbled in the dark toward the window that I'd shot. I heaved the planter. It fell short – sinking into the grass – then tipped hard against the bottom of the pane. A fracture rippled through the glass.

If I hit it with my shoulder, shards would rain over my face and body.

I kicked it.

The window exploded into the house. I ran through the empty

frame into the living room. The room was blacker than the night outside and smelled like metal and salt – the jagged odor of blood.

Somewhere nearby, Lynn Pritchard's babies cried. Outside, the sirens whined.

I moved through the dark toward the front hall. The babies were only a room away. I went up the stairs.

One light was on, in the room I'd seen from outside.

I stopped at the second-floor landing and tried to see into the dark at the ends of the hall. I saw only blackness – deep as the deepest hole.

Lynn Pritchard made a sound in the lighted room. A low sound. The sound of someone at the black bottom of the deepest hole.

I went in. I held the pistol in my sweating hands.

Lynn Pritchard was alone. The judge had tied her wrists and ankles to the bed. She stared at the ceiling and made that sound. She had wounds on her legs and hips. I pulled my eyes away and looked at her face – pale except for the wet red lipstick. Her tongue lolled against her lips.

The judge had taken the shade off a table lamp, converting the space into a kind of theatrical stage, as if he wanted to see *everything*, the way you see it in a burst of brightness before the world goes dark.

'Lynn,' I said.

She stared at the ceiling.

'Where is he?' I said.

She was lost in her pain and fear.

I said, 'I'll get—'

She turned her face toward me, sensing what I couldn't see. In the moment between her turning and the butt of the judge's pistol crashing against the back of my head, I knew that I was too slow – that I was already falling into a black tunnel even as my feet stood on the floor.

Then I saw a flash, as if the gun metal sparked against my skin.

I seemed to fly upward – my muscles jolting, my legs no longer mattering – and then I fell and kept falling.

I woke again – seconds or minutes later.

I lay on the floor next to the bed.

Crushed.

Fingers of blood caressed my neck and probed my ears.

I wondered if the judge had already shot me in the forehead.

I wondered if I was dead.

I touched my lips, my nose, my eyes. They felt like the lips, nose, and eyes of a dead man. I ran my fingers over my forehead. I found no hole.

Sounds came from the bed. Lynn Pritchard. The judge.

I tried to sit up to see. The edges of my vision collapsed, and blackness rained down on me.

I woke again to the sound of Lynn Pritchard. The sound of the judge.

The babies crying in a far-off room.

Sirens.

I felt my face. My forehead.

Then all went silent. Inches from me. Miles from me.

I pushed myself to my elbows. My vision narrowed – widened.

My ears flooded with sound. Babies. Sirens. The judge speaking softly, tenderly, incomprehensibly.

He straddled Lynn Pritchard. He wore pants but had removed his shirt. The graying hair on his chest was dabbed with blood. Blood wrapped a clownish mask around his lips.

He hung over her. His pistol lay on the mattress, touching her cheek, where she could have grabbed it if he hadn't tied her hands.

The babies cried.

The sirens came.

I sat on the floor by the bed, watching.

The judge seemed blind to all but the scene he'd created, deaf to all but his own pleasure. Whatever he was telling her. Whatever he was telling himself. Whatever judgment came from the hole that was his mouth.

I watched for the longest time.

Then he reached for the gun.

And I reached to my belt for mine.

It was gone.

The judge pressed his gun barrel against Lynn Pritchard's forehead.

I looked around the room for my pistol. It glinted in the light of the shadeless lamp – inches from me on the floor.

The judge was enjoying himself. He caressed the trigger as if he could give it a sexual thrill.

He spoke softly, tenderly, lovingly, his words creating worlds.

I drew the pistol into my hand.

I understood his words then. What he would do to Lynn Pritchard. In the minutes or hours before he shot her in the forehead. Or maybe – *maybe* – he would just shoot her now. He leaned and kissed her forehead. Gently. Like a loving father. Then he sat up and held his pistol barrel against the wet kiss stain he'd left on her skin.

I spoke to him. 'Judge.' The word felt like twisted wire in my throat.

He turned. Surprised to see me among the living. Irritated by the interruption.

So I shot him in the belly.

He whirled, as if I'd lashed him. He looked at his ribs – the blood streaking – and looked at me. Uncomprehending.

He raised his gun in an unsteady hand and aimed it at my face.

I shot him in the chest.

He looked down. Amazed at the new wound. His gun fell to the mattress, and he put a hand over the torn skin. If only he could stuff it back inside. He looked stricken and bewildered. And then he fell. Toward Lynn Pritchard – as though he would crush her in his own death – then sideways and down and down, over the side of the bed, on to the floor.

I pulled myself up and stood. More or less stood.

Lynn Pritchard stared at me.

'It's OK,' I tried to say, and my words sounded as incomprehensible to my ears as the judge's words. 'It will be.'

As if to answer me, the judge made a sound of pain and righteous anger. He seemed to think he might live to win another battle.

Lights strobed through the window then. Police cars and vans came up the driveway, and the sirens drowned out the crying babies and my mumbling and the judge's fury.

I set my pistol by the judge's gun on the bed and untied Lynn Pritchard's ropes. She drew her hands around her body as if she could pull them inside her and make herself disappear.

Downstairs, the cops hammered at the front door.

I untied one ankle and then the other.

'It'll be OK,' I said, and I made myself look her in the eyes.

But she picked up my pistol, wrapped a finger over the trigger, and aimed at me.

'No,' I said.

'No,' she agreed.

She turned and aimed the gun at the judge. He lay on the floor, his hand covering his chest wound. He stared back at her. Smiling stupidly.

She pulled the trigger. Once. Twice.

When the noise of the second gunshot rang in my ears, the judge no longer had a face – none that anyone would know.

Lynn Pritchard raised the gun, considered it, and put the barrel against her own temple.

'No,' I said, and I crawled over the bed to her. 'No.'

She looked at me with anguish, with eyes that seemed to ask the same question I'd asked a thousand times when looking in a mirror. *Why not?*

'No,' I said.

I eased the gun from her hand. It seemed to weigh nothing now. It had become bird bone.

Boots pounded up the stairs. A dozen men and women, led by Bill Higby and Deborah Holt. Shouting incomprehensible words.

As they burst into the room, I wrapped Lynn Pritchard in a bed sheet. She stared at them as if they'd come too late and she and I were already dead.

THIRTY-FOUR

Too much rode on the judge's reputation to let it collapse completely. Too many cops' and lawyers' jobs. Too many years of trials and verdicts.

The next morning, the city officials started to spin the story. A sheriff's spokesman said that, under pressure of his family crisis – Josh's recent death, Andrew's disappearance – Judge Skooner suffered a breakdown. Yes, the judge had encountered Lynn Pritchard and become fixated on her. Yes, the judge went to her house late at night pursuing an interest she didn't share. Yes, as he pressed himself on her, she shot him – once in the chest.

That afternoon, the District Attorney, while calling the shooting an act of self-defense, said Judge Skooner was more to be pitied than vilified.

When Higby and Holt visited Lynn Pritchard at the hospital, she agreed to go along with the story. She was still in shock. Scared to death of future trauma. Wanting – *needing* – to have all that had been out of reach since the murder of Duane Bronson when she was just a kid.

But when they visited me, I said, 'He wrecked me' – I looked at Higby – 'with your help.'

He said, 'I did my—'

'I want the story in the open,' I said. 'Every detail. I'll tell it if you won't.'

Holt said, 'All of Skooner's court cases would fall apart. That's hundreds and hundreds.'

'Maybe they *should* fall apart. Skooner must've railroaded others too.'

'This would shake everyone who's ever brought a case through his courtroom,' Higby said. 'That's a lot of the Sheriff's Office. You're talking about people's lives.'

'I'm talking about *your* life,' I said.

'And the lives of a lot of others.'

'I'll be happy to shake you,' I said.

'You don't want to do this,' Holt said.

'Yes, I do. I need to.'

'Sometimes it's better to tell only part of the story,' Higby said. 'Even if it's a lie.'

'And sometimes it's better to tell the whole truth,' I said.

'The truth can hurt all of us,' he said.

'But mostly you.'

He shook his head. 'Are you ready to tell the truth about what happened to Randall Haussen?'

A better man might have choked on his own hypocrisy. Not me. 'I've told you, I know nothing about him. You never had anyone other than the judge saying he saw us together.'

Higby said, 'And the judge is dead, so you're safe from his testimony.'

'That's right.'

Holt asked quietly, 'How about the testimony of a body in the Trail Ridge landfill?'

'Bullshit,' I said.

'The medical examiner found a single bullet in the cranium. How about the testimony it will give if we compare it with the bullets you and Lynn Pritchard shot into the judge?'

'Goddamn it,' I said.

'Or maybe we can rewrite that story too,' she said. 'Maybe the story could be about an unidentified body found at the landfill.'

'He was going to kill me.'

'That's your story now?' Higby said.

'Let's tell the stories the best way,' Holt said.

I wanted to lunge at her. 'What about Felicia Bronson? Doesn't she deserve to know what happened to her boys?'

'We'll never know exactly,' she said. 'Whatever was in the papers the Bronsons stole from the judge is buried.'

'What about you?' I said to Higby. 'You still have charges against you for shooting Josh Skooner. You'll go to trial.'

'We can protect the judge's reputation only so much,' he said. 'Next week, while doing yard work, one of the Skooners' gardeners will find the bullet you gave us. Our men must have missed it. An embarrassment to us. It'll be enough to get the charges dropped. The union will insist that the State Attorney drop them.'

Andrew Skooner, who, it turned out, was hiding in upstate New York only a few miles from Cornell, gave the eulogy at the judge's funeral, and, that evening, the news aired large portions of it. His father had been a hard man, he said, but he also called him a hero, while acknowledging that all heroes are flawed. He concluded by saying, 'I love you, Dad.' Terror never really dies. You can put it in a steel box and bury it in six feet of sand and dirt, but it will still breathe down the necks of its victims.

I stayed away from the service. Instead, that afternoon, I went to the Cineplex and watched *Singin' in the Rain* in the Golden Oldies Series, and afterward Cynthia and I went back to my room and pretended the world outside my four walls was black and white and tuned to the soundtrack of a happy musical.

I tried to go easy on myself. The doctors at the hospital said the judge had given me a concussion and I should expect head-aches, nausea, and double vision. When I said, 'Nothing new, then?' they looked at me as if I might be suffering from the effects of my smashed head. 'Take it slow,' they told me. 'Sleep. Protect yourself against further head injuries.'

When I went back to Dr Patel at the Medical Services Building, he agreed with those recommendations and added, 'Maybe freedom is too big of a word. What if you don't need to move a thousand miles an hour? What if you don't need to fly into the clouds? Maybe freedom comes from knowing how to live small and well.'

'Maybe that's a cop-out,' I said, though in the slow days that followed, I wondered if he might be right. Denial of big possibilities might mean contentment with the small ones. Complacency might make life livable.

So, when Jared knocked on my door one evening while Cynthia and I were lying in bed watching TV, I sent him away.

'What?' he said. 'We can't be brothers anymore?'

I said, 'My doctors tell me to avoid any head trauma.'

He looked at me as if I'd sunk below his lowest expectations. 'Did they also tell you to act like an asshole?'

But a week after the judge's funeral, I started waking up in the middle of the night again.

After the third night of that, I put my box cutter in my pocket, drove to the Sheriff's Office, and asked to see Deborah Holt. When the deskman sent me through to the Homicide Room, I found Higby sitting back-to-back with Holt in the cubicle they shared. He had returned to duty with apologies from the sheriff and the prosecutor for the regrettable but necessary moves against him in the aftermath of Josh Skooner's shooting.

'Hey,' Holt said, as if we were on the same side. 'What's up?'

'The double vision's gone,' I said. 'The headaches too, mostly.'

'That's great,' she said, and even Higby looked glad to hear it.

'I'm thinking clearly again,' I said. 'Or as clearly as I ever did.'

'Good, good,' she said.

I said, 'It's made me curious.'

'That can be dangerous,' Higby said. As if it was a joke.

So I asked him, 'You've lived on Byron Road for a long time, right?'

He smiled, unsure where I was going. 'Twenty-three years next spring.'

'Long enough to know what's happening in the neighborhood.'

'Sure.'

'If kids were breaking into houses and stealing liquor and jewelry and things, you would know that, right? And, because you're a cop, if those kids got arrested in another neighborhood for similar burglaries, you would see the link – you would have access to the reports and the files.'

'I'm busy with my own work,' he said. 'We have enough homicides—'

'Right. So if the kids who were doing the burglaries got killed, you would make connections. I mean, like the Bronson brothers. When they broke into Eric Skooner's house, they'd already gotten caught for other burglaries, and you would've seen the connection. Or if you didn't see it right away because you were so busy, you would've seen it once they died and you started investigating.'

'What are you implying?' he said.

'I'm saying, all the pieces were there. Before I went to trial, you also knew about the dead boys downriver near Tomhanson Mill – Jeremy Ballat and Luis Gonzalez. And you knew about the judge's connection to that area. You'd brought Josh back from there yourself. If you talked to Lynn Pritchard, you also knew that she and the Bronson boys had snuck on to the mill property and swum in a contaminated pond. All the pieces. You just had to put them together.'

'There were a lot of other pieces too,' he said. 'Thousands of them. Most didn't fit.'

So I asked the question that had been waking me at night. 'What did you get from protecting the judge? I mean, while it lasted.'

Higby looked shocked. 'Fuck off,' he said.

'It must have been something,' I said.

He shoved his chair back and stood. To the day he died, he would be a big man, graying but dangerous. 'Get the hell out of—'

Holt, who'd been listening with fascination, said, 'Bill?'

He spun toward her. 'What?' and when she just looked at him, 'What!'

I said, 'Tell me. You owe me that much.'

'I owe you nothing,' he said.

Again, Holt just said his name. 'Bill.'

He seemed to waver – as if he still might break me. He said, 'I had . . . suspicions. That's all. Nothing solid. Nothing I could do anything about.'

I stared at him.

He said, 'Putting the killings on Skooner too soon would do no good. You don't try to take down a man like him unless you know you can keep him down. If he gets up, you won't have a second chance. But I never stopped trying, never stopped working it.'

'You put me on death row and let me sit in prison.'

'I thought you did it – for a while.'

'You couldn't have.'

'If it wasn't him, it was you,' he said. 'That's the way it always was.'

'You're as evil as the judge was,' I said.

'No,' he said. 'I did my best.'

'It wasn't good enough. It never will be.'

If Holt hadn't stood up then – if she hadn't gotten between us – he would have grabbed me by the throat and I would have sliced him with a blade.

Outside, the September sun glared on the sidewalk. And on the hoods and roofs of cars parked at the meters. And on the curbside crepe myrtle trees, which were shedding tissue-like flowers. And on me.

I got into my car, started the engine, and rolled down the windows.

I felt as if I was made of broken pieces. Maybe we all were – at least men like me and Bill Higby.

I pulled into traffic, drove north on the Interstate, and exited on Dunn Avenue. Ten minutes later, I walked into a store called Music Time. The place was cluttered with used horns, drums, and violins, racks of sheet music, counter displays of guitar picks, valve oil, and clef-shaped key chains. Dust hung in the air. The lights were dim.

When I asked about French horns, the counterwoman took me down a step into an attached room, opened a disintegrating vinyl case, and removed a brass instrument. 'This came in four weeks ago. We refurbished it. It makes a lovely sound.'

She offered it to me, but, moved by an impulse I didn't understand, I stepped away.

She smiled. 'Wouldn't you like to try it? We have practice rooms in the back.'

'I don't know,' I said.

'Come, see how it sounds.' She carried the horn into the main room and took me back through a hallway that led to three closed doors. She tapped on the first and, when no one answered, opened it. She handed me the horn and said, 'Take your time. I'll be in front when you're done.'

Behind the closed door, I turned the French horn in my hands. It felt heavy – heavier than I remembered my grandfather's horn being when I was a child. I polished the bell with the bottom of my shirt, then polished the bell pipe and the slides. I looked at my reflection in the brass. A fun-house mirror. I looked at the mouthpiece. There was something as fearsome as teeth about it.

I raised it to my lips.

What incomprehensible sounds?

I pulled the horn away, touched my tongue to my lips, and brought the mouthpiece back up.

What kiss?

What breath of life?

I played a note. The first note of the *Star Wars* theme song 'Across the Stars.' The horn gleamed and blurred in the tears that ran from my eyes. I held the mouthpiece to my lips and played another note.

COUNDON

ACKNOWLEDGEMENTS

I owe much of my understanding of Franky Dast's circumstances to the large and growing literature on death row exonerations. Especially important have been Bryan Stevenson's *Just Mercy: A Story of Justice and Redemption*, Pete Earley's *Circumstantial Evidence: Death, Life, and Justice in a Southern Town*, and Lola Vollen and Dave Eggers' *Surviving Justice: America's Wrongly Convicted and Exonerated*, which includes a story told by death row exoneree Juan Melendez that inspired the death scene involving Frank's friend Stuart.

My deep thanks to Julia Burns, Philip Spitzer, Lukas Ortiz and all at Severn House. My love to Julie, Isaac, Maya, and Elias.

Lightning Source UK Ltd.
Milton Keynes UK
UKHW01f1938121018
330452UK00001BA/1/P